AGAINST *the* WIND

Books by Amanda Cabot

HISTORICAL ROMANCE

Secrets of Sweetwater Crossing

After the Shadows

Against the Wind

Mesquite Springs

Out of the Embers

Dreams Rekindled

The Spark of Love

Texas Dreams

Paper Roses

Scattered Petals

Tomorrow's Garden

Westward Winds

Summer of Promise

Waiting for Spring

With Autumn's Return

Cimarron Creek Trilogy

A Stolen Heart

A Borrowed Dream

A Tender Hope

Christmas Roses

One Little Word: A Sincerely Yours Novella

CONTEMPORARY ROMANCE

Texas Crossroads

At Bluebonnet Lake

In Firefly Valley

On Lone Star Trail

secrets of SWEETWATER CROSSING • 2

AGAINST *the* WIND

AMANDA
CABOT

a division of Baker Publishing Group
Grand Rapids, Michigan

Published by Revell
a division of Baker Publishing Group
Grand Rapids, Michigan
www.revellbooks.com

Printed in the United States of America

Library of Congress Cataloging-in-Publication Data
Names: Cabot, Amanda, 1948– author.
Title: Against the wind / Amanda Cabot.
Description: Grand Rapids, Michigan : Revell, a division of Baker Publishing Group, [2023] | Series: Secrets of Sweetwater Crossing ; 2
Identifiers: LCCN 2022057106 | ISBN 9780800740658 (paperback) | ISBN 9780800745035 (casebound) | ISBN 9781493443444 (ebook)
Classification: LCC PS3603.A35 A73 2023 | DDC 813/.6—dc23/eng/20221202
LC record available at https://lccn.loc.gov/2022057106

Baker Publishing Group publications use paper produced from sustainable forestry practices and post-consumer waste whenever possible.

23 24 25 26 27 28 29 7 6 5 4 3 2 1

For Diane Thomson,
with thanks for a friendship that has
stood the test of time and distance.
I miss our dinners together!

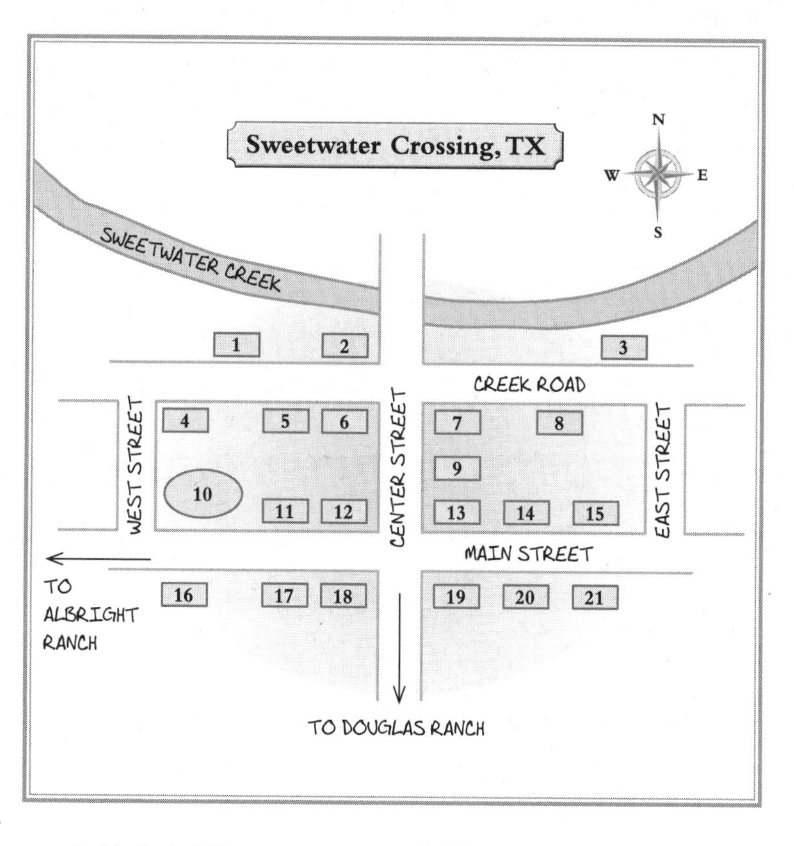

1 – Mrs. Sanders's Home
2 – Cemetery
3 – Finley House
4 – Saloon
5 – Mrs. French's Home (empty)
6 – Mrs. Locke's Home (empty)
7 – Parsonage Annex
8 – The Albrights' Home
9 – Parsonage
10 – Park
11 – Alice Patton's Home/Library
12 – School
13 – Church
14 – Mayor's Home and Office
15 – Mercantile
16 – Livery
17 – Sheriff's Home and Office
18 – Ma's Kitchen
19 – Doctor's Office
20 – Post Office
21 – Dressmaker

Chapter One

MONDAY, MARCH 12, 1883

"Louisa Vaughn, you're a fool to go back." Phoebe Sheridan propped her fists on her hips and glared as she repeated the words Louisa had heard half a dozen times since she'd announced her decision. "You have no future there."

Though Louisa couldn't deny the truth of her best friend's accusations, she wasn't going to admit how much she dreaded returning to Sweetwater Crossing and seeing the changes her oldest sister had made to their home. Instead, she continued folding the clothing she planned to take with her and said as mildly as she could, "You know your mother can't travel by herself. We'll be back as soon as she takes care of matters."

There was no reason to remind Phoebe that her father had died under what were euphemistically called difficult circumstances and that Louisa didn't want Mrs. Sheridan to be alone if she faced scorn or pity. After all, fear of the townspeople's reaction was the reason Phoebe refused to accompany her mother. "I won't give them a chance to laugh at me," she'd declared when Mrs. Sheridan had read the telegram to her. "I won't."

Louisa abandoned her packing and crossed the room she and Phoebe had shared for more than half a year to wrap her arms around her friend's waist and draw her close.

Though no one would call Phoebe beautiful, Louisa had always envied her blond hair and what Mama had called Phoebe's patrician nose. They were so much more distinguished than Louisa's medium brown hair and ordinary nose.

"But your eyes are prettier than mine," Phoebe had told her when they'd both been finding fault with their appearance. "Yours are like dark sapphires; mine are faded blue."

Right now, Phoebe's pale blue eyes were filled with apprehension, her need for reassurance evident.

"I doubt anyone will laugh," Louisa said softly. "Besides, going for the funeral doesn't mean staying there. We'll be back in a week." The journey would take two days each way, and surely three days would be enough to bury Doc Sheridan and close his office. "I wish you'd come with us." As heartbreaking as it had been, Louisa knew she would have regretted being absent when her father was laid to rest.

Phoebe shook her head. "I am never, ever going back to that town, and you shouldn't, either. You know Cousin Jake would accompany Ma, so don't use that as an excuse."

But Mrs. Sheridan hadn't asked Cousin Jake to drive her. She'd asked Louisa, and Louisa could not refuse, not after Mrs. Sheridan had helped Louisa escape Sweetwater Crossing.

"I know you want to help my mother." Phoebe wrinkled her nose. "You always want to help people, but you know you don't want to go back there."

Louisa wouldn't argue with Phoebe, not when she was right. "I don't, but I must."

"It's a good idea, Zeus. I know it." Joshua Porter tugged his hat lower. Though it wasn't officially spring yet, the Texas sun was bright enough that he was forced to squint unless the brim shaded his eyes, and when he squinted, he had the uncomfortable feeling that he was missing something. Traveling alone, he could not afford to miss anything, especially when the nearest town was miles away and hazards like poisonous snakes and javelinas were present.

"Don't you agree?" Josh wasn't surprised when his horse failed to respond. There were times when the black gelding with three white socks and a star would neigh or toss his head as if he understood, but Josh knew the horse that had carried him halfway across the country was responding to the tone of his voice, not the actual words.

Still, he continued, because speaking helped the miles pass more quickly than merely letting the thoughts bounce through his brain. "Grandfather will agree that a room featuring American foods is a good way to celebrate P&S's centennial." And a way to ensure that Josh's father's dream came true. That was one thought he wouldn't voice, even though there was no one other than his horse to overhear him. Some things were too important to be shared.

"It's a good idea." As he repeated the words, Josh wondered whether he was trying to convince Zeus or himself. The pickled eggs, the molasses pie, the maple-cured ham, the pumpkin bisque, and the dozen other foods he'd deemed special enough for the American Room of what Grandfather called the New World's answer to Fortnum & Mason were delicious, and unless Josh was greatly mistaken, they'd appeal to Porter & Sons' customers.

He'd traveled north, south, and now west, sampling foods, watching how they were prepared, and requesting recipes. Until this morning, he'd been certain that his idea was the right one, that Grandfather would agree that his concept was better than his cousin's. But now . . .

Josh stared at the scenery of what locals called the Texas

Hill Country. The combination of rolling hills with limestone outcroppings, verdant meadows, vivid blue skies, and more cactus than he'd seen anywhere appealed to him in ways that none of the other places he'd visited had. There was something different about this part of the Lone Star State, something that made his heart sing. Unfortunately, though his heart was singing, his brain was telling him his plan lacked something.

"What is it, Zeus? What am I missing?"

For a second, there was no response. Then the horse neighed and stopped abruptly, flinging Josh forward. *Protect your head.* His father's instructions echoed through his brain, but it was too late. As he hit the ground, excruciating pain radiated from Josh's skull down his spine, and he heard a bone crack just before the world turned black.

"It's only another ten miles." Louisa tried to sound encouraging, but the way Mrs. Sheridan was worrying a pleat in her skirt told her the older woman was even less anxious to reach Sweetwater Crossing than Louisa. Normally Phoebe's mother would no more have disturbed the lines of a garment than allow her graying blond hair to be anything but perfectly coiffed. Mrs. Sheridan was wrinkling her skirt and seemed oblivious to the strands that had escaped from her bun. Even more telling, she refused to meet Louisa's gaze, instead keeping her eyes—the same shade of blue as her daughter's—fixed on her lap.

Fortunately, the journey was approaching its end. They'd gotten an early start this morning, so unless the horse threw a shoe or one of the buggy's wheels broke, they should arrive by early afternoon.

"I appreciate your coming with me."

Louisa had done more than accompany the doctor's widow. Though they'd planned to take turns driving, Louisa had held the reins for the entire distance once she realized how distraught Mrs. Sheridan was. Louisa had insisted that the widow drink warm milk after supper in hopes that it would help her fall asleep in the unfamiliar bed of the inn where they'd spent the night. She'd been the one who'd insisted on eating a good breakfast and stopping every two hours, ostensibly to let the horse rest, but mostly because she wanted Mrs. Sheridan to relax by walking for a few minutes.

Relaxation, Austin Goddard had told Louisa the first day that she'd accompanied him on a house call, was essential to the healing process. And Mrs. Sheridan needed to heal, even though she had sustained no physical injuries. The emotional toll a loved one's death took could be as dangerous as a broken bone. Louisa hadn't needed Dr. Goddard to tell her that. She'd had firsthand experience with the effects of grief.

"You've been so kind to me," Mrs. Sheridan continued, raising her hand from her skirt to fidget with her hat ribbons. Though the doctor's wife had smiled more often in Cimarron Creek than Louisa could recall her doing in Sweetwater Crossing, perhaps because she'd been surrounded by family, she was not smiling now.

"It was the least I could do. If it weren't for you, I'd still be living in Sweetwater Crossing." *In my sisters' shadows, never managing to measure up to them, no matter what I did.* Though Louisa did not utter the words, the thoughts had been her companions for far too many years. Her sisters had mastered whatever they attempted. Louisa had failed countless times.

She fixed her gaze on the road, nodding when she realized there were no curves on this stretch and the horse would need no guidance. Turning to look at her passenger, she managed a small smile. "Cimarron Creek is wonderful."

Not only had the town's doctor and midwife helped her realize her dream, but there'd been no expectations to overcome. For the seven months she'd lived there, she'd simply been Louisa

Vaughn, not Louisa, the youngest daughter of Pastor Vaughn, the girl the parishioners had called the plain one.

"I always liked it," Mrs. Sheridan said, "but I also liked Sweetwater Crossing. Now I'm afraid of what's waiting for me. What are people saying? How will they treat me?"

Louisa knew the feeling. When it had appeared that her father had taken his own life, some of the townspeople had shunned her and Emily. That was one of the reasons she'd been so grateful when Mrs. Sheridan had invited her to accompany her and Phoebe to the town where Phoebe had been born. It was there Louisa had met the people who'd changed her life.

"You might be surprised. Everyone in town likes you." The doctor and his wife had been pillars of the community, both respected and liked by the other residents.

"But that was before Roger . . ."

"Died." Louisa completed the sentence, choosing the least offensive word to describe what had happened, though the actual events had been scandalous. "You're his widow. You deserve their sympathy." Just as Louisa and her sisters had deserved sympathy after Father's death.

Mrs. Sheridan brushed away the tear that had slid down her cheek. "I hope they'll understand, but even if they do, I know one thing: I won't stay there. Phoebe's all I have left, and you heard her. She won't leave Cimarron Creek."

Louisa couldn't blame her. Cimarron Creek was safe. Sweetwater Crossing was . . .

Uncertain how to complete the thought, she tried to dismiss her own worries about the reception she'd receive from Emily. If her sister was hostile, it was no more than Louisa deserved after the way she'd treated her. If the house where she'd grown up no longer felt like home, it wouldn't matter, because she'd be there only a few days.

As much to encourage herself as Mrs. Sheridan, Louisa said, "We'll be back in Cimarron Creek soon."

The widow nodded, then rested her head against the seat-back. "I hope you won't mind if I close my eyes for a bit. I'm tired."

Suspecting that dread rather than a lack of sleep was causing Mrs. Sheridan's fatigue, Louisa nodded.

Take a deep breath, she told herself when she felt her hands tighten on the reins. *Stop worrying*. How many times had Father preached about the futility of worry? Louisa had lost count, but she hadn't forgotten the way Father had insisted it was important to count blessings instead of fears. It was time to do that. She might not be able to escape what was ahead, but she could and would enjoy the rest of the drive.

The sight of ancient live oaks growing next to a small stream, their branches providing what would be welcome shade during Texas's hot summers, and the sound of two hawks greeting each other as they soared above made her smile. As Father used to say, God had given the Hill Country an abundant share of beauty, a reminder of the beauty that awaited them in eternity.

"Oh, Father, I miss you so much!" The words escaped before Louisa could control them. "I may not have been your favorite, but I know you loved me." She blinked away the tears that threatened to fall, then blinked again when the normally placid horse whinnied, apparently alarmed by something Louisa had yet to see.

She stared at the road, trying to determine what had startled the horse. There was nothing. A few seconds later, Louisa's breath caught at the sight of a dark form on the side of the road. Surely it wasn't . . . But it was. The horse had spotted a man. A man who wasn't moving.

"Whoa!" She stopped the buggy and leapt down, her heart pounding while she tried to remember everything Austin had taught her about serious injuries. If only she wasn't too late. As she ran toward the stranger, Louisa offered silent prayers for the man's safety. *Please, God, let him still be breathing. Grant me the skill to help him.* She didn't want to consider the alternative, for there'd been far too many deaths in the past year.

She knelt at the man's side, relief flooding through her when she saw his chest moving. Her first prayer had been answered. He was still alive. Alive but in desperate need of care.

The man's hat was nowhere to be seen, perhaps blown away, and his blond hair bore as much dirt as his obviously expensive garments. Unlike many men who favored muttonchop whiskers or large moustaches, this man's cheeks had only a light stubble, telling Louisa both that he was normally clean-shaven and that he'd been here at least overnight. Under other circumstances, she would have found him handsome. Now her primary concern was the extent of his injuries.

Though he might have heard her approach, her patient kept his eyes closed, giving Louisa an opportunity to catalogue his symptoms without distractions. The parched lips, flushed skin, and rapid breathing indicated he was suffering from dehydration, possibly heatstroke. The unnatural angle of his left leg told her he'd broken it, but he was alive. Blessedly alive. And, if her prayers were answered, he'd be coherent enough to answer a few questions, because before she could move him, she had to learn more.

"What happened?" she asked as she laid her hand on the injured man's forehead, confirming the fever she'd feared. "I'm Louisa Vaughn, and I want to help you. What's your name?"

"Zeus."

Though the reply surprised her, because Louisa had never met a man named Zeus, she was relieved that he'd understood her question and responded.

"All right, Mr. Zeus. Can you tell me what happened?"

The man's eyelids flew up, revealing vivid blue eyes. "I'm not Zeus. I'm Porter. Gotta find Zeus." His words were slurred, evidence of the severity of his condition, but at least Mr. Porter was coherent. "Help me stand."

Louisa shook her head. Even if he wanted to walk, it would be difficult with his broken leg. "First, let's get you some water." The leg could wait; his dehydration could not.

Mama had taught her daughters that ladies never ran, but this was no time for etiquette. Louisa raced back to the buggy and pulled out the jug of water she'd filled this morning, surprised that despite the unexpected stop, Mrs. Sheridan was still asleep.

When she returned to her patient, Louisa sat next to him and helped him raise his head, noting as she did that his shoulders were broader than many men's. "Just a sip now," she said as she held the jug to his lips. The water might help reduce his fever as well as quench his thirst.

Though it was clear that Mr. Porter wanted more, he followed her instructions. "That's better." His voice sounded better too. "Where's Zeus?"

"Is he your horse?" Louisa held the jug to his lips again, watching as he swallowed another mouthful of water. He'd need far more than the two swigs, but if he drank too quickly, his stomach would rebel.

"Yes." Mr. Porter looked around, searching for the missing animal. The horses Louisa knew would have stayed close to their riders, but Zeus had not.

"Something spooked him. He threw me off. Next thing I knew, I was here." Her patient rubbed the top of his head, drawing Louisa's attention to the lump that had formed on it.

She took a deep breath and offered another prayer. Austin had warned her about head injuries, saying they could be dangerous, but he'd given her little advice on how to treat them. She'd have to hope that this one was not serious. When she reached Sweetwater Crossing, she'd see what Doc Sheridan's medical books said. But first she had to get Mr. Porter there.

"You've broken your leg," she told him. "It needs to be set, but I can't do that here. We need to get you into the buggy."

When she glanced that direction, Louisa saw that Mrs. Sheridan had wakened. She beckoned her over, knowing it would take both of them to support the man's weight and help him climb into the carriage.

"I need your assistance, Mrs. Sheridan. As you can see, Mr. Porter is injured. I'm going to take him to Sweetwater Crossing."

When the widow nodded, Louisa's patient shook his head, then winced at the pain that must have shot through him from the sudden action. "I can't leave without Zeus and my saddlebags."

Louisa gave thanks that his speech was no longer slurred and that he was forming complete sentences, telling herself that the head injury was not as serious as she'd feared. Unfortunately, she could not reassure Mr. Porter about Zeus. "There's no sign of your horse."

This time his face registered dismay as well as pain. "There must be. I can't lose him or those saddlebags." Those eyes, as brilliant as the summer sky, beseeched Louisa to say she was mistaken, that the horse was grazing only a few yards away. "I can't lose them," he repeated. "Especially the bags. They're worth more than Zeus."

Louisa's optimism about Mr. Porter's condition faded with his insistence on finding his possessions. The head injury must have been more severe than she'd thought if he was so worried about saddlebags. Unless he was carrying gold or jewels, even finely tooled saddlebags weren't worth more than a horse.

"What's in the bags?" she asked as she helped him to his feet, draping one of his arms over her shoulders, the other over Mrs. Sheridan's.

Mr. Porter frowned. "My future."

Chapter Two

Josh winced as the buggy hit another rut. His leg hurt, his head hurt, his throat hurt. Every inch of his body hurt, but that pain seemed almost insignificant when compared to his heart. Zeus was gone, and unless by some miracle he could find him, so was his hope of winning the competition.

But miracles did happen. It seemed like nothing short of a miracle that he'd been found before the sun had leached the last bit of moisture from his body, leaving him like one of the dried-out cacti he'd seen on the side of the road. He'd not only been found, but he'd been found by a woman who'd surprised him with her calm and competence.

Even though she was composed under most circumstances, Winifred might have swooned at the sight of a man suffering from both dehydration and a badly broken leg lying on the side of the road. Not this woman. Miss Vaughn had assessed his situation and taken charge, just as she'd taken charge of driving the buggy. Though the black-clad older woman had helped him walk and climb into it, she'd said not a word, deferring to Miss Vaughn.

"Where are we headed?" Josh directed his question to the

woman who'd rescued him. The water she'd given him had relieved some of his discomfort, but the damage to his head must have been more severe than he'd realized, because he thought he recalled her saying she would set his leg. Obviously, he'd been mistaken. With her caramel-colored hair and those deep blue eyes, not to mention her self-assured air, Miss Vaughn was striking. But she was no more capable of setting his leg than Winifred.

Miss Vaughn turned slightly. "We're going to Sweetwater Crossing. It's about an hour away. Once we arrive, I'll be able to set your leg. As far as I can tell, the lump on your head will heal itself."

It hadn't been his imagination. Miss Vaughn had indeed claimed she would set his leg. "You're a doctor?" Josh knew there were a few lady doctors, but he hadn't expected to encounter one here.

Grandfather would have approved of Miss Vaughn. She had the cool composure he claimed was essential. If she had the business connections he craved, Grandfather would deem her worthy of being a Porter bride, but once she admitted she was a physician, he would . . . Josh tried but failed to imagine his grandfather's reaction to that revelation.

"She's your only choice." The older woman spoke for the first time, bringing Josh back to the present. "My husband was the town's doctor, but . . ." She paused for a second before saying, "He's gone."

Of course. Josh should have realized that the unrelieved black clothing she wore was widow's weeds. "I'm sorry." He struggled to recall the widow's name. "Mrs. Carrigan."

She shook her head. "Sheridan."

"I'm sorry for the mistake and for your loss."

When the widow returned to staring at the road ahead of them, Miss Vaughn gave Josh a small smile. "It's understandable. If you're in pain, it's hard to think about anything else. Names aren't important at a time like that. I'm Louisa Vaughn."

Josh nodded as the sun slipped behind a cloud, dimming its brilliance. At least his memory hadn't dimmed. "I remembered your name." And that each mile they traveled took them farther from the spot he'd last seen Zeus. Where was he? A horse as well trained as Zeus didn't simply wander away from his owner.

Oblivious to the direction Josh's thoughts had taken, Miss Vaughn spoke. "It's good that you recalled part of our conversation. I'm not a full-fledged doctor, but I have set several broken bones, including a tibia. Yours is badly broken—I won't deny that—but I believe I can ensure that you'll walk again."

Josh frowned at the realization that, even when he'd worried about dying from lack of water, he hadn't considered that he might not regain his mobility. "How long will it take?" He still had three and a half months before he had to be back in New York, but time had a habit of passing more quickly than he expected. If he was going to recreate the recipes he'd lost or find others to replace them, he'd need every minute of those three and a half months.

"You'll be in a cast for at least six weeks," the almost-doctor told him. "Once you learn how to use crutches, you should be able to walk."

"But not ride a horse."

"No."

"What about driving a buggy or wagon?" Josh couldn't imagine spending a month and a half in one town.

"It would be difficult, particularly at first. Driving wouldn't be a problem, but climbing in and out of the carriage would be a challenge. I don't recommend it."

The bad news seemed endless. No horse. No recipes. Six weeks of boredom. Josh settled back on the seat, trying to ignore the pain that continued to radiate up his leg and the sense that his plan for convincing Grandfather he was the man to control P&S was doomed. He couldn't have come this far to lose.

As he closed his eyes, his father's words echoed through his brain. *"Keep your eye on the goal, son. Do whatever it takes to win. Don't settle for second place. Jed may be older, but you're better. When it's your turn, prove it."*

Josh winced again, as much from the remembered ferocity of his father's words as from the pain. He'd do what Father wanted once he could walk and ride again. He'd been given the chance that had not been offered to his father, and he would not squander it. He would . . .

As the buggy jolted, Josh's eyes flew open. Somehow, though he hadn't expected it, he must have dozed off. He lifted his head, smiling when he saw the stretch of road ahead. Those weren't the first live oaks he'd seen. They'd been plentiful in South Carolina and Georgia, their limbs dripping with silvery Spanish moss. He'd seen some here in Texas, frequently marking the location of a small stream. This was the first time, however, that he'd seen oaks lining both sides of the road, their branches arching to meet in the center. Others might consider the oak canopy ordinary, but it gave Josh a sense of peace. Perhaps, despite all that had gone wrong, he would succeed.

Five minutes later, Miss Vaughn turned toward him. "We're almost there."

They crossed a stream, which she informed him was called Sweetwater Creek. "Our town founders weren't very imaginative," she said with a wry smile. "When they learned the name of the creek and realized that two roads intersected here, they decided to call the town Sweetwater Crossing."

Continuing south on what she said was Center Street—another less-than-imaginative name accompanied by another wry smile—they reached what was obviously the center of town. The school and a restaurant stood opposite each other, with the church and another stone building anchoring the other corners.

Miss Vaughn turned left, stopping the buggy in front of the two-story building whose identity Josh hadn't been able to discern from a distance. The minor mystery was solved by the presence of a small sign in the front window proclaiming it the doctor's office. They'd reached their destination and not an hour too soon, because the dull ache in Josh's leg had become an incessant throb.

Once the widow handed Miss Vaughn a large key from her reticule, the almost-doctor nodded at Josh. "Let's get you inside. Mrs. Sheridan, I'll need your assistance."

The way the older woman stared at the building with what appeared to be disgust surprised Josh, because if this was like other offices he'd seen, the doctor and his wife had lived above it. Hers was hardly a normal reaction to coming home.

"All right." The widow's tone underscored her displeasure. "But if you need someone to hold him while you set the leg, you'll have to find someone else. I never assisted my husband."

Together the two women helped Josh into the office. It was awkward and painful, but no worse than getting into the buggy had been.

As they made their way into the doctor's treatment room, the widow frowned again. "Once you're done here, you'll need to find him a place to stay."

"What about the infirmary?"

Mrs. Sheridan shook her head and continued speaking as if Josh weren't present. "There won't be anyone to help if he falls. I plan to stay with Lorena and Wilbur. I want nothing to do with this place."

There was a story behind her vehemence, but Josh knew better than to ask.

Miss Vaughn let out a sigh. "Then there's only one answer. He'll have to stay at Finley House."

It sounded like some kind of an institution. "What's that?"

"My former home."

Louisa studied the cast for a moment before nodding her approval. Austin would be proud of the way it looked, just as he would have approved the way she'd straightened her patient's tibia without assistance. The break had not been as bad as she'd feared, but Mr. Porter would still have a long recovery, and unless she was greatly mistaken, he would not relish the inactivity.

When he tried to rise, Louisa placed a hand on his shoulder, easing him back onto the treatment table. His color was better, and the fever had subsided, but it was too soon for him to attempt to move.

Fortunately, when Doc Sheridan had equipped his office, he'd made certain that the examining table in the room that also housed his desk, bookshelves, and the cabinets filled with medicines was comfortable enough for a patient to lie there for an hour or so. The infirmary on the opposite side of the hallway was reserved for longer stays.

"You need to rest." And she needed to visit her sister. "I should be back within an hour. By then, your cast will be completely dry." And Louisa would know whether Emily could forgive her.

Mr. Porter managed a small smile. "I don't know how to thank you. I can't imagine anyone could have done a better job."

The unexpected praise sent warmth flowing through her. "You were a better patient than the first one whose leg I tried to set."

"Who was that?"

Keeping her expression neutral, Louisa said, "The question is, *what* was that. It was a rabbit. I was about ten years old and was sure I could fix its broken leg. The bunny had other ideas and hopped away from me as fast as he could, even though he had only three good legs."

As she'd hoped, her patient smiled, and this time it was a

full-fledged one. "I can promise I won't be hopping anywhere, Miss Vaughn." He paused for a second, then asked, "Or should I address you as Dr. Vaughn?"

"I'd prefer that you call me Louisa." She wasn't a full-fledged doctor, so being addressed as such felt wrong.

"Thank you. I'm Josh."

Josh. The name suited him better than the more formal Joshua she imagined was on his birth certificate. Perhaps it was because of his slightly scruffy appearance, the result of his not having shaved for a day, but Louisa could not imagine him answering to his full name. The nickname fit.

Once she was assured that Josh was resting comfortably, she left the office. It would be faster to take the buggy that Mrs. Sheridan had left for her and her patient, but after two days in it, Louisa preferred to walk. Perhaps the exercise would settle her thoughts and prepare her for seeing Emily again.

I can do this, she told herself. *It won't be as bad as I've feared.*

She strode briskly east on Main Street, then turned north to head for what had been her home for as long as she could remember. When she rounded the corner onto Creek Road, Louisa paused, letting her gaze roam over the building that held so many memories. What would Josh think when he saw it? To her, Finley House looked the same as it had last year. Only she was different, both inside and out.

As she climbed the front steps rather than using the family's normal entrance, Louisa remembered how Emily had done the same when she'd returned to Sweetwater Crossing after her husband's death. Had she felt as out of place as Louisa did now? No matter how Emily had felt, Louisa should have been kinder.

She knocked on the front door, waiting until her sister opened it.

"Louisa?" Emily's expression registered surprise, and the blue eyes that were the only characteristic she and Louisa shared widened. "Is it really you?"

"Yes, it's me. Am I welcome?" She hadn't planned to be so blunt, but the question came out seemingly of its own volition.

Emily's response was immediate. She took a step forward and wrapped her arms around Louisa. "Of course you are. This is your home."

For a second, Louisa let herself savor the warmth of her sister's hug. The shortest of the three Vaughn girls, Emily was also the most slender, her petite stature, golden-blond hair, and deep blue eyes making some refer to her as a living doll. No matter what they called her, everyone agreed that Emily was the prettiest sister, the one true beauty.

As if recalling that they were on the porch in full view of anyone who might pass by, Emily let her arms fall to her side. "Why are we standing in the doorway? Come in and tell me what happened."

The formal parlor that had been the site of so many whispered conversations as the sisters shared the sometimes silly details of their lives hadn't changed. The horsehair settee still sat in front of the fireplace with two chairs perpendicular to it. The piano where Joanna had spent countless hours practicing was still on the opposite side of the door next to the pocket doors that led to the library. The only difference Louisa saw was the small chair between the two wingback chairs that Mama and Father had appropriated as their own. The chair, she assumed, belonged to Noah, the schoolmaster's young son.

By unspoken agreement, she and Emily sat on opposite ends of the settee. When they were both seated, Emily spoke. "I like your hair. It suits you, but at first I almost didn't recognize you."

Louisa raised a hand to her coiffure. "One of the women in Cimarron Creek used to live in France. She taught me how to fix my hair and what colors to wear."

Phoebe's hand-me-down clothes, which had been the staple of Louisa's wardrobe for more than a decade, had flattered Phoebe's blond hair and pale skin, but they'd left Louisa looking sallow. Aimee had chosen a different palette of colors for her and had insisted that Louisa's hair, which she'd always considered mousy brown and best hidden inside a snood, was one of her best features and needed to be treated as such.

"You're beautiful." Coming from Emily, whose beauty had never been in question, the compliment was particularly valuable.

"You look radiant." Gone was the saddened sister who'd greeted Louisa last year. In her place was a woman whose happiness glowed brighter than a full moon.

Emily's smile broadened. "If I look different, it's because of Craig. We're going to be married."

To Louisa's dismay, Emily's announcement brought a twinge of jealousy. She'd thought she'd outgrown her childish feelings of being inferior to her oldest sister, but the realization that Emily had found happiness a second time when Louisa had yet to have a single beau revived them. Deliberately, she squashed her envy and forced a smile.

"I'm happy for you." And, though she hadn't expected it, speaking the words made them true. She *was* happy for Emily.

"Craig's a good man," Louisa added. She hadn't approved Emily's decision to turn their home into a boardinghouse and offer the town's new schoolteacher, his son, and the woman who had agreed to care for little Noah during the day a permanent place to stay, but she'd never denied that Craig Ferguson was admirable. And if he made her sister happy, he was more than admirable. He was a hero like those in the stories Emily used to read.

"He is, but let's not talk about me. Are you home permanently?"

Louisa couldn't decipher Emily's expression. "Do you want me to stay?" Even though she didn't plan to remain, the answer was important.

"Of course I do. This is your home." Emily repeated her

earlier response, punctuating it with a smile that Louisa guessed was designed to reassure her.

"Even after all the horrible things I said and the way I abandoned you at the worst time of your life?" Though Emily sounded sincere, Louisa couldn't believe she could forget the way they'd parted. "I should have stayed here and helped you, but I didn't. I let my anger overrule my common sense."

The way Emily's smile faded told Louisa she was recalling how hateful Louisa had been, but her voice was calm as she said, "You'd been through a difficult time. Watching Mama die couldn't have been easy for you."

It hadn't been, particularly when both Father and Mama had refused to let her treat Mama. They'd insisted that Doc Sheridan was the expert and that he knew more than Louisa. Much more.

"That doesn't excuse me. I hurt you. Why, I didn't even try to comfort you over George's death."

An expression Louisa could not identify flitted across Emily's face. "That doesn't matter."

"But it does. I'm sorry, Emily, so sorry for all the things I said. I'm sorry I abandoned you, and I'm sorry I didn't answer your letters." Emily had written to her each week, and though Louisa had devoured the news greedily, she had not responded. "Can you forgive me for all that I did?"

In response, Emily slid along the settee until she was next to Louisa and wrapped her in another hug. "All is forgiven. I love you, little sister. I always have. I always will."

The reunion Louisa had feared had been far better than she'd expected or deserved. "And I love you."

"Does that mean you're here to stay?"

"I don't think so." No matter how good it felt to be with Emily again and know that the barriers Louisa had erected had tumbled, Phoebe was right. Louisa had no future in Sweetwater Crossing.

"You know I'm going to try to convince you otherwise, but at least you'll be here for a few days. I assume you brought Mrs. Sheridan back for the funeral."

"She's not the only one I brought." As quickly as she could, Louisa explained about Josh and his injury. "I was hoping you'd have a room for him while he recuperates. The problem is, climbing stairs will be difficult."

Emily was silent for a moment, her pursed lips telling Louisa she was pondering something. When she spoke, her suggestion startled Louisa. "We could bring a bed downstairs and turn the library into a room for him."

"Father's office?" Louisa looked at the pocket doors that separated the parlor from the large library where their father had written his sermons and counseled his parishioners. That had always been Father's room, his private sanctuary. Turning it into a bedroom seemed somehow wrong.

"Why not? No one's used it since Father died."

"You're right. It's the perfect solution. Thanks, Emily." That was Emily, always practical. Always determined to find a solution.

Louisa swallowed the lump that had lodged in her throat. Josh needed a place to stay, and this was it.

Chapter Three

"This is your home?" Josh stared at the house that looked decidedly out of place in this town of modestly sized buildings. When Louisa had mentioned that her father had been the town's minister, he'd envisioned a small parsonage, not a house that reminded him of plantation mansions in Mississippi and Louisiana.

Set farther back from the street than the other houses in Sweetwater Crossing, Finley House was surrounded by a stone wall, its sweeping driveway flanked by pillars topped with cement balls. And, in case anyone in town was unaware of the mansion's name, the pillars bore placards proclaiming it to be Finley House.

The entrance was impressive, the building even more so. Finley House appeared to have four stories, if you included the attic and the level that Europeans might have called the ground floor, located as it was beneath the twin curving staircases that led to the front door. The four columns that supported the front porch and the second-story verandah weren't as elaborate as some in the South, but they were grander than anything he'd seen in Sweetwater Crossing. Yet, though the building was large, its design wasn't garish. Instead, Josh would have described it as elegant. Much like the woman who seemed amused by his reaction.

"I sometimes forget how it must appear to newcomers," Louisa said as she parked the buggy at the side of the house. "I lived there my whole life, so I'm used to it, but my mother once admitted she found it ostentatious."

"Then why did your parents build it?" From what Josh knew of the Hill Country, most towns were only a couple decades old, meaning that Louisa's parents were probably the first owners of Finley House.

"They didn't. They inherited it . . . sort of." Louisa climbed down from the buggy and walked to the other side. "A man from Alabama named Clive Finley came to Sweetwater Crossing before the war," she said. "The story is that he wanted to bring his bride here, but her father wouldn't give them his blessing unless Clive could offer her a house as grand as the one she'd grown up in." When she reached Josh, she raised her arms. "Let's get you down from there."

How he hated being so dependent. Seeing him and Louisa struggling to maneuver him into the buggy, the postmaster had rushed out to assist them and volunteered to accompany them here, but Josh declined the offer, insisting he'd be able to get out by himself. As he looked down at the ground and estimated the distance, he wondered if his confidence had been misplaced. As much as he hated admitting he needed help, Josh leaned on Louisa as he swung his leg with the bulky cast onto the ground. It was only when he'd fitted the crutches under his arm and started walking that she continued the tale.

"The house was almost finished when the war broke out. When Clive returned to Alabama to fight alongside his neighbors, he asked my father to move in and take care of the house until he returned."

To Josh's relief, rather than entering the house from the

front, Louisa led him toward a side entrance with only one step rather than the more than a dozen on the front staircases.

"But Clive Finley didn't return."

"No. He was one of the many who perished in that horrible conflict. My family has been here ever since." Josh suspected that Louisa's frown was caused by her thoughts, not his halting gait. "After my parents' deaths last year, Emily—she's my oldest sister—turned our home into a boardinghouse. You'll meet the other residents at supper. Now, let me get the door for you."

Almost before Josh knew it, it was suppertime, and he was seated at the large table in Finley House's dining room. He'd been shown the room that would become his bedchamber once the furniture was rearranged to accommodate a bed, then had been escorted to the laundry room and given soap, hot water, a towel, and a razor as well as clean clothes that had belonged to Louisa's father. Feeling refreshed and still hungry despite the biscuits and jam Louisa had insisted he eat after he bathed, Josh was looking forward to supper.

The dining room wasn't as large or ornate as the one in Grandfather's mansion. Still, it wasn't what he'd expected of the Texas Hill Country. Neither were the other diners. Josh was grateful for his mother's lessons in how to remember people's names, because Louisa had thrown half a dozen at him before the meal. First came Craig Ferguson, the town's schoolmaster and Louisa's soon-to-be brother-in-law, and his son, a precocious three-year-old named Noah.

Craig, whose height matched Josh's six feet, had somewhat unruly dark brown hair, brown eyes, and a smile that offered the possibility of friendship.

"I can't tell you how glad I am to have another man here," the schoolteacher said when they were introduced. "As much as I love Emily, there are times when I crave masculine conversation." With a fond look at his son, he amended his statement. "*Adult* masculine conversation."

The boy, a miniature version of his father, was engaged in less-than-adult conversation with Mrs. Carmichael, the elderly widow who cared for Noah during the day. According to Louisa, the gray-haired woman was a longtime friend of the family who treated Noah like a grandson, not a charge.

"Those are the three permanent boarders," Louisa had explained, adding that her sister's friend, Alice Patton, and her daughter, whose name Josh had forgotten, normally came for supper each evening rather than depending on the town's sole restaurant for food.

"Alice is a terrible cook," Louisa had said with a wry smile. "Fortunately, her fiancé doesn't seem to care. He's taking her to Ma's Kitchen tonight. The last person is Beulah. Please be kind to her."

The reason for Louisa's admonition was evident when the girl entered the room. Though Beulah's blond hair arranged in a single plait was unremarkable, her almond-shaped eyes and somewhat halting speech told Josh that Beulah was what many would call simple. In his experience, children like her were kept hidden from guests or sent to institutions, but not here. According to Louisa, her sister and Craig had both recognized Beulah's desire to learn and had made it possible for her to attend school by having her board here during the week.

"Emily said it wasn't always easy, but it was the right thing to do."

Josh had to agree when he saw Beulah's eyes sparkle as she recounted what she'd learned in school today. She might not be the most intelligent pupil in Craig's class, but Josh had no doubt that she was one of the most eager.

"What brings you to this part of Texas, Mr. Porter?" Mrs. Carmichael posed the question when Beulah finished reciting a multiplication table. "I can tell from your accent that you're from the East, probably New York."

"You have a good ear. My home is in New York."

Beulah nodded solemnly. "I found it on Mr. Ferguson's map. It's far away."

"Yes, Beulah, it is."

The girl gave him an appraising look. "Is your wife there?"

Before Josh could respond, Emily fixed her gaze on Beulah. "You know it's not polite to ask personal questions."

The girl cringed, clearly chagrined by her error.

"It's all right, Beulah. I don't mind answering. I don't have a wife." Yet. He and Winifred had agreed that unless her father changed his mind, they would announce their betrothal when Josh returned to New York. "I live in my grandfather's house not too far from our store."

Josh saw the moment when recognition sparked in Louisa's eyes.

"Are you part of Porter & Sons?"

She seemed curious rather than avaricious. If Louisa had been one of the women Grandfather had introduced him to, she would have been calculating Josh's potential wealth and how difficult it would be to attract his interest. But her curiosity seemed focused on the store itself.

When Josh nodded, she continued, "Is it as wonderful as the advertisements make it seem?"

Grandfather would be pleased that someone almost two thousand miles from New York had seen the advertisements P&S had placed in several magazines.

"That depends on who you ask," Josh replied. *Wonderful* was not a word he would have used to describe the store. Large, traditional, staid—those adjectives came to mind, but they were overshadowed by *mine*. That wasn't yet the case, but it would be.

Though his pulse accelerated at the prospect of sitting behind the desk Grandfather had called his for half a century, Josh forced his voice to remain neutral. "Our customers seem pleased by the merchandise we carry."

It appeared that was enough. While Josh savored some of

the most delicious fried chicken he'd ever eaten, Craig handed his son a second roll, then turned toward Josh. "You're a long way from home. I imagine there's a story behind that."

There was indeed, but Josh wasn't ready to share it. Instead, he said, "I wanted to see more of the country while I still can."

"Before you assume more responsibility." It was Louisa who completed the sentence. "Your grandfather must be close to retirement."

"He is. We're also preparing to celebrate our centennial."

Noah looked up from the peas he'd been chasing around his plate with the roll. "What's a cen?"

"Cen-ten-ee-al." Emily enunciated each syllable clearly. "Can you say that?"

Noah tried three times before shaking his head and looking at Josh. "What is it?"

"A hundred years."

Beulah's eyes widened. "That's a long time. You must be old." She gave Josh a quizzical look. "Is that why you broke your leg? Mama told me old things break."

"In that case, I guess I am old." Josh's grin turned into a laugh that became contagious, causing everyone at the table to at least chuckle. And as they shared the moment, he realized he hadn't felt this contented since he'd left New York.

It made no sense. His leg was broken. Zeus and the recipes were gone. Even if he bought a carriage, Louisa had warned him it would be difficult getting in and out of it without assistance. All of that meant that he was stranded for six weeks.

He ought to be angry or at least annoyed. Instead, he was almost happy to be here, and that was totally absurd. Perhaps his head injury was more serious than Louisa thought.

Chapter Four

Someone was frying bacon. Louisa's mouth watered and her stomach growled as she forced her eyes open and fumbled for her watch, then blinked in disbelief. She hadn't slept this late in years, and of course it had to be today that she was a sluggard, lying in bed when she ought to be downstairs helping Emily prepare breakfast. That was the least she could do after Emily refused to accept any payment for giving Josh a place to stay, even when it was apparent that he had no financial worries.

"He'll need to buy a new horse," Emily had said. "A good one is expensive, so don't argue with me. You know you won't win."

They'd both laughed at the memory of how many times Emily had said that when they were children, asserting her superiority as the oldest. The words had rankled then, but yesterday they'd felt like balm on a wound, reminding Louisa of Emily's unfailing generosity.

She dressed as quickly as she could, then dashed into the hallway, stopping short when Beulah emerged from her room, her hair in disarray.

"Good morning, Miss Louisa. I'm glad you're here." A wide smile served as confirmation of her declaration.

Louisa returned the smile. "And I'm glad you're here. I was hoping to practice braiding hair this morning. Can I work on yours?" Louisa suspected Emily would normally have done that. It was a small task, but having someone else perform it might help her sister.

Though Beulah appeared dubious for a moment, she nodded. "Okay."

While Louisa brushed Beulah's hair in preparation for braiding it, she tried to engage the girl in conversation. "My sister told me you read stories to Noah." According to Emily, Beulah's reading skills were rudimentary, making her and Craig suspect Beulah was reciting from memory, but Noah didn't know the difference and enjoyed the time they spent together.

"I like books, and I like Noah, and I like you."

"I like you too." Louisa tied a ribbon around Beulah's braid, then hugged her, giving thanks for the easy acceptance that warmed her more than her first cup of coffee did each morning. "Let's see what Miss Emily's making for breakfast."

Beulah sniffed. "Bacon."

"I think you're right." Hand-in-hand, she and Beulah descended the stairs.

"I'm sorry I'm late. What can I do to help you?" Louisa asked as they entered the kitchen, where Emily was mixing pancake batter while Josh sat at the table, sipping a cup of coffee.

"Nothing more." As her eyes darted to Beulah's neatly braided hair, Emily's smile was as warm as the girl's had been. "I never say no to help doing the dishes, but you more than anyone should know that I prefer to cook alone."

That was true. Emily had always complained when Mama supervised her cooking.

"Would you like a cup of coffee?" Emily shook her head, correcting herself. "Why am I asking? I know you always start your mornings with one." She gestured toward the empty chair next to Josh, then filled a cup and handed it to Louisa. "Josh has been keeping me company, telling me about his travels."

While Louisa sipped her coffee, Josh continued to recount tales of the places he'd visited and the foods he'd eaten. Though Louisa suspected there was a deeper reason for his journey than simply wanting to explore the country, she didn't want to disrupt this conversation, not when Beulah was enjoying it so much.

As the young girl stared at Josh, clearly enraptured by the tales he was spinning, he kept his attention focused on her, freeing Louisa to study him. She'd known Josh was good-looking when she'd found him lying beside the road, and his appeal had only increased when he'd come to supper, freshly shaved and wearing some of Father's clothes. Now, with the lines of fatigue erased by a good night's sleep, he was even more attractive.

It was silly to be thinking about his appearance. After all, he was her patient—no more, no less. Even if Sweetwater Crossing's single women would view him as a potential suitor, Louisa knew he was only a temporary resident. A man like Josh Porter would never make a small town in the Hill Country his home. Why should he, when a bright and prosperous future and, in all likelihood, a dozen heiresses awaited him back in New York?

"How is your leg this morning?" Louisa asked when he finished a story. That was the question a physician should ask, not how many women were counting the days until Josh returned.

He wrinkled his nose. "Awkward, unwieldy, uncomfortable, and much better than yesterday."

"Exactly what I expected." She gave him another appraising look, telling herself her concern was purely professional. "You'll feel better when we get you some clothes that fit." Though Josh was the same height as Father, his broader chest and more muscular arms made the shirt strain. "I'll stop at the mercantile before I talk to the sheriff."

"Sheriff?" Beulah's face fell, and she stared at Josh in alarm. "Did Mr. Porter do something bad?"

He shook his head to reassure her. "Someone did something bad to me. He stole my horse."

"Ooh, that's bad."

"Very bad," Craig chimed in as he entered the kitchen with Noah at his side, "but if anyone can find him, it's Sheriff Granger. He'll do his best to track down your horse."

"I agree." Mrs. Carmichael stood in the doorway, a smile crossing her face when Beulah seemed to relax. Though the woman was close to seventy years old, she appeared to have the energy of someone a decade younger, a definite blessing when caring for an active toddler.

Emily turned from the pancakes she was flipping. "Breakfast is almost ready, so why don't you take your seats in the dining room?"

Growing up, the family had eaten breakfast every day except Sunday in the kitchen, but Emily had explained that she preferred to serve meals away from the clutter of pots and pans.

Noah jumped up and down, then tugged on Mrs. Carmichael's hand. "Let's go. I'm hungry!"

The meal was even better than Louisa had expected. Their mother had been a good cook, but Emily's skills surpassed hers. The bacon was crisp but not burned, the pancakes light and moist, the coffee exceptionally good. Noah smacked his lips with pleasure, and the other guests' comments echoed his approval.

"This was outstanding," Josh said.

To Louisa's surprise, though color stained her cheeks, Emily seemed unconvinced of Josh's praise.

"I'm sure you've had better food in New York."

He shook his head. "No, ma'am. I can honestly say that

these are the best pancakes I've ever eaten. If Porter & Sons served breakfast, I'd try to convince you to share your secret."

The smile Craig gave Emily reminded Louisa of the ones her parents used to exchange, a look so filled with love that the girls had sometimes felt like outsiders. How fortunate Emily was to have a second chance at love like that.

"Thank you, Josh," Craig said. "You just confirmed what I've been telling Emily ever since I arrived. She's an excellent cook and . . ." He paused for a second before adding, "So much more."

Blushing, Emily wagged her finger at the man she planned to marry. "And you, Mr. Flatterer, had better head for school. You don't want your pupils to beat you there."

Louisa felt another rush of pleasure at the sight of how happy Craig made her sister. If she married, and she hoped she would, this was the kind of deep and abiding love manifested in gently affectionate teasing that she wanted to share with her husband. But marriage was in the distant future. First, she needed to return to Cimarron Creek and continue learning everything she could from Austin and Thea.

When the others had left the room, Josh turned to Louisa, a question in his eyes. "I suspect I know the answer, but are you certain I can't walk to the mercantile myself?"

Louisa refilled both of their cups, then smiled at her decidedly impatient patient. "If the answer you're expecting is 'it's too soon,' you're right. I don't advise even getting in and out of a buggy for a few more days. The cast keeps your leg immobile, but you still need to rest and let the healing begin." When he'd taught her to set bones, Austin had stressed how critical the first days were for successful healing.

Josh raised his hand to salute her. "Yes, Doctor."

She couldn't help chuckling. "I should be back within an hour," she said as she pushed her chair away from the table and rose. "You need clothes, and we need Sheriff Granger to start the search for your horse."

She probably should have contacted the sheriff yesterday, but between setting Josh's leg and her reunion with Emily, Louisa had had no energy left. Not wanting to discourage Josh, she hadn't said how unlikely it was that Zeus would be found. Horses were one of the most valuable commodities in Texas, and even though horse thievery was punishable by death, stolen horses were rarely recovered.

When she left Finley House and headed west, Louisa saw Mrs. Sheridan deep in conversation with Mrs. Albright on the Albrights' front porch. Some things never changed, including the two women's friendship. But some things did. Mrs. Adams's former home boasted fresh paint, confirming what Emily had written in one of her letters, that the church was planning to make it an annex to the newly completed parsonage, a place for visitors to stay.

The biggest change was the parsonage itself. Twice the size of the former one and made of stone, it bore no resemblance to the place where Louisa's parents had spent the first few months of their marriage. Not only did the stone make it more impressive, but—more importantly—it was less likely to burn. After last year's fire, the parishioners were taking no chances.

One of Emily's letters had recounted the story of how fortunate the church elders felt when Raymond Knapp came to live with his aunt and uncle. Though the Bentleys had expected him to work in their mercantile and eventually inherit it, he'd been a builder in Mesquite Springs and had volunteered to take charge of constructing the parsonage.

"He did such a good job that he now has more work than he can handle," Emily had written.

The exterior of the parsonage confirmed the quality of Raymond's work.

Louisa smiled as she glanced across the street, the sound

of pupils singing reminding her of how Miss Albright had led them in song, even though her singing ability was nonexistent. Joanna, the musical Vaughn daughter, had cringed, but Louisa and Emily had found song time amusing and had tried to imitate their teacher's voice. Such good memories.

Her heart as light as the children's voices, Louisa entered the mercantile.

"Good morning, Louisa." Adam Bentley nodded as he greeted her, his light brown hair as unruly as ever, tumbling onto his forehead, since he refused to use the Macassar oil he stocked for his customers. "I heard you were back in town and trying to be a doctor."

There was no point in being annoyed by his assumption that medicine was some kind of game for Louisa. She knew the truth, and part of that truth was that, no matter how good it had felt to be with Emily yesterday, it was unlikely Sweetwater Crossing's residents would accept her as a physician. Her future was in Cimarron Creek.

"My patient is the reason I'm here," Louisa told the mercantile's proprietor. "You may have heard that his horse and all his belongings were stolen." The grapevine, probably fueled by Mrs. Sheridan and the postmaster, was as active as ever. When Mr. Bentley nodded, Louisa continued. "He needs new clothes." She looked around the store. "Is Mrs. Bentley here? She used to help me choose clothing for Father."

It wasn't simply because she was a woman that Louisa preferred to have Mrs. Bentley serve her. During those final weeks when Mama had been so ill, Mrs. Bentley had come to Finley House each day, spending at least half an hour with Mama. "You need a break," she'd told Louisa, "and I need time with your mother. She's my dearest friend." Her visits had been a boon to both Mama and Louisa, and Louisa wanted to thank her again.

Mr. Bentley shook his head. "I guess you haven't heard the

news. The missus and I bought a farm south of town. I reckon it was about a month after you left."

"I didn't know that."

"Tina had a hard time without Tillie. Doc said it would get better, but it didn't. After your mother died, Tina didn't want to stay here with all the memories, so we bought the farm. Now she has enough land to raise bees."

Louisa tried not to shudder at the image of swarming honeybees. Though she loved almost all of God's creatures, bees were an exception.

Wrenching her thoughts back to the present, she said, "I hope you're both happier there."

Louisa knew that their daughter's death had been particularly difficult for Mrs. Bentley. Before she'd been taken ill herself, Mama had spent hours trying to console Tina, only to admit defeat. "She's fragile," Father had said. "Healing will take a long time."

Mr. Bentley shrugged. "She seems better. Having her nephew here helps." As if he'd said too much, he gestured toward the stack of men's clothes. "What is it you need for Mr. . . ." He let his voice trail off, inviting Louisa to reveal her patient's surname.

Surprised that Mrs. Sheridan hadn't shared that piece of information, Louisa said, "Porter. Joshua Porter." She watched the storeowner's face carefully, looking for signs that he recognized the name. There were none, perhaps because Mr. Bentley had no reason to expect someone from Porter & Sons to be in Sweetwater Crossing. Louisa listed the garments she needed, adding, "I want two sets of everything."

Half an hour later, she headed west on Main Street to the sheriff's office.

"Glad to see you back in town."

Though Sheriff Granger was the same age and height as Mr. Bentley, the similarities ended there. The sheriff's hair was darker brown, his eyes lighter. While the owner of the mercantile was thin, the town's lawman carried a paunch around his midsection, the result, he told anyone who'd listen, of too many pieces of pie at Ma's Kitchen. Today there was one other difference between the men: the sheriff's welcome was warmer than Mr. Bentley's.

"I'm not sure how much success I'll have, but I'll try to find the horse," he said as he accompanied her back to Finley House. "No man should be without a good horse."

Josh propped his leg on the stool Louisa had placed in front of him when they'd taken seats on the front porch. "Sheriff Granger seems like a good man. An honest one."

He'd admitted that the odds weren't good that he'd be able to find Zeus. "If I were a horse thief," the sheriff said when Josh had finished his description, "the first thing I'd do would be to dye those white markings. A bit of boot polish would do the trick and make your horse look like just another black. Thieves are clever, because they know we hang them when we find them."

If we find them. Though the sheriff hadn't said it, Josh had known what he meant.

"I wish he'd been more encouraging," Louisa said as she set her rocker in motion.

"So do I, but let's not dwell on that."

The sense of peace he'd felt last night had vanished, evaporating like dew under a hot sun, and had been replaced by frustration over his situation. While Jed and his wife were in Europe searching for and probably finding something that would please Grandfather, Josh was marooned in a town so small it had nothing more than a single and probably mediocre mercantile to serve its residents. He, the man who had planned to impress Grandfather with his innovative ideas for the store as well as his alliance with the Livingston Bank, had lost his horse, the foundation for his proposal, and the use of one leg.

Though he'd wanted to rant and rail over his fate, Josh knew that would accomplish nothing. Instead, he did what he could to keep his future from unraveling any further.

Emily hadn't seemed surprised when he'd asked for stationery and a pen and had told him that she'd assure his letters were mailed today. "Mrs. Carmichael and Noah take a walk most afternoons," she'd said. "It'll make Noah feel like a grown-up to carry an envelope."

The first letter had been to Winifred, giving her his address and saying circumstances would keep him here for a while. Though Josh had written to her regularly, not wanting her to succumb to out-of-sight, out-of-mind, since he'd been unable to predict where he'd be next, she'd been unable to respond. Now she could.

"Good choice," Grandfather had said when Josh had announced that Winifred Livingston was the heiress he intended to pursue. "Her father's bank will be more useful to us than a shipping company or railroad. Just make sure you don't let her slip away." He'd pointed a finger at Josh as he said, "I still think you're making a mistake by not putting your ring on her finger before you leave."

But the timing hadn't been right, and though Josh knew what was expected of him, he was in no hurry to enter into the state of matrimony, for he knew all too well what that would be like.

The letter to Grandfather had included an explanation of where he was and what had happened and had ended with the promise that he'd have a proposal for him by the deadline. And he would, somehow. But he didn't want to think about that now.

"I heard you were in that other town for quite a while," Josh said, preferring to learn more about Louisa rather than consider what might happen if he couldn't recover his saddlebags. "I can't recall the name."

"Cimarron Creek. I was there for almost seven months."

"I'm surprised you'd leave home for so long." Though the women he knew traveled to Europe occasionally, those trips were shorter, and they took so many servants with them that it was almost like being at home.

"It wasn't hard to leave." The way her rocking increased suggested Louisa was telling only part of the story. "I needed a change, especially after both of my parents died within a few weeks of each other."

Josh's heart clenched at the memory of how he'd had change forced on him. "All of a sudden, you're an orphan."

Her blue eyes darkened. "I hadn't thought of it that way, but you're right. I wasn't ready to be an orphan." She was silent for a second. "You sounded as if you were speaking from personal experience."

"I was." There was no reason to hide his past. "My parents were killed when their carriage overturned on an icy street. They'd been at a party with my aunt and uncle." One of the endless series of parties, dinners, and other social engagements that had kept them away from home most nights.

"All four of them were killed instantly. At least that's what my grandfather said." That had been the one time Josh had seen tears in his grandfather's eyes. In little more than the blink of an eye, he'd lost both sons and had been saddled with the responsibility of raising his grandsons. It hadn't been the future any of them had anticipated.

"How awful!" Louisa stopped rocking and clenched the chair's arms as if they'd provide some measure of comfort. "You didn't have a chance to say goodbye. At least I was able to be with my mother." She swallowed deeply before speaking again. "Were your parents' deaths recent?"

"No. It was more than a dozen years ago." Before she could

ask, he said, "My cousin and I lived with our grandfather after that."

"And your grandmother?"

Josh shook his head. "She'd been gone for a few years." Even when she'd been alive, he'd rarely seen her. Unlike Mrs. Carmichael, who bestowed warmth on Noah, Josh's grandmother had been as cold as his grandfather, as distant as his parents. Those were things Louisa did not need to know.

"But you had your cousin. Were you two close?"

Josh nodded. "Most of the time. Jed and I had been best friends for our whole lives. When we moved in with Grandfather, we became almost like brothers." Josh didn't want to imagine what life would have been like without Jed.

Louisa resumed her rocking, apparently reassured by that. "You said you were close most of the time. Is Jed older than you?"

"Only a year."

Her nod was a sage one. "Did he sometimes act like he was an expert and that you should do exactly what he said?"

That was Jed to a T. "How did you guess?"

A small smile crossed Louisa's face. "Because that's what my sisters did. I'm the youngest of three. It didn't matter what the subject was. Both of them would insist that they knew better than I did. That's part of why I went to Cimarron Creek. It gave me a bit of independence. It also gave me a chance to let my anger cool."

Josh knew his surprise must be evident. "You haven't struck me as an angry woman."

"Believe me, I was. I was angry when Emily came back and started making all the decisions. She'd been gone for a year, but within an hour, she'd taken over."

The story was a familiar one. "Jed's tried to do that from time to time. Not so much at home, but when we're at P&S, he likes to assert himself."

"What do you do?"

Josh chuckled as the similarity of their responses hit him. "I'd walk away. I didn't go as far as you did—most times I'd simply go to a different floor in the store—but I kept my distance until my anger faded." He smiled when Louisa nodded in understanding. "Let's not talk about me. P&S may be my whole life, but it's boring. I'd much rather learn more about you. You said there are three daughters."

"That's right. Emily's the oldest. Joanna's the middle sister. I don't know whether you'll have a chance to meet her, because she's in Europe with her grandmother studying music, and we don't know when she'll be back."

The sound of small feet pounding on the floor told Josh that Noah had returned to the house. Though he enjoyed the boy's company, he hoped he'd stay inside, because Louisa's explanation had raised a new question in his mind.

"You said *her* grandmother."

Louisa nodded. "Our family is complicated. Both of my parents were married and widowed before they met each other. Emily is my mother's daughter from her first marriage, Joanna from Father's first. I'm the only one who grew up with both parents."

Though it was outside his own experience, Josh could see where those differences could cause friction among the girls. "I imagine there were times when the others resented you for that."

Louisa appeared startled; then her expression turned pensive. "I hadn't considered it, but you might be right. My sisters used to claim I was spoiled because I was the youngest—I assure you I wasn't—but maybe what they really meant was that I had something they didn't, because I was being raised by both of my parents."

She rested her chin on her hand in the classic pose of someone pondering deep concepts. "I thought our parents were careful to treat us all the same, but it's possible Emily and Joanna didn't see it that way." Louisa was silent for a moment, once again lost in her thoughts. Then she nodded shortly. "Thank you, Josh. You've given me a key to my sisters."

The smile she gave him made Josh feel like one of those heroes in fairy tales who conquered ferocious beasts to save the damsel in distress. He hadn't done anything so heroic, but being able to help this woman who'd helped him felt good. Very good.

Chapter Five

"This is the end."

"Or the beginning." Louisa studied the widow who stood dry-eyed next to her husband's grave. Though Mrs. Sheridan had shown no outward signs of mourning, this had to have been a difficult day for her. She had maintained her composure during the brief service, but now that the few other mourners had left, she seemed vulnerable.

"Reverend Grant was right when he said that only God knows what was in Doc's heart during those final seconds." Louisa wished the men who'd presided over her father's funeral had given her the same comfort that the town's new minister had tried to provide to Mrs. Sheridan, extending the hope that she and her husband might be reunited in heaven.

The doctor's widow shook her head. "Even if that's true, this"—she pointed to the grave—"is the end of my life in Sweetwater Crossing. I'm returning to Cimarron Creek tomorrow and have no intention of ever coming back."

Louisa wasn't surprised by her decision, for she herself had been eager to leave Sweetwater Crossing after her father's death. The rumors and the pitying glances had been more than she'd wanted to endure. It had to be even worse for the doctor's widow, and what Louisa was about to say would not help.

"I know I promised I'd take you, but I can't leave Josh without medical help. I need to stay here until I remove his cast and know that his leg healed properly."

Louisa hadn't expected it, but her desire to leave had lessened. A large part of that was due to Emily's willingness to forgive her, but another part was Louisa's sense that she was needed here. She might not be fully trained, but until the town could attract a new doctor, she was Sweetwater Crossing's only source of medical care.

Mrs. Sheridan took Louisa's arm and turned toward one of the benches in the cemetery where residents came to spend time remembering their loved ones. "I expected that," she said, "and I agree. That's why I hired Mayor Alcott's son to drive me. He'll bring his horse with us so he has a way to come back." When they were seated, she fished in her reticule and retrieved a key. "This is for you."

Louisa blinked in surprise when she recognized it as the key to the doctor's office. She'd returned it to the widow after she'd set Josh's leg and hadn't thought about it since. "What do you mean?"

Mrs. Sheridan's eyes reflected more pain than Louisa had seen since the day the telegram announcing Doc's death had arrived in Cimarron Creek. "I want you to have the building and everything in it. I told the mayor what I wanted to do, and he gave me some papers to sign. It's legal and it's all yours. Before you try to protest," she said as Louisa opened her mouth to do exactly that, "there are two reasons. First, I can never undo the past, but I owe your family for what happened."

She waited until Louisa nodded, wordlessly acknowledging that instead of saving lives, Doc had been responsible for a number of deaths, including Louisa's father's.

"Secondly, I don't want anything tying me to Sweetwater Crossing or my husband."

Surprise turned to shock as the magnitude of Mrs. Sheridan's gift registered. Louisa forced herself to take several deep breaths to slow her pulse and ease her light-headedness. Only when she was confident she could speak coherently did she say, "What about Phoebe? You could sell the building and give her an inheritance."

Mrs. Sheridan shook her head. "I have enough money from my side of the family for both Phoebe and me. Besides, you heard her. She wouldn't want anything from Roger any more than I do. Take it, Louisa. You deserve it."

But she didn't. She had done nothing to deserve this.

"I don't know what to say."

For the first time today, Mrs. Sheridan smiled. "Say thank you. I know my husband discouraged you when you said you wanted to become a doctor, but I saw how the people in Cimarron Creek trusted you and what you did for Joshua Porter. The mayor doesn't agree with me, and I suspect others in town feel the same way, but you're a healer, Louisa. Maybe having an office will help them accept you. Maybe it will also make up for my husband not trusting you. If there's one thing I know, it's that you'll be a better doctor than he ever was."

Tears of joy pricked Louisa's eyes. The day that had begun with solemn words at a gravesite had changed in ways she could not have foreseen. She owned a building, one that contained everything she needed to make her dream come true. It was an unexpected and incredibly generous gift. Even more, the widow's confidence in her abilities was as valuable as the building.

Her heart overflowing with gratitude, Louisa hugged the older woman. "Thank you, Mrs. Sheridan. This is the most wonderful gift I've ever received."

Hours later after she'd shared the almost unbelievable news

with Emily and explored every inch of the doctor's—no, *her*—office, Louisa locked the door and headed east on Main. This day, indeed, this whole week, had brought more surprises than she could have ever imagined, taking her life in unexpected directions. Father would have said it was the hand of God working in mysterious ways. Louisa agreed, but she would have said "wonderful" instead of "mysterious," because this was without a doubt a wonderful turn of events.

She'd returned to Sweetwater Crossing believing she had no future here. Now the future she'd dreamt of appeared within reach. There'd be hurdles, beginning with gaining the townspeople's trust, but the road was becoming clear.

Louisa's footsteps slowed and she smiled as she recognized the brunette emerging from the dressmaker's shop. Caroline Brownley had been her friend for as long as she could remember, part of the trio whose other members were Louisa and Phoebe Sheridan.

While none of them considered themselves beautiful, Caroline was the closest, with dark brown hair, eyes so green Louisa was convinced they'd outshine emeralds, and a pert nose that tipped up ever so slightly at the end, giving her a somewhat mischievous look, a look that had been confirmed during their childhood.

"I couldn't believe it when I heard you were back home, but I'm so glad you are. Although I shouldn't be welcoming you. I ought to be scolding you for not answering my letters."

"I didn't write to anyone." Even though she should have.

"I know. Emily said she hadn't heard from you either, but I'm not going to hold that against you. Not today, anyway."

Caroline gripped Louisa's hand, then tipped her head to one side in the inquisitive gesture Louisa remembered so well. "I can't believe how different you look."

"I'm happy to say you haven't changed. You're as lovely as ever." Louisa studied her friend's dress. While Aimee might have deplored the ruffles around the cuffs and hem, they suited Caroline. "Is that another of Thelma's creations?" Louisa asked, referring to the town's seamstress.

"Yes. I just ordered a new one, but I'm afraid it won't be as flattering as yours. I still can't believe the change in you."

Louisa shrugged. In the months since Aimee had helped her, she'd become accustomed to her new appearance. "Aimee insisted I wear bright colors." After the funeral, Louisa had changed into a royal blue dress. "She said Phoebe's hand-me-downs were too pale for me."

"I never thought of that, but this Aimee is right." Caroline linked her arm with Louisa's and began to walk down Main Street. "She sounds French. Where did you meet her?"

"Cimarron Creek. How she found her way there is a long story, but she's a native-born Texan who spent most of her life in France."

Caroline gave Louisa another appraising look. "That must be a French hairstyle. It's very attractive."

"Thank you. It's easier than curls." Aimee had shown Louisa how a simpler coiffure emphasized her cheekbones.

"Speaking of attractive," Caroline said as they strolled as slowly as if neither of them had any pressing engagements, "the town's been buzzing with the news that you brought a young man with you. Is he handsome?"

Caroline laughed. "It doesn't matter whether he's handsome so long as he's single. The girls all want to meet him." She gave another chuckle. "They had high hopes when Raymond Knapp came to town, but he doesn't seem interested in any of them. They hope this one's different."

Louisa wasn't surprised. When Emily's first husband had arrived in Sweetwater Crossing, almost every unmarried young woman had tried to find a way to meet him, some going so far as to spend hours inside the livery, waiting for him to come for his horse.

"I hate to disappoint them, but Josh will be leaving in six weeks when his cast is off."

They'd reached the corner of East Street, which was where they'd part ways if Caroline was going home. As if by mutual consent, they both stopped.

"Even if the handsome stranger isn't staying," Caroline continued, "at least you are. Now that you're back, it'll be like old times. All we need is for Phoebe to come home."

Louisa hated to keep disappointing her friend, but she didn't want Caroline to cling to a false hope. "Mrs. Sheridan is returning to Cimarron Creek. She and Phoebe plan to make it their permanent home."

"Oh." Caroline was silent for a moment. "I imagine they're afraid of gossip."

"That's part of it, but don't forget that Mrs. Sheridan has family there. That's where Phoebe was born."

"I'd forgotten that. I guess it won't be like old times, will it?"

"A lot has changed." Though Louisa couldn't explain why, she wasn't ready to tell Caroline about Mrs. Sheridan's gift. Instead, she turned her attention to her friend.

"Tell me about yourself. What have you been doing while I was gone? Your last letter said you were looking for work." After Caroline's parents died of scarlet fever when she was a child, she'd lived with her aunt and uncle. Though they claimed to love her, the older Brownleys had also insisted she pay for her room and board once she was old enough to work.

"I've been helping Thelma. That's why I was there today. She has more work than she can handle, so she pays me to sew and has started teaching me to design dresses. It's what she calls a mutually beneficial situation."

"I'm sure it is. You're an excellent seamstress."

Caroline shrugged. "That's what Thelma says, but . . ."

"But what?"

"I'm tired of sewing, and I don't think I'll ever be able to design a frock as pretty as the one you're wearing. I want to do something different. The problem is, the only position I've been offered is librarian once Alice leaves. I don't think I'd like that any better than sewing."

Louisa had to agree. "I can't picture you surrounded by books." Her friend had never been an avid reader, instead preferring almost any other pastime.

"Me either. I was hoping to work at Ma's, but Mrs. Tabor doesn't need any help with the restaurant."

"Something will turn up." Look what had happened to her. Three days ago, Louisa had been dreading her time in Sweetwater Crossing, believing as Phoebe did that she had no future here. Now she had the opportunity to create the future she'd dreamt of. Surely she could find a way to help her friend.

Chapter Six

"I still can't believe that Mrs. Sheridan gave you the office." Emily handed Louisa another plate to dry. "I hope that means you're going to stay here permanently."

Though she heard the enthusiasm in her sister's voice, Louisa had to be honest. Her initial euphoria had faded, and she woke in the middle of the night plagued by doubts.

"I want to, but . . ." A voice deep inside her told her that though the gift of the building and the widow's belief in Louisa's abilities had buoyed her spirits, they wouldn't be enough to sustain her. *This will be like all those other times you tried and failed.* In an attempt to silence the doubts, Louisa had lit a lamp, but the light had had little effect.

"I'm afraid," she admitted.

Emily abandoned the pot she'd been scrubbing to stare at Louisa. "Why?"

"Because I'm not strong like you. I make mistakes—lots of them—but you don't. You were always the perfect sister, the one who succeeded."

Emily shook her head. "You're wrong, Louisa. I've made plenty of mistakes. Some of them were huge."

"Like what?" Louisa couldn't imagine her sister doing anything worse than choosing the wrong ribbon to trim a dress.

Sorrow and something that looked almost like physical pain crossed Emily's face. "I can't talk about it. Not now. Maybe not ever. But believe me when I say I've made far greater mistakes than you ever will. Now, tell me why you're afraid."

Louisa was silent for a moment, trying to absorb what her sister had—and hadn't—said. She'd never thought of Emily as secretive, but it appeared that the woman she'd idolized and resented at the same time was harboring deep secrets.

"Thea claimed I was almost as good a midwife as her," she said at last, "but I'm not fully trained as a doctor. That makes me feel like a charlatan even thinking about taking over Doc's office. I can't call myself a doctor, because I'm not."

"But you can still help heal people." That was Emily, the encourager.

"If they'll trust me. I'm afraid no one will come to me when they're sick."

"Josh trusted you."

Louisa had to smile at her sister's attempt at reassurance. "Bad example, Emily. First of all, he didn't come to me. I came to him. Secondly, he had no choice. It was either accept my help or possibly die by the side of the road. And thirdly, he didn't watch me growing up. I'm afraid people who've known me all my life wouldn't view me as a real doctor even if I'd been to medical school."

"Maybe and maybe not." Once again, Emily had slipped into her role as the oldest sister, encouraging little Louisa to be brave the same way she had when Louisa had been afraid to get on the swing again after she'd fallen and scraped her knees. "The only way to know whether your fears are real or not is to confront them. Try being a healer. See what happens."

She made it sound easy, but it wasn't. Failing in Cimarron Creek would have been far easier than failing here where everyone knew her.

When Louisa said nothing, Emily continued. "You will stay at least until Josh's cast can be removed, won't you?"

"Yes, I need to do that." Six weeks wasn't a long time, but it might be long enough for Louisa to do what Emily had advised—confront her fears and decide whether she should remain here. "You can plan on that."

"Good, because there's something else I want to plan on and that's you being my wedding attendant." Emily's eyes softened at the word *wedding*. "I had hoped Joanna would be back and you could both stand up with me, but Craig and I don't want to wait that long. We want to be married while David is still here."

When he'd come to Sweetwater Crossing, David Grant had stipulated that he was only a temporary minister and had encouraged the elders to continue their search for a permanent pastor so that David could return to his home in Louisiana.

"We thought he'd stay until the end of June," Emily continued, "but the town has found his replacement, so he and Alice will leave in early May. That's why Craig and I chose April 21 for our wedding." Emily finished scrubbing the frying pan and handed it to Louisa to dry. "Will you be my maid of honor?"

"Of course."

Josh pulled out his watch to check the time. It was 10:30, which meant he'd been sitting on the rear verandah tossing a ball to Noah and watching him run for half an hour. As ridiculous as it was, he envied the boy both his energy and his ability to run. He'd become fairly adept at maneuvering the crutches, but he couldn't imagine how he would have climbed the stairs if his room had been on the second floor.

Although everyone at Finley House had done their best to make him feel welcome, the fear of failure weighed on him as heavily as the cast. He couldn't let his father's dream die. But without the recipes and Zeus, he was powerless. Telling himself there had to be a way to recover from what felt like overwhelming loss did nothing more than increase his frustration. He needed a diversion—something, anything—to take his mind off his problems.

"Would you like to go for a ride this afternoon?"

Josh turned, wondering whether the woman who'd walked so quietly that he hadn't heard her approach had read his mind. "If you have any doubt about my answer, you're not as smart as I thought."

Louisa settled into the chair next to him. Today she wore a dress the color of fine burgundy, her hair arranged in the simple but flattering style she seemed to favor. He'd expected her to spend the day in her office, but here she was, offering him what felt like a lifeline.

"The livery has a carriage that's a bit easier to get into than Mrs. Sheridan's was," she explained. "My father's horse needs some exercise, and he's pulled that buggy before, so we could accomplish a couple things at the same time."

"Alleviating my boredom and letting the horse stretch his legs. That sounds perfect. When do we leave?"

"As soon as I've helped Emily with the lunch dishes. Noah will be napping then, so he won't throw a tantrum when we go without him."

Lunch was delicious. Josh hadn't been flattering her when he told Emily she was an excellent cook, but he barely tasted the creamy chicken fricassee she'd served over flaky biscuits. Instead of savoring the food, he felt like a schoolboy counting the minutes until class was dismissed. And if that wasn't silly, he didn't know what was. He'd been in Sweetwater Crossing a mere three days. Finley House was a comfortable place to stay, with friendly people and good food. He shouldn't be this eager to escape, and yet he was.

Part of the reason was that he was looking forward to spending uninterrupted time with Louisa. Somehow, she'd come to dominate his thoughts. Perhaps it was because she'd rescued him. Perhaps it was because she was the only lady doctor he'd ever met. But perhaps it had nothing to do with her skill as a healer. Perhaps it was because there was no pretense about her, just an intriguing mixture of quiet confidence and unexpected vulnerability. All Josh knew was that he enjoyed Louisa's company and wanted to learn more about her, including why she seemed hesitant to settle into the former doctor's office.

At her suggestion, he was waiting at the west side of the house and had managed to descend the single step without falling on his face. Celebrating the minor victory, Josh smiled when he heard the steady clip-clop of a horse's hooves and watched as Louisa parked the carriage near the house and climbed out. Though he'd expected her to beckon him over, she headed for the stable, emerging with a wooden crate.

"Let me help you with that." Josh hated the idea that she was doing something better suited for a man.

Louisa chuckled and continued toward the carriage. "How do you propose to carry that when you need both arms to maneuver your crutches?"

She was right, of course. "I'm not used to being an invalid."

"You're not an invalid. I reserve that term for someone who's suffering from an illness. You're a man with a broken leg." She positioned the crate next to the buggy. "This will help you climb into the carriage."

And it did.

"Thank you. I feel less like an invalid now," he said as she guided the horse onto the street and headed west.

"The next time we go out, I'll show you the surrounding area, but I thought we'd explore the town today."

The next time. Three short words brightened Josh's mood

almost as much as sitting next to Louisa did. Somehow she knew exactly what to do and say to make his day better.

They rode silently until they crossed Center Street. He glanced to the right, spotting the bridge that spanned the town's namesake creek but averting his eyes from the cemetery. Today was not a day to think about death. Deliberately turning to the left, Josh found his attention snagged by two buildings.

"What are those? They look like houses, but they're so small." Small but perfectly proportioned. Someone had put a great deal of thought into their construction.

Louisa gave him one of those sweet smiles that never failed to make him smile in return. "We call them Sunday Houses. Many of the farmers and ranchers live a fair distance away, but they come into town each weekend to shop on Saturday and worship on Sunday. They built houses like this so they'd have a place to stay on Saturday nights."

"Instead of a hotel."

Louisa nodded. "Sweetwater Crossing has no hotel. Besides, paying for rooms each week would have cost more than building the houses."

It seemed the residents were both frugal and practical. Josh thought about the house he'd seen from Finley House's front verandah. "I noticed a small building next to the Albrights' home. Is that also a Sunday House?"

Louisa nodded again. "The church has turned it into an annex to the parsonage." She gestured toward the buildings that had caught Josh's eye. "These two are empty. All three belonged to Mrs. Carmichael's friends. They were widows who moved into town permanently when they sold their farms after their husbands' deaths."

As the carriage continued to move, Josh said, "Would you stop for a minute? I want to look at these a bit longer." He couldn't explain it any more than he could explain why his thoughts turned to Louisa as often as they did, but something about those Sunday Houses intrigued him. They were almost like magnets, drawing him closer.

"They're pretty, aren't they? I remember telling my mother I wanted one like them for a playhouse." The wistfulness in her voice told Josh Louisa hadn't gotten her wish.

"They're more than pretty. Not to disparage your home, but these look like they belong here." Finley House was magnificent, but it seemed out of place in Sweetwater Crossing. "These look like one house that was somehow cut in two."

Both were constructed of stone with two windows on one side of the door and a porch on the front. Each had an outside staircase that led to what Josh surmised was an attic. Where they differed was that the house on the west had its windows and stairs on the west side while the one on the east had them on the east. The symmetry was appealing.

Louisa looked at the houses for a second, then turned back to Josh. "The Frenches and the Lockes—those were the owners—knew each other before they moved to Texas. They wanted to be together on weekends and obviously had a common view of what their Sunday Houses should look like."

"They had good taste." Josh studied the buildings that had caught his attention. "I can't imagine living in such a small space, and I suspect you can't either." It would have been one thing to spend a single night there each week, but Josh thought it would have felt cramped as a permanent home. "Still, the houses have an undeniable charm."

"I agree."

"Which is why you wanted one as a playhouse."

"Exactly. Are you ready to continue our tour?"

As they drove slowly up and down each of the streets, Louisa pointed out various landmarks and establishments.

"I'm almost afraid to ask this," she said half an hour later, "but what do you think of Sweetwater Crossing? I've been trying to read your expression, but I couldn't, except for the Locke and French houses, that is."

"I have to apologize. My grandfather taught Jed and me not to show our feelings. He said we needed to cultivate a calm demeanor so we wouldn't offend customers. I'm afraid I learned that lesson too well." It had not been his intention to puzzle Louisa. "To answer your question, I like your town. It's very different from New York."

"A small town rather than a big city."

"The differences are refreshing. I can sense the slower pace. People seem industrious but not rushed, making me think they enjoy their lives more than many city dwellers do."

"That might be true." Louisa slowed the horse again, as if to match the slower pace Josh had noted. "My only experience is with small towns, so I can't say for sure, but you must have visited other small towns. Didn't you see the same differences there?"

"Yes and no. There was the same sense of being less hurried, but Sweetwater Crossing is different. It's hard to describe it other than to say that it has a unique appeal."

Louisa appeared surprised by his statement but said nothing.

"You're fortunate this is your home."

This time she did speak. "Believe me, I haven't always thought that, but now . . ." She paused for a second before saying, "It feels different now. I don't know whether the town has changed or whether I have, but since I've been back, I've seen things in a new way. Does that make any sense?"

"Do you feel like everything was blurry, but now it's clear?"

"I wouldn't say that it's clear, but it's becoming clearer. Why did you ask?"

"Because I still feel like I'm looking through a cloudy glass where things are distorted. I hope I'll find the clarity I need."

And he hoped he'd discover why the image of those Sunday Houses kept popping into his brain.

Chapter Seven

Louisa blinked back tears as Pastor Grant delivered the benediction. This morning's service had included the most moving Palm Sunday sermon she'd ever heard. Father had always focused on Jesus and the way that day had been foreshadowed in the Old Testament, but David Grant had taken a different approach. He'd spoken of the triumphant entry into Jerusalem from the perspective of the disciples rather than Jesus himself, asking the congregation to imagine the disciples' elation and then the total devastation they must have endured when their Lord was nailed to a cross five days later. "Do you think Palm Sunday made the crucifixion easier or harder for them to bear?" he'd asked.

Louisa was still pondering that when she emerged from the church. Josh, Emily, and Craig had stayed to talk to the minister, while Mrs. Carmichael had taken Noah home. Though she intended to compliment David on his sermon, she wasn't ready to answer his question, and so, hoping the sunshine might clear her mind, she'd come outside alone.

When she reached the bottom step, she found herself confronted by two men. How odd. Though she'd known them all her life, never before had they approached her. Growing up, they'd dismissed her as the little Vaughn girl, the one who couldn't compare to Emily's blond beauty or Joanna's dramatic darker coloring. Now they were staring at her with expressions that reminded her of when Mama would read the story about Red Riding Hood and bare her teeth when she pretended to be the big, bad wolf. These men weren't baring their teeth, but the way they were looking at Louisa was equally alarming.

"It really is Louisa Vaughn!" The hint of astonishment in Byron Wright's voice bothered her almost as much as his blatant leer. "The rumors didn't exaggerate your beauty."

Andrew Holt's lips curled as he said, "She's prettier than a field of bluebonnets."

They were acting almost as if she couldn't hear them. Louisa started to move past them, but Byron blocked her way, then glared at his companion. "Save your breath, Andrew. I saw her first, so she's gonna be mine."

As if she were an apple ripe for the picking.

"Pappy's right," Byron continued. "It's time I got myself hitched, and she's the filly for me."

Now she was a horse. Louisa was tempted to snort. Before she had a chance to tell them their words were as meaningless as the sounding brass mentioned in 1 Corinthians 13 and that a new hairstyle and more attractive clothing didn't make her a different person, a third man joined them.

Though she knew she'd never seen him before, he looked familiar. Shorter than the other two, he had medium brown hair, blue eyes, muttonchop whiskers, and a square face and big-boned frame that reminded Louisa of someone. The problem was, she couldn't remember who.

"Fellas, that's no way to treat a lady. My mama taught me that ladies deserve respect." The smile the stranger gave Louisa was genuine, not a leer. "I doubt these fellas will introduce me, so I reckon I'll have to do it myself. I'm Raymond Knapp."

The Bentleys' nephew. Now that she knew his name, the resemblance to Tina Bentley was unmistakable. This was the man who'd attracted the single women, the one who'd built the parsonage. Louisa seized on the last part of his identity. Looking pointedly at the building next door, she said, "The new parsonage is impressive—a big improvement over the old one."

When Byron and Andrew slunk away, either intimidated by Raymond or having gotten Louisa's message that she wasn't interested in their false compliments, Raymond's lips curved in another smile. "I know pride is a sin, but I'd be lying if I didn't admit that I'm proud of the way it turned out, Miss . . ." His voice trailed off as he waited for Louisa to introduce herself.

"I'm Louisa Vaughn."

His eyes lit with enthusiasm. "When Uncle Adam said you were back in town, my aunt was more excited than I've seen her in months. She was looking forward to talking to you today, but she woke with an awful headache. If this is like the last one, she'll spend the whole day in a dark room."

Austin had told Louisa about head pain like that, saying some called them migraines. He'd also told her they were difficult to cure but had shown her how to create a concoction that helped lessen the pain.

"I can give you something for her." It was the least she could do for the woman who'd tried to brighten Mama's final days.

Raymond shook his head. "You must not know my aunt very well. Ever since her daughter died, she's refused to have anything to do with doctors or medicine."

Though Louisa had seen Tina every day for more than a month when Mama had been so ill, doctors were one thing they had not discussed. It had been a painful subject for Louisa, whose suggestions had been dismissed as if they were worthless.

"I'm sorry to hear that, but I know some people are fearful. Please tell your aunt that if she changes her mind, I'm happy to help her."

Though the conversation with Raymond was pleasant, Louisa was concerned that Josh had been standing for too long. Emily and Craig were involved in a discussion with David and Alice, while Josh appeared to have been cornered by two men. Both Farnham Colter, one of the local ranchers whom everyone called Farnham Senior to distinguish him from his son, and the saloon owner, Jason Miller, wore serious expressions.

"I hope you'll excuse me," Louisa said to Raymond. "My patient needs to rest."

As she approached the trio, Louisa heard Farnham Senior say, "You're a braver man than I am." He made no effort to lower his voice, choosing instead to practically shout.

"What do you mean?" Josh's expression was as calm as ever, reminding her of the lesson he'd said his grandfather had given on deportment.

"I heard you let the littlest Vaughn girl set your leg. You'll be lucky if you can walk once you take the cast off."

"That's right." The saloon owner nodded. Like Farnham Senior, he had dark brown hair and eyes. Unlike Farnham Senior, he was taller and thirty or so pounds lighter. "Everybody knows gals got no business trying to be doctors. They ain't strong enough."

Farnham Senior clapped his friend on the back in a show of solidarity. "Weakness is only part of the problem. The fact is, gals ain't smart enough."

It was what Louisa had feared and what Austin had warned her might happen. "Men aren't accustomed to women doctors," he had told Louisa when she'd first approached him. "You won't have an easy time winning their trust."

Easy or not, she would do it. Let these men think what they wanted. She'd prove them wrong. When Josh walked without a limp, they'd realize she was a capable healer. And maybe sometime in the next six weeks, she'd have a chance to help someone else.

Louisa took another step toward the trio. She hadn't thought she'd made enough noise to alert him, but Josh turned slightly and inclined his head in a silent greeting.

"I'm afraid I have to disagree with you, gentlemen," he said. "I watched Miss Vaughn when she set my leg and put it into a cast, and I can tell you no one—man or woman—could have done better." When Farnham Senior scoffed, Josh continued. "My grandfather brought in the best doctor in New York City when my cousin broke his arm. I saw what he did, and that was exactly what Miss Vaughn did."

Farnham Senior made no attempt to hide his skepticism. "We'll see when the cast comes off."

"Yes, we will." Josh turned toward Louisa. "Are you ready to go home?"

"Yes." When they were far enough from the men not to be overheard, she gave Josh a long, appreciative look. "Thank you for defending me."

He shook his head. "All I did was speak the truth. You may not have all the training, but you did as fine a job as any doctor could have. Don't let anyone tell you otherwise."

They were simple words, but the feelings they evoked were far from simple. Josh's confidence in her abilities erased the sting of Farnham Senior's barbs at the same time that it increased her determination to prove she was worthy of his admiration. "Thank you, Josh. Once again, you've helped me."

When the sheriff entered the parlor the next morning, Josh wished Louisa were here, for the lawman's expression told him his news wasn't good. Unfortunately, Louisa was spending the morning in her new office. "Doc left me almost everything I'll need," she had said at breakfast, "but I want to reorganize the cabinets. He had different ideas of how supplies and medicines ought to be arranged."

Josh suspected that if Louisa had known the sheriff was coming, she would have stayed home, but this was an unscheduled visit.

"Good morning, Sheriff."

Frowning, the man took the seat across from Josh. "It would be a better morning if I had good news for you." He twirled his hat on one finger. "I'm sorry to say that I don't. My deputies and I looked around here and couldn't find anything. I sent telegrams to the nearby towns, and the answers were all the same. No one's seen any sign of your horse, either with or without the white markings. I'm afraid he's gone for good." The sheriff let out a mirthless laugh. "Whoever came up with that expression has a strange sense of humor. There's nothing good about your horse being stolen."

"No, there isn't, but I appreciate your help."

"I wish I could have done more."

After the sheriff left, Josh settled back in his chair, not liking the direction his thoughts had taken. His plan to win Grandfather's challenge seemed doomed. Even if he left Sweetwater Crossing right now, which he couldn't, there wasn't enough time to return to all the towns he'd visited and get another copy of the recipes. And even if he could, that wouldn't be enough. He'd hoped to find three or four more special foods as he traveled west, then take the fastest train back to New York. Now he had nothing and no plan.

He closed his eyes, trying not to let frustration overtake him, and as he did, he was assailed with the feeling he'd had right before Zeus threw him, that the concept of an American Room was good but not good enough. It was a moot point now that he had no recipes. Without regional foods, there would be no American Room. But Josh couldn't—he wouldn't—let Jed win. He'd promised his father he wouldn't settle for second best, and he wouldn't.

Sitting here was accomplishing nothing other than increasing his frustration. He grabbed his crutches and rose. His arms should be strong enough for what he wanted to do. After all, he'd managed to walk to and from church yesterday without stumbling or falling. There was no reason he couldn't walk again today.

Feeling more energized than he had since he'd wakened, Josh grabbed his hat, told Emily he was going out, and headed east on Creek, deliberately choosing the opposite direction from the one he'd traveled yesterday. His destination could be reached either way, but he was less likely to encounter people on this route.

The townspeople meant well, but Josh didn't need another man warning him that Louisa may have damaged his leg more than the fall itself or another young woman casting coy glances in his direction. He had confidence in Louisa's skill, and he wasn't in the market for a wife. Winifred, the perfect Porter bride, was waiting for him. What Josh needed was an idea that would impress Grandfather.

He wouldn't find that at his destination, but he might find a gift for the woman who'd shown him such kindness. When he reached the store, a quick perusal of the display windows confirmed the impression he'd formed when Louisa had driven him past it. Sweetwater Crossing's mercantile was ordinary in the extreme. Grandfather would have shuddered at the sight of items stacked in what appeared to be random order. Josh could only hope the interior was better.

"Good morning, Mr. Porter. I'm Adam Bentley, proprietor of this establishment." The man who greeted him was as ordinary looking as his establishment, with light brown hair, brown eyes, and a face that would not stand out in a crowd. "What can I get you? I understand you're from New York. My store may not be as big as you're used to, but we have a good selection of necessities and some luxuries." The man gestured toward two chairs in the front corner. "If you'd like to take a seat, I can bring things to you."

Josh knew he ought to appreciate the offer, but he wasn't an invalid and didn't like being treated like one.

"I'm not certain what I want," he told Bentley. "I wanted a small gift to thank Miss Vaughn for all she's done for me. I wouldn't be here if it weren't for her."

Bentley nodded. "I heard she set your leg. I hope it heals properly."

Biting back his annoyance that the store's proprietor shared the opinion of the men who'd approached him after services yesterday, Josh said only, "I expect it will. Do you mind if I look around?"

"Not at all, but if you'd like a suggestion, you can't go wrong with candy. That girl always had a sweet tooth."

That was one of the things Josh had noticed about small towns. Everyone knew almost everything about the other residents. There appeared to be no need for newspapers. Instead, the rumor mill transmitted everything from Louisa's preference for sweets to the fact that Josh was part of P&S.

What had surprised him yesterday was that few people commented on his being from New York; instead, they'd been more interested in his broken leg. He'd thought Bentley might ask him about P&S, since the owners of the other mercantiles he'd visited had asked for his advice, but the man had not, and Josh would not offer unsolicited opinions.

"Candy might be good, but I'd like to look around." When Bentley nodded, Josh walked in the opposite direction from the one the proprietor had indicated, quickly assessing the items on the counters and shelves. The store was filled with the same merchandise he'd seen in a dozen other mercantiles: canned goods, yard goods, ready-made clothing, everything residents would need for their everyday life. There was nothing wrong with the selection, but the displays were unimaginative and didn't encourage purchases.

Josh spotted a lady's shirtwaist trimmed with yards of lace.

It was the kind of item that would appeal to most women, a fancy garment they could wear to church or special events. But it was folded so that the lace was barely visible instead of being displayed in the window or the front of the store where women could admire it. Similarly, the store's one set of fine china was almost hidden in the back instead of being placed where it would be seen when a woman headed toward essentials like flour and sugar.

Though Josh was tempted to tell Bentley that he could improve sales by changing his displays, he doubted the man would welcome the suggestions, particularly now that he was helping two women select the best color ribbon to trim the calico they'd chosen.

"This one here is mighty pretty, ain't it?" one woman asked. Josh glanced in her direction, wincing when he saw what she'd chosen.

To his credit, the proprietor pointed out two other ribbons that were better suited. "I wish my wife was here. Tina's the one with the eye for color, but she's been spending her days at the farm."

The customer nodded. "You oughta hire another lady to help you."

"I will as soon as I can find the right one. Business has been better than ever this year."

Perhaps Josh had been too quick to criticize the mercantile. Perhaps Sweetwater Crossing's residents were content with it the way it was.

After he'd selected a box of chocolate creams for Louisa and one of caramels for Emily, he made his way to the cash register.

Bentley eyed the items and nodded. "A good choice."

There was no offer to wrap the boxes, leading Josh to suspect the mercantile didn't provide that service.

Spotting an open jar of honey next to a plate of toast pieces, Josh turned to the proprietor. "May I try that?" Even though there would likely be no American Room, he never missed an opportunity to sample a new foodstuff.

"Yes, indeed. It may sound like bragging, but the missus and I don't think anything can compare to Texas wildflower honey. That's why we're glad we live here. There's no place in the state with as many wildflowers as the Hill Country."

Josh spread the honey on a piece of toast and popped it into his mouth. To his surprise, the honey was as good as Bentley claimed. "You're right. This is the best honey I've ever tasted." The color was appealing, the flavor delicate but distinctive. It would be an excellent addition to the American Room, but even if that idea never became reality, he could picture P&S serving it with scones as part of their afternoon tea service.

Bentley grinned. "You ought to take a couple jars with you when you go back to New York."

Surely it was only Josh's imagination that the man seemed anxious for that to happen.

Chapter Eight

"Alice is so thin that she can wear ruffles, but you said she wanted this dress to be simple yet elegant, because it's her second wedding," Louisa said as she studied the sketch Thelma had made of the proposed gown. At Caroline's request she had come to the dressmaker's shop to provide what Caroline described as much-needed fashion advice.

"I'd suggest pleats instead of ruffles at the neckline, hem, and sleeves," Louisa told Thelma. "They're simpler, and I think they're more elegant."

Before the dressmaker could respond, the bell over the front door tinkled, announcing the arrival of a customer. Louisa smiled when she recognized her former schoolteacher.

"What a nice surprise to find you here!" The woman who'd taught Louisa the three Rs and countless other things made her way to her side, moving as deliberately as she had in the schoolroom. An inch or two shorter than Louisa, the schoolmarm had insisted that a lady was judged not by her height but by her demeanor as well as her appearance. Her light brown hair was always perfectly coiffed, her clothing plain but well-fitted, her blue eyes enhanced by the spectacles perched on her nose. Today there was no sign of the spectacles.

"I'm glad you're back home." The way Miss Albright's gaze moved from her head to her toes told Louisa she wasn't the only one performing an assessment. "I wanted to talk to you after church yesterday, but you were gone before I had a chance. I want to hear all about your time in Cimarron Creek."

"I learned a lot there, Miss Albright." Louisa bit her lip at the realization that she'd misspoken. "I'm sorry. I keep forgetting you're Mrs. Neville now." The wedding had been overshadowed by Mama's death only a few days later.

The new Mrs. Neville shook her head. "I hope I can convince you to call me Gertrude. It took a while for your sister and Alice to remember that I'm no longer a teacher."

"But you were a good one."

"A stern one." Caroline added her opinion. "I was always afraid of making a mistake and having you frown at me."

Gertrude pretended to frown, then turned it upside down. "You were one of my best pupils, even if you didn't enjoy reading as much as some. But I'm not here to talk about my years as a schoolmarm. Is my dress ready?"

"Almost." Caroline walked to the rack of dresses and reached for one of them. "I want you to try it on, in case I need to make any adjustments or in case Louisa has some ideas for changes. I made the seams extra wide so you can let them out when you need to."

For a second, Louisa was confused. Then she recalled Emily's letter saying Gertrude was expecting a baby. "Congratulations. You and Thomas must be excited."

Her former teacher nodded, her eyes brightening with anticipation of the happy event. "I'm also a little worried," she admitted. "My mother keeps telling me I'm too old to be having my first child."

Caroline scoffed as she urged Gertrude behind the dressing screen. "Nonsense. Now, let's get you into your new dress."

It wasn't all nonsense. Older women were more likely to have a difficult time during their pregnancy, but that didn't mean they shouldn't have children. "I hope you reminded your mother of the women in the Bible who became mothers when they were much older—like Sarah and Elisabeth."

Louisa's suggestion provoked a chuckle from behind the screen. "Spoken like a true minister's daughter. Your father would have told me the same thing. Unfortunately, my mother isn't happy unless she has something to worry about, and I may have inherited that. That's one of the reasons I'm glad you're back home."

Gertrude stepped back into the main room, her new dress still unbuttoned. "Emily told me you studied with the midwife while you were in Cimarron Creek. I hope you'll deliver my baby."

Happiness bubbled up inside Louisa. This was why she was here. Someone needed her. "When do you expect the baby to be born?"

"As best as I can tell, late August."

Caroline moved behind Gertrude. "Let me button it. Thomas will probably have to help you when you get bigger." She frowned as she began to fasten the gown. "I still think you should have let me put the buttons in front."

"Why? I'm not an invalid and I won't be in three or four months simply because I weigh a few pounds more."

Though the dress was attractive, Louisa understood Caroline's concern. "You might gain twenty-five or thirty."

Her face reflecting her horror, Gertrude stared at Louisa. "Now you really must promise to deliver this baby."

"Of course I will. Why don't you come to my office when you're done here. I'll make sure everything is progressing the way it should."

Gertrude shook her head. "I'll call you when I need you, and I'll expect you to come to the ranch. That's what midwives do."

Louisa was more than a midwife, but she wouldn't argue the point, since Gertrude was engaging her as one.

"Thank you for trusting me. I'm glad someone does." The last sentence slipped out seemingly on its own accord.

Gertrude turned from studying her reflection in the long mirror to look at Louisa. "Are you worried about the town accepting you?"

"Yes." There was no reason to pretend otherwise, not when doubts still filled her head.

Gertrude frowned, then turned to Caroline, her frown vanishing as she fingered the skirt fabric. "It's a beautiful dress. Thank you for suggesting this color. It's perfect." She raised her arms and began to unbutton the back, then shrugged. "All right. You might as well help me."

As Caroline worked on the buttons, Gertrude continued the discussion she'd begun with Louisa. "Let's talk about you, Louisa. Surely you don't expect to fail just because you're a woman."

"I don't want to think I will, but you should have heard the men yesterday. They're convinced I hurt Josh when I set his leg and put on the cast."

"But you didn't." Gertrude's words rang with conviction.

"How can you be sure?"

"Because I know you. I remember when you set a dog's leg because Doc Sheridan wouldn't consider helping an animal."

Caroline raised her eyebrows. "You did that?"

"She most certainly did."

"And the dog limped afterwards." Louisa couldn't let her friends' admiration stand unchallenged.

"That's true," Gertrude admitted, "but it was before anyone showed you the right technique, wasn't it?"

"Yes, but . . ."

"No buts. You need to stay here. Show all those doubting men they're wrong, because they are." Gertrude was once more in schoolmarm mode, giving Louisa a lesson.

"You're doing your best to persuade me, aren't you?"

Before Gertrude could respond, Caroline spoke. "She's right. This is your home, Louisa. This is where you belong."

Louisa hoped they were right.

The walk into town had tired Josh more than he'd expected. He wouldn't take a nap, but resting in the big leather chair in what was now his bedroom did not qualify as a nap.

Perhaps if he stayed here for half an hour, he'd feel refreshed by suppertime. That was his goal, and so while he shut the sliding doors to the parlor, Josh left the one to the hallway open as a connection to the rest of the household.

He'd closed his eyes for a second but opened them again when he heard the knock on the front door.

"I'll see who it is." Louisa's words were followed by her firm footsteps and the opening of the door.

"Good afternoon, Louisa." The man's voice echoed through the entry hall.

Though Josh tried to identify the man, he could not.

"Hello, Raymond. Would you like to come in?"

Raymond. The name triggered a memory, telling Josh this was the man who'd overseen the rebuilding of the parsonage. The day he'd met her, the minister's wife-to-be had sung Raymond Knapp's praises, saying she doubted anyone could have done a better job. "Sweetwater Crossing is fortunate to have him," she'd declared.

"I can't stay as long as I'd like," the builder said, "because my aunt and uncle are expecting me for supper, but I would like to come in."

Two sets of footsteps and the faint creaking of a chair told Josh they'd entered the parlor and taken seats there.

"First of all, I want to apologize for Byron and Andrew's behavior yesterday."

Though the names meant nothing to him, Josh assumed those were the men who'd confronted Louisa when she left the church. Josh hadn't heard their conversation, but her posture had left no doubt that she hadn't been pleased by whatever they were saying.

"There's no need for you to apologize." Louisa's voice was firm. "I've known them my whole life. I know what kind of men they are, and I don't worry about their opinion."

That raised the question of whose opinions mattered to her. Though he told himself he shouldn't care, Josh hoped she wouldn't discount anything he said so easily. Somehow—and for the life of him, he couldn't explain why it was so—he wanted her to trust him, to confide in him, to value his opinion.

"You're being too kind to them," Raymond said. "Men like that need to know there are consequences for poor behavior. I've warned them they won't get any more work from me if they're rude to you again."

"That wasn't necessary."

A flash of something—surely it wasn't jealousy—spread through Josh at the realization that this man wanted to be Louisa's champion, the one who slayed dragons and silenced boorish men for her.

"I thought it was. My mama told me gentlemen have responsibilities. But let's not talk about that now. The other reason I came was to invite you to have supper at the farm on Saturday. My aunt is eager to see you again, and so am I. Will you come?"

"Yes, Raymond, I will."

"Wonderful."

The unmistakable pleasure in the man's voice grated on Josh's nerves. This was the first time he could recall being annoyed by nothing more than a stranger's tone of voice. He couldn't explain his reaction; he only knew it was visceral, and it had to stop. No matter how intriguing he found Louisa, they had no future together, and he had no right to begrudge her an admirer. No right at all.

Chapter Nine

"You look better this morning." Louisa waited until everyone else had left the dining room after breakfast before she told Josh what was foremost on her mind. Though he'd tried to dismiss it, she'd been concerned by the fatigue he'd exhibited yesterday.

Emily had said he'd retired to his room during the afternoon, presumably to rest, and he'd been more subdued than usual at supper. When Louisa had asked whether something was wrong, he'd tried to assure her that everything was fine, but she had not been reassured. Josh might not have been in pain, but something had been troubling him. That was why she hadn't said anything about Gertrude's asking her to be her midwife. It had felt wrong to celebrate her success, minor as it was, when her first patient was in distress. Fortunately, there was no sign of malaise today. Instead, Josh appeared to have resolved whatever had bothered him.

"A good night's sleep helped." He wrinkled his nose, then grinned at her. "I should have listened to you and not tried to do so much yesterday. You were right, Doc."

As he'd intended, she laughed at the way he'd addressed her. "I'm not a full-fledged doctor yet." It was true that she'd posted a sign on Doc Sheridan's door—her door, she corrected herself—establishing daily office hours beginning today and advising anyone who needed treatment outside of those hours to come to Finley House, but she was realistic enough to know it would take more than that for the town to consider her a physician.

"You will be, and I'll have the honor of saying I was your first patient." Josh nodded when she raised the coffeepot to offer him another cup. "I still wish you'd let me pay you."

Though she had every intention of charging Sweetwater Crossing's residents who availed themselves of her services, it felt wrong to accept Josh's money. "The chocolate creams were more than enough." Candy had been a treat reserved for special occasions during her childhood; receiving a large box as a thank-you had pleased her more than a hefty fee would have.

"Hardly!" Josh made no effort to hide his disagreement. "If I'd broken my leg in New York, I would have paid a substantial amount to have it set."

"But you aren't in New York, and even if you were, you probably wouldn't have broken it there. Things are different here."

"But not so different that I shouldn't express my gratitude." The man was nothing if not persistent. "Since you won't accept my money, I hope you'll agree to have supper with me this evening. Mrs. Carmichael has already warned me that nothing can compare to your sister's cooking, but I thought you might enjoy a meal at Ma's Kitchen. Emily admitted that your family rarely ate there."

Louisa laid down her cup and stared at Josh, surprised and flattered that he'd gone to so much trouble. She couldn't imagine any other man she knew asking multiple women for advice about ways to please her. And please her, Josh had.

"I can only remember eating one meal at the restaurant." The Vaughn girls might live in the largest house in Sweetwater Crossing, but their family was far from wealthy. They learned frugality at an early age, with Mama saying they needed to be very careful about what they spent, because taxes took a substantial portion of Father's stipend. That was the reason the girls had few new dresses and relied on hand-me-downs from parishioners. A meal in a restaurant was a luxury.

"Thank you." Louisa hoped her smile would tell Josh just how much she was looking forward to their supper together. "I accept with pleasure." Even though it would set tongues wagging when she and Josh went to the restaurant without a chaperone. It was one thing for her to have supper at the farm with Raymond, since his aunt and uncle would be there. Even though Ma's was a public place and they'd never be alone, Louisa knew some of the busybodies would act as if she and Josh were having a tryst there. So be it.

"It's nice to see you again, Louisa."

The day had passed more quickly than Louisa had thought possible, the disappointment she'd felt when no one came into her office seeking medical help mitigated by anticipation of the evening. Now she and Josh were inside the town's only eating establishment.

Wrinkles formed at the corners of Mrs. Tabor's brown eyes as she smiled at both Louisa and her companion. Though her dark gray dress and simple white apron might be considered severe, and Louisa had heard others criticize the woman's tightly braided hair as old-fashioned, there was nothing severe or old-fashioned about her greeting. She radiated welcome.

"You must be Mr. Porter. It's an honor to have you at Ma's Kitchen." The woman whose hair had been the same shade of medium brown as Louisa's before silver threads had appeared led the way to a table for two in the front of the restaurant. It was, Louisa guessed, one of the most popular tables because of its location near the windows, giving diners the choice of looking outside or amusing themselves by watching other patrons.

"I hope you won't be disappointed," the restaurant's proprietor said as she waited for them to seat themselves. "I'm certain you've eaten at much finer restaurants in New York."

Josh shook his head, clearly disputing her assumption. "I've eaten in a number of restaurants, but none where the owner gave me such a warm welcome." When Mrs. Tabor blushed at the praise, Josh made a show of sniffing. "You must have known I was coming, because if I'm not mistaken, you have one of my favorite dishes on the menu: pot roast."

Louisa's already high opinion of Josh rose another notch at the way he made Mrs. Tabor feel valued. What a kind man he was!

"By this time tomorrow," Louisa warned Josh after Mrs. Tabor left for the kitchen to fill their orders, "half of Sweetwater Crossing will have heard that you like pot roast, whether or not you do."

"I do like it," he said, easing her concern that he had simply been trying to put Mrs. Tabor at ease when he'd claimed it was a favorite. "There's nothing as satisfying as a tender roast with the right vegetables. Unfortunately, my grandfather doesn't care for it, so that's one meal I rarely have."

Present tense, not past. "Do you still live with your grandfather?" Louisa remembered Josh saying his grandfather had given him and his cousin a home after their parents' deaths, but she hadn't realized he had remained there.

He nodded. "Grandfather's house is as large as yours. Now that we're grown, Jed and I have rooms on separate floors from Grandfather to give us more privacy. Jed stays there with his wife, but Winifred and I plan to buy a home of our own."

"Winifred?" Louisa felt the way she had when she'd fallen out of a tree she had been forbidden to climb, the breath knocked from her, the world turning black for an instant. It was ridiculous, totally ridiculous, that her heart skipped a beat and her stomach was roiling. Josh was a grown man. An attractive, eligible man. Of course he would have a sweetheart.

Clearly oblivious to the turmoil that had turned Louisa's insides upside down, Josh said, "Winifred Livingston. Her father owns a large bank that will be helpful in financing future expansions of P&S. Our alliance will be even more beneficial than the one Jed arranged. His wife's family has orange groves in Florida."

Louisa stared at the man she thought she knew, the man who was now spouting words that made no sense. Louisa ought to bite her tongue and pretend she wasn't shocked, but she could not.

"You make marriage sound like a merger between two companies."

"That's what it is. Marriage is designed to be beneficial for both families. My mother's father owned a tea plantation in India. When she and my father married, P&S obtained a reliable source of tea, and her family had a guaranteed market for their harvest."

The way he described it made it sound sensible, and perhaps it was, but he'd neglected to mention the most important aspect of marriage.

"What about love?"

Josh shook his head slowly. "A marriage based on love is a fairy tale. It's a fantasy created to entertain children, no more real than fire-breathing dragons or witches who can turn mischievous boys into toads."

He believed that. Louisa heard conviction in every word he uttered, but he was wrong. Totally, completely wrong.

"You're wrong," she said softly but firmly. "Love is real. It's the source of everything good in a marriage. It's what makes an ordinary day special. It's what ties people together and gives them the strength to endure tragedy. A marriage without love is nothing."

Josh looked at her as if she was the one spouting nonsense. He started to respond but waited when he saw Mrs. Tabor approaching with their plates. After he'd given thanks for the food and taken a bite of roast, declaring it as delicious as he'd hoped, Josh said, "It's clear you and I have different views of love. Let's not talk about them. When we came in, I noticed that Ma's is only open a few hours each day. Has it always been that way?"

Josh was wise to suggest a change of subject, because it would make the meal more pleasant. But Louisa wouldn't abandon it forever. More than Josh's leg needed healing. So did his heart. She had no idea how she could do it, but she was determined that by the time he left Sweetwater Crossing, Josh would know that what he called fairy-tale love was real.

Louisa had never considered the restaurant's hours. "I think they've always been the same. Mrs. Tabor took over last summer when her mother died. As far as I know, she didn't make any changes, because folks were happy with the way things were. Everyone knows she serves lunch from 11:00 to 1:00 and supper from 5:00 to 6:30, so they come then."

Though he appeared to be enjoying his food, the creases between Josh's eyes told Louisa something about the restaurant's hours bothered him.

"What if someone's hungry in the afternoon?" he asked. "Especially those who live out of town."

Louisa forked another piece of the tender roast, chewing it thoroughly as she considered Josh's question. "I never thought about that. My family didn't eat between meals, but if we were hungry, we were close to home. I imagine that the ranchers who have Sunday Houses keep food there. Others could buy something at the mercantile." She buttered a biscuit. "What would you do?"

His response was immediate. "If I were in New York, I'd have tea at P&S. Our tearoom is one of the store's most popular departments. When Grandfather started serving afternoon tea,"

Josh continued, "it was to keep shoppers in the store longer. Tea gave them a chance to sit down and rest a bit before resuming their shopping, but it soon attracted people who weren't already P&S customers. They came for the opportunity to feel pampered for an hour or so."

"Being pampered sounds intriguing." When they were in a bad mood, Louisa's sisters claimed that she was spoiled because she was the youngest, but she had never felt pampered. "What do you serve besides tea?"

"Small sandwiches, scones, several desserts. We use fine china and put the food on silver trays."

Louisa closed her eyes, imagining the scene. It sounded like something out of a novel, an elegant way to spend part of an afternoon. "You're making me hungry," she told Josh. "That shouldn't be possible when I've almost finished a delicious meal, but afternoon tea sounds so appealing. I wish Sweetwater Crossing had a tearoom."

It would be a change for the town. A good one.

Chapter Ten

As they'd finished supper, thoughts had bounced through Josh's brain, teasing him with possibilities. At the time, he hadn't minded the distraction, because anything was better than recalling Louisa's reaction when he'd mentioned the benefits that marriage to Winifred would bring. Astonishment had turned to horror, and then Louisa had started talking about fairy-tale love. She had been so passionate about it that Josh had felt as if she were delivering a sermon. Since it was one he hadn't wanted to hear, he'd asked her about the restaurant's hours.

His only intention had been to steer the conversation in a different, less disturbing, direction, but as they'd talked, the seeds were planted. Though he'd tried to dismiss them, they were stronger than ever this morning, refusing to be dismissed. That was why Josh wanted—no, he needed—to talk to Louisa. With the notable exception of love, she was clearheaded and would give him an honest opinion.

"Do you have a few minutes? There's something I'd like to discuss with you." The time after breakfast when he and Louisa remained to sip second cups of coffee was beginning to feel like their private time to talk.

She looked down at the watch she always wore pinned to her bodice. "My office doesn't open for another hour. Will that be enough?"

"It should be." Josh hoped she had at least one patient today. Though she'd tried to hide her discouragement, he knew she'd been disappointed when no one came into the office yesterday.

"Do you think others in Sweetwater Crossing would be interested in a tearoom?"

Louisa stirred a spoonful of sugar into her coffee, clearly trying to marshal her thoughts. "I can't predict how many, but I would expect some to like the idea. Mrs. Carmichael and her friends used to gather here for lunch. If there'd been a place like you described for tea, I could imagine them going there."

She paused for a second, then smiled at him, the sparkle in her eyes making Josh smile in return. "If it wasn't too expensive, I'd invite my friends to join me for tea. We could use some occasional pampering. Why do you ask?"

"Because this might be exactly what I need to win the challenge."

"What challenge?" Her curiosity obviously piqued, Louisa leaned forward. "Tell me about it, and don't worry if it takes more than an hour. I doubt anyone will notice if I open the office a bit late. I'm not expecting a rush of patients today."

And that was a shame. Not that Josh wanted Sweetwater Crossing's residents to suddenly develop illnesses or injuries, but he wished some of them would come to her for medical advice. Louisa had appeared pleased that he'd asked for her advice about business, but what she needed was to be acknowledged as a healer. In the meantime, perhaps his ideas would keep her from dwelling on the lack of patients.

"My grandfather has decided to retire. What he hasn't decided is who will replace him—my cousin or me. When my father and uncle were alive, there was no question about who would succeed him. Uncle John was older than my father, and in Grandfather's eyes, that made him the better choice—the only choice."

Louisa frowned. "That sounds like something from the British aristocracy, where roles are based on birth order."

"Exactly."

"But this is America. It should be different here."

"I agree. My father had no chance, but I do. Even though Jed is older, Grandfather challenged both of us to come up with an idea to celebrate P&S's centennial. Whoever gives him the idea he deems the best will receive the reins to the store."

The frown disappeared, and Louisa nodded, encouraging him to continue.

"Jed and Julia went to Europe, searching for new products to sell. Jed didn't say so, but I suspect he wants to expand beyond foodstuffs."

"And you don't." She took a sip of coffee, then placed the cup back on the saucer, carefully aligning the handle. It was a habit Josh had seen Louisa employ when she was pondering something.

"I'm not convinced that's the right direction," he told her. "Part of our appeal is being a specialty store. People come to P&S for high quality foods, tea, and coffee."

"Plus afternoon tea."

"Exactly." That seemed to be Josh's favorite word this morning. "I want to keep that as the core but find new foods to increase the appeal. That's what I was doing until the day I broke my leg."

He paused for a second as a wave of sorrow over losing Zeus swept over him. Before he could continue, Louisa spoke.

"You said your saddlebags held your future. What was in them?"

"Recipes. Recipes for distinctly American foods. P&S has specialized in British and Continental foods. My proposal was going to be to establish an American Room and sell foods from around the country. Most of our customers have never left New York. They haven't tasted pumpkin bisque or pickled eggs."

Louisa wrinkled her nose. "I can't say that pickled eggs sound very appealing."

"That's because you haven't tried them. They're surprisingly delicious." Once he accepted the purple color, which, the woman who introduced them to the delicacy had explained, came from using leftover beet pickling juice, he'd found the taste both unique and intriguing.

"I'll take your word for it." Louisa still appeared dubious. "How does a tearoom fit into your plan?"

"It doesn't. Just before Zeus threw me, I realized something was missing. An American Room was a good idea, but it wasn't good enough."

"And a tearoom is? I thought you already had one."

"We do. In New York. The way your eyes sparkled when I talked about afternoon tea sent my thoughts in a different direction. I'd been thinking about bringing different parts of America to New York, but maybe I should have been thinking about bringing parts of P&S to the rest of America. Towns the size of Sweetwater Crossing couldn't support a whole store, but a tearoom and a small shop with some specialty goods might be feasible."

The more he'd thought about the combination, the more he'd liked the idea. It was a way of expanding P&S's reach without destroying or diluting the essence of the company.

"What kind of specialty goods?" As they had at supper yesterday, Louisa's eyes radiated interest.

"Items that are part of the tea service—lemon curd, orange marmalade, clotted cream, savory biscuits, a half dozen varieties of tea—plus foods customers might not have considered—things like tinned lobster and escargots."

"Escargots? Isn't that just a fancy word for snails?"

"Yes, but before you say they don't sound appealing, I will

admit they're not for everyone, and that includes me. My grandfather refers to them as an acquired taste. Many of our customers consider them a delicacy, but I'd rather have pot roast." Josh took another sip of coffee before asking, "What do you think of the idea?"

"Other than the escargots, I'm intrigued by it, but I have a number of questions."

He wasn't surprised. One of the many things he admired about her was that Louisa considered every aspect of a subject before making a decision. "I'm not sure I have all the answers," he told her, "but I'll try."

She nodded. "Fair enough. First of all, why would you undertake a project like this when you'll only be here a few weeks? Even if you could construct a building in that time, you'd need someone to manage it."

As he'd expected, she'd raised several of the points that had bothered him. "There are two parts to that. Let's start with the easier one. I have an assistant who keeps telling me he'd like to live somewhere other than New York, at least for a few years. Richard would be an excellent manager. He's the kind of person everyone likes, so he'd fit in well here, and I think he'd enjoy the change."

Josh looked around the room, smiling at the memory of the delicious meals he'd had here. "If your sister is willing to offer him a room, he'd be an ideal boarder."

"I'm sure Emily would welcome him based on your recommendation." The frown that crossed Louisa's face was so brief that Josh told himself it was simply his imagination, but then she said, "He sounds like a good manager, but we'll miss you."

Her words warmed his heart and made Josh almost forget the second part of her question. Clearing his throat to chase the odd sensation away, he nodded. "I have an idea for a location for the tearoom. You were right in saying I wouldn't have time to build one, but I don't need to. The perfect place already exists." As her eyebrows rose, he continued. "I should have said the perfect *places* already exist." They had been one of the reasons he was so excited about the idea.

"I'm puzzled." Her expression confirmed her words. "There's nothing available on Main Street."

"I wasn't thinking of Main Street. From the moment I saw them, those empty Sunday Houses caught my fancy."

"Mrs. Locke's and Mrs. French's homes?"

"Yes. No one's using them. I could turn one into the tearoom, the other into the shop. I'm sure some work would be involved, and I'd want to connect them so customers could walk from one to the other without getting wet if it's raining, but it shouldn't be a major project." He'd been tempted to sketch his plans but had waited for Louisa's opinion. "What do you think? Am I crazy?"

The excitement he saw reflected in her eyes telegraphed her response. "If you're crazy, I must be too, because I think it's a wonderful idea. I'll help you in any way I can."

"That's very generous of you." It was more than he'd expected.

She shrugged. "As I told you, it's not as if patients are lining up to see me. Having something to do besides helping my sister with the dishes would be good."

"Where do we start?"

"We need to talk to Mrs. Tabor and Mr. Bentley to make sure they don't think you're trying to take business from them."

"I hadn't considered that." Once again, Louisa had provided valuable insights. "I thought the tearoom and shop would be complementary."

"They probably would be, but we need to convince Mrs. Tabor and Mr. Bentley. If either of them is opposed, you'll have more trouble attracting customers. No matter how appealing your tearoom and shop are, people won't like it if you're hurting one of their own."

An excellent point.

"I can help convince them. As someone who's lived here her whole life, my opinion should count for something."

"It counts for a lot to me."

Even though Louisa had raised possible stumbling blocks, Josh was more excited than he could remember. He looked down at his leg encased in the heavy cast, and for the first time he wondered if a broken leg and being stranded in Sweetwater Crossing were part of God's plan for him.

Chapter Eleven

The change was remarkable. In the ten days that she'd known him, Louisa had seen Josh in pain. She'd seen him bored, frustrated, and angry. She'd seen him intrigued by the Sunday Houses, but she'd never seen him looking like this. His eyes were wide and clear, radiating excitement. His face seemed to glow with an inner light. His posture was straighter, more alert. Everything about him reminded her of a picture she'd seen of a medieval knight preparing for a crusade. There was the same fervor, the same determination to succeed.

"Winning the challenge is important to you."

Josh nodded. Though they'd both finished their coffee, neither one was ready to end this conversation. "It's more than important. It's my duty."

Louisa knew she must have appeared surprised by his choice of words, because Josh continued. "I told you that my grandfather wouldn't consider letting my father run the company when he retired. He said the privilege—for he viewed it as a privilege as much as a duty—went to the oldest son. That was Uncle John. My father knew there was no way to change Grandfather's mind, but he told me that if I ever had a chance to be in charge, I should do everything I could to ensure that happened."

Josh paused, his eyes darkening with emotion. "That was one of the last things my father said to me on the day he was killed. I've always wondered whether he had some kind of premonition that he wouldn't return from that party."

What a burden to lay on a child. "The challenge gives you a chance to fulfill your father's wish and turn his dream into reality."

"It was more than a wish, Louisa. He asked me to promise, and I did. I know Father would have done a better job running P&S than Uncle John. He had a broader vision for the company, but no one would listen to his ideas, because he was the younger son."

Louisa felt a moment of guilt when she heard the clink of china as Emily washed the dishes, but she squelched it. Emily would be the first to tell her it was more important that she stay with Josh right now. The man might claim he did not believe in romantic love, but he clearly believed in love. It was love for his father that was driving him to win the challenge.

"It must have been hard for your father to accept second place. Age has nothing to do with wisdom." How many times had Louisa wanted to shout that at Emily and Joanna? "I understand how he felt and how you do whenever your cousin says he knows more simply because he's older."

Though Josh hadn't said it, she suspected that was another reason he was so determined to be the next head of P&S. Beating Jed would be a form of vindication. "I can't tell you how often my sisters told me I wasn't old enough to do something or that I was too young to understand. I hated it!"

Josh's smile radiated sympathy. "But look at you now. You're doing something they aren't and probably couldn't." He glanced around the room as if assessing it. "I'm not saying that running a boardinghouse isn't important. It is. But so is healing people. No matter what happened while you were growing up, I think Emily has realized that you have different talents and that one isn't better or more important than the other."

Tears pricked Louisa's eyes as Josh's words registered. She was supposed to be helping him, but he was the one providing comfort, his words like salve on a burn. "I hope you're right. We've had our differences—mostly my fault—but I think we're friends as well as sisters now, and that feels good. Are you and your cousin friends?" If they were, it might make the challenge more difficult and strain their friendship, because only one of them could win.

Josh shrugged. "We were before Grandfather issued his challenge. Now I'm not sure of that or much of anything other than that the idea of a tearoom and shop here is a good one."

"Then we'll make it happen." Louisa would do everything she could to ensure success.

"It seems to me the first step is to buy the houses. Who do I talk to about that?"

"Mayor Alcott. Emily told me he's handling the widows' estates. You'll find his office almost across the street from mine." It still felt odd to refer to Doc Sheridan's office as hers. "Do you want me to go with you? I'd be happy to, but I suspect he'd react better if I didn't. The mayor's a bit old-fashioned and thinks women shouldn't be involved in business."

Josh's shrug told her he wasn't surprised, perhaps because he'd encountered many men like Malcolm Alcott. "He and my grandfather would get along. I'll address him as Mr. Mayor and ask for his opinion. Do you think that'll get him on my side?"

"Without a doubt. You'll do fine. Just don't overdo the walking."

Josh kept his expression neutral as he left the mayor's office, not wanting the man to see his almost giddy reaction to their meeting. He'd waited until after the midday meal to approach Alcott, guessing a full stomach would make him more amenable to Josh's proposal. As he'd told Louisa he would, he'd shown the older man deference, then mentioned he was considering acquiring some property in Sweetwater Crossing, letting the mayor make whatever assumptions he chose about the purpose.

Alcott had nodded when Josh mentioned the empty Sunday Houses, agreeing that they might look appealing to someone from the East. After discussing the price, he'd given Josh the keys to both houses and told him to take his time looking at them. Josh planned to do that . . . once Louisa could join him.

He crossed the street and entered her office, setting the bell over the door tinkling. Seconds later, she emerged from the room on the left, her expression revealing disappointment mingled with pleasure.

"I know you were hoping I was a new patient, but at least I come bearing good news." He dangled the keys in front of her.

"You already bought the houses?" She made no effort to hide her surprise.

"I was waiting for you to visit them with me. I want your opinion."

Louisa looked at things differently, and that difference of perspective had already proven valuable. And while this was the first time he'd relied on a woman, he knew it wouldn't be the last. Louisa was an important part of this project. Grandfather would have scoffed at the idea, but Josh was not his grandfather.

Louisa reached for her bonnet, tying the ribbons beneath her chin. "Let's go. Office hours are over."

"Any patients?" Josh almost hated to ask, since he suspected the answer would be negative, but he wanted her to know that he cared about her professional life.

"No."

"Maybe tomorrow."

"Maybe, but I doubt it. Since it's Good Friday, I don't plan to have regular office hours."

There was no mistaking her discouragement, and so Josh did his best to lift her spirits, making the recounting of his meeting with the mayor as humorous as possible as they walked toward the Sunday Houses.

When they arrived at the houses and Louisa started toward the eastern one, Josh shook his head. "I want to see the other first. That's the one I envision for the tearoom."

If she'd asked, he couldn't have explained his reasons. All Josh knew was that his instincts told him that the building on the right was the one for the tearoom.

As a light breeze wafted the scent of flowers from the house across the street, Louisa smiled. "I don't know how she does it, but Mrs. Sanders has flowers blooming most of the year." Turning her attention back to the Sunday Houses, she said, "You probably remember that this was Mrs. French's house. I've never been in either, but I imagine they're virtually identical."

"There's only one way to know." Josh unlocked and opened the door, waving his hand in what he'd been taught was a gallant gesture while he did his best to keep his crutches from falling. "After you." Though his pulse was pounding with anticipation, Louisa should be the first to see the interior of the building that had captured his imagination.

She had no sooner entered it than she began to sneeze. "This needs a good cleaning."

It did indeed. The light from the open door and the windows revealed half an inch of dust covering the floor and furniture. Thankfully, Josh detected no smell of mold or evidence of rodents.

"Cleaning's easy enough." If he had to, he could do it himself, although his cast and crutches would complicate the seemingly simple task. "Let's see what else needs to be done."

As they walked slowly through the building, Josh's feeling

that this was the right place intensified. It might have only three rooms, but the house was filled with potential. A gathering room on the right extended the entire length of the house, while the left side held a bedroom in front with a kitchen behind it.

"This is even better than I'd hoped," he told Louisa when they'd finished the tour. Though another woman might have chattered while they looked at each of the rooms, she'd remained silent, seemingly unwilling to interrupt his inspection. "The kitchen is too small, and I'd like the tearoom to occupy the full width of the house, but if we move the bedroom walls, there'll be plenty of space for both."

When she nodded her understanding, he continued. "If the other house is the same, we could turn its kitchen into a stockroom and have two rooms for the shop."

Louisa seemed puzzled. "Why would you need two rooms? The mercantile has only one."

"The rooms will be very different. The larger one will be for British goods, the other for items from the Continent. The wallpaper and furnishings in each will reflect the origin of the products." Josh had lain awake for hours last night, envisioning how he'd decorate both the tearoom and the shop. "I'll have models of Big Ben and Buckingham Palace in the British one and the Arc de Triomphe and Brandenburg Gate in the other."

Those blue eyes that reminded Josh of a summer sky were filled with enthusiasm. "That sounds wonderful. I'm surprised there weren't any illustrations of those rooms in the advertisements I've seen for P&S. They would have made me want to go to New York if only to see them."

Louisa had no way of knowing how much her response meant to Josh. "We have nothing like that at P&S. Every part of the store has the same wallpaper and style of furniture."

"Then this was your idea."

The admiration he heard in her voice made Josh's heart sing with pleasure. When the image of uniquely decorated rooms had popped into his brain, he'd been more than intrigued. He'd been convinced it was a good idea. But then the doubts crept in. Louisa's enthusiasm banished those doubts.

"It was."

Her smile broadened. "It's a brilliant idea! People will come just to see the rooms."

"Hopefully they'll stay to buy something."

"Oh, they will." Louisa's confidence more than buoyed Josh; it assured him that he was headed in the right direction.

After they'd toured Mrs. Locke's house and confirmed that it had the same basic floor plan as her neighbor's, he escorted Louisa back outside. "I want to connect the two porches," he told her, "so customers can walk between the tearoom and the shop. Besides serving as a walkway, the porch will have a number of rocking chairs for the men."

"What about the women?"

"They'll be inside shopping. In my experience, husbands prefer to stay outdoors."

She chuckled at the idea. "You've thought of everything."

"Hardly. We're just beginning. As you said, we need to convince Mrs. Tabor and Mr. Bentley that this won't be a threat to their livelihood."

"We should probably wait until tomorrow morning. That's the least busy time for both of them."

Oh, how Josh liked the way she'd used the plural pronoun!

"If we go ahead, we'll need a name."

"Wouldn't you call it Porter & Sons?"

He shook his head. "That seems premature and maybe even presumptuous. I suspect Grandfather wouldn't be pleased, since I haven't asked for his permission. Besides, this is mine, and I have no sons."

Yet. If all went as planned, he and Winifred would have their first child in less than two years. There was no way of predicting whether it would be a son or a daughter, but they'd agreed that they wanted two children, maybe more, since neither of them had enjoyed being an only child. God willing, there would be young Porters to carry on the family tradition.

Josh pictured himself with a baby in his arms. His son or daughter. A tiny infant with Louisa's smile. Ridiculous! Winifred was the woman he was going to marry.

Oblivious to the direction his thoughts had wandered, Louisa tipped her head to one side in the endearing way she had when she was pondering something. "In that case, why not call it Porter's? Singular Porter, that is."

"Porter's." Grateful for something that would help banish the image that seemed indelibly etched on his brain, Josh let the name roll off his tongue. "I like that."

Chapter Twelve

"You've mastered those crutches amazingly well."

The feeling of satisfaction that welled up inside Josh was out of proportion to Louisa's words. "I had a strong incentive," he told her as they walked slowly toward Ma's Kitchen the next morning. "I want to win Grandfather's challenge, and I can't do that unless I can walk, even if it's with crutches."

"We could have taken the buggy."

"But that would have made me look and feel like an invalid, and that's something I can't afford." He wasn't particularly concerned about Mrs. Tabor's reaction to seeing him riding, but he suspected Adam Bentley would view the buggy as a sign of Josh's weakness.

When they reached the restaurant, Louisa led the way to the back entrance and knocked on the door.

"Louisa and Mr. Porter." Though her smile was as welcoming as it had been the night they'd dined here, Mrs. Tabor's surprise was evident. "I'm not open yet."

Josh sniffed, then grinned. If there was one thing a lifetime at P&S had taught him, it was to identify and evaluate foods based on their aroma. This might be a small restaurant in a small town, but the dishes Mrs. Tabor served were equal to those Josh had eaten in famous New York establishments.

"You've already started making pot roast. I hope you'll save a plate for me, because I plan to come back for lunch." Though Emily offered to let him share the midday meal with her, Mrs. Carmichael, and little Noah, he didn't want to take advantage of her generosity today, particularly since Louisa wouldn't be there. She'd packed a sack lunch to eat in her office.

The restaurant's proprietor dusted the flour from her hands. "I doubt that's why you're here. Come in and sit down while you tell me what brings you out this early in the morning."

When they were seated at the round table in the corner of the large kitchen, Louisa spoke. "Josh has a plan he'd like to discuss with you."

"A plan. That sounds interesting." Mrs. Tabor's brown eyes mirrored her curiosity, raising Josh's hopes that she'd be amenable to his idea.

"I hope you approve of it, because I won't proceed unless you do." As succinctly as he could, Josh outlined the concept he and Louisa had devised, watching Mrs. Tabor's reaction. Though she nodded occasionally, her expression didn't reveal her opinion. Feeling as if he were in a court of law awaiting a judge's ruling, Josh said, "I want to assure you that the food I'd like to offer is different from what you serve here."

The older woman nodded again. "I can see that, and your hours wouldn't overlap with mine." Josh had decided to have the tearoom open from two to four, although the store would be open from ten until five, allowing customers to shop before and after they visited the tearoom.

Mrs. Tabor was silent for a moment. Then she nodded briskly. "I like your plan. It might even help my business if it encourages ranchers to stay in town longer and possibly have supper here." Her smile was genuine as she added, "It's a good idea, young man. You have my blessing."

"I hope Mr. Bentley is as easy to convince," Louisa said when they were back on Main Street, "but I doubt he will be."

Josh harbored the same doubts, and the shopkeeper's scowl while Josh was outlining his plans did nothing to make him think he'd approve of Porter's. Josh had once heard a woman say that while blue eyes could appear cold, brown could not, that they always looked warm. That woman had never met Adam Bentley. His eyes might be brown, but they were as warm as a January sleet storm.

There was silence when Josh finished his explanation, confirming his fears. Then the man let out a deep sigh. "I won't stop you. That wouldn't be the Christian thing to do, but I don't like the idea of having competition. This is a small town. Folks don't need two places to buy tinned goods." He gestured toward his shelf of canned fruits and vegetables.

Before Josh could point out that he planned to carry different merchandise, Louisa nodded as if she understood Bentley's concerns. "As I recall, your wife was worried about losing business when Thelma Scott opened her dressmaker shop, but your sales increased, because Thelma bought all of her materials from you rather than from the manufacturers."

Though she'd intended to placate the shopkeeper, her words appeared to have no effect.

"Mr. Porter won't be buying things from me."

"That's because nothing Josh is planning to sell is the same as your merchandise." Louisa's voice was low and pleasant but firm.

Bentley shrugged, clearly not believing her.

"That's only partially true." It was time for Josh to argue his case. "The goods in the store will come from P&S, and they're different from what you offer, but I was hoping you'd be able to provide the dishes and flatware for the tearoom. I'll need service for at least four dozen."

As Josh had expected, the man's eyes lit with barely concealed interest and perhaps a bit of avarice.

"How will you fit that many people into one of those houses? They're too small."

"You're right. Neither house is big enough for that many. I'll have six tables for four, but I can't have customers waiting while dishes are being washed. That's why I need a second set. I assume you have catalogs. I'd like Louisa to help me choose patterns."

"Are you going to be washing those dishes?" Bentley gave Louisa a patronizing look that annoyed Josh almost as much as his question.

To her credit, she smiled sweetly. "If Josh can't find someone better qualified, yes, I'll wash dishes. I want him to succeed, because I think the tearoom will benefit Sweetwater Crossing."

The man appeared mollified by the prospect of a large order, but Josh knew he wasn't completely convinced.

"There's one more thing." Josh pointed to the jar of honey on the counter. "I wondered if you'd allow me to offer that as part of the tea service. P&S sells several good honeys but none as delicious as your wife's."

The scowl turned into cautious appraisal. "I suppose you could do that."

"I'm planning to sell the other items we use for the teas in the shop, but it would be wrong to have your honey there. Instead, we'd tell people where we bought it and encourage them to come here for a jar or two to serve at home."

Though Josh suspected the man knew that might result in higher sales, he said only, "Tina would like that." Bentley was silent for a moment. Then he pursed his lips and gave a quick nod. "I'm not sure Sweetwater Crossing is ready for a tearoom and shop. We're simple folks here. But it's your money to waste. Go ahead."

He reached under the counter and withdrew two large books. "Here are the catalogs." He flipped through the pages of one and pointed to a set of china. "This is a popular pattern."

It might be popular, but Josh knew it wasn't the right one. "Please give us a few minutes to see what else is available."

He and Louisa spent the next half hour debating which design would be the best.

"Grandfather said ladies like flowers." Josh pointed to a teapot covered with roses described as various shades of pink.

"Most do," Louisa agreed. "That's why the first pattern Mr. Bentley showed you is so popular." She tipped her head to one side. "Does P&S use floral china in its tearoom?"

When Josh nodded, she turned the page and studied the picture on it. "You said the décor at Porter's would be different from anything at P&S. Shouldn't the china be different too?"

It was a good point and one he hadn't considered. This was why he'd wanted Louisa to accompany him today—she provided a different and valuable perspective.

"What would you suggest?"

Without hesitation, she pointed to a design so simple he'd dismissed it as too plain. It was nothing more than white china with a dark border that the catalog called royal blue on the rims of the plates and saucers and around the top of the cups.

"This is simple and elegant. It will appeal to both men and women. Best of all, it won't detract from the wallpaper and furnishings you've planned."

The more he studied the design, the better Josh liked it. When his gaze moved from the catalog page to Louisa's face, he grinned. The tearoom's china would match Louisa's eyes. Perfect.

"Mr. Bentley made a lot of money from you today," Louisa said when they were outside and far enough away from the store that no one would overhear them. "I don't claim to be an expert, but his prices seemed high."

"They were, but it was worth it to get his agreement."

"Grudging agreement."

"Even so, he won't discourage others from patronizing Porter's when his wife's honey is being featured."

As they walked east on Main Street, Louisa slowing her steps to keep pace with him, she gave Josh what appeared to be an approving look.

"I've never known anyone who approached business the way you do. I'm learning a lot by watching you."

And he had never known a woman so interested in his business.

Though his heart expanded at the praise implicit in Louisa's words, Josh tried to make light of it. "Should I be worried that you'll decide to compete with me?"

"Never! I'll be the one who treats your customers when they eat too much of the delicious food you're planning to serve."

"Ah, I see. You think this will be a mutually beneficial arrangement."

As he'd intended, she chuckled. "I think many will benefit from Porter's. I can't wait to have afternoon tea there."

Smiling at the prospect, Josh swung his crutches with more force than normal, regretting it when he almost tripped.

"Are you all right?"

He nodded. "Simply excited about the idea of Porter's. Once I get past the formality of the sale, I need to hire a builder. Who's the best in town?"

"There's only one. Raymond Knapp. I've heard he's very busy, but if you'd like, I'll talk to him about Porter's when I see him on Saturday."

Though he'd been grateful for Louisa's assistance in approaching others, this felt wrong. It wasn't merely that he didn't want her to be beholden to Knapp if the man put aside other work at Louisa's request. Josh's stomach churned at the prospect of working with the man who appeared to have a romantic interest in Louisa.

He pushed back his discomfort, telling himself this was business. Simply business. He didn't need to like the man. He needed Knapp to be competent. The fact that he might want to court Louisa shouldn't matter.

But somehow it did.

Chapter Thirteen

"'It is finished.'"

Tears filled Louisa's eyes as the minister recited Jesus's final words on the cross. Today marked David Grant's only time delivering a Good Friday sermon, and it had been the most moving one she'd ever heard, increasing her wish that he would remain in Sweetwater Crossing. But he wouldn't. Couldn't, because he'd committed to return to his hometown and his replacement had already been hired.

She fished a lace-trimmed handkerchief from her reticule and dabbed the tears, noting that she wasn't the only one who'd been affected by David's sermon. Several women including Emily had tears streaming down their faces, and Josh, who sat at her right, wore the most somber expression she'd seen as the minister urged them to reflect on what had happened that Friday almost two thousand years ago.

"Let us pray. Dear Lord . . ."

A loud cough interrupted the minister. It began as a single cough but turned into a spell that grew louder the longer it persisted. And while it continued, David stood silently in the pulpit, waiting to finish his prayer.

Louisa turned, wondering who was coughing so vehemently. It didn't sound like bronchitis or croup, but there was no doubt that it was painful. She spotted a girl about eight or nine years old, her face red with the effort of trying to suppress the cough that refused to stop. Though she couldn't recall the child's name, she recognized her mother.

Mrs. Storm and her husband had moved to Sweetwater Crossing soon after their wedding ten years ago. Louisa might not have remembered their arrival had both Storms not been outspoken in their criticism of several of Father's sermons, claiming he was too lenient with sinners. It was one of the many times that Father had asked the family to pray for an unhappy parishioner.

Today Mrs. Storm, whose brown hair, dress, and bonnet made her look like a sparrow, was once again unhappy, although this time the minister was not to blame.

"Outside," one of the women whose patience had evaporated hissed. "Take her outside."

The command only increased the child's distress and the strength of the coughs. Though Louisa longed to help her, she would do nothing without the mother's approval. Finally, Mrs. Storm wrapped an arm around her daughter's shoulders and led her from the sanctuary.

Louisa followed. When the church doors closed behind them, she pulled a key from her reticule. "I can help her, Mrs. Storm. If you come to my office, I have a syrup that will soothe her throat and lessen her cough."

The woman stared at Louisa as if she'd proposed inserting a flaming torch down her daughter's throat. "Why should I trust you? You're not a real doctor. For all I know, you might poison Violet."

As her coughs continued unabated, the girl gave Louisa an imploring look. Her potential patient was willing to be treated.

"It's the same syrup Dr. Sheridan would have given her. It's part of his supply."

Mrs. Storm was not convinced. "I don't know that." She tugged her daughter's hand. "Come along, Violet. I'll give you some sarsaparilla when we get home."

But sarsaparilla wouldn't help her. Louisa clenched her fists in frustration as the mother and child climbed into a buggy and drove away. This was worse than last Sunday when the men had dismissed her abilities. Now a child was suffering needlessly, simply because her mother wouldn't trust Louisa.

It wasn't right, but there was nothing Louisa could do to change it.

"You're a picture of loveliness," Raymond said as he bent his arm to escort Louisa to the wagon.

She didn't feel lovely. Even though more than twenty-four hours had passed since Mrs. Storm had refused her help, she kept thinking of Violet and praying that the girl's cough had subsided. As often as she reminded herself that it took time to gain trust, the rejection hurt. For years, the townspeople had trusted Doc Sheridan, not realizing that he had betrayed his oath to do no harm and had been responsible for multiple deaths, but they wouldn't give her even the smallest measure of trust. She'd known men would be more skeptical of her abilities, but she'd thought the women might at least give her a chance. If they were all like Mrs. Storm, her time as Sweetwater Crossing's healer would be short.

Louisa forced a smile, reminding herself that Raymond was not to blame for what had happened. "Thank you. I'm looking forward to seeing your aunt again. This will be my first visit to the farm."

Raymond chuckled as he helped her into the wagon. "It's an ordinary farm, but don't tell Aunt Tina that. She thinks it's special because it has a smokehouse and space for her bees. My parents' farm had that plus a larger barn and an icehouse."

"If she's happy, that's what matters." Look at Emily. Though she'd lived on a large ranch when she and George were married, she seemed content to stay in her childhood home even after she and Craig were wed.

"She's happy, and so am I. Sweetwater Crossing is a nicer place now that you're here. I hope we get to know each other better."

Louisa felt color rise to her cheeks as the implication of Raymond's words registered. Caroline had said he'd shown no interest in the women who'd vied for his attention, but now, though he hadn't asked to court Louisa, Raymond's smile made it seem that he wanted to explore that possibility. It was an intriguing possibility, but it was too soon. They'd only just met, and Louisa was still trying to find her place—her new place—in Sweetwater Crossing.

"I'm sure we will get to know each other better," she said, "since we both live here. As your uncle reminded me, it's a small town. Everyone knows everyone."

They'd left the town and were headed south. When the road straightened and the horse needed no guidance, Raymond turned to look at Louisa. "That wasn't what I meant, and I think you know that, but I won't rush you. I'm a patient man."

"And, from what I've heard, a busy one. I wondered whether you'd have time for a new construction project. You may have heard that Josh Porter bought the Locke and French houses."

Raymond nodded. "My uncle said he's planning to have some kind of tearoom and shop. He didn't sound too happy about that."

Though Louisa didn't want to cause friction between Raymond and his family, she wanted him to help Josh. "Porter's won't compete with either the mercantile or Ma's. Josh explained that to both your uncle and Mrs. Tabor. The houses are in good shape, but they need some renovations to turn them into commercial spaces. In addition, Josh wants to connect them by extending the porches. I was hoping you'd be willing to do the work."

To Louisa's relief, Raymond smiled. "If we can agree on a price and schedule, sure. There's nothing I wouldn't do for you, Louisa, but please don't tell my aunt and uncle until everything is settled. I don't want to upset them unnecessarily. They're still unhappy that I'm not interested in running the mercantile, so I try not to do anything that would aggravate them. Talking about building would spoil the day."

As it turned out, there would not have been an opportunity to discuss Porter's. From the moment Louisa stepped down from the wagon, Mrs. Bentley kept her by her side.

"Louisa, my dear, I'm so glad you're here." The woman wrapped Louisa in a hug that highlighted their physical differences. They were the same height, but Mrs. Bentley was heftier and stronger. "Let me look at you."

While her hostess scrutinized her, Louisa studied Raymond's aunt. Though her hair was blond while his was brown, their eyes were the same shade of blue, their features the same shape, their builds similar. No one would question their kinship.

"Come in, come in." Mrs. Bentley led Louisa into the parlor, then waved her hand at Raymond, shooing him away. "Adam wants your opinion about something in the barn, and I want to talk to Louisa." When Raymond had left, she smiled at Louisa. "Would you like something to drink?"

"No, thank you, Mrs. Bentley."

Once again, the older woman gave a dismissive wave with her hand. "Call me Tina, and you must call my husband Adam. We want you to feel like part of the family."

Mama would have been shocked. Elders, whom she defined as anyone ten or more years older, were to be addressed formally, and yet Mrs. Bentley seemed determined.

"Did you know that your mother was the first to call me Tina?" When Louisa shook her head, she explained, "My full name is Augustina. All my life, people called me Gussie. After Adam and I moved here, I told your mother how much I hated that name. She suggested Tina, and I've been Tina ever since."

That sounded like something Mama would have done. She considered it her mission to make parishioners comfortable, no matter what that involved.

"It's wonderful that you're back home." Tina wrapped her hands around Louisa's. "An answer to prayer. I wanted another daughter, and now you're here."

"My mother was a special person." Louisa hoped Tina would understand that she wasn't looking for a substitute for Mama. No one could take her place.

"She was indeed." Tina's lips quivered, and for a second, Louisa thought she might be on the verge of tears. "She was the only one who knew how to comfort me when Tillie died. That's why when she told me she worried about you more than her other daughters, I said I'd take care of you. It was the least I could do when she'd done so much for me. You understand, don't you?"

What Louisa understood was that Tina needed someone to mother, and she was the person she'd chosen. She also knew that if Mama were alive, she'd urge her to be kind to the woman who'd been so devastated by her daughter's death.

"Of course I do."

"Then come help me get supper ready."

Chapter Fourteen

Easter was a day for rejoicing, and that was exactly what Louisa planned to do. As she slipped her favorite blue dress over her head, she smiled. Easter morning had always been her favorite time of the year, sitting in the front pew with her sisters and Mama, listening to Father speak of the empty tomb and the promise it signified. Today would be different. Joanna was in Europe, and Mama and Father were no longer on Earth, but the sense of rebirth and hope still filled her.

She and Emily were closer than they'd been since her sister's marriage and, despite the discouragement she'd felt on Friday and the momentary uneasiness she'd experienced with both Raymond and Tina, Louisa was glad she was spending this special day in Sweetwater Crossing. Her own future might be murky, but it felt right to be with Emily. It also felt right to have Josh accompanying them to church.

Josh. As she coiled her hair the way Aimee had taught her, Louisa's smile broadened. He was more than her first patient. He needed her, and oh, how good it felt to be needed. Helping Josh choose china might not seem important to someone else, but the knowledge that he'd relied on her had mitigated her disappointment over having no other patients.

With one final look at her reflection, Louisa gathered her shawl and reticule and headed toward the staircase. Today was a day to worship, but tomorrow morning would bring a new adventure as she helped Josh turn those two vacant Sunday Houses into a thriving business. Her instincts told her Porter's would be a success, and when it was, Josh would win his grandfather's challenge. That would give her another reason to rejoice.

"This is a first for me," Josh said an hour later as they filed out of the church. Though the clothing he wore wasn't as finely tailored as the suit that had been ripped by his fall from the horse, there was no ignoring Joshua Porter's good looks. With his blond hair carefully combed, his vivid blue eyes, and those full lips unhidden by a moustache, he was strikingly handsome. And right now, he was smiling at her.

"Your first time attending Easter services?" Somehow, Louisa found that difficult to believe.

"No. My family went to church every Sunday. What's new for me is the community breakfast." He gestured toward the park where Louisa had told him the townspeople would gather immediately after the service.

"I don't know whether other towns have the same tradition, but Sweetwater Crossing has had Easter breakfast for as long as I can remember."

"But not forever." Mrs. Carmichael, who'd preceded them down the steps, shook her head slightly as she faced them. "Your father started it when he moved here. It seemed like a revolutionary idea the first year and not everyone attended, but those who did enjoyed it so much that the second year almost everyone in town came." Her smile became wry. "The women tried to outdo each other with their egg casseroles."

As Mrs. Carmichael may have intended, Josh appeared intrigued, making Louisa suspect he had not abandoned the idea of an American Room, even though he'd lost Zeus and the recipes the horse had carried. "Are there any particular casseroles you can recommend?"

Louisa didn't wait for the widow's response. "If Mrs. Tabor brings her mother's sausage and egg bake, you should try it." When Mrs. Carmichael nodded and turned to speak to Alice, Louisa returned her attention to Josh. "Were you thinking about the American Room?"

"Good guess. It's probably foolish since I have no recipes, but the idea still intrigues me. I'm convinced it would be a good addition to P&S."

Before Louisa could reply, she felt a tap on her shoulder and turned to see Tina.

"May I speak to you for a moment? Privately." Though the older woman was dressed in her Sunday finery, her bonnet secured with what appeared to be a new light green ribbon that complimented her darker green gown, her expression was solemn, more suited to a funeral than an Easter celebration.

"Of course."

When they'd moved to a spot where they would not be overheard, Tina said, "I want to apologize for last night."

"There's no need for apologies. Supper was delicious, and I enjoyed hearing how you and Adam decided to open a mercantile." It was surprisingly like Josh's decision to create Porter's—a seemingly impulsive decision but one that had proved successful for the Bentleys. Louisa hoped Josh would have the same or even greater success.

"Not that. I'm afraid I spoke out of turn and made you uncomfortable when we were alone. If I did, I'm sorry. If I sounded a bit maudlin, it was because yesterday was the anniversary of Tillie's death."

Louisa's heart ached for the woman who'd suffered—and continued to suffer—over the loss of a child. "I'm sorry. I didn't know."

"There's no reason you should have remembered. I just hope you won't hold what I said against me or Raymond."

Though Louisa could not imagine why Tina had included Raymond in her plea, she saw no reason not to reassure the older woman.

"As I said before, there's no need for an apology."

"Thank you." Tina's relief was apparent in her more relaxed posture. "It would please me greatly if you'd come to the farm for lunch occasionally. Please say you will."

"I will."

As Louisa walked back to the gathering, she looked at the members of the congregation who were walking toward the park but saw neither Mrs. Storm nor Violet. Had the girl's cough worsened? She hoped not.

Ten minutes later when they were making their way through the serving line, Louisa pointed to one of the large pans of food. "You're in luck," she told Josh. "This is Mrs. Tabor's casserole." With bits of sausage poking through the delicately browned crust, it looked as appealing as it smelled.

Josh took a healthy serving. "If it's as good as you say, do you suppose she'd share the recipe?"

"I imagine she'd be flattered, especially if you put her mother's name on it."

"I was planning to do that with all the recipes. It's only fair to credit the women who so generously contributed them. Besides, everyone wants to be famous."

"Not me." The words came out so quickly that they surprised Louisa. She hadn't spent much time thinking about fame, but when Josh mentioned it, it felt wrong.

He gave her a puzzled look as they moved to the next table laden with food. "Then what do you want?"

"To heal people. If only they'd let me." Though she'd lowered her voice so much she wasn't sure Josh had heard her, he nodded.

"You're thinking about the girl with the cough, aren't you?"

"Yes, but how did you know?"

A small smile tilted the corners of his mouth upward. "I'm getting to know you."

She shouldn't allow a smile to affect her, not when she knew the man who'd bestowed it on her was planning to marry another woman, but Louisa was unable to control her heart. After taking a deep breath in an attempt to slow her pulse, she said, "You'll have a chance to get to know something else this afternoon," she told him.

"And what would that be?"

"A surprise."

"A picnic? This is a nice surprise." Though he'd declared he'd eaten so much at the breakfast that he wouldn't need another meal today, the aromas escaping from the basket Emily had packed for them were making Josh salivate. This was not a traditional Easter dinner, but Josh was learning that the Vaughns were not as bound by tradition as many of his acquaintances in New York.

He rested his leg on the crate Craig had placed in the buggy, impressed with the amount of thought that had gone into today's excursion. Not only had Emily created what smelled like a delicious meal for them, but Craig had arranged for Mrs. Carmichael to stay with Noah, freeing the four adults for an afternoon without the distraction of a young boy. Even the crate showed that everyone had been thinking of Josh's comfort.

"I've never been on a picnic," he told Louisa as they settled in the backseat, leaving Craig to drive and Emily to direct him.

"I thought that might be the case." When a light breeze teased her hat ribbons, Louisa tightened them, then returned her attention to him. "The picnic is only a small part of the surprise. The real surprise is where we're going."

"And you won't give me any hints?"

"Nope." Craig tossed the word over his shoulder. "You'll have to be patient. I hope you're better at that than most of my pupils."

"I can't say that I have an abundance of patience."

"Then we'll have to distract you with other things." Emily turned to look at him. "You and Louisa were all anyone could talk about this morning."

"Except for the food, that is." Craig corrected his soon-to-be-wife.

"What did they say?" Though he'd known her less than two weeks, somehow hearing his name coupled with Louisa's filled him with a sense of rightness, and that was totally ridiculous. Louisa was serving as his doctor. She was helping him establish Porter's. That was all. Winifred was the woman he would marry.

It was Emily who answered. "Folks, especially the women, are excited about the idea of Porter's. No one's experienced a formal tea, and now that the solemnity of Lent is over, they can't wait. They're saying you're the best thing that's happened to Sweetwater Crossing in a long time."

What about Louisa? Why had people been talking about both of them? Few knew the role she was playing at Porter's.

"See, Josh. That's exactly what I predicted. Porter's will be a success."

As Louisa shifted slightly, the scent of her perfume wafted through the air, a scent as appealing as any he'd ever encountered. Though he suspected he'd met other women wearing the same perfume, never before had it smelled so good.

"They were like bees buzzing," Emily said.

Though they seemed innocuous to him, Louisa shuddered at her sister's words. "You said they were talking about both of us. What did they say about me?"

"I heard most of it," Craig said. "People were surprised—

shocked might be a better word—that Mrs. Sheridan gave you her husband's office."

Louisa nodded as if she'd expected that. "Because I'm not a real doctor."

"I wouldn't go that far."

This time she shook her head. "You're trying to be kind, Craig, but I know how many of them feel. Mrs. Storm wasn't willing to let me prescribe cough syrup for Violet, even though it would have come directly from Doc's cabinet."

The resignation in Louisa's voice bothered Josh more than outright pain would have and made him determined to encourage her. "They'll come around."

"You don't know that."

"I know human nature. Change is difficult for many people, and you have to admit that having a woman as a healer here is a big change. My experience is that it takes people a while to become comfortable with change, but many of them do . . . eventually." He wouldn't try to convince her that it would happen immediately, because she knew as well as he did that that wasn't realistic.

"I want to believe you're right," Louisa said at last, "and so I will. At least for today."

When Craig and Emily resumed their conversation, Josh turned his attention back to Louisa and asked the question that had bounced through his brain more times than he could count. "What made you decide to become a doctor?"

"Bees."

"Bees? I thought it might have been the rabbit with the broken leg."

She smiled. "I'm surprised you remember that."

"I remember most of what you've told me." That was another thing Josh could not explain. Though conversations with Louisa were easy to recall, he had difficulty remembering any he'd shared with Winifred. The only reason he could imagine was that it had been months since he'd spoken to Winifred.

"What happened with bees?"

"They stung me, and I almost died. Doc Sheridan said he'd never seen anything like it and didn't know why I had such trouble breathing."

That sounded extreme. All Josh knew about bee stings was that they hurt but that the pain lasted only a few hours. "What did he do?"

Louisa shuddered. "He made me drink something that tasted worse than anything I'd ever had, and he put poultices on my skin. None of that helped, but eventually my breathing returned to normal."

"But you wanted to be able to do better."

A small shrug accompanied Louisa's answer. "I was convinced I could do better, but I've learned there's nothing other than prayer that will help if I'm bitten again."

No wonder her sister's casual mention of bees had made Louisa shudder. "How old were you?"

"Seven."

"And you never wavered?" If true, that was remarkable.

"Oh, I certainly did." Louisa chuckled, as if the memory amused her. "I wanted to be a famous opera singer, a painter, and to play the trombone. I was a dismal failure at all of those."

"But you're not a failure as a healer."

"That remains to be seen."

Louisa turned her gaze back to the road in front of them and smiled, the melancholy their discussion had raised disappearing. "Close your eyes, Josh. The surprise is coming."

Though it was an odd sensation to be in a moving vehicle without being able to see where he was going, Josh complied. Judging from the way his body pressed more tightly against the seatback, he surmised they were climbing a steep hill. When they reached the summit, Louisa laid her hand on his, the warmth making him smile.

"You can look now."

Josh blinked for a few seconds, letting his eyes adjust to the sunshine, then grinned. The valley before him was unlike any he'd ever seen. Instead of a green meadow, he saw fields so blue that if he didn't know otherwise, he would have believed he was looking at water.

"Flowers?"

Louisa nodded. "Bluebonnets. Aren't they beautiful?"

They were more than beautiful. "They're incredible. I hope this is where we're going to have our picnic."

"It is." Emily turned to flash a smile at him. "Louisa and I wanted you and Craig to experience one of the most impressive sights of the Hill Country. Our family used to come here each year, but this is the first time we've been able to do it on Easter."

The reason, Josh suspected, was that, as the town's minister, their father had other responsibilities on Easter Sunday.

"Emily and I'll get lunch ready," Craig said when he'd parked the buggy. "You and Louisa should enjoy the flowers."

They walked even more slowly than they would have on level ground, with Josh watching each time he swung his crutches, lest he place them on an uneven patch and fall. But even at the snail's pace—or perhaps because of it—he was able to savor the beauty of the wildflowers. The bluebonnets, he discovered, weren't pure blue spikes but had white tips, and interspersed with the sea of blue was the occasional red flower, something Louisa called an Indian paintbrush.

"It's hard to believe this is real," he said as he stared at the vast expanse of blue. "If I saw it in a painting, I would have thought it was an exaggeration, that there couldn't be so many flowers in one spot."

She smiled, as if she'd once had the same reaction. "They

only last a few weeks, but when they're in bloom, I'm convinced nothing can compare to their beauty."

Louisa pointed toward a rock outcropping on top of a nearby hill. "I wish you weren't in a cast, because the view from there is spectacular. My sisters thought it was too far to walk, but I climbed up every year." She chuckled. "One time, a gust of wind caught my shawl, and for a second I felt as if I was being swept off my feet. I wondered if that's what it would feel like to fly."

"So you were turning into a human kite?"

"Maybe. It only happened once, but I've never forgotten how thrilling it was to feel the wind's power."

The picture she painted was an intriguing one, and Josh took a deep breath, exhaling slowly as an unexpected thought assailed him. "Seeing this makes me wish I lived here."

"You do now, so enjoy it."

He did. He stood silently for a moment, drinking in the beauty of the Texas countryside. The blue of the flowers that seemed to mirror the faultless sky was almost the same shade as Louisa's dress and contrasted vividly with the green mesquite bushes on the perimeter of the field. The occasional call of a hawk soaring above broke the companionable silence he and Louisa shared, while the faint scent of the flowers mingled with the light perfume that tantalized his senses whenever she moved.

It was odd how everything made him think of Louisa, or perhaps it wasn't so odd. She'd probably saved his life, and now she was helping him create a future. It was only natural he'd think about her.

Chapter Fifteen

Josh was still thinking about Louisa the next morning when they parked the buggy in front of what would become Porter's. Though he had insisted he could walk, she'd been adamant that he save his energy.

"You'll be on your feet more than you realize," she'd said.

While she unlocked both of the houses, Josh checked his watch, nodding in approval when he saw Raymond approaching right on time. The man looked at the two Sunday Houses for a second before his attention turned to Louisa.

"I didn't expect to see you this morning." He moved to her side, his smile broadening.

Josh shouldn't have been surprised. Raymond's interest in Louisa was no secret. If it affected Porter's, it would be in a positive way, which meant there was no reason Josh should be rethinking his approval, wondering whether Raymond was the right man for the job. Surely it wasn't jealousy.

When Raymond gave Louisa what appeared to be a proprietary look, Josh said, "She's my unofficial partner."

Louisa's flush, which looked like pleasure, sent Josh's thoughts in a new direction. Perhaps he should make her an official partner. Even though he knew she longed to spend her days healing people, if that didn't happen, she could manage Porter's once he returned to New York. She'd do it as well as—possibly better than—Richard. Perhaps even if she did succeed as a doctor, Louisa would have time to oversee his business. It was something worth considering.

Raymond raised an eyebrow, clearly questioning Josh's statement, but asked only, "What do you want done here?"

"Come inside. We'll show you." The plural pronoun was a deliberate choice, further evidence that he valued Louisa's opinions.

As the three of them walked through what would become the tearoom, with Josh explaining his plans, Louisa interjecting an occasional comment, and Raymond making notes, the man's expression was professional, easing Josh's initial concerns.

"It's a big job." Raymond frowned as he studied the notes he'd made.

"But you can do it, can't you?" Louisa's words were infused with confidence.

"Of course, but it's not as easy as constructing a new building."

Recognizing that this could be part of a ploy to charge him more, Josh refused to let the comment stand. "I'm surprised you said that. The builders I've worked with told me everything's easier once the shell of a building is complete, because then they can work regardless of the weather."

Raymond's expression revealed his surprise that Josh knew anything about construction. "That's true. Still, it will take a couple months to complete everything."

Again, Josh questioned the man's motives. Perhaps because he was Bentley's nephew, he wanted Porter's to fail or at a minimum be delayed. "I want to have the grand opening on May 1."

Raymond studied his notes. "That will be difficult."

"But you can do it, can't you?" Louisa repeated her question. "This is important."

The man who would transform two ordinary Sunday Houses into Porter's smiled at her. "Of course." He scribbled a few more numbers on the sheet of paper he'd been using, then handed it to Josh. "This is what it'll cost."

Josh studied the estimate. While it was less than he would have paid in New York, he suspected it was inflated. "What's the last item?"

"That's the cost of working extra hours to finish by May 1. I'll have to pay my men more if they work after supper and late on Saturday."

Though that was plausible, the look on Raymond's face made Josh suspect he was being fleeced. It wouldn't be the first time someone tried to take advantage of him, assuming that as a Porter he had unlimited funds at his disposal. What bothered him was that this was a man who wanted to court Louisa. She deserved someone whose integrity was unquestioned.

"I see. So, if you don't complete the renovations in time for me to open then, which means the work needs to be finished no later than the preceding Thursday, you will forfeit that amount."

Josh almost laughed at the man's discomfort. Raymond swallowed and looked at the ground, then mumbled, "Well . . . um . . . all right."

Extending his hand, Josh smiled. "We've got a deal."

Louisa waited until the other man had left before she spoke. "He'll do a good job. He can't afford to do anything less."

"Not when he knows the whole town will be watching."

"And we'll be checking on his progress every day."

"Yes, we will." The plural pronoun had never sounded so good.

"You have a visitor, Louisa." Emily poked her head into the parlor where Louisa and Josh were sitting after supper that evening. "Shall I show him in?"

"Who is it?"

"Raymond."

"No. I'll meet him on the porch." She rose and started toward the door, reaching for her shawl.

"Good evening, Louisa," Raymond said as soon as she closed the door behind her. The light of the almost-full moon illuminated his face, revealing a smile that seemed more genuine than the ones he'd given her when they'd walked through the Sunday Houses. He'd seemed tense then. "I was hoping you'd go walking with me."

"That would be pleasant." Though the evening was cool, her shawl would make a short walk enjoyable. When she'd been in Cimarron Creek, Louisa and Phoebe had walked each evening, but since she'd returned, she had stayed home, preferring to spend the time with Josh rather than remind him of something he could not do.

"Did you like living in Cimarron Creek?" Raymond asked as they strolled west on Creek.

"Very much. There was a time when I was convinced I'd never come back here. I was learning so much there."

In retrospect, Louisa realized she'd needed to leave Sweetwater Crossing to heal. The grief over her parents' deaths and her anger at Emily had been open wounds that only the salve of being with people who did not know her past could heal. The training she'd received had helped the process, but it was the novelty of Cimarron Creek itself that had been most valuable.

Raymond nodded as if he understood. "You learned to be a midwife."

"And a doctor, although I still need more training for that." Louisa felt Raymond's arm stiffen beneath her hand and suspected he did not approve of lady doctors. Rather than spoil a pleasant evening, she changed the subject. "How does Sweetwater Crossing compare to Mesquite Springs? That's where you used to live, isn't it?"

"You have a good memory. I was born and raised in Mesquite Springs and probably wouldn't have left if Uncle Adam hadn't asked me to come here. The job he offered at the mercantile sounded appealing, since it came with the promise that one day the store would be mine."

As the light breeze turned into a cold gust, Louisa wrapped her shawl more tightly around her shoulders. "But you're not working there."

Raymond let out a chuckle. "It didn't take long for me to realize that I wasn't cut out for working in a shop. I found everything about it dull and couldn't imagine spending the rest of my life stocking shelves and talking to customers. I like building things."

He paused for a second. "My uncle's not happy that I'm working on those Sunday Houses, but when we walked through them today, I saw they'd be a good opportunity. Folks have seen me turn an empty lot into the parsonage. Now they'll have a chance to see that I can renovate a building. If I do a good job—and I assure you I plan to—it'll lead to more work. Within a year, I should be able to afford what I want."

Raymond's voice had deepened, telling Louisa how important this dream was to him.

"And what is it you want?"

"A home for me and my wife."

Chapter Sixteen

The rain stopped shortly before dawn, and the sun had already begun to dry the streets, turning what had been a dismal night into a beautiful Wednesday morning that filled Louisa's heart with hope and tempted her to skip on her walk to the office. She couldn't do that, of course, not if she wanted people to take her seriously. And she did. She had to appear to be a sensible young woman, not a carefree little girl. But, despite her admonitions to herself, she was still humming as she unlocked the front door and set the "doctor is in" sign in the window.

Today would be different. Today she'd have some patients, she told herself as she opened the shutters. Since the office faced north, there was no direct sun, but the daylight was enough to confirm what she already knew. The cabinets were filled with the bottles and jars of medicines Doc Sheridan had ordered. The only change Louisa had made was the order in which they were arranged, since she preferred the alphabetical system Austin used, while Doc had grouped them by symptoms they treated.

The black bag he'd carried on house calls contained everything she would need if she were summoned to a patient's home. She'd started taking it home each day but kept it close at hand on top of a small bookcase while she was here. The floor had been swept, the desk and examining table dusted. Louisa and the office were ready for the day. All that was lacking were patients.

Settling behind the desk, she began leafing through the two journals where Doc had kept records of whom he treated and what medicines he'd dispensed, trying not to sigh when she realized how many of Sweetwater Crossing's residents had consulted him on a regular basis. Unless they began to trust her, they would be without medical care, and that could be dangerous. Her earlier optimism faded, leaving her disheartened. But then the bell over the front door tinkled.

Louisa rose to greet her neighbor. "Good morning, Mrs. Albright. How can I help you?" She gave the woman, whom she knew to be just shy of sixty, an appraising look. Mrs. Albright's blue eyes appeared clear, her gray hair was glossy, and her skin normal for her age. As immaculately dressed as ever, she walked without a limp. Nothing was visibly wrong.

The woman shook her head as she took the chair Louisa had indicated. "It's not me," she said when Louisa had returned to her position behind the desk. "It's Gertrude. When I visited her yesterday, she looked peaked. She insisted nothing was wrong, but I'm worried about her." The lines that formed between Mrs. Albright's eyes confirmed her concerns. "This is my first grandchild, you know. Will you call on her?"

Louisa nodded, trying to contain the excitement that bubbled through her. She'd been right. Today she would see her first patient.

Mrs. Albright opened her reticule and withdrew a small purse. "I'll pay whatever you ask. You don't have children of your own yet, but when you do, you'll understand why I'm worried. Wilbur and I want our daughter to have the best care possible." She looked around the room, perhaps trying to determine whether anything had changed. "I heard you studied with a midwife in Cimarron Creek and that you delivered several babies."

"Yes, I did. And, of course, I'd be happy to check on Gertrude." It still seemed odd to call her former teacher by her given name, but Gertrude had insisted on the informality.

"And you'll tell me what you find." Gertrude's mother made it a statement rather than a question. "My daughter can be secretive at times. She probably thinks she's protecting me, but she's wrong. I know she's a grown woman, but a mother's worry never ends."

"I understand that you worry." Mama had said the same thing when they'd received that horrible letter from Emily only two months after her wedding, declaring she wanted no further contact with the family. "Something's wrong," Mama had said, and it appeared she'd been right, for though Emily said nothing, even now, almost two years later, the few times she spoke of her husband, her eyes radiated pain.

"I'll go to the ranch right away," Louisa told Mrs. Albright, "and when I return, I'll stop by your house." She wouldn't tell Mrs. Albright anything Gertrude didn't want her to know, but she could at least reassure the anxious grandmother-to-be that her daughter was receiving good care.

Her spirits higher than they'd been in days, Louisa saddled Horace, knowing her father's horse preferred being ridden to pulling a buggy, and headed west.

Befitting the home of Sweetwater Crossing's wealthiest family, the Albright ranch was large and obviously prosperous, its entrance driveway well-graded and free from potholes, the grounds surrounding the house and outbuildings freshly mowed, the house itself sporting newly painted trim.

When she reached the sprawling building that formed the main house, Louisa grabbed her black medical bag and knocked on the front door.

Seconds later, Gertrude opened it. "Oh, Louisa." She frowned as she looked down at her slightly faded light blue dress, clearly chagrined to be caught in less-than-perfect attire. As had been true the last time Louisa had seen her, Gertrude wore no spectacles.

"It's nice to see you, but I wish I'd known you were coming." Gertrude extended her hand. "Come in and stay for a while. Would you like some tea or coffee?"

"Later perhaps. I'm here as your midwife."

Gertrude ushered her into the parlor, a room filled with furniture that clearly favored style over comfort. Louisa could not imagine curling up in one of the straight-backed chairs and spending hours reading a book.

Her former teacher pointed toward one of the least uncomfortable-looking chairs. "My mother sent you, didn't she?"

There was no reason to dissemble. "She's concerned."

"I imagine she told you I'm too old to be a first-time mother."

Since Mrs. Albright had been considerably younger than Gertrude when she'd borne her child, the concern was probably based on her own experience. "She didn't mention that," Louisa assured her patient. "She only said she wanted to be sure you were well cared for. How have you been feeling?"

Gertrude wrinkled her nose, deepening the lines at the corners of her eyes. "Other than being sick every morning, I've been fine. By noon I'm filled with energy."

"That's normal. Let's go to your room so I can make sure everything else is normal."

When she'd completed the examination, Louisa smiled. "It's as I thought. You're a healthy mother-to-be, and your baby is progressing well."

Gertrude's relief was palpable, making Louisa suspect she'd been as worried as her mother, even if she'd been reluctant to voice those worries. "Will you stay for lunch? I'd welcome the company."

"I'm afraid I need to return to the office." Even though she doubted she'd have other patients. "If I stay away too long, your mother will be convinced something's seriously wrong."

A chuckle greeted Louisa's words. "You're probably right, but before you go, let me show you my favorite part of the ranch."

As they stepped down from the front porch, Louisa said, "I noticed you're not wearing spectacles. Are they broken?"

Gertrude laughed. "I don't need them anymore. And, no, my vision hasn't miraculously improved. It's always been good, but I thought I'd look more like a schoolmarm in glasses, so I ordered a pair with clear lenses. Not even my parents knew they weren't necessary."

Was this one of the secrets Mrs. Albright thought her daughter was hiding?

Walking slowly and deliberately, Gertrude led the way over a small rise to a part of the ranch that wasn't visible from the house. There, close to a spreading live oak but far enough away that the branches did not shade it, was a flowerbed. It was small—perhaps three feet wide and seven feet long—but every inch was covered by plants. "This is it, my favorite spot. In another month, they'll be flowering. You need to see it then."

"It's beautiful even now." The seedlings were in various shades of green, telling Louisa that Gertrude had planted a variety of flowers. It wasn't difficult to see why she liked it, but one thing puzzled Louisa. "Why is it so far from the house? I would have thought you'd want to see it from there." The single flowerbed Mama had planted had been located where it could be seen from all the rooms on the rear of the house.

Gertrude bent down and touched one of the seedlings. "It started as a secret. My mother believes gardens are meant for growing vegetables and that flowers are frivolous. I didn't agree, so I decided to have my own flowerbed." Gertrude straightened up and smiled at Louisa. "I didn't tell her about it until everything was in bloom. Even she had to admit it was pretty, and Thomas says it's the best part of the ranch."

Another secret. No wonder Mrs. Albright thought her daughter might be harboring them. "Thank you for showing it to me."

"I knew you'd like it." Turning her attention back to the bed, Gertrude said, "What do you think about Clive for a name if the baby's a boy?"

"Not Thomas?"

Gertrude shook her head. "He agrees it would be confusing to have two Thomases in the house."

"The only Clive I've heard of was Clive Finley." The man who'd built Finley House for his sweetheart, the man who'd never returned from the war.

Hooking her arm with Louisa's, Gertrude headed back to the house. "Clive Finley was one of my father's best friends. Even though it's been years since he left Sweetwater Crossing, my father still talks about him. I thought having his grandson named Clive might please him. What do you think?"

"Clive Neville is a fine name."

"Thank you, Louisa. I knew you'd agree." Gertrude gave her a quick hug. "I'm so glad you're back home."

"You're making good progress." Josh smiled as he walked through the first of the Sunday Houses. Raymond's team had already moved the walls in the future tearoom, giving Josh a good idea of what the finished room would look like. He might be biased, but in his mind, it would be the perfect size—large enough to accommodate the six tables he wanted, small enough to feel cozy.

He nodded at the man he'd hired. "I'm glad to have you doing the renovations. Louisa was right when she said you were the man for the job."

Leaving Raymond and his team, Josh made his way to the other building. Perhaps it was foolish to climb the steps when he knew nothing had changed inside, but he enjoyed visualizing what it would be like when finished. What would Grandfather think? He'd urged Josh and Jed to think boldly, but this might be too bold for him.

Josh was unlocking the door when he heard footsteps behind him. Turning, he saw a pretty brunette whose dark green dress highlighted her eyes. Though he'd seen her talking to Louisa, they'd never been introduced.

"Hello, Mr. Porter. I'm Caroline Brownley, and I'm looking for Louisa. I went to her office, but it's closed, so I thought she might be here."

"No need for formality. Please call me Josh. Louisa usually comes here at the end of her office hours." He pulled out his watch and checked the time. "That's two hours from now. She must be on a house call." It was the only reason he could imagine for Louisa closing the office, and oh, how he hoped that was the case.

Caroline tipped her head to one side, seemingly drawn by the sound of hammering in the other building. "When you see her, would you tell her Thelma has a question for her."

"Certainly." Grandfather would chuckle over the fact that one of his grandsons had been designated a messenger, but Josh decided to take advantage of the woman's arrival. "I'd like your opinion. What do you think about the idea of a tearoom and specialty shop in Sweetwater Crossing? Is it somewhere you'd go more than once?"

"That would depend on three things—how good the food is, what merchandise you sell, and who you have managing it. The right person can make the difference between success and failure."

Impressed with Caroline's insights, which told him she knew

more about business than most people, Josh nodded. "That's exactly what my grandfather would have said."

"He sounds like a wise man."

"He is." Josh gave Louisa's friend a long look. "I was about to go inside and check a few things. Would you like to see what we have planned?"

"Very much."

When Josh had finished showing Caroline around what would become the shop, she paused at the doorway to the kitchen. "Are you sure this will be big enough for a storeroom?"

It was a question few would have asked, more evidence that this was no ordinary woman. "That depends on how well things sell. I plan to keep a few of everything here. The rest will be upstairs. I haven't been there yet"—he gestured toward his crutches in explanation—"but Louisa assures me there's plenty of space there."

Caroline nodded. "There should be."

As they left the store, Josh saw Louisa approaching on horseback and felt both envy and worry. Envy that she was able to ride while he was still weeks from being able to mount a horse, worry about what had happened to Zeus. For what felt like the millionth time since he'd found himself lying abandoned on the edge of the road, he wondered what had happened to his horse.

"It looks like you can deliver your message yourself," he told Caroline as Louisa reined in Horace.

To give the two women privacy, Josh took a few steps away from them, and as he did, he heard one of the workers say, "Look at him, will you? He's trying to spark every pretty gal in town."

But he wasn't. He wasn't sparking any of the gals.

Louisa studied the piecrust her sister had just finished. "I'll never be able to flute a piecrust like you." It was midafternoon on Friday, and the two women's work preparing food for Alice and David's wedding the next day was far from finished.

"Maybe so," Emily said, "but I wouldn't even try to set a man's leg or deliver a baby. You're amazing, Louisa."

What was amazing was that they were having this conversation. In all the years they'd been growing up, though they'd shared many things, they'd never complimented each other like this.

"You're the amazing one, Emily. Turning our home into a boardinghouse was one of the best decisions you've made."

At the time that Emily had proposed it, Louisa had been vehemently opposed, thinking it little short of sacrilege. Now she knew the move was exactly what this house—and her sister—needed.

"I think so too." The sweetness of Emily's smile told Louisa her thoughts had turned to the man she would soon marry even before she said, "It brought Craig into my life."

"It's obvious he makes you happy, and that makes me happy too. You deserve to be happy."

Emily shook her head. "Not just me. We all deserve happiness. I hope Joanna has found it in Europe. I worry, though, that I haven't heard from her. I know you said she used to write at least once a month, but since I've been back, there was only the one letter that I forwarded to you."

"I wrote to her and gave her my address in Cimarron Creek, but I didn't receive a response."

"The silence bothers me."

Though Emily didn't say it, Louisa suspected she was remembering how Louisa had not answered any of the weekly letters she'd sent. Other than one letter, a rather gloating one saying she was happy in Cimarron Creek, Louisa had ignored her oldest sister.

Emily shrugged. "I want to believe everything's fine and that either Joanna's letters were lost or she's been too busy to write. She never was one for writing. All she cared about was her music."

And all Louisa had cared about while she was in Cimarron Creek was furthering her education as a healer.

"That's true." Louisa couldn't dispute anything Emily had said. "Not everyone writes as many letters as Josh does." Louisa had taken several of his letters to the post office and knew that he'd written to both Winifred and his grandfather, although he'd yet to receive any mail.

Though Louisa couldn't imagine what had caused it, Emily appeared uncomfortable with the conversation.

"Is something wrong?" she asked.

Her sister looked back at the piecrust for a second before she said, "I probably shouldn't say anything. Josh seems like a very nice man, and Craig assures me we can trust him, but I worry that you're having your head turned by someone who's little more than a stranger."

"Oh, Emily, I'm not having my head turned. Josh is practically engaged to a woman named Winifred. All I'm doing is helping him with Porter's." There was no need to tell her sister that while it was true that she'd met him only a few weeks ago, Louisa felt closer to Josh than she did to most people she'd known for her entire life.

Emily did not appear convinced. "Practically engaged is not the same thing as engaged. I've seen the way you two look at each other, and it's more than casual friendship. Be careful, Louisa. That's all I ask. Think long and hard before you give your heart away."

"I haven't given my heart away." Yes, she enjoyed Josh's company. Yes, she took satisfaction from being able to help him. Yes, she'd even dreamt of him, but that wasn't giving her heart away.

Emily's frown said she didn't believe Louisa's denial. "Raymond would be a better choice, but you need to be careful even with him. Make sure you know who he really is."

Louisa poured the pecan filling into Emily's perfectly fluted crust. "I'm not ready to marry Raymond or anyone."

"That's wise. Marriage is a big step. When George came to town, I was so flattered by his attention that I didn't look beneath the surface. That was a mistake."

Louisa stared at her sister, shocked by what she'd said and even more shocked by what it implied. Despite the letter that had disturbed the family so much, the one Emily had said George had written and sent without her knowledge, Louisa had believed her sister's marriage had been happy.

"What do you mean?"

Emily shook her head. "I'm not ready to talk about it yet. Just be careful. There's a difference between infatuation and love."

Louisa couldn't define what she felt for Josh, but she knew it wasn't infatuation, nor was it love. But, try though she might, she couldn't explain why thoughts of him were her constant companions.

Chapter Seventeen

"What a beautiful wedding." Caroline's smile was almost as bright as Alice's had been when she'd walked down the aisle toward her husband-to-be. "Alice looked even happier than she did the first time."

Louisa nodded in agreement as she gazed at the bride and groom standing at the other side of the yard. The town had converted what had once been Mrs. Adams's Sunday House into an annex for the parsonage, making the combined backyards the perfect place to host the reception for its minister and his bride. The grass had regrown, leaving no reminder of the fire that had destroyed the original parsonage last summer, and the oak trees on the perimeter provided shade for those who found the late-March sun too strong.

Now that every bit of the food she and Emily had prepared yesterday had been consumed, the guests stood in clusters, waiting for the dancing to begin. As Caroline had said, it had been—and continued to be—a beautiful wedding.

Almost everyone in town had come to celebrate the nuptials. The only surprise so far had been that Noah, who was normally content to stay with Mrs. Carmichael, had insisted on spending the day with Josh. "He tells better stories," Noah had announced. Apparently other children shared his opinion, because Josh had half a dozen youngsters clustered at his feet, listening intently.

"He'll make a wonderful father," Caroline said, apparently having noticed the direction of Louisa's gaze. "It's a shame he's going back to New York, because you and he would make a handsome couple, but you're lucky. You have the most eligible man in town wanting to court you."

Caroline gestured toward Raymond, who seemed engrossed in a conversation with Andrew and Byron, the men who were working on Porter's. It seemed they'd taken Raymond's threats seriously, because whenever Louisa had encountered them, they'd been unfailingly polite.

"If you weren't such a good friend," Caroline continued, "I'd be jealous of you. Raymond was smitten the first time he saw you."

Smitten seemed like an exaggeration, although Raymond had made no secret of his interest in Louisa.

"She's right." Louisa hadn't heard her approach, but there was no mistaking Tina's voice. "Raymond doesn't say much to Adam and me, but a woman can always tell when a fellow fancies someone. Caroline's right about two things: Raymond fancies you, and you're a lucky girl that he does. He's a fine young man, and if I'm not mistaken, he's heading this way to ask you to dance."

"It's nice to see Louisa getting so much attention."

Once the dancing began and the children decided that playing hide-and-seek was more fun than listening to stories, Gertrude had settled into the empty chair next to Josh and appeared to have made it her mission to tell him everything she knew about the woman who'd rescued him from the side of the road.

Though he was no fan of gossip, there was no stopping Gertrude. And, if he were being honest with himself, he wanted to learn more about Louisa. She had more facets than a diamond, and Josh wanted to explore each one.

"The whole town's surprised at how she's blossomed. That time in Cimarron Creek was good for Louisa. It really changed her."

That surprised Josh. In his experience, people didn't change—not fundamentally. They might adopt different styles of clothing; age might add wrinkles and gray hair; but inside, they were the same.

"I didn't know her before, but what I know now is that Louisa's a remarkable woman." One who seemed to dance as well as she set broken bones. One who made Josh regret that he wasn't dancing with her.

He and Winifred had shared many dances, and they'd all been pleasant. Years at a boarding school had polished Winifred's social skills, turning her into an accomplished dancing partner. Dancing with Louisa would be different. Unlike Winifred, who maintained a faint smile that was considered proper, Louisa was laughing at something Raymond said. Unlike Winifred, who never missed a step, Louisa appeared to have faltered once, precipitating another peal of laughter. Unlike Winifred, who'd never hesitate to refuse an offer to dance if she deemed the partner unsuitable, Louisa accepted every one, including one from a man old enough to be her grandfather and another from a boy whose head came only to her waist.

Oh, how Josh wished he could take her into his arms and guide her across the grass while the fiddlers played.

"She used to be like a little mouse who'd fade into the background when she was around her sisters." Gertrude's words brought Josh back to reality. "You've met Emily, so you know how beautiful she is. Joanna's almost as pretty, but in a different way. She doesn't have Emily's classic profile, but she has dark brown hair and eyes and a perfect smile. And then there was Louisa, the girl with nothing special about her."

Josh felt his hackles rise. How could the woman be so blind? She was basing her opinion on superficialities. "I beg to differ. Louisa is very special." Craig might consider Emily the most beautiful woman in Sweetwater Crossing, but Josh knew that true beauty was found below the skin. Even Grandfather had agreed with that, telling Josh and Jed not to let their heads be turned by a pretty face but to search for a woman with the strength to become a Porter and the right connections to help the business. The fact that Winifred was attractive, if not a conventional beauty, was merely a bonus.

The way Gertrude smiled at his retort made Josh wonder if she'd deliberately baited him, wanting him to reveal his feelings about Louisa. "You're right," Gertrude agreed. "Since she came back, she's been different. It's not just the fashionable clothes and hairstyle. Louisa's more confident."

Josh, who'd kept his attention on the woman they were discussing, had seen her confidence each time she accepted an offer to dance. "She's more than confident. She's strong."

"I might have said courageous. It takes courage for a woman to try to be a doctor here. A midwife's one thing, but a lady doctor . . ." Gertrude shook her head.

"No one should underestimate her. She'll succeed. I'm sure she will."

"You don't have to convince me." Gertrude seemed almost annoyed by Josh's defense of Louisa. "It's the rest of the town that needs to recognize that she can help them. I suspect they're waiting to see whether your leg heals properly."

Josh looked at his cast-covered leg. "It feels stronger every day."

"But you won't know for sure until the cast comes off." Gertrude turned her attention to the crowd, then frowned. "It looks like Adam Bentley is headed this way. Judging from his expression, whatever he has to say isn't good."

As Gertrude had predicted, the owner of the mercantile stopped in front of them. "I hate to spoil the day, but I thought you should know that there's a problem. Just got a telegram saying the shipment of dishes you ordered has been lost. What do you want to do?"

"Reorder them."

Bentley's pursed lips made Josh think he needed some of his wife's honey to sweeten his disposition. "I'm not sure they'll arrive in time. What about another pattern? I checked, and they have the one with the roses in stock. Those dishes could be here next week."

Josh shook his head. Both he and Louisa had agreed that while the roses might appeal to some, it was the wrong pattern for Porter's. "Do what you can to get the one we chose."

"It'll cost more to have them rush the order." If it weren't so implausible, Josh would have said that Bentley's voice held a note of satisfaction.

"Just do it."

The shop owner shrugged. "All right. It must be nice not to worry about money."

Josh was concerned about spending too much on an experiment, but he also knew that the china Porter's used for tea was too important to substitute a pattern neither he nor Louisa thought was right.

An hour later, when he was certain he could bear no more of Gertrude's conversation, no matter how well meaning it was, Josh's spirits rose at the sight of Louisa heading his way.

"You look happy," he told her. Louisa's face was wreathed in a smile, and her eyes sparkled as she greeted first her former schoolteacher, then him. Something was afoot, and his instincts told him it was more than having danced every dance.

"I am. I'm also ready to go home."

"I should probably leave too." Gertrude rose and, after rejoining her husband, led him toward the street.

Josh grinned at the reprieve combined with the prospect of spending time with Louisa. "And you're going to make me wait until we get there before you tell me why you're happy."

"I am." Her laughter sent a bubble of happiness through his veins.

"Then let's go."

As they made their way through the crowd, moving slowly because of Josh's crutches, Louisa said, "I saw Adam Bentley talking to you. Was it about Porter's?"

"Yes."

When Josh completed his explanation, Louisa frowned. "I hope he wasn't trying to cheat you. A year or so ago, there were rumors that he overcharged customers."

As he recalled Bentley's expression during their conversation, Josh wondered if he'd sought to increase his profits by claiming there was a need to reorder and pay for faster shipment. "I hope that's not true, but I'll ask to see the telegram about the lost shipment." If there was one thing that mattered to Josh, it was integrity.

Louisa looked solemn. "You probably should do that. I don't want to believe he's lying, but it never hurts to be certain."

"Let's talk about something happier," Josh suggested.

And they did until they reached Finley House. There they found Mrs. Carmichael and Noah in the kitchen, Noah nibbling a cookie while Mrs. Carmichael sipped a cup of tea. When they'd greeted both of them and admired the haphazard pile of blocks Noah had arranged in the corner of the kitchen, Louisa led the way to the parlor, her earlier enthusiasm once again evident in her expression.

"All right," Josh said when they'd both taken their seats. "We're here. Tell me what's making you so happy."

She giggled softly, the childlike sound so unusual for her that Josh knew whatever it was, it was important. "Three women asked me to be their midwife. Oh, Josh, I'm so happy and so excited. People are finally beginning to trust me."

Chapter Eighteen

The tinkling of the doorbell was a sound filled with promise, at least for Louisa. Each time she heard it, she stopped whatever she was doing and walked toward the door, hoping it meant a new patient. Most often, her visitor was Caroline, taking a break from sewing or coming to ask Louisa's help in selecting trim for a gown. Today, however, a young girl stood in the hallway.

"We need you, Miss Vaughn." Louisa recognized Susan Johnson, one of Craig's most advanced pupils. Though her features were ordinary and her hair almost as boring a shade of brown as Louisa's, her green eyes shone with intelligence. This afternoon, concern radiated from them.

"Is something wrong?" Other than the obvious worry, the girl appeared healthy.

"It's Beulah." Susan turned and beckoned to the girl who'd been hiding behind her. "Mr. Ferguson says she has measles and needs to go home."

Louisa reached for Beulah's hand and drew her into the examining room, hoping Craig's diagnosis was mistaken but suspecting it wasn't, since he'd mentioned that several other pupils had contracted the highly communicable disease.

Louisa hadn't observed any symptoms when Beulah had eaten breakfast this morning. Most children became drowsy and irritable before the telltale rash appeared, but Beulah was rarely irritable, even under circumstances that would have annoyed another child. Her sweet disposition was one of the reasons Emily and Craig had been so insistent that she attend school, despite being slower to learn than other pupils.

The child squinted and kept her free hand on her forehead, shading her eyes. "It hurts."

"I know it does." Louisa helped Beulah climb onto the examining table, then closed the shutters. She didn't need a lot of light to confirm that the rash was beginning to appear on Beulah's face.

"Have you had measles?" she asked Susan.

"Yes. Six years ago. That's why Mr. Ferguson sent me."

Of course. Craig would have done his best to minimize the other pupils' exposure, although at this stage, everyone in the classroom would have been close enough to Beulah to become infected.

"I'd like you to stay with Beulah while I get the buggy." It would take a few minutes to return home and harness Horace. She touched Beulah's forehead, nodding at the evidence of a fever. "You'll feel better if you lie down and close your eyes," she told her patient. "Don't worry if you fall asleep. I'll wake you when I return, and Susan will make sure you're okay."

Louisa had seen Beulah's uneasiness when she'd realized the table was higher than an ordinary bed and wanted to reassure her that she would be in no danger of falling off it. The child nodded, relaxing when Susan pulled a chair next to the table so she could hold her hand. The girls would be fine.

Once she had Beulah lying on the buggy's backseat, a towel over her face to protect her eyes, Louisa headed south toward the Douglas ranch. Even though she'd been gone only a quarter of an hour, the rash on Beulah's face had become more prominent and was spreading quickly. By the time they reached her home, it was likely to alarm her mother.

Louisa drove as quickly as she could, wanting to get her patient inside and under her mother's care. When she reached the ranch, she set the brake on the buggy, then hurried toward the front door.

"Louisa!" A worried expression crossed Miriam Douglas's face as she answered the knock. Several inches taller than Louisa, Beulah's mother had brown hair and blue eyes, both of which were several shades lighter than Louisa's. Her clothing, like that of most ranchers' wives, was sewn from a practical calico that would hide the inevitable stains from life on a ranch.

"What's wrong?" Even without seeing her daughter, Miriam was concerned simply by Louisa's presence.

"I brought Beulah home because she has the measles."

When Louisa had finished her explanation and done her best to reassure the worried mother, she led her to the buggy where Beulah lay listlessly.

"That's normal," Louisa assured Miriam. "She needs a lot of rest."

In response, Miriam wrapped her arm around her daughter's shoulders, pressed a kiss on her head, then helped her out of the buggy. "You'll be all right. Mama's here to take care of you."

Louisa waited until Beulah was in bed, her skin coated with the chamomile lotion she'd brought to assuage the itching, before she prepared to leave. There was nothing more she could do for this patient today, but she'd return tomorrow to check on her.

"I shouldn't have been surprised," Miriam said as they walked toward the front door. "When I saw Nancy McIntyre in the mercantile last week, she told me Will had the measles. We were both surprised that our children hadn't caught them when they were younger. Will's a year older than Beulah, so he should have had them years ago."

Louisa wasn't too surprised that Beulah hadn't contracted the disease, since until last year, she'd had little contact with other children outside of church each week. Even then her parents arrived late and departed early, leaving little time for her to be exposed. But since Will McIntyre attended school, there was no way to explain why he was only now infected.

Knowing that measles were often more severe in older patients and that Nancy had no one to help her, Louisa decided to stop at the McIntyre ranch on her way back to town to see if there was anything she could do.

"I'm concerned about Nancy," Father had said a month or so after Nancy's husband died from a snake bite. "She's all alone now."

The once-prosperous ranch bore signs of neglect, from the rutted road to the peeling paint on the house, evidence that Father's worries that Nancy would be unable to maintain it after her husband's death had been well founded. "She's a proud woman," he'd said, "and won't accept help. Says she's not a charity case."

Louisa understood pride but was concerned about the effect that Nancy's refusal might have had on her son. Losing his father and seeing his mother struggling had to be difficult for a boy who was old enough to know there were alternatives. It was possible that he resented his mother and had become sullen. Louisa hoped that was not the case, because the Will she remembered was a cheerful boy, eager to help.

One of Louisa's worries eased as she approached. It appeared Will had recovered from his measles, for he was grooming a black horse in the corral. The fact that he was out in the bright sunshine suggested his eyes were no longer affected.

She climbed out of the buggy and approached the gangly boy whose carrot-red hair made him stand out in a crowd. "I heard you had measles. How are you feeling?" A quick inspection revealed that the rash had faded, leaving only a few inflamed spots, but the way he squinted revived Louisa's earlier concerns.

"Okay." When his voice cracked, Will's face flushed with embarrassment, and he turned back to the horse, running the currycomb through its mane. "Ma says I'm almost ready to go back to school."

"You need to wait until you have no more spots. More importantly, you shouldn't be out here in the sun." The possible damage to his eyes made it dangerous.

The boy shook his head, sending a shock of hair over his forehead. "I have to take care of Blackie. Ma's not good with horses."

And a boy his age would prefer being with a horse rather than cooped up in the house. That was natural. What concerned her was the horse itself. This was an unusually fine specimen with a distinctive shiny black coat, three white socks, and a star.

Louisa's mind began to whirl with disturbing possibilities, and she searched her memory for Josh's description of Zeus. Three socks, a star, a midnight black coat. Exactly like the horse Will called Blackie. Though it might be a coincidence, she doubted it. Horses this distinctive were rare, and the odds of the McIntyres being able to afford one were practically nonexistent. Still, she had to explore every possibility before accusing the boy of theft.

Before she could ask Will about the horse, Nancy emerged from the house, wiping her hands on her apron as she approached the corral. "Louisa, I didn't expect you." Though her hair had darkened to an attractive auburn, her green eyes and her slender frame left no doubt that she was Will's mother, while her threadbare apron and twice-turned skirt hem along with Will's pants being two sizes too small, revealing skinny ankles, confirmed the financial difficulties Louisa had feared.

"Beulah Douglas has measles. When I took her home, her mother said Will was also infected, so I thought I'd stop by and see how he was recovering."

A hint of something—perhaps embarrassment—flitted across Nancy's face, making Louisa wonder why she was so uncomfortable with her. Perhaps she thought Louisa was making a house call and would expect to be paid.

"I'm here as a friend," she said to allay that concern. The way Nancy relaxed told Louisa she'd not been mistaken.

"That's mighty kind of you, but as you can see, Will's doing fine."

The boy had returned to his grooming, checking each of Blackie's hooves for stones.

Louisa turned her attention back to the horse.

"Did Will have a birthday recently?"

Nancy shook her head, clearly confused by the question. "No. Why?"

"I thought Blackie might have been a gift. He seems like a very fine gelding."

Nancy shook her head again and darted a glance at her son. "Will found him abandoned on the road a few weeks ago."

If this was Zeus—and Louisa was certain it was—it had been three weeks. And the horse had not been abandoned. He may have wandered a few yards from Josh while he grazed, but he would not have abandoned his rider.

"Will was out riding that day," Nancy continued. "He said there was no sign of his owner, so I figured we might as well keep him. A boy needs a horse of his own."

The woman hadn't been thinking clearly. That much was obvious. Everyone knew how important horses were. That's why the penalty for stealing one was so severe. Nancy should have realized this was no ordinary horse. And even if he'd been old and swaybacked like the McIntyres' sole mount, she should have told the sheriff about him. If she had, Josh would have been spared weeks of worry. He would have had both his horse and the recipes he'd spent so much time collecting.

Louisa took a deep breath, trying to control her anger. Nothing would be gained by berating Nancy. Instead, Louisa turned toward Will. "Were there no saddlebags?"

He stared at his boots, scuffing a line in the dirt. "Um . . . no." Both his posture and the way he'd almost whispered the denial told Louisa he was lying, just as he'd been lying about the horse being abandoned.

"Really? I heard Zeus had fancy tooled saddlebags. Right, Zeus?" As she'd expected, the horse neighed in response to his name.

"Zeus?" Nancy looked from Louisa to the horse to her son, furrows forming between her eyebrows.

"That's the name of Josh Porter's horse. You know. The man whose leg I set. The man who's going to open a tearoom and shop in town." Louisa made no effort to soften her words. "As far as we can tell, Zeus caught his leg in a prairie dog hole and threw Josh. By the time I found him, the horse was gone. Josh couldn't understand that, because he said Zeus would never have left him. He figured he must have been stolen."

Nancy strode to her son's side, placed her hands on his shoulders, and forced him to face her. "Where did you find this horse?"

"On the road, just the way I told you."

"Was Mr. Porter there?" Nancy's voice was stern.

Will shrank under the force of his mother's displeasure. "No. Blackie was all alone. When I found him, he was grazing way off the road."

This time there was no evidence that Will was lying, and Louisa's anger began to fade. It was possible Zeus had moved far enough that Will hadn't seen Josh and that the boy was so excited by the idea of a horse of his own that he hadn't searched for Zeus's owner. That scenario was far preferable to the one where Will had abandoned a seriously injured man, caring for nothing but having a horse.

Louisa kept her gaze fixed on Will. "What about the saddlebags?" They wouldn't have fallen off.

"Um . . ."

"Tell the truth, Will." Nancy tightened her grip on her son's shoulders. "Did the horse have saddlebags?"

"Um . . . yes, but there was nothin' important in them. Just clothes and some papers."

Papers that might hold the key to Josh's future.

"Why didn't you tell me that?" Anger and frustration colored Nancy's words.

Will's face flushed with anger of his own. "Because I wanted him to be my horse. I knew you couldn't give me one. You can't give me anything I want."

The accusation was filled with the frustration Louisa had feared might have resulted from Nancy's refusal to accept help. Her grief and pride had kept her from seeing how her choices had affected her son. Now she was faced with the realization that her son considered her a failure.

Her shoulders slumped. "We'll talk about this later. You go into the house and stay there until Miss Vaughn and I are done. If you think you're going to run away, think again."

Though she was reluctant to interfere, Louisa had one more thing to resolve. "First Will needs to show me the saddlebags." Though she had no doubt this was Zeus, the saddlebags were almost as valuable to Josh as the horse itself.

Less than a minute later, Will emerged from the barn carrying the saddlebags. The bits of hay that clung to them revealed their hiding place.

It took only the briefest of glances to confirm that these were indeed Josh's. "See these initials?" Louisa asked as she pointed to the center of the intricately carved flap. "JEP. That means they belong to Mr. Porter."

She opened one of the bags and pulled out a stack of papers. While they might have no value to Will, these were the recipes Josh had feared were lost forever. Louisa almost smiled at the thought of how relieved he would be when he saw them, but the situation was too serious for smiles.

"What are you gonna do to my boy?" Nancy asked when Will was out of earshot. "Are you gonna tell the sheriff?"

Louisa saw the fear in Nancy's eyes and knew she was remembering that horse thieves were hanged. Will might be only thirteen, but that was old enough to face the consequences of his crime. Though Louisa might argue for leniency, she was not the one who'd been wronged.

"That will depend on Josh."

"I know what my boy did was wrong, but Sheriff Granger can be harsh." Nancy swallowed deeply and blinked to keep the tears that had formed in her eyes from falling. "Will's been different since his pa died. I do my best, but I know he's suffering. Underneath it all, Will's a good boy."

The last of Louisa's anger melted in the face of Nancy's distress. "I've never heard anything bad about Will, but he needs to pay for what he did. He can't go scot-free."

Nancy bit her lips. "I wasn't suggesting that. All I'm asking for is some mercy."

Though Louisa's heart ached for the mother who was suffering as much as her son, she could make no promises. "I'll see what Josh says."

Chapter Nineteen

Josh looked up in surprise when he heard Louisa enter the tea shop. Though she hadn't said a word, the delicate perfume she always wore announced her arrival.

"This is a pleasant surprise." He pulled out his watch, confirming what he'd thought. "Isn't your office supposed to be open for another hour?"

"I closed early today."

Louisa's smile warmed him more than time in the sunshine, but it was the barely concealed excitement as well as a bit of apprehension in her expression that intrigued him the most.

Louisa fiddled with the strings of her reticule, an anomaly on what was turning into a day filled with puzzles.

"I hope you can leave, because I have something to show you at home."

"Of course. Just give me a minute." After telling Raymond he'd be back in the morning, Josh joined Louisa at the base of the steps. "I suspect this will be like the Easter picnic and your good news after the wedding, and you won't give me a hint."

"You're right. That would spoil the surprise. The only thing

I'll say is that I think you'll like it even more than the bluebonnets." As they headed toward Finley House, she flashed him another smile, making Josh wonder if he'd imagined the apprehension. "How is the work coming?"

"Raymond keeps complaining that he needs more help but can't find anyone. If it were summer, he said he might hire some of the older schoolboys to do basic things, but no one's available now." As the sun slid behind a cloud, Louisa shivered. "Cold?"

"Not really. I should have brought a shawl, but I was too excited to think about that. And, no, I won't tell you anything more. Is there any solution to Raymond's problem?"

Josh wrinkled his nose, thinking about the man who was turning his dream into reality. "I'm not convinced it's as much of a problem as he claims. I think he likes to complain."

"I've never heard him complain. Maybe he's worried about having everything finished on time. I know he's counting on that final payment." Louisa paused for a second before asking, "Did you learn anything more about the lost dishes?"

That, at least, was good news. "When I talked to Adam Bentley this morning, he showed me the telegram. The shipment really is missing."

There was no mistaking Louisa's relief. "So he wasn't lying. I'm glad. I know no town is perfect, but I hated the idea that someone who's always been a pillar of the community was cheating people."

They walked in silence for a few minutes. When they reached Finley House, instead of going to the west side entrance they normally used, Louisa led the way to the other side of the house, her smile widening as she gestured toward the small corral next to the barn. "There's your surprise."

Josh stared, not believing his eyes. The corral, which usually held two horses, now had three. Emily's mare and Horace were nose-to-nose with a magnificent black horse. Josh's breath caught at the sight of the gelding that had carried him for so many miles, listening to his rambling conversations, never complaining when they rode through rain or fog. Whoever claimed that miracles had ended when Jesus returned to heaven was wrong.

"Zeus." At the sound of his name, the black gelding raced to the fence and neighed. "Oh, Zeus!" The relief flooding through him made Josh's legs weaken, and he gripped the crutches to avoid falling. Though he wanted nothing more than to run his hands over Zeus's neck, assuring himself he was not dreaming, Josh could not forget the woman who'd brought his horse home.

"You're right. This is much better than the bluebonnets. Where did you find him?"

The hint of apprehension he'd seen before once again colored Louisa's expression. "It's a long story, but there's more good news. Your saddlebags were with him. I put them in your room."

"Zeus and the saddlebags?" Josh had given up hope of finding either, and now he had both. If it weren't for his casted leg, he would have whirled Louisa around in excitement. "I don't know how you did it, Louisa, but you're a miracle worker. Tell me everything."

She shook her head. "Later. Right now I think you and your horse deserve a reunion." Pulling a carrot from her pocket, she added, "He might enjoy this. I'll be inside whenever you're ready."

Josh hobbled to the corral as quickly as his crutches would allow, then stroked Zeus's head while the horse neighed his approval. "Where were you, my friend?" He made a quick appraisal, looking for signs of mistreatment, breathing a sigh of relief when he saw none. Whoever found Zeus had taken good care of him.

"I'll be back," Josh promised before heading to the house.

"Tell me everything," he said once he and Louisa were seated in the parlor.

"It started with Beulah's measles."

He listened, filled with a sense of wonder that something as simple as a child's illness had led to the discovery of his horse.

"What do you want to do about Will?" Louisa asked when she'd finished her explanation. "His mother begged for mercy, but I told her the decision was yours." The faint quiver in Louisa's voice confirmed this was the cause of the apprehension Josh had seen.

He was silent for a moment, trying to formulate a response. The anger he'd felt when he'd heard of the boy's deception had faded when he learned about Will's father's death. The boy wasn't much older than Josh had been when his father had died, but Josh had had advantages Will did not. Josh had Jed, who'd suffered a similar loss, by his side. And though Grandfather had been a strict taskmaster, he'd ensured that neither Josh nor Jed lacked anything material.

"What Will did was wrong," Louisa continued. "He knows it and so does his mother. I told her there would be consequences and that you were the one who'd decide what they were."

His hand resting on the intricately tooled saddlebags that held months of work, Josh nodded. "Part of me wants to throw the boy in jail for a week or so, but the other part remembers how I felt when my parents died. I was lost and believed my life had ended. Nothing made me happy."

It had been the worst time of his life. Despite his grandfather's efforts to buoy his spirits, Josh hadn't wanted to do anything other than remain in his room, staring out the window, waiting for his parents to return, even though he knew that would never happen. For the first few weeks, even Jed's company had been no solace.

Louisa nodded her understanding. "Zeus made Will happy.

When I saw them together, I could tell that he loved the horse, and you can see how well he cared for him."

"That's true. One of my biggest worries was that Zeus was being mistreated. I'm glad he wasn't." Josh opened one of the saddlebags and pulled out a recipe, remembering how the woman who'd given it to him claimed it was the only legacy she'd received from her mother.

"You said the family has very little money."

Louisa nodded. "Nancy's barely holding on to the ranch."

"What if the consequence—we won't call it punishment—of Will's theft is that he has to work. He'll pay me three-quarters of what he earns. The other quarter will go to his mother." Josh wouldn't tell Louisa that when he left Sweetwater Crossing, he'd give Mrs. McIntyre the rest of the money. He had no need for it, and if it made life a bit easier for someone who was struggling, he'd be content.

"That's incredibly generous of you, but where's Will going to work?"

"At Porter's. Whether he likes it or not, Raymond will have a new helper."

Louisa nodded, then gestured toward the paper in Josh's hand. "And you have your recipes for the American Room."

"There are fewer than I'd originally planned, but with Mrs. Tabor's sausage and egg casserole, I have enough to take to Grandfather."

His heart overflowing with gratitude, Josh looked at the woman who'd done so much for him. "Thank you, Louisa. This was the best surprise ever."

Chapter Twenty

"What style of house do you prefer?" Raymond asked as he and Louisa strolled west on Creek.

Though their walks were brief, Louisa found herself looking forward to them, because they provided the opportunity to forget what had—or hadn't—happened at her office. While Josh never failed to inquire about her patients, Raymond did not. Instead, he asked about her childhood, admitting that he envied her having siblings. He asked about her time in Cimarron Creek, contrasting that with his experiences in Mesquite Springs. He asked about her favorite foods and flowers. And tonight he was asking about houses.

"Should it have more than one story? What about dormers? Aunt Tina said you favor them."

"My mother must have told her that." Louisa wondered what else Mama had shared with the woman who'd been such a faithful visitor. "My sisters and I used to wish those were our rooms, mostly because they were farther away from our parents. That was the real appeal."

"There was no getting away from my parents," Raymond

told her, "and until Aunt Tina married, I slept on a cot in the pantry. I wouldn't want my children to have to do that."

Louisa nodded, thinking about how different their lives had been. "If there's one thing we have at Finley House, it's plenty of space. When I have to clean the rooms, it seems too big."

"So you won't be like Clive Finley's sweetheart and expect a huge house."

"The story is that it was her father who insisted on that. But no, I don't need a mansion. If Emily and Craig decide they want Finley House to themselves, I can move into the apartment over my office." That might scandalize some people, but it was a possibility.

"Or you could have your own house—you and your husband."

The idea was attractive.

"What's wrong?" Louisa appeared to be studying him. "I thought you'd be happy since you have Zeus and your recipes back."

Josh tried not to sigh. Though he'd done his best to participate in the discussion over breakfast and had thought he'd smiled at all the right times, somehow she had sensed that he was preoccupied. There was no point in pretending otherwise, not when this all-too-perceptive woman was watching him.

"I'm both happy and relieved, especially about Zeus. It may seem strange to you, but he's more than a horse to me. He's a friend." And that friend had been as happy to see him as Josh had been to have him safely in the Vaughns' barn.

Louisa took a sip of coffee, then placed her cup back on the saucer before she spoke. "That doesn't seem strange at all. My father used to say the same thing about Horace. When he was stymied over something—his next sermon, a parishioner's problem, something one of us had done—he said talking to Horace helped."

She let out a little chuckle. "When we were young, my sisters and I used to think Horace answered. Later Father explained that the simple act of speaking his concerns aloud helped him find the answers that had eluded him." It was an ordinary story, but the warmth in her voice told Josh how much she'd loved her father.

"That's exactly what I do when I'm on Zeus." Wrinkling his nose in annoyance, Josh tapped a finger on his cast. "I wish I could ride him. That's one of the things that concerns me. Even though he now has your family's horses for company, Zeus isn't happy unless he's ridden regularly."

"Just like Horace. On the other hand, Blanche seems content to stay here."

Josh wondered whether that was because Emily's horse was a mare. If Grandfather and Father were correct, females were happiest when they were settled in a home. They didn't have the same craving for adventure and new places that males did. Whether or not it was true, that did not resolve his concerns.

"Do you suppose Craig would ride Zeus until my cast is off? I know Will would jump at the chance, but I can't let him do it. That would be like rewarding him for stealing Zeus."

The boy had seemed chastened when Louisa had brought him, his mother, and Raymond to Finley House to outline their decision, and while Raymond had rolled his eyes at the idea of a young helper, he'd agreed that Will could work after school each day and all day on Saturday. He'd even agreed—admittedly, grudgingly—to pay Will the same amount he did his adult workers. The way Will's shoulders had straightened when he'd heard that made Josh grateful he'd insisted.

"Craig and Emily take Horace and Blanche for rides at least once a week," Louisa said. "He might be willing to ride Zeus instead of Horace."

"I was hoping for more than weekly."

She nodded as if she understood. "Would you trust me with Zeus? I could take him for a short ride almost every day."

It was an appealing offer but not one that alleviated all of Josh's concerns. "I'm not sure how he'd handle a sidesaddle."

"Don't be shocked." The smile that accompanied Louisa's admonition indicated that she expected that reaction. "This is Sweetwater Crossing, not the bridle paths of Central Park. I know how to ride astride."

His mother and Winifred would have been shocked. Josh was only amazed and almost amused. "Is there anything you can't do?"

Though he'd meant the question to be rhetorical, Louisa's smile dimmed. "Many things, starting with convincing people that I can help them."

"Give them time." As much as he wished he could speed the process, Josh knew some things could not be rushed.

Setting her cup back on its saucer, Louisa frowned. "You're more patient than I am. I sometimes wonder whether I've made a mistake in thinking I should stay here. At least in Cimarron Creek, folks trusted me."

He hated the discouragement he heard in her voice and searched for a way to lessen it. "But you were an assistant there. Here you have your own office."

"And few patients. Oh, let's not talk about me. I may be wrong, but I think you're concerned about more than Zeus."

It seemed there was no limit to her perceptiveness. "You're right. I looked through all the recipes last night." Josh had spent hours reading them, trying to recapture the enthusiasm he'd felt when he'd collected them. "When I finished, I felt the way I did the day Zeus threw me, that the idea is good but not good enough. It doesn't excite me."

Louisa showed no sign of surprise. "What does?"

"Porter's."

"You sound a bit surprised by that."

"I am. It's unlike anything I've done or ever thought about doing. Even though it excites me, I'm not sure Grandfather will like the idea."

"And if he doesn't, your cousin gets to run P&S."

Josh nodded, picturing Jed's expression when Grandfather made the announcement. The boy who'd been his friend and as close to a brother as Josh would ever have had become a man as driven to succeed as Josh himself. The prize was something they both wanted, but only one would win it.

"I promised my father I'd do my best to ensure that didn't happen. I can't let him down."

Louisa raised an eyebrow, as if questioning him. "I know you feel an obligation to your father and that you think that would have made him happy, but what about you? What would make you happy?"

"Fulfilling my father's wishes." The answer was automatic, but even as he gave it, Josh wondered whether it was still true. From the moment he'd hit the ground, his life had changed in ways he could never have anticipated, and now he was questioning the future that had once seemed so clear. What was happening?

"I heard you've been calling on some women who are in the family way."

Louisa tried not to smile at the discomfort she heard in Raymond's voice. Like many men, he seemed to find it difficult to discuss the very natural state of pregnancy. She was certain it was no coincidence that he'd waited until the sun was low enough that his embarrassment would be less obvious, although she had no idea why he'd introduced the subject in the first place, since he'd never before asked about her work. Most evenings when they walked around town, he spoke of the progress he was making on Porter's and the house he wanted to build.

"I have three patients in addition to Gertrude Neville." When Raymond said nothing, Louisa continued. "It seems hard to believe my former teacher is married and expecting her first child. Growing up, we were all convinced she was a confirmed spinster."

"That's something no one would say about you." Raymond squeezed the hand Louisa had laid on his bent arm. "Anyone can see you should be a wife and mother. I'm surprised you're not already married, but my aunt says that means you were waiting for the right man to come around."

The tone of Raymond's voice indicated that he hoped he was that man. There were times when she thought he might be, for there was no denying that she enjoyed the time they spent together. Being with Raymond was comfortable. They shared many of the same opinions, and they both envisioned a future in Sweetwater Crossing. Raymond would be a good husband, but Louisa could not encourage him tonight.

"It's too soon for me to think of marriage," she said firmly. "I need to establish myself as the town's doctor first." No matter how discouraged she had been, she was not ready to abandon that dream.

"You mean midwife, don't you?"

Louisa shook her head. "Not just a midwife. I want to be accepted as a doctor too. I know I'm a woman and that I don't have a degree, but Austin told me that not all men who call themselves physicians went to medical college. Some of them are self-taught or worked with other doctors, the way I did."

Raymond was silent for a moment, perhaps surprised by the vehemence of her declaration. "What if that doesn't happen? What if folks don't accept you? What will you do then?"

"I don't know."

"If I never have to thread another needle, I'd be a happy woman," Caroline announced as she settled into one of the chairs on the opposite side of the desk from Louisa. As she did many days, Caroline was spending her lunch hour with Louisa, and as she did more often than not, she was grousing about how unhappy she was.

The subject of happiness had weighed heavily on Louisa ever since she'd challenged Josh to identify what would make him happy. It had been almost a week since then, and while he'd said nothing more, she wasn't convinced that running P&S would bring him the satisfaction he expected. She knew very little about his life in New York, but Josh's enthusiasm for Porter's was obvious. Whether he was supervising the renovations or interviewing people to work in the tearoom and shop, he was visibly happy. If only Caroline could be so contented.

"Are you tired of working for Thelma?"

Caroline shrugged. "It's not Thelma. She's as good a boss as anyone could want. But I'm tired of pricking my fingers and I'm tired of women who take an hour to choose a piece of soutache braid. Mostly, I'm bored. The only good thing I can say about working as a dressmaker is that Thelma pays me more than anyone else has. I'm saving as much as I can, because I want to move out of my aunt and uncle's house."

This was the first time Caroline had mentioned that possibility. "Where would you go?"

"I'm not sure. I'd like my own house, but it'll take a long time before I can afford one."

Unless she married, but as far as Louisa knew, no one was courting Caroline. As Louisa took a bite of the sandwich Caroline had brought for her, the image of an empty seat at the dining room table flashed through her brain. Now that Alice and David were married, Alice had begun cooking meals for them at the parsonage, saying it was time for her to learn to feed her family.

"What about Finley House? Would you like to live there?" Louisa almost cringed as she heard the words emerge from her mouth. Emily had always called her the impulsive Vaughn sister, and this would only cement that opinion. Still, it felt right.

A smile transformed Caroline's face from ordinary to pretty. "That would be wonderful!" She paused, perhaps remembering other times when Louisa's impulsiveness had gotten them into trouble. "Is Emily taking new boarders?"

"I don't know," Louisa admitted. "I shouldn't have offered without asking her. It's almost ironic that I'd suggest you stay there after I was the one who told Emily she was making a huge mistake by turning our home into a boardinghouse, but I agree that it would be wonderful to have you there. The room across the hall from mine is empty."

Caroline's smile broadened. "It would be almost like old times. Remember how we used to sit on the verandah and pretend we were royalty when we waved to everyone who passed by?"

As Louisa chuckled at the memory, the front door slammed against the wall, drowning out the sound of the tinkling bell.

"You've got to help me!"

Louisa rushed into the small hallway, reminding herself of the first rule Austin had taught her: remain calm. When she recognized her visitor, she knew that would be a challenge. Though she'd seen Alice in many moods, she had never seen her so distraught, her face flushed, her lips pursed in anguish as she stared at her daughter from her first marriage.

"Jane is dying."

The child in Alice's arms was unnaturally stiff, her fists clenched, her eyes rolled back into her head, her pinafore reeking of vomit. It was a sight that would have frightened anyone, but for a mother, it would be terrifying. Fortunately, the regular movement of Jane's chest told Louisa the child was not on the verge of death.

"Bring her in here." Louisa led the way to the office and gestured toward the examining table. "I'll see you later," she told Caroline as her friend gathered the rest of her lunch and headed for the door.

"How long has she been like this?" Though Alice was clearly reluctant to release her grip on her child, Louisa took her from her arms and laid her on the table, continuing to assess Jane's condition.

"Too long." Alice shuddered. "What's wrong? This has never happened before. She wasn't breathing."

"But she is now." Louisa laid her hand on Jane's forehead, the heat radiating from it confirming her initial diagnosis. "Let's make her comfortable. There's a kettle of water and a basin in the storage room. I need you to fill the basin about halfway with water and bring it here. You'll also find some towels. Bring a couple." The items would be helpful, but most helpful of all would be having Alice out of the room. Her distress was only worsening Jane's condition.

"It's all right, Jane." Louisa began by stroking the girl's forehead, then moving to her cheeks and chin, all the while speaking in soothing tones. "You'll be all right." As she'd hoped, the stiffness in Jane's limbs began to ease, she unclenched her fists, and her breathing deepened. The worst was over.

"Here you are." Alice laid the basin and towels on the desk, then rushed to her daughter's side. "How is she? Is she going to die?" The frantic tone grated on Louisa's ears and made Jane clench her fists again.

Though she was tempted to tell Alice to wait in the infirmary, Louisa knew the young mother would not agree, even though her fear was worsening her daughter's condition.

"Thank you, Alice." Louisa used the same low and soothing voice that had helped Jane relax. "What I need you to do is sit down, close your eyes, and take deep breaths. Count to four as you inhale. Hold your breath for a count of four, then count to four again as you exhale."

Alice stared at her as if she'd suggested she sprout wings and fly. "Why? There's nothing wrong with me."

"Jane senses how upset you are, and that's making her worse. You need to trust me to do what's best for both of you."

Tears welled in Alice's eyes, her tightly fisted hands confirming these were tears of anger. "She's my baby."

"And I'm your doctor." Amazingly, that seemed to convince Alice, and she settled into the chair. Still speaking softly, Louisa removed Jane's stained clothing and bathed her in the cool water, then wrapped her in the largest of the towels. As she'd expected, the child's breathing returned to normal, and her eyes closed as she drifted into sleep. On the opposite side of the room, Alice seemed almost on the verge of sleep.

"It's over, Alice. Jane is fine."

Alice's eyes flew open, and she leapt to her feet, covering the distance to the table in three quick strides. "She's sleeping!" Her voice was filled with wonder.

When Alice reached to pick up her daughter, Louisa shook her head. "Not yet. She needs to rest."

Alice pouted for a second before nodding her acquiescence. "What was wrong?"

"It's called a febrile seizure." Louisa took Alice's hand in hers and laid it on her daughter's forehead.

"She's very hot. I can't remember her ever having such a high fever."

That confirmed Louisa's diagnosis. "Seizures like that are rare. Few children have them, but when they occur, it's before the fever reaches its peak." She looked down at the slumbering girl. "The combination of the seizure and the fever is very tiring, so Jane will probably sleep for the rest of the day. Just to be sure, I want to keep her in the infirmary for a few hours. We'll both watch over her." That would ensure that Alice did not disturb Jane's sleep.

Alice stared at her daughter, and this time the tears that slid down her cheeks were tears of relief, not anger. She brushed them away as she met Louisa's gaze. "How did you know what was wrong if these seizures are so rare?"

Father would have said it was the hand of God at work, and Louisa couldn't dispute that. "One of the children in Cimarron Creek had one while I was there. Austin taught me what to do."

Alice wrapped her arms around Louisa's waist and drew her close. "I don't know what I'd have done if you hadn't been here. Thank you, Louisa. You saved my daughter's life."

Chapter Twenty-One

"I want to propose a toast." Emily raised her water glass and waited until everyone else at the table followed suit. "No, not you, Louisa. You're the one we're toasting."

As color rose to her cheeks, Louisa placed her glass back on the table. Though she suspected she knew what Emily was about to say, she didn't like being the center of attention.

The way Emily straightened her shoulders before speaking again reminded Louisa of their father standing in the pulpit, preparing to deliver his sermon, but unlike Father, who'd always been serious, there was a hint of amusement on Emily's face as everyone waited to hear her.

She lengthened the pause for drama, then said, "To my sister, who proved she's a gifted healer today. I'm proud of you, Louisa."

"To Louisa." Josh's voice echoed through the dining room, and the warmth in his expression made Louisa's pulse race.

"Who was the patient?" Mrs. Carmichael asked.

"Alice's daughter, Jane. She had some kind of seizure." Emily looked at Louisa, silently asking her to complete the sentence.

"Febrile seizures. They're caused by a high fever."

"And my sister—my brilliant sister—knew how to help both Jane and her mother. Sweetwater Crossing is fortunate to have her." After the briefest of pauses, Emily continued. "And now I hope everyone's hungry, because I made a chocolate cake with lemon filling to celebrate."

Louisa smiled in anticipation of her favorite dessert. A very good day had just gotten better.

"You are the best friend anyone could wish for." Caroline brushed the lock of hair that refused to stay in her chignon as she settled into a chair on the opposite side of the desk from Louisa. Though her friend was usually meticulous about her appearance, today had been her moving day. Thelma had given her the day off, but she had still come to Louisa's office for lunch.

"It's going to be wonderful living at Finley House." Caroline's voice resonated with enthusiasm, and her smile threatened to stretch her cheeks out of shape. "Emily made me feel like part of the family, and little Noah asked if I'd read him a story every day until Beulah is back."

The laughter that bubbled up inside Louisa owed as much to the prospect of having her friend staying with her as the thought of Noah's excitement. As she'd hoped, Emily had been supportive of the idea of Caroline as a boarder, saying she would help fill the hole left when Alice and David moved to Louisiana.

When she'd first broached the subject, Louisa had thought the move might take longer to arrange, but Caroline was so eager to leave her aunt's home that she'd packed her belongings last night and brought them to Finley House before breakfast today, joining everyone for some of Emily's scrambled eggs and bacon.

Noah had pronounced Caroline a nice lady, an endorsement that Mrs. Carmichael had seconded. "I always did like her," the older woman had declared at supper last night when Emily had made the announcement that Caroline would be joining them. And while Josh admitted that as a temporary resident, he had no right to pass judgment on a potential boarder, he added his approval. "There's no nonsense about her, and I like that." Everyone was happy about the change.

"I'm glad you don't mind being roped into reading stories," Louisa said with another chuckle. "Craig realized Beulah couldn't read when she started school, so he and Emily think she had the stories memorized. It didn't matter, though. Both she and Noah are happy when they have a book in front of them. That's all that's important."

"Because making people happy is what you Vaughn girls do, especially you." Folding her hands and placing them on the desk, Caroline leaned forward. "Phoebe and I always knew that if we were upset about something, all we had to do was tell you, and you'd fix it."

"What do you mean?"

Caroline seemed as surprised by Louisa's question as Louisa had been by her friend's statement. "Don't you remember when we wanted a private place of our own? Phoebe was convinced that the oak tree out back"—Caroline gestured toward the rear of the building—"would be perfect for a treehouse, but her parents wouldn't even consider it. Doc said his patients wouldn't like it, and Mrs. Sheridan told Phoebe girls shouldn't climb trees. She said if anyone caught Phoebe in a tree, she wouldn't be allowed to play with us."

"I had forgotten that." Louisa wondered why she couldn't recall something that seemed to have been important to Caroline. "All I remember is the tent where we played." She'd asked her mother for an old sheet, and the three of them had used that and a couple sticks to create a tent.

"Exactly. That was your idea."

"My sisters claimed it was the ugliest thing they'd ever seen."

The memory of how she'd insisted they were simply jealous that they hadn't thought of it made Louisa laugh again.

"It was ugly, but we didn't care. It gave us a place to play." Caroline unfolded her hands. "You're always doing things like that. That's what makes you special."

Louisa was still thinking about her conversation with Caroline an hour later as she mounted Zeus and headed toward Opal Smith—no, Opal Gleason's—home. She had never thought of herself the way Caroline had described her, but she couldn't deny that Caroline was right in saying Louisa wanted to make people happy. She did.

Caroline was happy. Emily was happy. Alice was happy. Now if only there were something Louisa could do for Josh, something more than giving this magnificent animal a bit of exercise. Horace was a good horse, a reliable one, but there was no comparison between him and Zeus. Even though this was the first time Louisa had ridden him, he seemed to anticipate her commands. It was uncanny.

So was the way her thoughts turned to Josh so often. He'd become an important part of her life, and that meant it was important—more than that, it was vital—that he be happy. But that, Louisa was certain, would happen only if he learned that what he called fairy-tale love was real and was willing to give and receive it.

Mama had said that love was like a plant. It grew, becoming more beautiful as it matured, and like a plant, it began with a seed. Had the seed of Josh's love for Winifred been sown?

Louisa's doubts made her heart ache. Josh was a wonderful man who deserved everything life had to offer, especially love. If only he was willing to let the seed take root.

"What can I do, Zeus?"

There was no answer.

Louisa's spirits rose when she reached the Gleason home. Unlike many of their neighbors, the Gleasons raised goats rather than cattle or crops, and Opal's stories of the mischievous animals' behavior never failed to make her smile. Today she'd meet the critters that ate laundry and climbed on top of the chicken coop for no apparent reason other than sheer orneriness. Even more importantly, she'd have the opportunity to help another woman prepare for what Mama called a blessed event.

While Louisa was hitching Zeus to the front porch, Opal emerged from the house, her face wreathed in a smile almost as wide as her midsection.

"Look at you." Louisa returned the smile as she gave her patient a professional appraisal before mounting the steps. This was the first time she'd seen Opal since she'd returned to Sweetwater Crossing, and the intervening months had brought more changes than Opal's expanding waistline. The younger woman's blond hair, which she'd always worn in ringlets, was now braided and arranged in a coronet, and her skin bore evidence of too much time outside without a bonnet. But Opal's chocolate brown eyes still shone with happiness.

"The prospect of motherhood seems to agree with you."

Opal led the way inside the house, then laid a protective hand on her stomach. "I can't wait to hold the baby, but I'm scared about the actual birth. Mark is so much bigger than me that everyone says I'll have a hard time."

Louisa understood why other women would have told Opal that. She stood a mere five feet tall, and her husband was more than six feet with broad shoulders. It was possible her baby would be larger than most. More concerning was Opal's petite frame, which might make delivering any but the smallest child difficult. But, despite her own concerns, Louisa wouldn't frighten her patient. Both Thea and Austin had stressed the importance of maintaining an air of calmness.

"Every birth is different," she said, keeping her voice low and reassuring. "I can't predict how large your baby will be, but I'll be here to help you. Labor—particularly first labors—can be long, but I'll come as soon as it starts and will be with you the whole time. Now, let's see how you're doing."

When she completed her examination, Louisa gave the expectant mother a reassuring smile. "It looks like you have another two weeks to go. Of course, babies arrive on their own schedule, not when we think they should."

Straightening her dress as she stood up, Opal nodded. "That's what everyone tells me. My mother's friends said they'd come for the birth, but I'm glad you're here. I wanted a midwife. Is there anything I should do to prepare?"

"You should have a few things ready." Louisa handed Opal the list she'd prepared. "And, of course, you and Mark should be thinking about names."

"We've already chosen them. James if it's a boy, Penelope for a girl."

As they left the bedroom, Opal gestured toward the kitchen table. "Will you stay for a piece of cake? I want to hear about your beaus. It's not every girl who has two."

"But I don't."

"Sure, you do. Everyone knows Raymond Knapp is interested, and I heard Mr. Porter was courting you."

"You heard wrong. I'm helping Josh get the tearoom and shop ready. That's all."

Opal wagged her finger at Louisa. "Then why do your eyes twinkle when you talk about him? I know you're not a betting person. I'm not, either, but if I were, I'd bet that you and Mr. Porter will be married and expecting your first child by this time next year."

Josh's heartbeat accelerated at the sight of Louisa walking toward Porter's. He couldn't explain why it did that. It was silly—more than that, it was ridiculous—that his heart threatened to break through his chest whenever he saw her. That had never happened with Winifred or any of the other women he'd considered making Mrs. Joshua Porter, and yet it happened every single time he was near Louisa.

"Good day?" Josh asked when she was close enough that he didn't have to raise his voice. Her smile and relaxed posture told him Louisa was happy about something.

She nodded, the motion wafting her perfume toward him, making his pulse race again. "The best. It looks like I'll be delivering my first baby in about two weeks."

No wonder she was so happy. A successful delivery combined with what she'd done for Alice's daughter would help establish her reputation as a skilled healer.

"Will that be before or after you remove my cast?" Josh had been counting the days until he could ride Zeus and walk unencumbered by a cast. Both of those would make him feel like his old self, not an invalid. Even better would be the ability to do more things with Louisa without worrying that he was overdoing and might harm his leg.

"I can't predict that. Babies don't arrive on any schedule other than their own. That's part of what makes being a midwife so challenging. I can schedule checkups for the mothers before and after the baby's birth, but I can't control when they'll hold their child for the first time. It's the baby who's in control."

Though she wrinkled her nose as if annoyed by that, Josh heard the satisfaction in her voice and knew that that uncertainty was part of what Louisa enjoyed about midwifery.

"I'm glad I'm not a midwife. I like being in control." That was one reason winning Grandfather's challenge was so important. It would give Josh the opportunity to put his mark on P&S.

"I'm not surprised to hear you say that. There's a big difference between running a company like P&S and delivering babies." Louisa turned her attention to the porches that would one day connect the two buildings. The underpinnings for the extension had been constructed, and workers were beginning to lay the floor.

"It looks like Raymond's making good progress," she said.

"He still complains, but yes, he is. They should be finished on schedule. In fact, now that Will's here, they might even be done a day or two early."

Josh wouldn't count on that, although the extra time would ease the rush of getting the interior ready. The furniture he'd ordered was on its way, and Grandfather had confirmed shipment of the merchandise for the shop.

"How is Will doing?"

Josh smiled at the realization that while he'd been focused on things, Louisa was concentrating on people. No wonder she wanted to be a healer, while he was content to run a store.

"As far as I can tell, he's doing well. Every time he sees me, he apologizes for what he did. I don't know whether his mother told him to do that, but the apologies seem genuine."

"I think he's a basically good boy."

"Don't let him hear you call him that. He views himself as a young man."

"Like Noah."

This time Josh's smile turned into laughter at the memory of how the three-year-old insisted on being referred to as a man.

"Let me show you Raymond's latest idea. I'd like your opinion." When they were inside the store where work had been halted pending his decision, Josh gestured to the space on the right. "You know how I wanted this to be two separate rooms. After he took out the first wall, Raymond suggested making it one large space and using columns to delineate the areas. What do you think?"

Louisa moved to the middle and squinted, trying to visualize the finished room. "He might be right," she said at last. "It'll feel more spacious, but even more importantly, having a single showroom will encourage customers to explore both parts. You could still have the different decors you were planning, but I'd limit the wallpaper to the outside walls and have a neutral color paint for the center and the columns."

She paused for a moment. "Maybe a neutral color isn't the best idea. Don't both of the wallpapers you've chosen have blue in them?" When Josh nodded, she continued. "You could paint the columns the darker blue and use a lighter one for the walls. That would tie everything together and highlight the differences between the British and Continental sections."

Josh didn't need to squint to imagine the room Louisa had described. "You've convinced me. The single room will be better for customers, and it'll make it easier for Richard to supervise everything."

"So you're still planning to have him manage the store."

"If he's willing." Turning Porter's over to anyone felt wrong, but there was no choice, not if Josh was chosen to assume the helm of P&S. And he would be. He had to be.

Though his stomach churned at the idea that he might fail, Josh refused to burden Louisa with his worries. "I realized, though, that I need a second person for the store and someone to be in charge of the tearoom. Do you have any suggestions?" She would. He was far more confident of that than of his ability to convince Grandfather.

"You might hire Mrs. Sanders to work here. She's the widow who lives across the street, the house with the flowers. I doubt she's had experience in a shop, but I've heard that she's quick to learn, and I know she could use the money."

Louisa paused, her expression turning hesitant. "I should tell you that Mrs. Sanders used to be considered scandalous, but Emily said she's changed, and the town has accepted her. I think she'd do a good job."

Josh nodded. "I'll talk to her today. Until Richard comes, she'll be working with me, so I'll have a chance to see if she's the right choice. What about the tearoom? That's my biggest concern now."

When she'd mentioned Mrs. Sanders, Louisa had walked to the window, perhaps to see if the widow was in her yard. Now she turned around to face Josh.

"Since most of the customers are women, the manager should be one. That'll make the women feel more comfortable spending time there." Her voice was filled with confidence. "I remember Mrs. Webster—she was the original Ma of Ma's Kitchen—saying that even though men ate at the restaurant, it was most often because their wives had been there first. They convinced the men to come."

As Josh had hoped, Louisa had an opinion, and it was a valuable one. "Your smile tells me you have someone in mind."

"I do. Caroline. She's tired of working as a seamstress. This could be the change she needs."

"What if she tires of the tearoom?" Though he'd spent only a few hours in Caroline's company, Josh had learned that she'd worked at various stores, never staying more than a year.

"I don't think she will. This will be different, because she'll be the one running it. Instead of taking orders, she'll be giving them. I think Caroline will thrive on that."

Just as he was thriving on the idea of having his own business. Once again, Louisa was right.

"It's a good suggestion. I'll ask her tonight."

After Louisa returned to Finley House, Josh walked slowly around the buildings that would become Porter's, his eyes cataloging things that still needed to be done while his mind whirled at the memory of his time with Louisa and the realization that he'd changed.

In the past, he'd wanted to make decisions and had chafed when Grandfather had overruled him. Creating Porter's had given him the opportunity to make every decision, and yet he'd consulted Louisa, which the old Josh would never have done.

He'd not only asked for her opinion, he'd accepted it, recognizing that she had different insights and that those insights were valuable.

Why had he done that? Josh didn't know. All he knew was that it was a heady experience, one he liked, one he wanted to continue.

Chapter Twenty-Two

"I'm so glad you could come." Tina rushed out the front door only seconds after Louisa rode into the yard and drew her into a hug when she reached the porch. "I was afraid you might have a patient."

"No patients today." Despite all the praise Alice had heaped on her.

"Then we can spend the whole afternoon together. I've been looking forward to it."

Tina kept her arm wrapped around Louisa's waist as they walked inside. "I hope you don't mind a cold meal. I made chicken salad."

"That's one of my favorites," Louisa said truthfully. "It reminds me of my mother."

"I'm using her recipe. After Tillie died, your mother brought me a dish of it, saying I might appreciate something I didn't have to heat. She was right."

Once Louisa was seated at the kitchen table, Tina brought out the salad, a plate of flaky biscuits, and a jar of honey. "Even cold, Adam says there's nothing as good as my biscuits and honey. He's convinced the best bees in Texas made their way to my hives."

Louisa bit back the shudder that even a casual mention of bees caused. "I've heard your honey is delicious." As much as she did not want to offend her hostess, Louisa couldn't take the risk of eating honey. "I wish I could taste it, but Doc Sheridan warned me that I was likely to be allergic to honey. I'm sure you heard what happened when I was stung by a bee."

As the blood drained from Tina's face, she grabbed the jar and carried it to the counter, returning with one filled with peach jam. "I'm sorry, Louisa. I wouldn't do anything to hurt you. Mind you, I don't believe Doc was right. The man didn't know how to save my Tillie, so what would he know about honey? But I don't want you to worry that something awful might happen. The jam is almost as good."

It was delicious, as was the salad. When they'd both cleaned their plates and Tina had refilled their cups with fresh coffee, she leaned forward, her expression earnest.

"Are you certain you want to be a midwife?"

Feeling as if she'd been ambushed, Louisa took a deep breath before she responded. "A midwife and a doctor. I want to help women bring their babies into this world and keep them healthy once they're here."

Tina pursed her lips in obvious disapproval. "You're young and you're idealistic, but you're not being realistic, Louisa. Women aren't supposed to be doctors. They're supposed to be wives and mothers."

She wasn't saying anything Louisa hadn't heard dozens of times, but that didn't make it any easier to hear. "I understand some people aren't ready for a woman to be a doctor, but women have been helping other women give birth for a long time. There were midwives as far back as Moses."

"Maybe so, but Sweetwater Crossing has never had a midwife. I didn't need one for Tillie."

"Didn't Mesquite Springs have one? Weren't you still living with your sister when Raymond was born?"

A wistful expression softened Tina's face. "Yes, but Mabel wouldn't call for the midwife. She said we didn't need one, and she was right. Raymond was the most perfect baby I've ever seen."

"So, you were with her for the birth." Louisa was surprised that Mabel would have wanted an unmarried woman to attend her, but perhaps she'd had no one else close by.

Tina nodded. "Every minute. It was the most wonderful day of my life, holding that beautiful boy in my arms." For a second, she appeared lost in thought. Then she said, "That's how I knew I didn't need anyone when Tillie was born. I could do it on my own."

"But some births are difficult. It's important to have someone who's been trained to help with deliveries."

Tina shook her head. "You'll never convince me, but I hope you'll listen to me. Give up your fantasy of being a doctor. God made you to be a wife and mother. That's enough."

But it wasn't.

"Are you sure you don't mind?"

Louisa put down the tablecloth she'd been folding to stare at her sister. Though Friday wasn't their normal laundry day, when she'd heard that Alice needed another tablecloth for tomorrow's wedding supper, Emily had offered one of hers, saying it would be no problem to wash and iron it.

To Louisa's astonishment, Emily had planned to prepare all the food for her wedding, even though both Louisa and Craig had protested. Fortunately, Ada Tabor had insisted that the meal would be her gift to the bridal couple, and Alice had offered the parsonage's yard.

"David and I may be leaving town soon," she'd explained,

"but we want to start a tradition. Having our wedding reception there was perfect, and we'd like everyone in Sweetwater Crossing to have the same experience."

Neither Emily nor Craig had needed to be persuaded, and so the plan had continued. Now only a few hours remained before Emily would become Mrs. Ferguson.

"Of course I don't mind taking over for the weekend," Louisa told her sister. "No one expects my meals to be as good as yours, but I promise you they won't starve. I can cook two breakfasts plus Sunday lunch and supper."

Emily's eyes, the same shade of blue as Louisa's, still reflected doubt. "Yes, but . . ."

"Don't forget that I prepared all the meals while Mama was ill." At first, Mama had directed her, but during her final weeks, Louisa had been on her own in the kitchen, learning to make dishes that would encourage Mama to eat, even when her appetite had fled.

"I know, but Finley House is my responsibility."

"Emily, Emily, Emily." Louisa propped her hands on her hips and glared, mimicking the posture Mama had used when she was annoyed with one of them. "Listen to yourself. Tomorrow is your wedding day. Your only responsibility is to Craig. You two deserve some time alone."

David had offered them the parsonage's annex for a brief honeymoon. They'd go there after the wedding and remain there until Monday morning when Craig left for school.

Louisa didn't know whether it was the reminder of Mama or her own words that had convinced Emily, but her sister's shoulders relaxed. "You're right. It's just that I worry about everything here. It'll be the first time Noah's been separated from Craig."

"He's so excited about spending the night with Caroline that he'll barely know you're gone. I brought two books from the library so she'd have something new to read to him."

"You've thought of everything, haven't you?"

"Probably not, but it's only two nights. I'm sure we'll all be fine."

Closing the distance between them to enfold Louisa in a hug, Emily said, "I'm so glad you're back home. It wasn't the same without you."

And, as wonderful as Louisa's time in Cimarron Creek had been, it wasn't the same as being here with her sister. Mama had claimed nothing took the place of family, and she'd been right.

Emily took a step back, her expression once again solemn. "If only Joanna were here, tomorrow would be the happiest day of my life."

"I miss her too." Joanna's long silence was disturbing, since she had sent monthly letters when she'd first arrived in Europe, but nothing would be gained by saying that. Instead, Louisa sought to encourage her oldest sister. "She and her grandmother are only supposed to be gone for a year. Even if the trip is extended, I'm sure Joanna will be back before your first child is born."

Emily closed her eyes and bit her bottom lip in a gesture Louisa remembered from their childhood as one Emily used when she was struggling to keep tears from falling. Though she didn't understand the reason, Louisa's attempt at encouragement had failed.

"There won't be a child." The words were so soft Louisa could hardly hear them. "I'm barren, and please don't tell me I'm wrong. George and I were married for over a year. If I was able to have children, it would have happened."

The agony in her sister's voice wrenched Louisa's heart. She'd wondered why there'd been no children, but since Emily had discouraged any discussion of her marriage, she hadn't asked.

"George might not have been able to sire a child."

A violent shake of her head was Emily's first response. "He

told me that wasn't true. I don't know how he could be so sure, but he was." Emily folded her arms, gripping her upper arms and letting out a small shudder.

The only explanation Louisa could imagine was that a child had resulted from a dalliance with another woman, but that wasn't something she wanted to suggest, especially not today when her sister was preparing for her second wedding. "Maybe he was wrong."

"I doubt it, but it doesn't change anything. Craig says he's happy with only one child, and I love Noah as if he were my own. He'll be enough for us."

The words were brave ones, designed to convince Louisa, but though she heard the words, Louisa also saw the pain in her sister's eyes. Being barren was breaking Emily's heart, and no matter how much she wished she could solve this problem, Louisa knew she couldn't. Only God could give Emily the child she so desperately wanted.

Please, God, make my sister's dream come true.

Chapter Twenty-Three

Josh stared at his legs stretched out in front of him on Louisa's examining table, the one perfectly normal, the other with the pants leg slit up the seam to accommodate the heavy cast.

"I was beginning to think today would never come," he told her. "There've been so many things I couldn't do with that thing on my leg." He gave the cast a little thump.

Louisa smiled as she withdrew a saw from a drawer in the tallest of the cabinets that lined one wall. "Things like riding Zeus."

"And dancing with you. I was the only man under fifty who didn't have a chance to be your partner at your sister's wedding. You were the belle of the ball."

The deep purple dress she'd worn had made her look like royalty, and the matching hat with some kind of fluffy feathers had given her a slightly mysterious look. A look that had appealed to him and, judging by the crowd that had surrounded her, every other man there. Although he'd known it was ridiculous to feel even a shard of jealousy when Winifred was waiting for him back in New York, Josh would have given almost anything to have been able to sweep Louisa into his arms and twirl her around the makeshift dance floor.

"Hardly the belle of the ball!" The blush that stained Louisa's cheeks was even more appealing than her wedding attire had been. "It's customary for everyone to dance with everyone else on special occasions like weddings."

"And everyone did, except for me and your former schoolteacher." He'd noticed that Louisa had shared more than one dance with Raymond and that the builder had worn the same expression Josh had seen on Craig's face when he and Emily had exchanged vows. They'd both displayed a tenderness he'd only seen once before. The day of his wedding, David Grant had looked the same way, almost as if he could not believe his good fortune.

Josh had been to numerous weddings, but he'd never seen a groom look like these men did. Jed certainly hadn't. If Josh had had to describe his cousin's expression the day he and Julia were married, he would have said "satisfied." It was the same way Grandfather looked when he completed a particularly important business deal.

Louisa's frown as she tested the saw's sharpness on a piece of paper made Josh wonder if she'd read his thoughts. Her next words reassured him that she had not. "Gertrude's being cautious. Her mother convinced her that activity is bad for her baby."

"Is it?" Gertrude's declaration that she wasn't fond of dancing had not rung true, but Josh hadn't challenged her, since he'd assumed her reluctance was somehow connected to what he'd heard described as her delicate state.

Louisa shook her head as she walked back to the examining table. "No, but this is one time when Gertrude won't believe me."

He heard the regret in her voice and resolved to do nothing to deepen it. "I won't make that mistake. When it comes to medicine, you're the expert."

"Then you'll believe me when I tell you you'll probably be shocked when you see your leg again." She positioned the saw on the ankle edge of the cast.

"Why would I be shocked?"

"Because you haven't used those muscles for six weeks, and they've started to atrophy."

"That sounds ominous." Josh didn't recall Jed having any difficulty using his arm after the cast was removed, but perhaps he'd simply forgotten. After all, it had been ten years, and it hadn't been his arm.

Louisa gave him a smile designed to reassure him. "It's only temporary. Your muscles will regain their strength, but it'll take a while. Let's get started."

Though he trusted her, the sight of the saw gave Josh a moment of discomfort. "Now I know why doctors are called sawbones. That looks like it could hurt."

"It would if it hit your leg," she agreed, "but that won't happen unless you move. And there won't be any bones being sawed—just the cast. The best thing for you to do is relax. That might be easier if you didn't watch."

But Josh could no more look away than he could fly. This was his leg, and he wanted to see everything that was happening.

As the edge of the saw bit into the cast, Louisa nodded with approval. Apparently, the cast removal was going the way she'd expected, and that helped reassure him, despite the ominous sounding rasp of the saw. *That's normal*, he told himself, not wanting to speak and possibly distract Louisa.

She worked carefully, slowly moving the saw up the cast until she reached its top. Then, just as carefully, she pulled the two sections apart and laid them on the desk behind them. All that remained was to remove the cloth she'd wound around his leg to protect it from the plaster. When she'd unwrapped it, she ran her fingers along the length of his leg and smiled.

"It's done."

As Josh studied the pasty-white leg, he was grateful Louisa had prepared him. Had she not warned him, he would have been appalled. As it was, he was moderately concerned by both the color and the size of his leg. "You're right. It shrank, but it's straight." The calf might be thin and pale, but there was no sign that the bone had once been snapped in two, leaving his leg bent at an unnatural angle. Louisa had done what she promised: she'd healed his leg.

"No one should ever doubt your skill," he told her, gratitude making his voice crack a bit. "You knew exactly what to do, and you did it."

He raised his leg, reveling in being free from the cast. "I feel like I've shed a hundred pounds."

"Not quite that many." A chuckle accompanied Louisa's response. "The next step is to try walking." She returned to the cabinet where she'd found the saw and pulled out a cane. "You'll need this."

Josh wrinkled his nose at the sign that his healing was not yet complete. "You're making me feel like my grandfather. His doctor told him he'd need a cane for the rest of his life."

"Don't worry. *Your* doctor says this isn't permanent. Like the muscle weakness, it's temporary. You'll rely on it less each day. Let's see what you can do."

Josh swung his legs over the side of the table, then grabbed the cane when his left leg threatened to buckle. Louisa was right. He required the cane for stability. She moved to his other side, ready to support him if he needed it, and that made him all the more determined to walk on his own. Gingerly, he took a step, then another. Having to depend on the cane was awkward, but this was a major step forward from walking with crutches.

When he'd taken half a dozen steps, he stopped and faced Louisa, grinning. "Thank you, Dr. Louisa. No one could have done a better job."

When she smiled, Josh wasn't certain whether it was because

of the compliment or the salutation. All he knew was that the flush that colored Louisa's cheeks turned her from pretty to downright beautiful.

"You'll need to be careful." Though her color was high, her voice was calm. "No dancing and no riding for a couple weeks."

He'd expected that. What he hadn't expected was the feeling of euphoria that coursed through him. It was more than having the cast off, although that felt like a victory. It was the knowledge that Louisa had successfully healed his leg, and while there might still be naysayers, no one could deny the evidence of her skill.

"Even if I can't dance, I want to celebrate. Will you let me take you to dinner at Ma's tonight?"

Louisa's smile broadened. "I'd like that."

She might have said more, but the front door banged open, and a man rushed into the office. "You've got to come!" The man's hat was askew, his face flushed with exertion, as if he'd run all the way from his home, wherever that was. "Opal's labor has started."

Louisa nodded as if she'd expected it. "Right on time. You can go home, Mark. I'll be there soon." When the expectant father left, Louisa turned to Josh. "Do you mind if I take Zeus again?"

"Of course not. As you said, it'll be a while before I can ride him, and he enjoys the exercise."

Louisa opened her black doctor's bag, checking the contents. When she looked up, apparently satisfied that she had everything she needed, she said, "Supper may have to be postponed."

"I understand. Babies have their own schedules."

She grabbed the bag and her cloak, then handed him her key. "I don't want you to rush and hurt your leg, so please lock up when you leave."

He would. And then he'd go next door to see if the postmaster had a letter for him from Winifred. Even though she'd once told him she disliked writing notes, it seemed odd that she hadn't responded to the news of his broken leg. Didn't she care?

The day Louisa had heard a man boast that his horse rode like the wind, she had thought he was spouting nonsense. Today she understood what he'd been saying.

"Let Zeus gallop," Josh had said when she was leaving her office. "He'll enjoy it, and so will you."

She had. It was more than the knowledge that she'd reach her patient quickly. It was the sensation that she and Zeus were moving as smoothly and effortlessly as the wind.

Almost before she knew it, Louisa reached the Gleasons' ranch. Nothing had changed from the last time she'd been there except for the laundry flapping on the line. Opal must have been doing the wash when her pains began.

Inside, Louisa found the mother-to-be lying on the bed, screaming, "This hurts too much! I can't go through it!" while her husband stood at her side, beads of sweat rolling down his face.

The look Mark gave Louisa was so filled with anguish that she knew she had to do something, or she'd have two patients. "I need you to take care of my horse." That would occupy him for a few minutes.

When he practically ran from the room in relief, Louisa moved to Opal's side and laid a hand on her shoulder, trying to comfort her. "I know it hurts."

"How do you know?" The woman who'd always been kind snarled at her. "You've never had a baby."

"No, but I've helped other women deliver theirs. The first thing we're going to do is see how far along you are." Louisa examined her patient, and as she'd suspected, Opal was hours away from giving birth. Lying here with nothing to think about other than the pain would make each minute feel like an hour.

"You need to get out of bed."

Opal's expression said she was convinced Louisa was out of her mind. "Why? Babies are born in bed."

Sometimes. Thea had told Louisa that some midwives used birthing chairs in the belief that gravity helped speed the process, but since she had no birthing chair, Louisa would try a different approach.

"I think we should go outside and check on your goats. I saw laundry out there."

This time when Opal blanched, it had nothing to do with her pain. "How could I forget? My best tablecloth is on the line! I can't let them eat it."

"Then we'd better rescue it." As Louisa had intended, her patient was distracted, at least temporarily. And when the next contraction began, she'd be upright and better able to handle it.

Opal climbed out of bed and slipped on a wrapper, then led the way toward the back door. When they reached the kitchen, the door opened, revealing Mark, his arms filled with a ball of laundry, laundry that now had horsehairs sticking to it.

"Mark! What are you doing? Don't you know anything?" The angry shrew was back. "You're supposed to fold things when you take them off the line. Look at all those wrinkles."

Her husband stared at her, his satisfaction at being able to help changing into frustration that she'd berated him. "Why? What are a few wrinkles? I'll still have to iron everything."

Opal's expression turned to horror. "You, iron? What do you know about ironing? And look at that." She pointed to one of Zeus's black hairs. "What have you done? Can't you do anything right?"

When Mark dropped the laundry onto the table, his exasperation overcoming his patience, Opal burst into tears and flung herself into his arms. "Oh, Mark, I'm sorry. I don't know what's come over me."

"You're having a baby." Louisa kept her voice low but firm

as she tried to defuse the situation. Thea had warned her that women's moods could be volatile during this stage of labor, that they'd lash out at anyone who came too close, saying things they'd later regret . . . if they remembered them.

Louisa gave Mark a look of commiseration. "She'll be fine once the baby comes."

As if on cue, Opal screamed and doubled over in pain. "Another one!"

Mark, clearly unable to cope with seeing his wife in pain, appeared on the verge of fainting.

"This might be a good time for you to feed the goats," Louisa suggested.

"But I already . . ." His voice trailed off as he recognized her intention. "Oh, all right. Call me when it's over."

As soon as the pain subsided, Louisa touched Opal's shoulder. "Let's get that laundry folded. If we brush off the horsehair, no one will ever know it was there."

In another mercurial change of mood, Opal laughed. "No one told me I'd be doing laundry while I was in labor."

No one had suggested it to Louisa, either, but she wouldn't tell her patient that. "It's better than thinking about when the next pain will come, isn't it?"

"Yes."

Four hours later, Opal sat propped up against the headboard, her son cradled in her arms, an expression of pure joy on her face.

"He's perfect." She pressed a kiss on his forehead, then smiled at Louisa. "Thank you. I couldn't have done it without you."

It had been a difficult delivery. Besides being large, the baby was breech, and there'd been times when Louisa had feared she lacked the strength to save both mother and child, but with God's help, they were alive and healthy.

"I'm glad I was here." Louisa wouldn't frighten her patient

with the knowledge of how difficult she'd found the delivery or how she'd feared that she would fail. She hadn't failed. And because she hadn't, the Gleason family now numbered three.

Louisa returned Opal's smile, remembering the moment when she'd told her she had a son. A son with a well-developed set of lungs. There was nothing as satisfying as hearing that first angry scream when a child left the warmth of its mother's womb.

A mischievous smile crossed Opal's face as she caressed her son's button nose. "I wonder what Mark will say if I call him Laundry."

"Let's ask him." It was time for the father to meet his son. The baby was clean and obviously happy to be in his mother's arms, and Opal had changed into a fresh nightgown, allowing Louisa to braid her hair and wash her face, erasing the signs of the tears she'd shed.

When Mark entered the bedroom, his smile rivaled his wife's. "You did it," he said, looking as proud as any father Louisa had seen. He stared at Opal for a second, as if assuring himself that she was no longer suffering, then knelt by the bed and clutched her free hand. "Oh, sweetheart, you did it. Our son is here!"

"Thanks to Louisa." Opal tightened her grip on her husband's hand. "She won't admit it, but I might have died if she hadn't been here."

Mark's expression sobered, and he turned his gaze toward Louisa. "Is that true?"

Refusing to alarm him, Louisa said simply, "What's important is that you and your wife have a healthy son."

Mark nodded and gingerly touched the baby's forehead. "Hello, James."

Opal shook her head. "We need to talk about that. James doesn't sound right. He doesn't look like a James to me."

Mark studied his son. "I agree. What would you suggest?"

"I told Louisa I was thinking about Laundry."

Perhaps recalling his wife's irrational anger over the laundry, the young father pretended to consider the suggestion. "I don't know, sweetheart. Laundry Gleason doesn't sound right to me. Why don't we call him Louis?" When Opal nodded, Mark turned to Louisa. "How do you feel about having a namesake?"

She stared at him, speechless for a moment before saying, "Honored."

It was a wonderful way to celebrate her first Sweetwater Crossing delivery. Though the memory of Opal's struggle to birth her son would fade, Louis would remain as a reminder that Louisa had succeeded, a reminder that nothing in her life had brought her as much satisfaction as helping with the birth and being able to place a screaming Louis Gleason in his mother's arms.

Thank you, dear Lord, for being with me.

Chapter Twenty-Four

"Are you sure you don't want to wait until tomorrow?" Josh studied the woman who'd just come downstairs. She'd changed into a different dress, a dark blue one this time, and had done something that made her hair look fancier, but there was no ignoring the circles below her eyes.

"You look tired." The words were no sooner out of his mouth than Josh realized how wrong they were. "Oh, I shouldn't have said that, should I?"

Though he'd thought she might have been offended, Louisa chuckled. "You were only telling the truth. I am tired, but I'm too excited to sleep."

"Then let's go to Ma's. We have two reasons to celebrate."

"Do you want to take the buggy?"

Josh shook his head. "I can walk. My leg's doing better than I expected considering your warnings." He flexed it to demonstrate his newly found mobility. "Being able to bend my knee again makes everything so much easier. Stairs no longer feel like almost insurmountable obstacles."

They walked slowly, talking about nothing and everything, greeting the few pedestrians who were out at this hour, and enjoying the cool evening air as they made their way to the restaurant. Though the thump of the cane reminded him that he wasn't completely healed, Josh relished not being reliant on crutches and looked forward to the day when he needed no assistance.

When they entered Ma's Kitchen, Mrs. Tabor hurried across the room to greet them. "Look at you! No crutches, no cast." Her excitement was almost as great as his.

Josh nodded. "My leg may be free, but I still have the same appetite. Maybe even more. I may have to order both of your specials tonight."

She gave Louisa's dress and hairstyle an appraising look. "Are you here to celebrate?"

"We are." Josh answered for both of them. "The successful healing of my leg and Louisa's first delivery."

"Tell me all about it. I can see that Josh's leg is fine, but whose baby was it?"

As Mrs. Tabor led them to a table in the corner where they'd have more privacy, Louisa said, "Opal Gleason had a boy. They named him Louis."

Josh hadn't heard the details, merely that the delivery had been a difficult one and that she'd feared she would lose both mother and baby. "Is that a family name?"

Mrs. Tabor shook her head. "The father's Mark. The grandfathers are Aaron and Samuel. I wonder why they chose Louis."

The flush that colored Louisa's cheeks gave Josh the answer. "I bet I know. Am I right?"

She nodded. "I still can't believe they honored me that way." The flush deepened, confirming that she was both honored and embarrassed. While another woman might have been proud, Louisa seemed humbled by her namesake.

"I'm glad they did." Mrs. Tabor patted Louisa's shoulder. "It's about time folks recognized your gift. The Lord has blessed me with good health, but if I was sick, you'd be the person I would want to help me."

"Thank you."

Josh wondered whether Louisa had noticed that Mrs. Tabor had raised her voice for the last sentence, ensuring that everyone in the restaurant could hear her. If she did, she gave no sign, instead saying, "We have a third reason to celebrate tonight. It's one week until Porter's opens."

"Counting the days, are you?" Mrs. Tabor chuckled. "So is most of Sweetwater Crossing, but you didn't come here to listen to me. Let me tell you about tonight's specials."

The food was as delicious as it had been the last time he'd eaten there, but Josh found himself paying more attention to his companion than his meal. It wasn't simply the attractive clothing or hairstyle. That was the outside, and while Grandfather had told him and Jed that if boxes and jars had a pleasing appearance, customers were more likely to buy the product once, he'd stressed that whether they repeated their purchase depended on what was inside.

What was inside Louisa intrigued Josh. She was different from Winifred and the other women he'd known in New York. There was no pretense, no need to wear fancy clothing to impress. If he'd had to describe Louisa in one word, it would be *genuine*.

The woman who occupied so many of his thoughts smiled as she cut another piece of roast chicken. "Thank you for suggesting this. It's the perfect way to end a very good day."

"I agree. I have a feeling neither of us will have much time to relax for the next week. There's still a lot to do on Porter's."

Knowing how important the final days of preparation were, Louisa had said she'd close her office, leaving a note on the door to tell patients where they could find her, so that she could help. It was a generous offer, more evidence of how selfless this woman was.

"I rode by it on my way home and was surprised to see that the roof over the new part of the porch isn't finished."

Josh buttered another bite of roll as he said, "It should have been, but Raymond ran out of nails. How could there be a shortage of something as basic as nails? The only good news is that the shipment's due in tomorrow, so they'll be back to work on it on Thursday."

"What about the interior? I was hoping to see the Continental Room's wallpaper."

Louisa had been coming to the site every afternoon to witness the progress, but Baby Gleason's arrival had kept her away today.

"It's almost finished. The supplies from P&S are scheduled to be delivered Friday morning. By then, everything should be ready for us to stock the shelves." Josh could hardly wait to arrange the displays.

"Did your grandfather question why you needed so many things?"

"Surprisingly, no. I told him I wanted to see if our products would be popular here, and he accepted that explanation. It's not like him not to demand more details." Grandfather had always been a stickler for controlling even the most minute aspect of the store.

"Maybe he's more concerned about your leg."

Although that was a possibility, Josh doubted it. "His first telegram asked whether he should send his doctor to check on it, but once I assured him that wasn't necessary, he hasn't mentioned it again. I suspect he's busier than he expected with both Jed and me gone and doesn't have time to worry about why I ordered our most popular items."

Josh savored the final bite of roast beef before adding, "He did remind me that my proposal and I were due in New York on June 30th." As if Josh could forget either his obligation or the date. Both were indelibly etched on his brain.

"We need to ensure that Porter's is so successful that he has no choice but to approve your proposal."

Louisa made it sound simple, but it wasn't. "I believe Porter's will succeed. The question is whether Grandfather will like that concept better than whatever Jed brings from Europe or whether I should propose the American Room."

"But Porter's is what excites you."

As was so often the case, Louisa was right, but that didn't solve Josh's dilemma. "What's important is choosing the idea that will excite Grandfather. I wish I could read his mind, but I can't."

Seeing their empty plates, Mrs. Tabor came to their table. "Was everything satisfactory?" When they'd assured her it was, she suggested dessert. "You said you were hungry," she reminded Josh, adding that many customers claimed her bread pudding was their favorite dessert.

Louisa waited until they'd taken their first bites of the sweet that was as delicious as Mrs. Tabor had claimed before she returned to the subject of Josh's grandfather.

"I hate to ask this, but what will you do if your grandfather doesn't choose whichever idea you propose?"

"I've been asking myself that ever since I left New York. The answer is, I don't know."

It might affect his betrothal to Winifred if her father decided Josh's role was not important enough to secure his daughter's future. Mr. Livingston had made no secret of his ambitions for both himself and Winifred. That and the absence of letters from her despite the ones Josh had sent made him wonder whether her father had already chosen a more suitable son-in-law. Oddly, those concerns seemed trivial compared to the potential change in his relationship with his cousin.

"I can't imagine working for Jed." Josh took another spoonful of pudding while he considered how to explain his feelings. "Jed and I are friends as well as cousins, but we have very different ideas about how to run the store. I'm afraid he'd make changes I don't like, and there would be nothing I could do about them."

Frown lines appeared between Louisa's eyes. "Wouldn't he listen to you?"

That was the crux of the problem. "He never has. When Jed makes up his mind, nothing changes it. He's like Grandfather in that." Josh had accepted the sometimes-authoritarian decrees because Grandfather was older, but it wouldn't be easy—maybe not even possible—to give Jed the same deference.

"The problem is, P&S is my life. It's hard to imagine a future without it."

Louisa laid her spoon on the plate and fixed her gaze on Josh. "Then there's only one thing to do: make Porter's such a resounding success that your grandfather will have no choice but to put you in charge of the company." Her voice was filled with conviction as she said, "You know that's the right proposal, because it's the one you care about. You can make it a success. I know you can."

Josh wished he had the same confidence.

Louisa pulled another book from the shelf and began leafing through it, looking for information about breech deliveries. Even though she'd managed a successful birth, perhaps there were techniques Thea hadn't mentioned. But Doc Sheridan's medical books held virtually no information about childbirth. Doctors, it seemed, were too busy treating infections, fevers, and wounds to bother themselves with women's needs.

No wonder Thea had told her that every town should have a midwife. Perhaps that was why even though Austin was a competent and compassionate doctor, many of the women in Cimarron Creek brought their concerns and those of their small children to Thea.

Still mulling over the absence of sections devoted to women, Louisa started when the doorbell tinkled. A patient! She laid the book back on the desk and entered the hallway, then stopped in surprise.

"Raymond. Is something wrong? Was someone hurt?" Josh had told her they took many precautions but that construction was inherently dangerous.

Raymond stroked his muttonchop whiskers as he shook his head. "No one was hurt. This is a friendly visit. I heard about the Gleason baby and wanted to help you celebrate." He pulled a box from inside his coat. "This is for you."

Louisa smiled as she recognized her favorite candy. Someone—most likely Tina—must have told him which flavors she preferred.

"Thank you, Raymond. That was kind of you." She opened the box and extended it to him. "Would you like a piece?"

He shook his head. "They're all for you. I hope you'll think of me when you eat them."

"I will."

The smile he gave her made Louisa wonder whether celebrating Baby Gleason was only an excuse and whether the candy was Raymond's next step toward courtship. Perhaps it was time for them to take that step.

Chapter Twenty-Five

Louisa could barely control her excitement as she turned onto Creek Road and looked at the buildings that were almost complete. Josh's dream was close to becoming reality. Unless something unforeseen happened, today would be the last day of construction. It was also Caroline's last day as a dressmaker. Tomorrow she would join Louisa and Josh as they readied the interior of the tearoom. Mrs. Sanders would start work on Monday, becoming familiar with the merchandise as she helped Josh stock the shop's shelves. And then Tuesday . . .

Louisa smiled in anticipation of the grand opening. The way everything was falling into place filled her with both excitement and a sense of rightness. Josh might not be convinced, but she was certain this was the right project for him.

Her smile broadened at the sound of pounding, evidence that the nails had been delivered. Byron and Andrew were working on the steps to the shop, securing the loose board Josh had noticed yesterday, but the loudest hammering came from above. Louisa looked up, expecting to see someone working on the porch roof. Instead, she spotted Will McIntyre kneeling on the peak of the tearoom, fastening a loose shingle.

He was staring at the shingle with the single-mindedness Josh had said he gave to all of his assignments. When he was convinced it would not come loose in the wind, Will turned and scrambled to his feet, his expression as triumphant as if he'd built the entire Sunday House without assistance.

"I'm done here," he announced, his voice filled with satisfaction.

Byron and Andrew paid no attention to him, perhaps because they'd grown weary of his exuberance. Louisa started to reply, then gasped.

It couldn't be, and yet it was. An older man might have crouched or crawled across the steeply pitched roof, but Will was standing upright, oblivious to the precariousness of his position.

It happened so quickly that Louisa couldn't tell whether he'd somehow become unbalanced or whether his feet lost their grip. All she knew was that Will was in danger. Seconds, minutes, hours—afterwards she could not have said how much time elapsed as the young man fell forward, his arms flailing uselessly as he plummeted toward the ground.

"No!" Louisa raced toward Will, determined to catch him, to somehow break his fall. But she was too late. By the time she reached him, Will lay on the ground, his neck bent at an unnatural angle.

"Breathe," she commanded, kneeling at his side and pressing her ear to his mouth. "Breathe." But Will had no more breaths to give.

Seconds later, perhaps alerted by her scream, Josh hurried out of the tearoom, followed closely by Raymond, Byron, and Andrew. All four men's faces mirrored the horror Louisa knew colored hers.

"What happened?" Josh demanded, his voice harsh with shock.

Not rising from her spot next to the boy who was beyond

help, Louisa said softly, "When Will stood up, he lost his balance and fell. Death was instantaneous." That was the only good thing she could say about what had happened.

Louisa was no stranger to death. She'd been with her mother when she'd drawn her last breath. She'd seen her father soon after he'd died. She'd been with Austin when one of his elderly patients hadn't recovered from a virulent fever. But none of those deaths had hit her with the intensity of this one. Will had been a young man with his whole life ahead of him, and that life had been snuffed out.

She closed her eyes, trying to fight back the feeling of failure that threatened to overwhelm her sorrow. This boy shouldn't have died. Her brain told her there was nothing she could have done, that Will was like many boys his age, taking foolish chances simply because he did not have the wisdom to realize they were foolish. Louisa knew that, but the knowledge did nothing to lessen the ache in her heart.

"It wasn't your fault." Had Josh read her mind? "It was an accident, a terrible accident. If anyone's at fault, it's Raymond and me. We should have known Will was too young to be on the roof."

Though Raymond's lips tightened, he did not contest Josh's statement. "I'll get the sheriff." He stared at Will, then shook his head, perhaps trying to deny what had happened. "He'll take him back to his mother."

Nancy. Poor, poor Nancy. She'd told Louisa that Will was the only thing she had in her life, and now he was gone. Louisa couldn't let the sheriff be the one to break the news to her.

"I want to do that."

Josh's expression radiated concern. "Are you certain? It won't be easy."

"I know it won't, but I owe it to his mother."

In less than half an hour, the sheriff had concurred with Louisa's assessment of the cause of death and returned with a wagon to transport the body to the McIntyre farm. Though he'd insisted it was his responsibility to notify Nancy, he'd allowed Louisa to accompany him. "She might appreciate having a woman with her when she hears what happened to her boy," he'd acknowledged.

"This is a sad day for Mrs. McIntyre," Sheriff Granger said as they headed out of town. His face bore the same lines of sorrow and resignation Louisa had seen the day he'd investigated her father's death. "I sure hate to be bringing her news like this. It's the worst part of my job."

"And mine." This was the first time she'd had to explain a death.

They were silent for the rest of the drive, both lost in thought. When they arrived at the ranch, Louisa took a deep breath, trying to prepare herself for what she knew would be a difficult conversation.

Alerted by the sound of the wagon's approach, Nancy emerged from the house before the sheriff had put on the brake. Though her hair was neatly coiled around her head, her apron bore red stains, evidence that she'd been cooking.

"Sheriff Granger, Louisa, why are you here? Is something wrong?" Worry lines formed between Nancy's light red eyebrows.

"I'm sorry, ma'am, but there's been an accident." Without dismounting, the sheriff glanced at the back of the wagon, where a blanket covered the still form that was unmistakably a human body.

Nancy covered the distance between the porch and the wagon in a few swift strides, then began to wail. "No! It can't be true! Not Will!" As she peeled back the blanket, tears streamed down her cheeks. A second later, she turned toward Louisa, her grief transformed into fury. "You claim to be a doctor. Where were you when he needed you? Why didn't you save him?"

"There was nothing she could have done." Sheriff Granger

spoke before Louisa could reply, his voice conciliatory. "Your son broke his neck falling from the roof at Porter's. Miss Vaughn was there, but there was nothing she or anybody could have done."

Perhaps the sheriff thought repeating his declaration would console the grieving mother. It did not.

Her face contorted with anger, Nancy pointed a finger at Louisa. "It's your fault! If it hadn't been for you, he wouldn't have been working there. That was your idea, yours and that awful man's."

"Now, Mrs. McIntyre, it was no one's fault. Will slipped and fell." Once again, the sheriff was trying to calm or at least placate her.

But Nancy would not be consoled. "It is her fault," she insisted. "I tell you, Sheriff, she's to blame." She took a step closer and poked Louisa. "You're gonna pay for this."

"How are you feeling this morning?" Wanting to speak to her privately, Josh had been waiting for Louisa to descend the stairs before he went into the dining room for breakfast. Though her steps were firm, the dark circles under her eyes told him she'd slept poorly, as had he. Yesterday had marked them both.

It should have been a day for a minor celebration, because despite Will's death, the construction of Porter's was complete. Perhaps because a final payment hinged on it, Raymond had sent the men back to work as soon as the sheriff and Louisa left for the McIntyre ranch. There'd been none of the usual bantering among the workers, but they'd accomplished everything on Josh's list.

"I'm feeling better than last night." The shrug that accompanied Louisa's response said that the improvement was minimal, and that concerned Josh, for last night had been a difficult one.

The only word he could use to describe supper was solemn.

Emily's meal was as delicious as ever, but Louisa had eaten only a few bites, and Josh had struggled to concentrate on the savory pork roast. Though Craig had tried to lighten the mood with stories of Noah's attempt to imitate a duck, only Beulah had laughed. The adults were all affected by the afternoon's events.

Josh had no trouble understanding how deeply disturbed Louisa had been by Will's death. That was only natural. Violent death, even if it was an accident, was difficult to accept. There had been fatal accidents at P&S, but this was the first time the person who'd been killed had been someone Josh had hired, someone he knew personally, and it had shaken him. How much worse must it have been for Louisa, who'd witnessed the boy's fall?

"Were you able to sleep?" Perhaps he shouldn't have posed such a personal question, but Josh wanted to do everything he could to help Louisa, and understanding how she'd fared was the first step. The way she gripped the newel made Josh wonder if she feared her legs would collapse.

"Not much," she said. "I kept remembering Nancy McIntyre's face when she saw Will and the way she blames me for his death."

"That was grief speaking. It's natural to blame the closest person." He'd blamed the coachman for the accident that had taken his parents' lives, even though Grandfather had assured him the man was not responsible, that he'd done everything he could when the heavy wagon had plowed into the side of the carriage, overturning it and flinging the occupants onto the ground.

"I know that, but it doesn't help. I don't think I'll ever forget Will saying 'I'm done here' and then falling. One minute he was alive; the next he wasn't."

Though her voice was even, Josh saw the anguish in Louisa's eyes. "What he did is not your fault," he said firmly, willing her to believe him. "You didn't tell him to stand up, and you couldn't have stopped him from falling. If anyone deserves the blame, it's me. I should have insisted Raymond assign Will less dangerous tasks, and Raymond should have remembered how rash boys that age can be."

Josh paused, hoping Louisa would accept what he'd said. When she remained unconvinced, he added, "It was a tragic accident, but that's all it was. An accident."

Her lips descended into a frown. "You can say that, but a boy is still dead, a mother is still devastated, and I still wonder whether I could have prevented it. Austin warned me there would be times like this, but it's much worse than I could have imagined."

Though Noah's excited chatter told Josh his time alone with Louisa was coming to an end, there was one more question he needed to ask. "Are you sure you want to work today? It's all right if you don't." As much as he wanted her to be part of furnishing the interior, he didn't want to do anything that would increase her suffering.

She nodded slowly. "I know you're right. I can't change what happened. Working at Porter's today will be good for me."

Four hours later, Josh realized she'd been right, just as she'd been right in insisting that they not delay the opening of Porter's. "Nothing can bring Will back," she'd told him, "and the town needs a reason to celebrate. Will wouldn't have wanted it any other way." Today as she'd worked alongside him and Caroline, moving tables into place and stocking the storeroom with the china and accessories, Louisa's shoulders had relaxed, and the haunted expression that had worried him disappeared. Though her smile wasn't as brilliant as usual and her eyes reflected grief, she no longer seemed to be carrying the heavy burden of guilt.

Brushing back a tendril of her dark hair, Caroline smiled, then gestured around the tearoom. "This is even better than I expected."

Once they'd arranged the tables, Louisa had brought out table linens and two place settings of dishes and silverware for one of the tables, calling this a dress rehearsal. The result was everything Josh had hoped for and more. At Louisa's suggestion, they'd purchased pale blue linens rather than the traditional white or ivory. Since the china had only arrived yesterday afternoon, this was the first chance they'd had to see everything together.

To Josh's delight, it couldn't have been more perfect. The descriptions in the catalog had been accurate, and the pale blue tablecloth highlighted the deep blue rims on the plates, cups, and saucers. And, though he hadn't been convinced, the flatware appeared to shine more brightly on the colored cloth. Louisa might claim she had no artistic talents, but there was no doubt she knew how to set a beautiful table. And, while he expected the majority of the customers to be women, the décor wasn't so feminine that it would discourage an occasional man from having tea with his wife or sweetheart.

"You were right about everything," he told Louisa.

She shrugged off the compliment and focused on Caroline. "Do you think you'll like working here?"

Caroline nodded vigorously. "I'll *love* it. This looks like something out of a storybook. I can imagine duchesses eating here."

To Josh's surprise, Louisa laughed. "And here I thought you didn't read much."

"But you and Phoebe did. You were always talking about dashing dukes and charming counts."

Josh joined in the laughter. "I can see that my education was sorely lacking. I'll admit that I met a duke once when I was in England, but I never read about them."

"Your books were probably about soldiers and pirates," Louisa said as she moved one of the teacups a quarter of an inch to the right.

When she looked up, Josh shook his head. "I'm afraid I'm like Caroline. I didn't read much when I was growing up, because I was too busy working."

Louisa's raised eyebrow encouraged him to continue. "From the time I was six or seven, my father would take me to P&S every Saturday. At first, I helped in the stockroom. When I was older, I assisted the salesmen."

Though Caroline appeared interested, it was Louisa who asked, "When did you play?"

"Sunday afternoon." Josh smiled at the memories of the years when life had seemed simple. He suspected it hadn't been simple for his parents, but they'd sheltered him from the problems of everyday life.

"We all had dinner with my grandparents. Afterwards while the grown-ups talked about boring things, Jed and I played ball or skated or—"

"Got into mischief." A grin accompanied Louisa's words.

Josh chuckled. "How did you know I was going to say that?"

"I don't know. It just seemed logical."

This time it was Caroline who chuckled. "You sound like an old married couple, completing each other's sentences."

Josh couldn't recall his parents or his grandparents doing that. What he remembered was that no one interrupted, because no one would have presumed to know what someone else was thinking. And yet, having Louisa guess what he'd been about to say felt right. More than that, it felt like fun, and fun was one thing his life had lacked.

Chapter Twenty-Six

"Are you ready?"

Louisa took a deep breath, trying to calm her nerves as she looked around the tearoom, assuring herself that everything was in place for their grand opening. "I think so," she told Josh, "but I can't ever remember being so nervous." Everything had to be perfect, because she couldn't bear the thought that he might fail to win the challenge.

"We've done all we can. Now it's up to the townspeople." His voice was as even as if this were an everyday occurrence. She knew it wasn't, but perhaps he wasn't as worried about the possibility of failure as she was, and that kept his nerves under control.

Louisa moved to the window and peeked outside, gratified by the size of the crowd waiting for Josh to emerge from the tearoom and officially open Porter's. "It looks like most of the women are here, even some of those who live quite a ways away."

She and Josh had discussed having the opening on a Saturday when whole families would be in town, but he'd been adamant about the May 1 date, explaining that a smaller number of customers might be preferable for the first day. "Inevitably, there are problems, and it's easier to resolve them if we're not overly crowded," he'd said.

But judging from the number of women in front of the tearoom, both it and the store would be crowded.

"Special pricing draws people."

Louisa knew that was true, but there was another reason so many had come. "So does curiosity. Caroline said women were lined up to reserve tables for tea an hour before she started taking reservations." She glanced toward the back of the room, where Caroline and her staff were preparing food. "She's almost as excited as we are." And that pleased Louisa. If this turned out to be a job Caroline enjoyed enough to remain here indefinitely, both she and Porter's would benefit.

"You were right to recommend her. She'll be good for Porter's. So will Mrs. Sanders." Josh pulled out his watch and nodded. "It's time. After you, my lady." He feigned doffing his hat, perhaps remembering Caroline's comments about dukes and duchesses.

Though Louisa had protested, saying this was his store, not hers, Josh had insisted she accompany him onto the porch to greet the first customers. She looked at the women who'd assembled in front of the store, smiling at the familiar faces. Women of all ages were there, from her former classmates to some who were old enough to be her grandmother.

Though last Sunday had been David's final day in the pulpit, he and Alice had delayed their trip to Louisiana so that she could attend the opening. She and Gertrude stood together, with little Jane between them, holding their hands. The only surprise was the sight of Nancy McIntyre at the far edge of the group, apparently deep in conversation with Tina Bentley. After she'd forbidden Louisa to attend Will's funeral, once again telling Louisa she was responsible for her son's death, Louisa had not expected Nancy to come near the site where Will had died.

"Welcome, friends." Josh paused as cheers rang out. When the crowd was once more silent, he continued. "For those of you who haven't met me, like the little one there"—he pointed toward the Gleason baby, provoking both a round of good-natured laughter from the group and a proud smile from Opal—"I'm Josh Porter, and I want to welcome you to the tearoom and shop that bear my name."

Though he didn't turn around, Louisa saw people's gaze move to the sign hanging from the porch that connected the two buildings. The blue background and white lettering coordinated with the colors she and Josh had chosen for the interior of both buildings.

"Now, you may think I could have found a more imaginative name, and you'd be right," he continued. "The truth is, even though it's Porter family tradition to have our name on our businesses, this should probably be named after the person who made it possible, and that's Louisa Vaughn."

Louisa let out a gasp. Not once had Josh hinted he'd say anything like this. Not only was it unexpected, it was undeserved. The concept had been Josh's. What she'd done was trivial.

Ignoring Louisa's gasp and the surprised expression on some of the women's faces, Josh continued. "Louisa rescued me from the roadside when my horse threw me. She set my broken leg so well that I can now walk without a limp." He took a few steps forward, then moved back to his original position to demonstrate the healing. "She introduced me to Sunday Houses. She even chose the colors for the tearoom. In short, she's been with me every step of the way." Josh turned to smile at Louisa before he concluded. "Please join me in thanking Louisa for everything she's done."

When he began clapping, the women gathered in front of the store joined in, the exceptions being Nancy McIntyre and Tina Bentley, whose frowns proclaimed that they did not share Josh's admiration for her. Louisa wasn't surprised by Nancy's reaction, but she couldn't understand Tina. There was no reason she should look so annoyed.

Though she suspected her face was almost as red as an Indian paintbrush from the unexpected praise, Louisa knew she had to say something. She took a deep breath, then stepped forward to address the group.

"Josh told me he's taken several trips to Europe. I thought he meant England, but it's clear to me one of those trips was to Ireland and that he kissed the Blarney Stone. That's the only logical explanation for what he just said."

As the women laughed, Josh sputtered. "Ladies, I assure you that's not true. But you have better things to do than listen to me talk, so"—he turned and opened the door with a flourish—"Porter's is now officially open."

Knowing Caroline and the girl she'd hired as a waitress would welcome the tearoom guests, Josh and Louisa made their way to the shop, unlocking the door and ushering customers inside. Until he returned to New York, Josh planned to spend each day in the shop with Mrs. Sanders, but realizing there would be more customers than normal today, Louisa had volunteered to handle some of the sales while Josh provided advice and recommendations.

"What a nice man!" Opal Gleason said as she cradled Louis with one arm so she could pay for the marmalade she'd chosen. Though the baby was only a week old and most mothers would have stayed home with him, when Louisa had made a brief house call yesterday, Opal had insisted nothing short of an earthquake would stop her from coming to Porter's today.

"I don't care what Nancy McIntyre says. Mr. Porter is a good man, and this is what the town needs." Opal gestured toward both rooms of the shop. "The mercantile can't compare to this, and what Nancy said is just plain mean."

"She's grieving." When Tina had stood up in church and denounced Doc Sheridan, claiming he should have been able to save her daughter, Father had told Louisa that people who were in the early stages of mourning said and did things they wouldn't ordinarily consider and that others should excuse what might be seen as poor behavior. Louisa still cringed at the memory of how she'd behaved toward Emily when their father had died. Even though she'd been grieving, her behavior had been inexcusable. Fortunately, Emily had been quick to forgive.

"I know Nancy's grieving, but she has no call to tell people that Porter's will fail." Opal looked at the line behind her, lowering her voice so she could not be overheard. "I don't know what she and Tina were saying, but they looked thick as thieves. I'd watch out for them if I were you."

Remembering the camaraderie she'd seen between the two women, Louisa nodded. Josh didn't need any enemies, not when so much was riding on Porter's success.

Half an hour later, the two women who'd occupied too many of her thoughts entered the shop, picking up jars of jams, studying the labels, then putting them back on the shelves.

"You were right, Tina. Nothing here can compare to your honey." Nancy raised her voice, leaving no doubt she meant everyone to overhear her conversation with her friend. "Who would buy pickled onions? Mark my words, this place will be closed within a month." She plunked the onions onto the shelf with more force than needed, then headed toward the door. "Don't waste your time here," she told the women who were waiting their turn to enter the shop. "The Bentleys sell better merchandise."

Louisa kept a smile on her face, refusing to let Nancy's pettiness spoil an otherwise good day. Customers continued to enter the store, undeterred by Nancy's warning, and everyone bought at least one item. At this rate, almost every shelf would need restocking tonight.

Only a few minutes before the shop was scheduled to close,

Emily and Alice came inside, their smiling faces leaving no question of their opinion of Porter's.

"This is even more impressive than you said," Emily said as she approached the shelf closest to the cash register and began inspecting the jars that lined it.

"I wish we'd gotten reservations for tea today." Alice ruffled her daughter's hair when Jane tugged on her hand, apparently attracted by the brightly colored label on one of the jars. "No, sweetie, we're not buying that."

"It'll be more relaxing tomorrow, and the food will be just as good. Besides, having tea here will be a good way to spend your last day in Sweetwater Crossing." Though Emily punctuated her words with a smile, Louisa knew she was dreading her friend's departure.

"What's this?" Emily asked when Jane continued to point at the brightly labeled jar. "Chutney. I've heard of it but have never tasted it."

"It's spicy," Josh said as he joined them. "I find it goes well with roast beef."

Nodding, Emily laid a jar on the counter. "All right. I'll take one."

"So will I." Alice reached for a second jar. "The last roast I made was too dry. Maybe this will help."

Emily chuckled at the evidence that Alice's culinary skills had not improved. "Did I hear David say he's going to hire a cook when you get back to Grant Landing?"

"I think it's a matter of self-preservation." Alice wrinkled her nose, then grinned.

"Ladies, Porter's will close in five minutes." Josh raised his voice to be heard over the hum of conversation that had filled the store since its opening. "If you can't decide what you need today, we invite you to return tomorrow."

When he locked the door behind the final customer and assured Mrs. Sanders there was nothing else she needed to do today, Louisa breathed a sigh of relief. Her feet hurt from standing all day, her cheeks from smiling more than she could recall. And yet, despite the aches, she wouldn't have traded this day for anything. It had been wonderful being here, sharing Josh's success.

"Mrs. Sanders will be busy restocking tomorrow morning," Josh said as he moved to Louisa's side. "Even without tallying the sales, I can tell you we sold more than I'd expected." He smiled as he looked at the almost bare shelves. "Thank you, Louisa."

"The credit goes to you. This was your idea—your vision." Though his words had echoed through her brain all day, this was the first time she'd been able to tell him what they'd meant to her, how they'd warmed her heart and made her feel like a success. "Thank you for what you said this morning. The praise was very nice, even if it wasn't deserved. Porter's is yours. I only played a small part."

Josh shook his head. "You're underestimating your contribution. I couldn't have done this without you. Don't you see, Louisa? The idea may have been mine, but you've become its heart. It was because of you that it came to life."

Before she could speak, before she could still the pounding of her heart, he set his cane aside and wrapped his arms around her waist, drawing her close to him. Then slowly, ever so slowly, he pressed his lips to hers.

Chapter Twenty-Seven

What had he been thinking? Josh scoffed as he slid his right arm out of the coat sleeve. There'd been no thinking involved. He'd been so exhilarated by the success of the day, so excited by the way he and Louisa had turned an idea into reality, that rational thought had fled, leaving only raw emotion. And in that moment of pure emotion, he'd given in to the longing he'd been suppressing and had drawn Louisa into his arms.

The kiss had been wonderful. More than that, it had felt right to hold Louisa close to his heart, to feel her lips beneath his, to hear her soft sigh of contentment.

But it hadn't been right. Josh tugged the coat off and tossed it onto the bench at the foot of his bed.

He'd never kissed Winifred, not once in all the months they'd been courting. The one time he tried, she informed him that her mother claimed a man should not kiss a woman's lips until the day they were wed. But Josh had kissed Louisa. One kiss had led to another, and if it hadn't been for the shadow passing the window and the sound of footsteps on the porch, he would have continued, for nothing was as sweet as Louisa's lips.

"Thank you," he'd said when they'd broken apart. There

was so much more that he wanted to say, but that was the wrong time and Porter's was the wrong place. Before he could tell Louisa what was in his heart, he needed to make sense of everything that was in both his heart and his mind. And that, Josh knew, would not be easy.

"What happened between you and Josh?"

Louisa looked up, startled by the unexpected interruption and the way her traitorous face reacted to her sister's question. "We're not children anymore, Emily. You could have knocked. This is my bedroom, not yours." Not bothering to hide her annoyance, Louisa continued brushing her hair in an attempt to control the flush in her cheeks. "Besides, what makes you think something happened?"

Undeterred by Louisa's curtness, Emily perched on the end of the bed only a few feet from the stool where Louisa sat, brush in hand as she prepared to braid her hair.

"When you came home, you were glowing—that's the only way I can describe it—and Josh looked happier than I've ever seen him."

"He had a good reason to be happy. Porter's first day was better than either of us had expected." Perhaps Emily would accept that and leave Louisa alone to savor her memories of what had happened after Josh turned the sign to "closed."

"That may be true, but it's not the whole story." Big sister Emily had always been perceptive, and today was no exception. "Something else happened. I know it, and I won't leave until you tell me what it was." Perceptive and persistent. That was Emily.

"Did I ever tell you that you're the most annoying big sister anyone could have?"

"Only about a million times. And don't think I didn't notice that you're trying to change the subject. Whatever happened must have been very important for you to act like this."

There was no point in dissembling. Emily had always been able to either coax or coerce Louisa into revealing her secrets. Abandoning her braid, Louisa faced her sister.

"He kissed me." Only three words, but the memory of that kiss sent tingles up and down Louisa's spine. When she'd been in Josh's arms, she had felt cherished. More than that, she'd felt as if they were the only people on Earth, a man and a woman in a world of their own. Without question, it was the single most wonderful moment of her life, and even if it was never repeated, it would remain a priceless memory.

Josh had kissed her out of gratitude—the way he'd said thank you when he ended it had told her that—but Louisa could not dismiss the belief that he felt more than gratitude. The warmth in his eyes, the tenderness of his smile, the gentle way he'd touched her cheek before they left Porter's all pointed to something deeper than simple gratitude.

Was it love? Louisa had no way of knowing, because although they'd smiled at each other during supper, they had not spoken of the monumental moment when their lips had met.

"I thought so." Emily's smile was one of satisfaction. "The way you said 'he kissed me' told me just how special that kiss was. Louisa, you look and sound like a woman in love."

Love. There it was again, the word neither she nor Josh had spoken. Mama had told her daughters that they'd know when they met the man they were destined to love, but when Louisa had asked how she would know, Mama had simply smiled. "Deep in your heart, you'll know," she'd said when Louisa pressed for a better explanation, her response leaving Louisa as confused as before. Maybe Emily would be more helpful.

"How do you know if it's truly love?" Louisa asked her sister. "You've loved two men. How did you know it was love and not infatuation when you married George? You married him only a few weeks after you met."

Emily and Craig's courtship had spanned months, and even

though she hadn't been here for most of that time, Louisa would never question their love. It was apparent from the way they looked at each other, the way they gave each other tender touches when they thought no one would see, the way their voices softened when they spoke to each other. All of that had been apparent before the wedding, and it had only increased since then.

Emily's smile faded and she was silent for a long moment, the furrows between her eyes telling Louisa she was debating whether or not to respond. Unlike Mama's enigmatic answer, which had been accompanied by a radiant smile, Emily's response appeared to bring her pain. She bit her lip, almost as if she were trying not to cry, before she said, "Marrying George was the biggest mistake of my life."

Louisa took a deep breath as she considered what she'd just heard. Emily had said little about her marriage during the few days they'd been together before Louisa left for Cimarron Creek last summer, but she had attributed that to grief. First Mama, then George, and then Father. Three deaths in such a short time would have overwhelmed anyone. Though Louisa had been concerned by the letter that George had written, claiming it was from Emily, and the ones he'd apparently withheld from her, she hadn't realized just how troubled her sister's marriage had been.

"Why was it a mistake?" Louisa asked.

Emily leaned forward and took Louisa's hands in hers, a gesture they'd used as children when they sought comfort. "When I came back to Sweetwater Crossing, I vowed no one would know what happened. I was ashamed of how I'd been duped."

Louisa stared at her sister, trying to understand what she was saying. How could Emily, always the most sensible of the three Vaughn girls, have been duped?

"I was so flattered that George chose me rather than you or Joanna that I didn't look beneath the surface. If I had, maybe

I would have realized that he didn't love me. All he wanted was a woman who could give him blond children."

More than one parishioner had commented on how different the Vaughn sisters were in appearance. Emily was the blond, Joanna the dark brunette, Louisa the one with mousy brown hair. Like Josh, George had been a blue-eyed blond, but surely that hadn't mattered.

"That can't be true," Louisa protested. "No one would marry for a reason like that."

"George did." Her sister's voice was filled with anguish.

Louisa tightened her grip on Emily's hand, wanting to assuage her pain. "I wish I'd known, but I had no idea. I envied you for having such a handsome husband. It was like one of those stories we read about the dashing duke who found his true love and cherished her for the rest of her life."

Emily shrugged. "He might have cherished me if I'd given him the son he wanted, but when I didn't, he became violent."

Louisa gasped as the words registered, her brain shrieking denial. It couldn't be. And yet as she remembered catching glimpses of bruises on Emily's arms the day she'd returned, Louisa knew it was the truth. She'd been so distraught with grief over their father's death and angry that her life had been turned upside down that she hadn't said anything. Even worse, she'd been cruel to her sister. Louisa cringed at the memory of the angry words she'd flung at Emily, never realizing that her sister had suffered far more than she had.

"That's horrible. No one should be treated like that."

"It *was* horrible." Emily's eyes darkened with remembered pain. "Each month was worse than the one before, but it's over and now I have Craig." This time her lips curved into one of the smiles she wore whenever she mentioned her husband. "Craig is as different from George as day is from night. I tell him he's my life after the shadows."

Though Louisa's heart overflowed with gratitude that her

sister had found a kind and loving man who'd brought light and happiness into her life, it ached at the thought of what Emily had endured.

"I wish I'd known. I wish I could have helped you."

Emily shook her head. "There was nothing you could have done. George did everything he could to make sure no one knew what was happening. It's probably terrible of me, but when the sheriff told me he was dead, all I felt was relief."

"That wasn't terrible," Louisa assured her. "That was human."

"Maybe so." Emily waited until Louisa met her gaze before she said, "Be careful. Before you marry anyone, be sure you know who he really is. Be sure you know how he reacts when things go wrong. Don't make the mistake I did."

Louisa nodded. Though there'd been many times when she'd resented her sister's advice, everything Emily said rang true.

"Josh seems like a good man, but so is Raymond. Make sure you choose carefully."

"You act as if I'll have a choice. No matter what happened today, Josh's future is in New York with Winifred and mine is here."

Her sister raised an eyebrow. "Is it?"

Chapter Twenty-Eight

"Here's the honey."

When Caroline laid only one jar on the table in the tearoom's kitchen after Josh had requested a minimum of three, he raised an eyebrow. Today's guests were eating even more honey than yesterday's had, exhausting Porter's supply. It was a minor problem but one Josh welcomed because it kept him from dwelling on the question of Louisa. He'd hardly slept last night, at one point abandoning his bed to pace the floor, but even that had done nothing to calm his turbulent thoughts and make sense of his emotions.

"The mercantile only had two jars," Caroline explained, "and Nancy wouldn't sell both of them to me."

The name surprised Josh even more than the refusal. "Nancy McIntyre? Will's mother?"

"Yes. I wondered what she and Tina Bentley were talking about yesterday, and now I know. Apparently Nancy needs money, so Tina suggested she help at the mercantile."

Josh suspected the widow needed something to do with days that must seem empty now that she was alone as much as she needed the money. "It seems like that's a good arrangement for both of them. I remember someone saying that Mrs. Bentley refused to continue working there after her daughter died."

As she opened the jar and began spooning some of the honey into the small serving dishes they used for jams, Caroline frowned. "It might be good for them, but it's not good for Louisa, at least not today. When I arrived, Nancy was telling half a dozen women not to trust Louisa. She claimed she would have been able to save Will if she was a real doctor."

That was balderdash—pure, unadulterated balderdash. Josh struggled to tamp down his anger that anyone could think, much less say, that Louisa was less than competent. "No one could have saved Will."

"You don't have to convince me, Josh. I know that, but folks listen to Nancy."

"And they won't listen to Louisa."

Caroline's nod confirmed his assumption. "She still has to prove herself. I tried to defend her, but the women said my friendship with her keeps me from seeing clearly, even though Nancy's grief colors her opinion of Louisa."

It was the way of the world. A still-grieving widow who'd recently lost her only child would garner more sympathy and be seen as more credible than a woman trying to establish herself in what many considered a man's profession.

"I suppose there's nothing I can do."

Other than possibly convince her to leave Sweetwater Crossing and accompany him to New York. But as appealing as that idea seemed, Josh knew it wasn't the answer. Louisa wanted to prove herself here. More than that, she needed to show the doubters just how competent she was.

Caroline placed the dishes on a tray, ready to be taken into the dining area. "You're a newcomer. And everyone knows you're only here temporarily. They'll put a resident's opinion ahead of yours. It may not be like that in New York, but that's the way it is in small towns."

Josh was still reflecting on what Caroline had said hours later. At his suggestion, he and Louisa were strolling along the creek, savoring the warmth that remained after supper. It was an ideal evening for a walk, even for a man whose thoughts were troubled.

"You must be pleased that today's sales were even higher than yesterday's."

To his relief, Louisa had not alluded to their kiss, perhaps because that was not something a lady should do. And until he was able to determine exactly why the kiss had affected him the way it had and what—if anything—he should do about it, he welcomed her reticence.

"I am pleased." But that pleasure was diminished by the town's lack of acceptance of Louisa. The story Caroline had recounted and his desire to do everything he could to counteract Nancy's vitriol had taken precedence over Josh's need to sort through his emotions.

"At the rate we're going, we'll run out of merchandise in a couple weeks, so I placed another order with my grandfather."

Louisa slowed her pace and looked up at him. "Did you tell him what you're doing?"

"No." He'd simply sent a telegram asking Grandfather to ship the merchandise. "Two days' sales aren't enough to prove this is a good idea. Even a whole month won't be enough, but it's all I have."

"I was a little surprised when Caroline said you've already had some repeat customers. Surely that's more evidence that Porter's is a good concept."

Though Caroline had touted the second-timers as proof that Porter's was exactly what Sweetwater Crossing needed, Josh knew it could have been an aberration. As he'd told everyone at the supper table, it was too soon to make any generalizations.

He shrugged as he looked at Louisa. "Apparently people are developing a taste for chutney and marmalade." Neither was his favorite P&S product, but that was of no account. All that mattered was what customers here preferred.

"It's good that people come back for more."

Josh laid his hand on top of the one Louisa had placed on his arm. Though Winifred had laid her hand in the same place numerous times, he'd never felt the desire to touch her. With Louisa, everything was different.

"It is good," he agreed. "If the trend continues, I'll include it in my proposal. Of course, there's no way of knowing how Grandfather will react to the whole idea, even if I can show that it's popular here. He may claim that the experience in one town proves little."

"Which is why you won't tell him until you're back in New York. You want to be able to address his concerns in person."

A week ago, Josh might have agreed with Louisa's assumption. Now he wasn't so certain. "The truth is, that's only part of the reason. As I was tallying sales this afternoon, I realized I was reluctant to share the idea of Porter's with him."

"Why?" Understandably, Louisa was confused.

"Because if he likes it, it might mean relinquishing control of the whole concept. Even if he agrees that I should run P&S, Grandfather might insist on changing the name of the tearoom to P&S." And that thought had caused Josh's stomach to churn more than if he'd eaten spoiled meat.

"Would that be awful? You've always seemed proud of Porter & Sons."

To Josh's surprise, Louisa laid her other hand on top of his. Winifred had never done that, but the warmth and, yes, the comfort from the gentle pressure of Louisa's fingers on his made Josh's heart race.

He took a deep breath in an attempt to calm himself before he spoke. "It might not be awful, but it feels wrong to me. Porter's is my creation. Even though I think it would be a valuable part of the company, I don't want it to have the same name as the store in New York. I can't explain why I feel that way. I just do."

They'd reached the bridge over the creek. By unspoken consent, they'd moved apart and were now standing side by side at the railing. Louisa remained silent for a moment, staring down at the water as if it contained answers. "Maybe you feel that way because it's yours and yours alone. It's your mark on the world."

The idea lodged deep inside Josh, igniting a spark that quickly turned into a flame. Once again, Louisa—kind, caring, perceptive Louisa—had proven she knew him better than he knew himself.

"I hadn't thought of it that way, but you're right. How did you become so wise?"

She gave her head a gentle shake. "I'm not wise. It's just that I have similar feelings about being a doctor here. When I went to Cimarron Creek, I thought I might never return, but once I came back, I realized that even though I could be a healer somewhere else, helping people I grew up with is more rewarding than treating strangers. That's why I keep reading Doc Sheridan's books, trying to learn everything I possibly can."

Josh nodded slowly, impressed with both her insights and her enthusiasm. Though he'd intended to tell Louisa what Caroline had heard at the mercantile, he wouldn't, at least not tonight. He wouldn't spoil the satisfaction Louisa felt, but oh how he hoped the poison Nancy McIntyre was spreading wouldn't taint the townspeople's attitude toward this wonderful woman.

"Louisa."

Though she had been in the middle of a dream, it vanished the instant Louisa heard her sister's voice and the firm rapping on her door. Something was wrong. That was the only reason Emily would have woken her.

Louisa sat up in bed. "Come in and tell me what's wrong."

"Thomas Neville is here," Emily said as she entered the room. "Gertrude needs you."

Please, Lord, don't let it be serious, Louisa prayed as she dressed more quickly than she could recall and grabbed the medical bag she always kept close at hand.

"What's wrong, Thomas?" she asked as she descended the stairs. The man whose hair was almost as dark a brown as Joanna's ran his hand through it, his agitation visible. His coat was misbuttoned, and unless Louisa was mistaken, he wore one brown and one black sock. The normally fastidious rancher was obviously distressed. First-time fathers were frequently nervous about their wives, Louisa reminded herself, but Thomas's reaction seemed extreme.

"Gertrude's having horrible pains. I didn't want to leave her, but she said you were the only one who could help her." He turned to gesture toward the front door. "I brought the wagon so you wouldn't have to take the time to saddle a horse. She thinks she's having the baby."

Louisa's heart sank. It might be nothing more than false labor, but if it wasn't . . . She paused, reviewing everything Thea had told her about premature births. This was much too soon for the Nevilles' child to leave the womb.

The ride was silent. Though Louisa wanted to reassure the frantic husband, she wouldn't offer promises she might not be able to keep. Instead, she spent the time praying for the wisdom to know what to do for Gertrude and her baby.

When they reached the house the Nevilles shared, Louisa jumped down from the wagon, not waiting for Thomas's assistance, and rushed inside, retracing her steps to the room where she'd last examined her patient.

As she'd expected, Gertrude was in the bedroom. What Louisa hadn't expected was that she was standing, a pool of blood at her feet.

"Help me, Louisa." The mother-to-be's face was pale and drawn, her nightgown and hands blood-stained, but her voice was as firm as if she were addressing a classroom of recalcitrant pupils.

"Save my baby. You've got to save him." It was a command, not a request.

The amount of blood Gertrude had lost made Louisa fear she was too late and that only a miracle would save this child. "I'll do my best."

But Louisa's best wasn't good enough. As she'd feared, Gertrude had gone into labor far too early, and the boy—Gertrude had been right about that—was too small to live outside his mother's womb. Less than a foot long and weighing no more than a pound, he had no chance of survival in a world where babies four times his weight struggled and often failed to breathe on their own.

"I'm sorry, Gertrude. There was nothing I could do," Louisa said as she washed the still form and wrapped him in a soft cloth, all the while praying for the words to comfort the bereft mother. One look at Gertrude told her nothing she could say would provide that comfort.

Her blue eyes brimming with tears, Gertrude held out her arms. "Let me hold him."

"Of course." Louisa laid the infant who would never laugh or cry in his mother's arms.

"I'm sorry, Clive." The tears Gertrude had been holding back dripped onto her son's face. "I loved you." She touched each of the tiny features, perhaps trying to memorize them. "I've always loved you."

She stayed there, her back propped against the headboard, staring at her son for what seemed like an eternity but was only a few minutes. Finally, she handed him back to Louisa. "You'll find a white gown in the top drawer. Will you dress Clive in that? Thomas and I'll bury him tomorrow."

Though the gown was much too large, Louisa did what Gertrude wanted. When she'd finished and laid little Clive back in his mother's arms, she asked, "Do you want me to call Pastor Lindstrom?" The new minister had been in Sweetwater Crossing only a few days, but he'd already assumed full responsibility for the church and its parishioners.

Gertrude shook her head. "I don't want strangers looking at my son." She stared at him, her face contorted with grief. "I should have realized I wasn't intended to be a mother. Every one of my dreams has died."

That couldn't be true. Gertrude was still a relatively young woman, able to bear another child. "You could have another baby." Perhaps that hope would comfort her.

Gertrude shook her head again, this time more vigorously. "You don't understand. This was my one chance, and now it's over. Go home, Louisa. I know you did your best. I don't blame you for Clive's death, but I need to be alone."

"Let me send your mother." Though Gertrude was grieving, her sorrow seemed to be colored by bitterness. Was this normal? Louisa did not know. What she knew was that Gertrude should not be alone. Perhaps Mrs. Albright would be able to console her daughter.

"I don't need anyone! This is between me and the God who won't let me be happy."

She wasn't being rational. Louisa knew that, just as she knew nothing she said would help. This was another instance of the effect of grief that Father had described. Like Nancy and Tina before her, Gertrude needed time to heal.

"I'll get Thomas," Louisa told her patient as she prepared to leave.

"No. Not even him."

As she told Thomas what had happened, Louisa tried to hold back her tears. This was part of being a midwife. Not all deliveries were successful. Not all babies lived to be adults, but oh, how she wished today could have been different.

Perhaps it was knowing the high price Emily had paid for her infertility, perhaps it was simply grief that her former schoolteacher was suffering. Whatever the reason, Louisa felt as if her heart were breaking.

Chapter Twenty-Nine

What was he doing there? Josh hadn't expected to see Raymond other than in passing now that the work on Porter's was complete, but there he was, sitting on the bench in front of the store. Josh had arrived earlier than usual, because there'd been no second cup of coffee with Louisa; no first cup, either, since she'd been summoned to the Neville ranch.

"Morning, Raymond. Is there something I can do for you?"

The man who'd turned Josh's vision into reality stood, his stance surprisingly adversarial. "You can go back to New York. There's nothing left for you to do here, Porter."

If the harsh words hadn't told Josh the man was spoiling for a fight, the use of his last name would have. Josh had no intention of fighting. Instead, he pretended that Raymond was an irate customer. Keeping his voice calm, he said, "There's plenty for me to do in the next month." Now that Porter's was open, he hoped to spend more time with Louisa and planned to talk to Craig about another Sunday picnic.

Raymond took a step closer, moving like an animal stalking its prey. "That *plenty* better not have anything to do with Louisa. Just because her sister had her head turned by a stranger and left town to marry him doesn't mean Louisa will. She's more sensible than that. She knows this is her home."

Josh forbore pointing out that Louisa had left that home for an extended period, although not for marriage. "As you said, Louisa's a sensible woman. She knows what she wants."

His face reddening with anger, Raymond glared at Josh. "Look, Porter, I want what's best for Louisa, and it's not you. You may have thought you'd sway her with those pretty words you threw at her at the opening, but she saw right through them. Blarney. That's all you have to offer her. That and plenty of money."

The man was acting like a dog staking out his territory, but he was mistaken if he thought that would discourage Josh. Porters knew how to win, and it didn't involve fists. "What do you think you can offer her?"

"What she needs." A smug smile accompanied Raymond's words. "I can give her what every woman needs: a home close to her family, a little garden so she can grow flowers, a passel of children to raise."

"I see." What Josh saw was that Raymond spoke of needs rather than wants and that there'd been no mention of Louisa's medical practice. "And you think that's what Louisa wants?" He stressed the last word.

"Of course it is. Admit it, Porter. You're not the right man for her. She's just a temporary distraction for you."

That wasn't true, but Josh had no intention of adding fuel to the fire Raymond was kindling. "What is she to you?"

"The woman I love."

It was almost noon by the time Thomas and Louisa arrived back in Sweetwater Crossing after one of the most difficult mornings Louisa could recall. If the weather had matched her mood, it would have been dark and damp, mirroring her discouragement. Instead, the sun shone from a brilliant blue sky, making this a close-to-perfect Thursday morning. But it was far from perfect. Though she'd done her best to comfort both of the Nevilles, her heart ached over the loss Gertrude and Thomas had sustained, and she'd remained outside the bedroom, refusing to leave until Gertrude had fallen asleep.

"My wife's a stubborn woman," Thomas said as he drove the wagon toward town, "but she needs her ma at a time like this." Despite Gertrude's protests, her husband was determined to take Mrs. Albright to the ranch.

"Do you want me to go with you?" Delivering unwanted news was one of a physician's responsibilities, Austin had told Louisa, and though her experience with Nancy had shown her how painful it could be, she didn't want Thomas to face the Albrights alone. "I could assure them there was nothing anyone could have done and no reason why you can't have another child."

"Thank you, but the news would be better coming from family."

And Louisa was not family.

"In that case, you can leave me at my office." She needed time to accept what had happened before she returned to Finley House and faced Emily's and Mrs. Carmichael's questions. Though their concern would be well-intentioned, it was more than Louisa could handle right now. Besides, while it was unlikely she had anyone waiting for her, Louisa wanted to be in her office in case someone came.

Though the events of the morning weighed heavily on her, Louisa straightened her shoulders and held her head high as she descended from the wagon. *This is the day which the Lord hath made; we will rejoice and be glad in it.* The words of Psalm 118:24 echoed through her brain. She might not be able to rejoice, but she could—and she would—try to find at least one reason to give thanks.

As she unlocked the front door and spotted a piece of paper that had been slid under it, her spirits rose. This was her reason to give thanks. Emily had posted a sign saying Louisa had been called away and that anyone who needed care should leave a note. Someone had!

She bent down to retrieve the sheet, unfolded it, and gasped. She would give no thanks for this. Far from it. Anger rushing through her, Louisa crumpled the paper and tossed it onto the floor as she stormed into her office. The only thing to do with a message like that was burn it, but today was warm enough that she didn't need to light the stove, and her hands were shaking so much that she wasn't certain she could strike a match. She slumped into the chair behind her desk and rested her head on her hands.

Forget it, she told herself. But forgetting was impossible. The words were etched on her brain.

"What's wrong?"

Louisa's head jerked up. "Josh. I didn't hear you come in. Shouldn't you be at Porter's?"

Though his eyes mirrored the concern she'd heard in his voice, his reply was calm. "I took advantage of a lull and left Mrs. Sanders in charge. She's more than capable of handling our customers, but I'm the one who needs to place orders at the mercantile. When I saw Thomas leaving, I realized you were here."

As if he sensed that she wasn't yet ready to answer his questions, Josh responded to Louisa's unspoken query while he settled into the chair across from her. "Caroline thinks we need more teapots. It seems there was an argument yesterday when the women at one table couldn't agree on which flavor of tea they wanted. She suggested we have individual pots so each of the ladies can have her favorite."

"That's a good idea. Did you order the smaller size?" His matter-of-fact explanation helped Louisa relax, and she seized the opportunity to think about something other than Gertrude's baby and the crumpled paper. When they'd chosen the china, she and Josh had debated whether to order the medium or large teapots, finally settling on the medium size. Now it appeared they should have selected the individual-sized pots.

"Yes. Adam says he can have them here next week." Josh leaned forward, his expression serious. "Now, tell me why you're so upset."

The respite was over. Even though she'd told herself she wouldn't talk about what had happened until much later, Louisa knew that rather than questioning her abilities, Josh would simply listen, allowing her to unburden herself.

"It was a horrible morning. Gertrude lost her baby." Somehow she managed to say the words without tears filling her eyes.

Josh's expression changed from concern to compassion. "I'm sorry. It must have been difficult for both of you and for her husband."

He understood. "It's not the first time I've witnessed a stillbirth, but it was the first time the mother was someone I've known my whole life. I felt like my heart was breaking along with hers."

Louisa took a deep breath, trying to calm the racing of her pulse as she struggled to find the words to explain why this loss had been worse than others. "It makes me wonder if I was wrong when I said there was more satisfaction in treating people here. When I left Cimarron Creek, Phoebe told me I was a fool to come back. I think she may have been right, especially when I saw that." She pointed to the crumpled paper that had landed under the examining table.

Josh rose and retrieved the sheet, straightening it and reading aloud. "'Ladies aren't supposed to be doctors. You'll never be a real doctor. Stop trying.' Printed, not written. No signature. The only thing distinctive about it is the loop on the *L*." A scowl marred his handsome face. "You were right to throw this away.

It's the mark of a coward, because only people who are afraid to be held accountable for their words choose anonymity."

A bird perched on the windowsill and pecked the glass, perhaps mistaking his reflection for a rival. On another day, Louisa might have tried to shoo him away, but today she was unable to muster the energy.

"I know you're right," she told Josh, "but the note still hurts, maybe because it confirms my fears. It makes me feel like a failure." And that had happened too many times.

Instead of returning to his seat, Josh perched on the side of the desk. Though he wasn't touching her, he was close enough that she could feel the warmth from his body. This wasn't like those wonderful moments at Porter's when she'd stood in Josh's embrace, but still his nearness comforted her.

"You're not a failure. You helped Alice when Jane had a seizure. You knew how to successfully deliver Opal Gleason's baby." His words were designed to provide comfort, but they failed.

"I couldn't save Gertrude's son. I think that's why someone left that note. They heard about Gertrude's baby and they're blaming me."

Josh shook his head. "First of all, you're not to blame. You know that. Secondly, no one other than you and Thomas knows about Gertrude yet."

Louisa was silent for a moment as the significance of his words registered. When she'd read the hateful message, she had made an assumption. An erroneous one.

"You're right. The note was here when I returned from the ranch, so it wasn't related to what happened this morning." Although her father had cautioned his daughters about blaming someone without proof, one name stood out in Louisa's mind. "Nancy might have written it. She's made no secret of blaming me for Will's death."

"Unjustly." The way Josh turned his gaze to the far wall told

Louisa he was debating what to say next. "I didn't want to tell you this, but Caroline heard her disparaging you to some ladies in the mercantile yesterday."

And neither Caroline nor Josh had told Louisa. She couldn't fault her friends' desire to protect her, even though the truth would become apparent at some point.

"I'm not surprised. Nancy's grief over Will is still fresh. So is mine." Louisa knew she'd never forget the sight of his broken neck and the knowledge that none of her training could have helped him. "I know it's not the same grief their mothers are feeling, but I wish I could have saved both him and little Clive." When Josh raised a brow, she explained, "That's the name Gertrude gave her baby. All along she's insisted it would be a boy, and she was right."

After a moment of silence, Josh spoke again. "Death is part of being a doctor or midwife, just as birth and healing are. You must have known that when you decided to become a healer."

"I did. Both Austin and Thea warned me, but it's harder than I'd expected. Maybe I should give up." The anger the anonymous note had provoked had faded, replaced by sorrow that someone felt so strongly that she shouldn't try to be a healer.

This time there was no hesitation before Josh replied. "You'll regret it for the rest of your life if you do. You're not a quitter, Louisa. You're a strong, determined woman. You can't let some coward chase you away." He slid off the desk and extended a hand to her. "Close the office for the rest of the day. We'll start by going to Ma's for lunch, because I doubt you've eaten all day."

"I haven't."

"Everything seems better when you have a full stomach."

"What about Porter's?" Afternoons were busy times there.

"Mrs. Sanders will handle it."

"All right." Louisa took his hand and rose from the chair.

To her surprise, lunch helped lift her spirits from the doldrums. Josh had been right. Eating a bowl of stew and two of Mrs. Tabor's biscuits made her feel better, and the dried apple pie he'd insisted she order was so delicious she'd almost asked for a second piece. By the time she'd swallowed the last bite, she was feeling better. The credit went to Josh. His careful assessment of the situation had helped her accept what had happened and realize that it wasn't her fault.

"Be sure you know who he really is." Emily's warning echoed through Louisa's brain. With each day, she knew Josh better. He was kind. He was caring. He made her feel as if she'd succeeded, not failed. Just being with him buoyed her through bad times and let her dream again.

Even though the circumstances had been difficult, the day Louisa had met Josh had been one of the best in her life. Looking back, she realized it had been a turning point. If it hadn't been for his injuries, she wouldn't have stayed in Sweetwater Crossing, and if she hadn't stayed, she wouldn't have restored her relationship with Emily, nor would she have been able to help Alice and Opal. Most of all, she wouldn't have gotten to know Josh.

Was this love? Louisa wasn't sure. All she knew was that she cared for him and that the times they spent together were the best part of her days.

"I'm sorry we missed our walk last night." Raymond bent his arm, waiting for Louisa to put her hand on it when they reached the bottom of the porch steps.

Clouds had rolled in this afternoon, and the air was heavy with moisture, but Louisa had not wanted to disappoint Raymond a second time, and so she'd agreed to an evening stroll.

"I was exhausted." Both physically and emotionally. "It was a difficult day."

Raymond nodded as if he understood. "I heard what happened to Mrs. Neville's baby. It must have been hard for you."

"It was." It was also something Louisa did not want to discuss with Raymond or anyone else. Thanks to Josh, her determination to serve Sweetwater Crossing's residents had been renewed. There was no reason to relive the hours she had spent with Gertrude.

"My mother would probably tell me I'm out of line saying this, but Aunt Tina assured me a man should learn everything he can about the woman he plans to marry."

Louisa wasn't certain which surprised her more—that Raymond had discussed her with his aunt or that he'd so calmly announced his intention to marry her. While it was true that he'd made no secret of his desire for a formal courtship, wanting and planning were two very different things.

"It's too soon to be speaking of marriage," she said as calmly as she could.

"You're right. I'm sorry if I made you uncomfortable. That was not my intention." Raymond sounded abashed. "You must know that I care for you and that I hope you'll one day feel the same way about me. It's because I care that I worry about you. That's why I have to ask you whether you're certain that being a midwife is right for you."

Though she had asked herself the same question only yesterday, Louisa's hackles rose at the idea that someone else was questioning her calling.

"Yes, I am." She made her voice firm, hoping Raymond would understand that this was not up for discussion.

"Wouldn't it be better to devote yourself to your family? That's what most ladies do."

For a second, Louisa wondered whether Raymond had written the note she'd found under the door. The words were different, but the sentiment was the same. She dismissed the idea, realizing that unlike the author of the note, Raymond was not a coward. The fact that he'd openly challenged her proved that.

"I'm not most ladies, Raymond. I believe God intends me to be a healer, and that's what I plan to do."

Though Raymond's lips tightened, he nodded slowly. "I hope you'll change your mind, but even if you don't, my feelings for you won't change."

Chapter Thirty

Josh reached for the cane, wishing he could leave it behind but knowing Louisa would protest if he did. She was undoubtedly right, especially since they'd walked farther than normal last night. Now, he joined the other residents of Finley House as they left for church.

"It's the perfect day for our new minister's first sermon," Louisa said as they walked slowly along Creek.

The day was beautiful, the sun bright but not too hot, the breeze light enough that it didn't muss the ladies' hair. The week that had just passed had been far from perfect, but some good things had happened. Most importantly, Louisa seemed at peace after their time at Ma's. Josh hoped that would continue.

In addition, sales at the store had exceeded his most optimistic estimates, and the tearoom was filled every day. Some women had even reserved tables for a number of weeks in the future, saying they wanted tea at Porter's to become a weekly tradition. Both the shop and the tearoom were closed for the Lord's Day, giving everyone who worked there a chance to rest and rejoice. Josh intended to do both.

"It looks like most people agree with you about it being

a perfect day," Josh told Louisa. As they turned onto Center Street, he gestured toward the larger than usual number of people outside the church, proof of the new minister's appeal or at least their curiosity about him.

Louisa nodded. "Everyone I've talked to seemed excited about Pastor Lindstrom."

When her husband paused to explain something to Noah, Emily joined Josh and Louisa. "That's probably because he's permanent," she said, making it clear that she'd been listening to their conversation. "David was a wonderful minister, but we all knew he was only temporary."

"And now he's gone, taking Alice with him." Josh had seen how close Emily had been to her friend and imagined she missed her.

The first few weeks after he'd left New York had been lonely ones for him. Despite the undeniable excitement of meeting new people and searching for foods to feature in the American Room, he'd missed Jed's companionship. They didn't always agree, but they'd shared their thoughts and respected each other's opinions. Gradually, the loneliness had subsided, and once he'd arrived in Sweetwater Crossing, it had disappeared, replaced by the new friendships he'd forged here.

"I hated to see Alice leave," Emily admitted, "but Craig has promised we can visit them once school's out for the summer."

"Will you close the boardinghouse?" He'd be gone by then, but Josh wondered what would happen to Caroline if Finley House became a private residence again. He knew Mrs. Carmichael was considered part of the family, but Caroline was simply a boarder.

"No. Mrs. Carmichael said she'd prepare the meals, and Susan Johnson—she's one of Craig's best pupils—will clean the house and do the laundry to earn some extra money. She told me she wanted two new dresses, and her parents can only afford one."

"It sounds like everything's arranged."

Louisa chuckled. "That's my sister: organized Emily."

Conversation ceased as they entered the church and walked to the second pew from the front. The others took their seats first, leaving the spot by the center aisle for Josh in case he needed to stretch his leg during the service. It was the same place he'd occupied last week, a seat he appreciated not only because of the extra space but because Louisa was at his side. There was an unexpected pleasure in sharing a hymnal with her and observing her reaction to the sermon.

As Josh had predicted, by the time the first hymn was announced, every seat was filled, and the sense of anticipation was palpable. A collective sigh arose as Sweetwater Crossing's new minister walked to the pulpit. Physically, Harold Lindstrom could not have been more different from David Grant. Close to fifty years old, he was an almost painfully thin man with graying brown hair and brown eyes, rather than being young, blond, and blue-eyed. But when Pastor Lindstrom began to speak, Josh realized that both ministers shared an enthusiasm for the Word of God.

Basing his sermon on Psalm 100, Pastor Lindstrom encouraged his congregation to praise the Lord and give thanks for the many blessings he'd bestowed on them. The reminder was a welcome one, and Josh found himself keeping a mental count of the reasons he had to give thanks, one of which was that Louisa had begun to relax as the minister spoke. Perhaps the sermon would help her focus on what was good in her life, not the loss of Gertrude's baby and Nancy McIntyre's pettiness.

The respite was short-lived. Josh and Louisa were among the last to leave the sanctuary, because Emily and Craig had remained to congratulate the minister, and Louisa had wanted to add her own thanks. When they descended the steps into the bright sunshine, Josh saw a dozen women standing near Nancy.

"I'm sure you've all heard what happened to Gertrude Neville's baby," Nancy said, her voice pitched to reach far beyond the cluster of women. "It's such a shame. A needless tragedy." Her voice rose again. "Mark my words. That child would be alive if Gertrude had had a real midwife. Louisa Vaughn killed him just like she did my son."

Josh heard Louisa's intake of breath and turned to give her a reassuring look, but she was staring at the woman who was spouting poison. Someone needed to stop Nancy, and it was apparent none of the women who listened so intently would do that.

"Two deaths in one week. Who will be next?" Nancy demanded.

The anger Josh tried to tamp down began to reassert itself. Hadn't this woman listened to the sermon? She should be giving thanks that Louisa was here to fill the gap that the death of Sweetwater Crossing's previous doctor had created. She should be giving thanks that Gertrude was still alive and that the Gleasons had a healthy son because of Louisa's skill.

Before he could speak, a woman he recognized as Mrs. Colter did. "My husband says women ain't fit to be doctors. I think Farnham Senior's right. If something happens to Farnham Junior, I wun't take my boy to her."

"You're right, Millie." Nancy gave the other woman an approving smile. "No one else should, either."

Josh's anger turned to fury, but when he took a step forward, intending to tell both women exactly what he thought of their opinions, Louisa laid a hand on his arm.

"If you were thinking of defending me, don't. It will only make it worse. Nothing will change Nancy's mind."

"But she's wrong, and she's convincing the others."

Though Josh saw the pain in Louisa's eyes, her voice was firm. "We can't stop her. Farnham Senior's the same way. My father used to say he was a good man but stubborn as a mule. When he makes up his mind, nothing changes it."

"I can be stubborn too."

She tightened her grip on his forearm. "Please, Josh, don't say anything. People have to form their own opinions. We can't stop them if they choose to rely on the wrong people."

Josh nodded slowly, knowing she was right but hating feeling powerless. He wanted to help Louisa. More than simply righting the wrong Nancy was sowing, he wanted to do everything he could to make Louisa's life happy. She was always helping others. Surely she deserved to be recognized for that and to have her dreams come true.

"Why don't you wait here?" she asked as she lifted her hand from his arm and looked at the group of women. "I need to talk to them."

And that was an extraordinarily brave thing for her to do when their anger and fear had been incited. But that was Louisa.

She wasn't like anyone Josh had met—strong but tender, caring, and loving, determined to think the best of everyone. He watched as she approached the women, her smile genuine as she spoke civilly to each of them. He couldn't have done that. He couldn't have put aside the ugly and unkind remarks. But Louisa had. And in that moment, Josh realized that what he felt for her was more than admiration. It was love.

Louisa was right. Love wasn't a fairy tale. She'd told him that it was what made an ordinary day special, that it tied people together and gave them strength. He hadn't believed her, but he'd been wrong, so very wrong.

The kiss they'd shared had been more than an impulsive act, more than a way to celebrate the result of their hard work. It had been more than a passing attraction to an extraordinary woman. Though he hadn't realized it at the time, it had been the culmination of feelings that had developed so gradually that he hadn't recognized them for what they were—not admiration and not respect, although he admired and respected Louisa. No, the kiss had been the manifestation of his deep and abiding love for the woman who'd changed his life in so many ways.

There was no question about it: Josh wanted Louisa to be part of his life. He wanted to build a future together, but how could he? His future was in New York with Winifred; Louisa's was here. Though she'd been discouraged this week and had questioned whether she should remain, she wasn't defeated. She would stay in Sweetwater Crossing, because it was both her past and her future.

If he asked her to marry him—and the idea was incredibly appealing—he'd be asking her to abandon her dreams, to put his desires ahead of hers.

Josh stared at the woman whose smile did not falter, even though the women around her were clearly berating her. Another woman might have fled or at least returned their criticism with some of her own. Not Louisa. That extraordinary woman stood her ground, refusing to cower, refusing to capitulate to their demands that she cease practicing medicine. That was her dream, and no one should take it from her, least of all Josh.

He couldn't—he wouldn't—ask Louisa to put her dream aside. That would be the act of a selfish man, not a loving one. And oh, how he loved her.

Chapter Thirty-One

Louisa took a deep breath, savoring the fresh air as she headed out of town, determined not to let yesterday's unpleasantness after church weigh on her. Both Josh and Emily had urged her to think about the good things in her life, and there were many, including being able to ride Zeus. He was the most responsive horse she'd ever encountered. While she wouldn't say he could read her mind, he reacted so quickly to her commands that it almost seemed he did.

"You're the best of horses," she said softly, smiling when Zeus pricked his ears as if he understood. "I'll miss you when you're gone."

Not being able to ride him was one of the many reasons Louisa was dreading the day Josh left Sweetwater Crossing. Her life would be so different without Josh, but she wouldn't dwell on that now. It was a beautiful day, and she'd take pleasure in what lay ahead of her this morning—a visit to the Ellis ranch to check on Charlotte, one of the women who'd engaged her services as a midwife.

Though the ranch was among the smallest in the area and Louisa had heard rumors that the Ellises were struggling to make ends meet, the house was well cared for, with brightly colored flowers blooming along the foundation. When Louisa had admired them on her first visit, Charlotte had explained that they were a small luxury she allowed herself.

Louisa was still smiling as she climbed the porch steps and knocked on the front door. Strangely, there was no answer. The other times, Charlotte had been waiting for her and had opened the door even before she knocked. Louisa checked her watch. As she'd thought, she had arrived at the designated time. She knocked again, and once again, there was no answer.

At last, the door swung open, and the expectant mother took a step onto the porch, her hands cupping her midsection in the protective gesture Louisa had seen other women employ. Charlotte's blond hair was neatly braided, her dress freshly pressed. Only her light blue eyes betrayed what appeared to be fear.

Instead of ushering Louisa indoors, Charlotte shook her head. "I'm sorry you rode all the way out here, but Mr. Ellis and I decided we don't need your services any longer. This baby is too important for us to risk what happened to poor Mrs. Neville."

The almost mechanical way Charlotte spoke made Louisa think she'd memorized the short speech, but nothing could dilute the shock she felt upon hearing it. When she'd been here last week, Charlotte had told her how grateful she was for Louisa's expertise. Now she was being dismissed.

She took a deep breath, trying to keep her voice calm. "You more than most women know that not every baby lives." Though she hated reminding Charlotte of her three previous miscarriages, a child's life was at stake, and Louisa had to do everything she could to ensure that it had the best chance at survival.

"That's why I won't let you harm this one. Mrs. Bentley said she would help me when my time came."

But Tina had no experience other than having given birth

more than ten years ago. If the delivery was normal, that might be enough, but if it was a difficult delivery . . . Louisa didn't want to consider what might happen.

"I wish you would change your mind. I'm concerned there might be complications."

Charlotte's eyes darkened, and her face flushed with anger. "You're just trying to scare me."

That was the last thing Louisa would do. "I'm trying to help you," she said, wishing she could assure the young woman that her labor and delivery would be easy, but knowing she could not. "Deliveries can be difficult for a woman as small as you." Charlotte was slender and only five feet tall, and from what Louisa could tell, the baby was larger than most.

The look Charlotte gave Louisa was scornful. "Nancy told me I have good hips, so it won't be a problem. Besides, women have been giving birth without midwives for a long time."

And more women and babies died than should have. As much as Louisa wanted to persuade her patient to reconsider her decision, she wouldn't fuel fear. "If you change your mind, I'm still willing to be your midwife."

"I won't change my mind, so you'd best leave." Charlotte's voice was as firm as steel. "Maybe someone else will trust you, but I don't. Nancy warned me, and I trust her more than I do you."

The words reverberated through Louisa's mind for the rest of the day. Trust. It was a matter of trust, and what she'd established had been destroyed.

Dear Lord, what do I do now?

There was no answer.

Josh settled behind the desk in what had once been his bedchamber and brought out a piece of paper and a pen. It was time to tell Winifred what had changed.

Everything.

Though he didn't want to hurt her—after all, she was the woman he'd once planned to marry, the woman who'd once seemed to be an ideal companion for the rest of his life—he now knew that marriage would have been a mistake for both of them. Even though his future with Louisa was unclear, one thing was clear: he would not settle for second best.

He'd believed that love was nothing more than a fairy tale; now he knew that it was real. Not only was it real, it was what made life worth living. Louisa had been right about that, as she had been about so many other things.

Dear Winifred,

There is no easy way to say this, but I find myself in the position of realizing that I am not the man you should marry.

Perhaps that was too blunt a beginning, but Josh didn't want to waste time on trivialities.

You are one of the most admirable women I've ever met, and you deserve a man who can give you everything you deserve, including love. I am not that man.

Please be assured that I wish only the best for you.

Sincerely,
Joshua Porter

He frowned as he reread the letter. It was hardly eloquent, but he was not an eloquent man. All he could do was hope that Winifred understood and that she found a more suitable husband.

Josh slid the letter into an envelope, grabbed his hat, and headed for the post office. If he hadn't been so determined to ensure that the letter went out in today's mail, he would have waited for Louisa to return to her office, but now that he'd made his decision, Josh would allow no delays.

"Mornin', Mr. Porter." Jake Winslow's greeting was as cheerful as ever. Though the man whose hair was almost as black as ink and whose brown eyes were so dark that Josh had once mistaken them for black would never be considered handsome, the postmaster's ever-present smile more than made up for less-than-perfect features.

"Another letter to mail?" When Josh nodded, Jake's grin widened. "I'm glad you stopped in today, cuz you've got a letter waitin'." He turned to pull an envelope from one of the slots. "If I ain't mistaken, this one smells like perfume. Reckon you've got a lady friend back in New York."

Only one woman in New York knew where Josh was. How ironic that after all the weeks of waiting to hear from Winifred, her letter arrived the day he was about to mail what would be his final one to her.

After sliding the missive he'd penned into his coat pocket, Josh accepted the letter from the postmaster and opened it. Normally, he would have taken it back to Finley House to read, but he wanted to see what Winifred had written before he mailed his letter to her.

The message was even shorter than his.

Dear Joshua,

My father has decided that Nicholas Barton would be a more suitable husband for me, and I agree. We will be wed before you return to New York.

Josh laughed aloud as relief flooded his veins. He'd met Nicholas Barton on several occasions and agreed with Winifred's father's assessment. As heir to a prosperous railroad, Barton brought more to the marriage than Josh could. Even more importantly, Barton and Winifred had similar opinions. They might not be in love, but their marriage would be a peaceful one.

What wonderful news! What perfect timing!

"You gonna mail your letter?" Jake asked.

"Nope. There's no longer any need."

The chicken and dumplings Emily served for supper were as delicious as ever, but they might as well have been cardboard for all the pleasure they gave Louisa. Try though she might, she was unable to erase the feeling of failure that Charlotte's dismissal had created. Even though she told herself she'd done all she could and that no one could have saved Gertrude's baby, she hated that other lives were in danger because of one premature birth. And so, though Louisa did her best to act as if this had been a normal day, she suspected she was falling short.

"Was it another good day at Porter's?" Emily directed her question to Caroline and Josh.

"Yes." Caroline was the first to answer. "The tearoom has been full ever since we opened. I know that might change as the novelty wears off, but today several women told me they plan to bring their daughters for tea once school is out for the summer. They want them to learn how high tea is served."

Louisa smiled, grateful someone had good news. "Have you thought about offering etiquette lessons?" Craig's and Josh's raised eyebrows told her she needed to explain. "When Gertrude was the schoolmarm, she used to teach etiquette, but I suspect you haven't made it part of your curriculum, have you, Craig?"

His lips twisting into a wry smile, Craig shook his head. "You're right. I haven't. To be honest, I wouldn't know where to start."

"Caroline may be too modest to tell you, but she knows everything there is to know about etiquette." Louisa welcomed the chance to praise her friend. "She was the star pupil for that part of our classes. She could easily teach young boys and girls what she learned."

Though Caroline's eyes sparkled, Louisa saw hesitation cross her face as she turned to Josh, who was helping himself to a second serving of dumplings. "What do you think?"

"I like the idea. My grandfather always said our goal should be to meet our customers' needs, and this sounds like a good way to do that." He gave Louisa a smile so full of approval that it warmed her heart. "Thanks for suggesting it. Etiquette lessons will make Porter's an even better place."

Beulah, who'd been silent but listening intently, spoke for the first time. "I want to learn etty—" She paused, searching for the rest of the word.

"Et-tea-ket," Louisa prompted her.

"Et-tea-ket." The girl beamed with pleasure when Louisa nodded in approval.

"You'll be part of the first class," Josh assured her.

As Beulah grinned, Louisa addressed Josh. "How were sales in the store?"

"Good, although we ran out of marmalade. When I suggested the customer buy peach jam at the mercantile as a substitute, she said the price was too high. I hadn't realized Adam was raising prices."

Emily shrugged. "I'm afraid he sees you as competition."

"If that's true, raising prices makes no sense." Louisa didn't claim to be an expert in salesmanship, but logic told her Adam Bentley's approach was wrong. "If he wants to keep his customers, he should sell the same quality merchandise you do but at lower prices."

Mrs. Carmichael finished buttering a roll, then placed it carefully on her plate before she spoke. "I agree, but Adam Bentley isn't always sensible. Buying that farm just so Tina didn't have to look at the doctor's office seemed frivolous to me."

Louisa disagreed. "She's happier on the farm than she was living in town, because there are no memories of Tillie out there."

"I still think it was a foolish move. No matter what you do, you can't escape your memories."

Her discomfort with the direction the conversation had taken obvious, Emily turned to Louisa and asked the question she'd been dreading. "How was Charlotte Ellis today? Her baby's due soon, isn't it?"

"Yes, but I won't be delivering it."

"What?" Emily's shock was almost as great as Louisa's had been, and the way her sister tightened her grip on her water glass left no doubt that shock had turned to anger.

"She told me my services were no longer needed."

"That's preposterous." Josh made no effort to mask his disgust.

"I agree." Emily turned to Louisa, her face radiating both anger and concern. "Isn't there any way to change her mind?"

Louisa shook her head. "She was adamant. It seems everyone blames me for Gertrude's baby being stillborn."

"Not everyone. You said Gertrude and her husband don't blame you. Doesn't that matter?" Josh posed the question Louisa had asked herself so many times.

"Apparently not."

"Have you ever thought that Charlotte's decision might be a sign from God?"

Louisa looked up from the carrots she was peeling to see whether Tina was joking. When she'd accepted the invitation to supper, though Raymond had volunteered to drive her, Louisa had insisted on coming early to help Tina prepare the meal. Now she wondered whether she'd made a mistake, because Tina appeared perfectly serious.

"What kind of sign do you think it might be?"

Tina continued dicing potatoes, acting as if this were an ordinary conversation. "I think he's showing you that you're hankering after the wrong thing. The good Lord meant us ladies to marry and raise children. Even though he took my Tillie before her time, the years she walked this earth were the happiest of my life."

As tears welled in Tina's eyes, she laid down her knife and faced Louisa. "If your mama was here, she'd say the same thing. You should find yourself a good man and settle down with him."

Though Louisa did not share Tina's belief that her mother would have said that, she wouldn't contradict the older woman. "A woman can be a doctor or a midwife and still have a family of her own. Cimarron Creek's midwife has a husband and an adopted son. And I wouldn't be surprised to learn that she's expecting a baby."

Tina's pursed lips signaled that she wasn't convinced. "Maybe so, but are you certain that's the right life for you? I'm not saying this only because he's my boy, but Raymond would make you a fine husband. He's a fine man."

"Yes, he is."

Chapter Thirty-Two

Louisa drew the comb through her hair, wishing it were as easy to dismiss the sense of foreboding that hung over her like a dark cloud as it was to untangle the knots in her hair. There was no reason to feel the way she did, she told herself an hour later as she unlocked her office door, and yet the feeling remained.

It was a beautiful May morning, one that should have sent her spirits soaring. So too should the memories of what had happened yesterday. There'd been no unpleasantness after church. Instead, while not everyone spoke to her, those who had had been friendly. Sunday dinner had been particularly delicious, and the obvious love between Emily and Craig assured Louisa that her sister was happy.

As if that weren't enough, the afternoon stroll she and Raymond had taken had been enjoyable. More than enjoyable. It filled Louisa with a sense of anticipation, for the smile he gave her when he'd invited her to have supper with him at Ma's this evening showed such warmth that she'd caught her breath in surprise. She'd seen admiration before, but never this depth of emotion. That and his smile had told her he intended tonight to be a special one.

Though she'd been shocked by Tina's obvious matchmaking on Saturday, Louisa knew the older woman wanted only the best for her. And she was right. Raymond had much to offer—a comfortable life in Sweetwater Crossing and, if they were blessed, children. Raymond was a good man, a kind man, one who would do all that he could to make her happy. As Tina had said, he would be a fine husband.

As the word *husband* reverberated through her mind, Louisa pictured Josh and the way he'd looked when he'd kissed her. Was that the way a husband looked at his wife? In her memory, Josh's expression was similar to Craig's when he was with Emily, but memories were notoriously fallible. Though Josh had comforted, complimented, and supported her since that day, not once had he mentioned the word *love*, nor had he made any effort to repeat the kiss.

Of course he hadn't, for he was promised—or almost promised—to Winifred. That wonderful, unforgettable embrace they'd shared had been the result of excitement and gratitude. She and Josh were friends, partners in the establishment of Porter's, nothing more. Their time together was temporary, and though Louisa might wish otherwise, that was no reason to be downcast.

If Mama were still alive, she would have quoted Robert Browning, saying, "God's in his heaven, all's right with the world." But something wasn't right, and it was more than the fact that Josh would leave Sweetwater Crossing next month. The problem was, Louisa couldn't identify whatever was causing her malaise.

She pulled out the chair and settled behind her desk, waiting for the patients she doubted would come. Perhaps that was what was bothering her, the sense that being here was futile, that no one would trust her with their care. Even as the thought made its way through her brain, she knew that wasn't the cause of this morning's foreboding. Unless she heard otherwise from him, Louisa would continue to believe that God intended her to be a healer. Something else was wrong, but she had no idea what it might be.

She looked around the office, assuring herself that everything was where it should be, then glanced out the window. At the sight of a customer entering the mercantile, she rose and reached for her reticule. Emily had mentioned that Mrs. Carmichael's birthday was approaching. Rather than sit here and mull over what might or might not be happening, Louisa would spend a few minutes choosing a gift for the older woman.

"Good morning, Nancy," she called out as she opened the door to the mercantile. The other customer had left, and there was no sign of Adam. Instead, the woman who seemed to blame Louisa for everything that went wrong in Sweetwater Crossing stood behind the counter, her back to the door.

When Nancy turned, Louisa's heart plummeted at the sight of her visible distress. Nancy's eyes were red-rimmed, her face weighed down with sorrow.

"What's wrong?"

"It's Charlotte." Tears thickened Nancy's voice. "She's gone. Tina and I tried, but we couldn't stop the bleeding."

Gripping the edge of the counter as her knees buckled under the realization that what she'd feared had happened and that this was the reason she'd had such a sense of foreboding, Louisa managed to ask, "What about the baby?" Surely Tina and Nancy had been able to save it, even though the delivery had obviously been a difficult one.

Nancy shook her head. "The cord was wrapped around his neck. Tina said he was strangled."

Louisa felt as if a cord had been wrapped around her heart, squeezing the life from it. Poor Charlotte. A week ago, she'd been defiant; now she was dead, her husband alone. The magnitude of the tragedy made Louisa want to shriek with horror. Two lives lost. A husband bereft.

There was no way of knowing whether she could have saved them, but if Louisa had been there, perhaps the outcome would have been different. Perhaps her training and her experience with Opal Gleason would have ensured a successful delivery. Perhaps Charlotte could now have been holding a healthy boy in her arms. *Oh, Lord, why did this happen?*

"How is Mr. Ellis?" Louisa said a silent prayer for Charlotte's husband.

"Adam's with him. He thought he might need a man by his side." Seeming to realize she had a business to run, Nancy straightened her shoulders and took a step forward. "What were you looking for?"

It didn't matter. Nothing mattered but finding Josh and telling him what had happened. He'd understand; he'd help her sort out the thoughts that were even now clashing with each other inside her brain.

Something was wrong. Terribly wrong. Josh's heart ached as he glanced out the front window and saw Louisa approaching. It was the wrong time for her to be here. More than that, only something desperately wrong would make her shoulders slump. Though the store was crowded with customers, Josh had to go to her.

"I don't know when I'll be back," he told Mrs. Sanders, "but there's something I need to do."

The woman he'd come to regard as his right hand nodded. "Take your time. I can manage the store."

He grabbed his hat and hurried outside, wanting to intercept Louisa before she entered the store and was subjected to questioning looks from the customers.

"What's wrong?" he asked when he reached her. It was hardly a congenial greeting, but her posture indicated that she was not looking for a discussion of the weather or something equally trivial.

"Oh, Josh." The tears that welled in Louisa's eyes and her inability to say anything more told him the situation was worse than he'd thought.

"Let's go to the park." It wouldn't be the first time they'd cut through Porter's backyard to approach the small but attractive area where the town's residents came to relax and occasionally celebrate. Being there might help her cope with whatever was bothering her.

When they reached one of the benches beneath a spreading live oak, he waited until they were both seated before he spoke again. "Do you want to tell me what happened?" The anguish he'd seen on her face made him fear someone had hurt her again, perhaps by spreading lies or sliding another note under the office door.

She bit her lip, then said, "Yes. No. I don't know."

Though Josh wanted nothing more than to take Louisa in his arms and find a way to comfort her, he knew this was neither the time nor the place for that. He needed to wait until she was ready to speak, then search for the right words to assuage whatever hurt she'd sustained.

It seemed like an hour, but Josh knew it was only a few seconds before she nodded slowly. "Saying the words will make it seem real. Even though I wish with all my heart that it hadn't happened, I know it did." She paused again before adding, "I don't know whether I could have prevented it, but I would have tried."

Her pain was real, and yet Josh felt a sense of relief at the realization that whatever had caused her anguish hadn't been directed at her.

"Talking can be like lancing an infected wound," he told her. "It's painful at first, but that starts the healing."

To his amazement, Louisa gave him a weak smile. "I thought I was the doctor."

"You are," he assured her. No matter what had happened, he

wanted her to know that he had confidence in her abilities as a healer. "That's what my mother told me when the splinter in my finger became infected. She was right. Being poked with a needle hurt, but almost immediately after, I felt better because the infection was draining." Louisa had no physical wounds, but Josh knew that emotional ones could be even more painful.

"You're a wise man."

"I wouldn't say I'm wise. What I am is a man who cares about you and wants to help you. Will you trust me enough to tell me what happened?"

At the other side of the park, two men emerged from the livery, their raucous laughter proof that they were having a better day than Louisa.

She looked at him, the tears in her eyes threatening to tumble down her cheeks. When she spoke, her voice was bleak. "Charlotte Ellis and her baby died."

"Is she the patient who dismissed you last week?" Although the story had infuriated him, he hadn't recalled the woman's name.

"Yes." It was one word but so filled with pain that Josh knew how difficult simply saying that was for Louisa. "I wish she'd sent for me. In my heart, I believe I could have saved her and her baby, but I wasn't given the chance." She brushed a tear from the corner of her eye and shook her head, as if trying to prevent others from falling.

"It's all right to cry."

"I don't want to cry. I want to scream with anger, because this should have been different. I tried to warn Charlotte, but she wouldn't listen, and now it's too late. Oh, Josh, this shouldn't have happened."

His heart aching over the anguish he heard in Louisa's voice, Josh wrapped an arm around her shoulders and drew her closer to him. He'd told himself he wouldn't subject her to possible criticism by providing physical comfort in a public place, but that no longer seemed important. What was important was helping Louisa in every way he could.

"It's true that it shouldn't have happened, but you can't blame yourself. We all make choices and have to bear the consequences of them. Charlotte made hers."

"And it cost her her life." A sob that might have been sorrow or frustration or perhaps both accompanied Louisa's words.

"That's true." Josh hoped what he planned to say next would provide at least a small measure of comfort. "But who knows what other consequences there may have been? Perhaps what happened to Charlotte will keep another woman from making the same mistake. Doesn't the Bible say that God can turn all things to good?"

Another weak smile accompanied Louisa's nod. "Romans 8:28. I know it's true, but my heart still aches."

"Because you're not only a healer, you care deeply about others—your family, your friends, your patients, even those who've been unkind to you."

Josh squeezed Louisa's shoulders, wanting her to know how much he admired her, how much he wanted to help her regain confidence in herself. For, even though she hadn't said it, the fact that Charlotte hadn't trusted her had made Louisa doubt her abilities.

"That's all part of you, and it's what makes you so special."

Special. Louisa frowned as she fastened the last button on the dark green dress she'd chosen for tonight. She did not feel special. Instead, she felt as if her heart had been carved out of her chest, leaving an empty spot that nothing—neither Josh's attempts to comfort her nor Emily's assurance that the pain would recede—could fill.

When she'd returned from the park, Louisa had tried reading the Bible, seeking the peace she normally found in it, but it had opened to the eleventh chapter of Luke. She'd cringed as she'd read how both Mary and Martha had told Jesus that if he'd been there, their brother would not have died. Even though she knew the rest of the story and that Jesus raised Lazarus from the dead, all she could picture was Mary and Martha's grief over their brother's death. Charlotte wasn't Louisa's sibling, but the grief Louisa felt was real.

She turned slowly, ensuring that the skirt draped properly. The fact that this was one of her most flattering dresses did nothing to boost her spirits. She was in what Mama would have called the doldrums, a place where things like pretty dresses provided no comfort. If she'd been thinking clearly this afternoon, she would have asked Raymond to postpone their supper, but it was too late now. He'd be here in five minutes. Taking a deep breath and praying for peace to settle over her, Louisa descended the staircase.

"You look more beautiful than ever," Raymond said when she opened the door for him. "I'll be the envy of every man in Sweetwater Crossing tonight."

"Thank you." The tinted face powder Mama used to wear had hidden the blotches her crying had caused, and the smile Louisa forced onto her face must have looked convincing, because Raymond returned it, his own smile almost a grin.

"You look especially fine tonight," she told him. Freshly shaven, dressed in his Sunday suit, and sporting a tie she'd never seen before, he was clearly ready for a special occasion.

Special. There it was again, but in a different context. Louisa could only hope she did nothing to spoil the evening for Raymond.

"If I look fine, it must be because you're with me," he said, bending his arm so she could place her hand on the crook of his elbow.

They walked slowly toward the center of town, talking about nothing in particular, a fact for which Louisa gave thanks. If

Raymond had heard what happened to Charlotte and her baby, he gave no sign of it. Tonight would indeed be special if it provided a respite from the grief and guilt that had plagued Louisa all day.

"Good evening." Mrs. Tabor gave them both warm smiles as she led them to a table.

When Raymond pulled out her chair in a gentlemanly gesture, Louisa noticed the speculative looks other diners were sending their way. Undoubtedly, by tomorrow morning, half of Sweetwater Crossing would know that they had been here.

"Tonight's choices are ham with scalloped potatoes or fried chicken with mashed potatoes," Mrs. Tabor told them. "Both come with green beans and rolls."

Louisa considered the options, then shook her head. "They both sound delicious. I can't decide which I'd prefer."

"I agree. It's a difficult choice." Raymond winked at Louisa, then turned to their hostess. "Could you give us each a half serving of both of them?"

Though she looked taken aback for a second, Mrs. Tabor nodded. "Certainly."

When the restauranteur had left, Louisa felt the tension that had been a constant companion since the morning begin to recede. "I doubt she's ever done that before," she told Raymond, "but it was an excellent idea. Thank you for thinking of it. It was the perfect solution to my dilemma."

"Our dilemma," he corrected her. "By now you should realize that I'll do anything I can to make you happy." He reached across the table to take her hand, seemingly heedless of the protocol he was breaking. "I was going to wait until we'd finished our meal, but I don't want to wait a minute longer."

Giving her hand a gentle squeeze, Raymond continued. "I love you, Louisa, and I hope you love me." Without waiting for a response, he raised her hand to his lips and pressed a kiss on her knuckles. "Will you marry me?"

She wasn't surprised by the question—after all, Tina had told her Raymond was smitten—but Louisa was surprised by her reaction. As she looked at the man who'd been nothing but kind to her, the man who was so earnest about his feelings for her, Louisa felt the same sense of foreboding that she'd had this morning, and she knew that marrying him would be the biggest mistake of her life.

If she married, her husband should be foremost in her thoughts, the one she turned to first, the one she wanted to share every moment of her life, both the joyful and the sorrowful times. This morning had proven that Raymond was not that man. She hadn't even thought of him when she'd heard the news about Charlotte and her baby. It had been Josh—only Josh—that she'd needed.

Tears sprang to her eyes at the knowledge that she would hurt Raymond, and yet Louisa knew there was only one answer she could give. He deserved a wife who would love him with all her heart.

"I'm sorry, Raymond, but I cannot."

Chapter Thirty-Three

Raymond stared at her, his shock apparent. "What do you mean?"

When he tightened his grip on her hand, Louisa pulled it away, hoping the other diners hadn't noticed the drama unfolding at this table. There was a reason most proposals took place in the privacy of the lady's home. That way, if she did not accept the offer, her suitor was spared public humiliation. But in his eagerness, Raymond had eschewed custom, and now others would witness Louisa's refusal.

"I can't marry you." She spoke softly, not wanting anyone to overhear her reply. It was bad enough that she was hurting Raymond. Pain filled his eyes and his lips turned down as she repeated her words. "I wish it were otherwise, but I'm not the right woman for you."

Mama had been correct when she'd told Louisa she would know when she'd found the man she was intended to love. The signs had been there from the beginning. It had simply taken Louisa a while to recognize them. And even though she knew that love did not always lead to marriage, she knew that marriage without true love would never satisfy her. It would be better to remain single.

Raymond continued to stare at her as if she were a stranger speaking a foreign language. "You can't mean that. I thought you cared for me." His voice was harsh, filled with disbelief.

"I do care for you. Very much. You're a wonderful man, but—"

Before she could complete the sentence, Raymond interrupted. "But I'm not rich like Porter."

How could he think that? How could he believe that money had any bearing on her decision? Didn't he know her at all? Perhaps he didn't. Perhaps, like Louisa, Raymond had mistaken the friendship they shared for something deeper.

"That's not it," she said firmly. "I don't need wealth. My family never had much money, but that didn't stop us from being happy." While it was true that she'd sometimes longed for the luxuries Phoebe's parents had lavished on her, Louisa knew how blessed she and her sisters had been to have parents who lavished love on them.

"Then what's the problem? Why won't you marry me?" Raymond's questions were plaintive, telling Louisa more clearly than his expression how deeply she'd hurt him.

"You deserve someone who can give you her whole heart."

"Why can't you do that?" Confusion mingled with pain as Raymond lowered his voice in a futile attempt to avoid attracting the attention of the other diners. "Does this have something to do with wanting to be a doctor? Aunt Tina doesn't agree, but I'd let you continue to be a midwife once we're married. Isn't that enough for you?"

He'd let her? Louisa bristled at the idea that she needed her husband's permission to use her God-given talents. If that was Raymond's view of a woman's role after marriage, Louisa was thankful she'd recognized how ill-suited they were. Emily's advice to be certain she knew a man before committing to a life with him echoed through Louisa's brain. She'd believed she knew Raymond, but it appeared she did not. Fortunately, she'd discovered that before she made a serious mistake.

"No, being a midwife is not enough. I want to do more than deliver babies."

The pain that colored Raymond's eyes turned to anger. "So you'll trade your chance for happiness for a dream that will never come true? I thought you were more sensible than that."

"I guess I'm not."

As Mrs. Tabor approached with their meals, Raymond waved her aside. "I'm not hungry anymore." He reached into his pocket and withdrew some coins, placing them on the table as he rose. Turning back to Louisa, he said, "You may think you know what you want, but you're wrong. Make no mistake, Louisa. You'll regret this."

Josh stared at the blank sheet of paper in front of him. It ought to be simple to begin drafting the proposal, but though he'd sat here for close to an hour, he'd yet to write a single word. He could blame it on his indecision over which idea to propose, but he knew that wasn't the reason his mind was filled with turbulent thoughts.

"You look like you could use a friend," Craig said as he took a seat on the opposite side of the desk. Now that Josh was able to climb the stairs, Finley House's library had been returned to its original function. "What's wrong?"

It was the question Josh had asked Louisa less than twelve hours ago.

"I'm concerned about Louisa," he told his friend. "This morning's news was hard on her." And though he'd done what he could to comfort her, he knew the grief would linger.

"That's understandable, but I imagine tonight will boost her spirits." Craig tipped his head to one side as he often did when he was thinking. "The way Raymond looked when he came for Louisa reminded me of the day I asked my first wife to marry me. Even though I knew she loved me, I was as nervous as a schoolboy."

Marriage. The supper that had tasted so delicious only minutes ago curdled in Josh's stomach. "You think that's what he's doing?" He shouldn't have been surprised after the way Raymond had confronted him a couple weeks ago, but Josh hadn't expected the man to move this quickly.

A short nod was Craig's answer. "I'm not a betting man, but if I were, I'd say it was a sure bet." He narrowed his eyes as he rested his arms on the desk. "He'll make her a good husband. Not as good as you, but she'll have what she wants—a home close to Emily and, once she returns, Joanna. From what Emily has told me, the three of them always expected to stay together."

Craig was right. Though he loved Louisa, a life in Sweetwater Crossing was something Josh couldn't offer her, not unless he was willing to forget his promise to his father and abandon his future at P&S. He'd told himself he wouldn't ask Louisa to give up her dreams. The question was, would he give up his own? That was a moot point if Louisa married Raymond.

"Family's important." Josh understood Louisa's desire to be near her sisters, especially since their parents were gone. "I learned that at an early age." Even though he and Jed were rivals now, Josh still considered him a friend as well as a cousin, the closest thing he had to a brother. Nothing would destroy that. If Grandfather decided Jed was the one to take over the helm, Josh would be disappointed—deeply disappointed—but he wouldn't leave the company. He couldn't abandon his family's legacy.

"Then you'll be happy for Louisa?" Craig's question was infused with doubt.

"Of course." When Craig lifted an eyebrow, Josh nodded. "Of course," he said, uncertain whether he was trying to convince his friend or himself.

Before Craig could challenge him, Josh heard the front door open. Surely it was too soon for Louisa and Raymond to have returned from the restaurant, particularly if the evening included a declaration of love and proposal of marriage. Surely there would have been excited voices and two sets of footsteps as Raymond came inside to receive everyone's congratulations. But the only sound Josh heard was a single set of heels clicking on the floor, followed by Emily's rushing out of the parlor.

"You're back early. What's wrong?" Emily asked. It was the question of the day.

"I told Raymond I couldn't marry him."

Perhaps it was wrong, especially when he heard the anguish in Louisa's voice, but Josh was unable to control the surge of happiness that filled him.

Louisa opened the jar of meadowsweet to check the contents. Satisfied that she did not need to reorder it, she moved to the next bottle on the shelf. Though she'd taken inventory only a week ago, she needed something to occupy her mind this morning, something other than memories of refusing Raymond's offer of marriage. It had been the right decision—she had no doubt of that—but she hated having caused him so much pain.

She was a healer, someone whose mission was to alleviate pain, and while her primary focus was on physical ailments, she knew that emotional wounds could be equally dangerous. Though Tina had suffered no visible injuries when her daughter died, her spirit had been damaged. That was why she'd sworn she would have nothing to do with doctors, why she'd insisted on moving out of town so that she did not have to look at the building where Doc Sheridan had failed to save Tillie's life.

Louisa doubted that the pain she'd inflicted on Raymond had been that severe, but there was no denying that she'd wounded him, even though she'd done it to save him deeper anguish in the future. If only there had been a way to avoid hurting him.

Lost in her thoughts, Louisa was startled when the front door banged against the wall and heavy footsteps echoed through the hallway.

"Tell me it's not true!" Tina burst into the office, her face reddened with exertion.

For a second, Louisa was so shocked that Tina had entered the building where Tillie died that she was speechless. She took a shallow breath before asking, "What is it you want me to deny?" Even though she suspected she knew the answer, Louisa did not want to make any assumptions.

"That you refused Raymond's proposal."

She'd been right. Tina was upset that her attempts at match-making had failed. "I did." Louisa wouldn't add that it had been difficult to give him that answer or that she knew it was the right decision. Neither would satisfy the woman who was staring at her as if she'd suddenly sprouted horns.

"I never thought you were a fool, but I can see that I was wrong." Tina pressed her hand to her chest, as if trying to slow her heart's pounding. "Raymond offered you everything a woman needs—a home, a chance for a family, a comfortable life. What else did you want? Surely you're not still holding on to the hope that the town will accept you as a doctor."

When Louisa did not respond, Tina continued. "If you are, you're even more foolish than I thought."

Nothing she could say would satisfy the distraught woman, and so Louisa simply shrugged. "I did what I had to."

"You fool!" Tina practically spat the words. "I'm glad your parents aren't alive to see this. As it is, I daresay they're turning over in their graves."

She spun on her heel and stormed out of the building, leaving Louisa no doubt that the friendship she and the older woman had cultivated was another casualty of her decision.

"Would you like to go for a ride before supper?"

Though he didn't normally leave the store this early, Josh was waiting on the front porch when Louisa returned home that afternoon. It had been a quiet day once Tina left. A few women had come into the office with minor complaints, but if they'd heard that wedding bells would not be ringing for her anytime soon, they gave no indication of it. She'd tried not to dwell on the consequences of refusing Raymond, but knowledge of the pain she'd caused clung to her like morning mist to the grass. Josh's suggestion might be what she needed, a figurative sun to evaporate the mist.

"That's a wonderful idea." When they'd saddled and mounted their horses, she suggested they head east. There'd be little chance of encountering either Tina or Raymond if they went that direction.

"It feels good to be on Zeus again," Josh said as they left Sweetwater Crossing.

"He and Horace are friends." Louisa leaned forward to pat her father's horse's neck. Even though it had been months since Father's death and she'd become the person who rode him regularly, she still thought of Horace as her father's horse. "I'm afraid he'll be lonely once you take Zeus back to New York." Just as she'd be lonely without Josh's company to brighten her days.

"I can't promise to bring Zeus with me, but I'm planning to return. No matter what Grandfather decides, I want to introduce Richard to Sweetwater Crossing and show him what we've done with Porter's." Richard, Louisa remembered, was the assistant Josh had said would probably manage Porter's once he left.

Though her heart swelled at his use of "we," one question hung over her almost as heavily as the pain she'd caused both

Raymond and Tina by refusing his proposal. "What if your grandfather prefers Jed's idea? I can't imagine anything being better than a way to bring P&S to new parts of the country, but you said he's conservative."

Wrinkling his nose, Josh nodded. "Stuck in his ways. At least that's how it seems most of the time. That's why I'm not sure I'm going to tell him about Porter's."

Josh paused, his expression making Louisa wonder whether he was seeing the beauty of the rolling hills, the lush green of the grass that lined the road, and the brilliant blue sky or whether his thoughts were so heavy that he was oblivious to the magnificence of God's creation.

"I tried to write the proposal last night," Josh admitted, "but I felt stymied every time I picked up the pen. I'm starting to believe that the American Room would be a better idea for Grandfather, because it's a logical expansion of the current store without being too much of a change."

"Even though it's not the idea that excites you?" Louisa hated to think Josh would settle for less than the best. That no one should do that was a lesson she'd learned yesterday.

Josh slowed Zeus to a walk and turned to face Louisa, his expression somber. "You're right that it's not as exciting for me, but if it means that I get to sit behind that big desk, it would be worth it."

As confident as he tried to appear, Louisa suspected Josh was trying to convince himself. She also suspected that the American Room was not the right direction for him, even though he had not yet admitted that. "Have you prayed about it?"

"Many times, but I haven't heard an answer." A hint of frustration colored Josh's words.

"Maybe God's telling you to wait. You have more than a month before you leave for New York."

"True, but right now I'd rather talk about something more pleasant—like whether Zeus and Horace want to race to that tree." He pointed to a large oak whose branches formed a canopy over the road. "Shall we find out?"

Josh won, but it didn't matter. By the time she reached the tree, though several of her hairpins had come loose, Louisa felt better than she had all day. Being with Josh was what she'd needed.

Chapter Thirty-Four

Josh was unlocking the door to the store the next morning when Caroline emerged from the tearoom, her flour-spotted apron confirming that she'd been baking scones.

"Don't forget that you promised Louisa two jars of marmalade for Mrs. Wilcox," she called from the other side of the porch.

"Thanks. I did forget." Apparently, forgetfulness was part of the price he was paying for a night with little sleep. Each time he closed his eyes and tried to relax, snippets of his conversation with Louisa began bouncing through his mind. Which was the right proposal to give Grandfather? The man who'd run P&S for over fifty years had been adamant that no matter how many ideas appealed to them, he and Jed could each propose only one.

Despite Josh's prayers, there'd been no answer, just as there'd been no answer to what he'd do once he was back in New York with more than a thousand miles separating him from Louisa. His life would resume its familiar routine. The question was whether that would be enough to satisfy him. It was becoming more and more difficult to imagine life without Louisa, and yet he saw no way for both of them to realize their dreams and still be together.

He'd worry about that later. Right now, he owed Louisa some marmalade.

As soon as Mrs. Sanders arrived, Josh grabbed his hat and the bag with the jars, telling her he'd be back shortly. He'd almost reached Louisa's office when he heard a blood-curdling scream coming from inside. Louisa! Something was happening to her! Fear propelled Josh at a speed his leg protested, but he didn't care. All that mattered was saving Louisa from whatever was frightening her.

Josh flung the door open. "Louisa! What happened?" He raced in to find her standing on top of her desk, her face unnaturally pale, her eyes wide with fear as she continued to scream.

"What is it?" Josh had seen her upset, but never had he seen such sheer terror. What on earth could have upset normally calm Louisa so greatly?

"S-s-snake." Her hands shaking like a leaf in a windstorm, she pointed down at the floor. There, curled up in a patch of sunshine, was a young brown rat snake.

Josh breathed a sigh of relief that the serpent that had frightened her wasn't poisonous. He'd had no experiences with snakes in New York, but before he'd embarked on his journey, Josh had learned as much as he could about the wildlife he might encounter. Recognizing the difference between poisonous and harmless snakes could have made the difference between life and death.

"It's a rat snake. He won't hurt you." He kept his voice calm, hoping the tone would reassure Louisa as much as his actual words.

She shuddered, then covered her face with her hands. "It's a snake. I hate them. All of them. Take it out and kill it." Her voice trembled as much as her hands, leaving no doubt that she was not reassured.

Josh wouldn't tell her that, no matter how much the creature had frightened her, he wouldn't kill it. Instead he picked it up by the tail and strode to the back door. Once the snake was on the ground, it slithered away in search of another sunny spot.

"It's gone," Josh told Louisa when he returned. Though a bit of color had returned to her face and her hands shook less than before, she was still perched on the desk. "It was probably as scared as you."

Louisa shook her head vehemently. "That's impossible. I'm more afraid of snakes than anything other than bees. They can both kill me."

Josh knew that some snakes' bites could be lethal, and after her reaction to a bee sting when she was a child, it was no wonder she feared them. "You can't be comfortable there." He held out his arms. "Let's get you off that desk."

When she did not protest, Josh wrapped his arms around Louisa's waist and lowered her to the ground. Perhaps he should have released her as soon as her feet touched the floor, but he did not, for she was still trembling from the shock and fear. While she was in the grip of terror, he would do everything he could to comfort her, even though he was flouting convention by holding her so close.

"You're safe now," he told her. "As long as you keep your back door closed, it won't return."

Louisa tipped her head up and stared at him. "What do you mean, keep it closed? I always keep that door closed and locked."

Not today. "It was ajar. The opening was only a couple inches, but that was enough. Snakes can get through amazingly small spaces." Or so the book he'd read had claimed.

She shook her head, clearly confused. "How can that be? I didn't unlock it, and no one else has a key."

"Are you certain? Isn't it possible the Sheridans gave someone a key?" As far as Josh knew, Louisa hadn't changed the locks since she'd taken over the office.

"I suppose it's possible, but that means someone wanted to hurt me." As her legs started to buckle, Josh helped her into one of the chairs in front of the desk and took the other. Though he was no longer touching her, he wanted to be close enough to catch her if she collapsed or if she needed more comfort than mere words.

"The snake wouldn't have hurt you, and it wouldn't have frightened most people." Josh assumed that almost everyone who lived where snakes were common would easily identify poisonous ones. "Who knows you're scared of snakes?"

Louisa shrugged, as if the answer should be apparent. "This is a small town, Josh. Everyone knows everything. I doubt there are many who don't know that I'm deathly afraid of snakes and that I almost died from a bee sting."

"Then the question is, who would want to frighten you?" Whoever had let the snake into the office hadn't wanted to harm Louisa, merely to scare her.

"It could have been the same person who wrote that note. The message is the same. Someone wants me to stop being a doctor. When the note didn't convince me, the snake was supposed to make me afraid to be here."

"Who do you think that is? You thought Nancy wrote the note."

"I did, but it could also have been Farnham Senior. Recently, he's been more vocal about women not being qualified to be doctors." Louisa paused for a second before saying, "Or it could have been . . ."

When she didn't complete the sentence, Josh prompted her. "Who?"

"Raymond." The admission was clearly painful. "When I refused to marry him, he told me I'd regret it." Louisa closed her eyes for a second, perhaps remembering his anger. "My mother warned my sisters and me that people who were hurt and angry might do unpredictable things."

"You could be right." But Josh doubted it. While he could picture Nancy being vindictive, he couldn't imagine a man who loved Louisa wanting to hurt her like this. "Someone's sending you messages, and they seem to be escalating." Josh didn't want to consider what might be next. "What are you going to do about them?"

Louisa straightened her shoulders and lifted her head high. "Ignore them. I was angered by the note and terrified by the snake. You saw that. But I won't give in." The fear that had left her trembling was gone, replaced by steely determination. "You were right when you said only cowards would do things like this anonymously. I wish I knew who was responsible so I could confront them, but since I don't, my only recourse is to ignore the attempts to get me to stop being a doctor."

Pride filled Josh as her courage confirmed his opinion of her. "You're a strong woman, Louisa."

Those beautiful blue eyes began to cloud with doubt. "I don't feel strong. I feel as if I'm fighting against the wind. I take two steps forward; then I'm pushed back one."

"But you're still making progress. If you're only pushed back one, you're still ahead." When she didn't appear convinced, Josh continued. "Did you ever think that fighting against the wind could be good?"

Doubt changed to incredulity. "I can't imagine why unless it's because it makes me stronger."

"Not only that." Josh waited until he was certain he had Louisa's full attention before he said, "You've probably never seen seagulls."

As he'd expected, her expression mirrored confusion and curiosity. "You're right; I haven't. What do seagulls have to do with fighting the wind?"

"They don't appear to fight it. When they start to fly, they move into the wind. I can't explain why. All I know is that somehow the wind helps them, because that's how they become airborne. Perhaps it's like that day you told me about, when you thought you might fly."

For the first time since he'd entered the office, Louisa smiled. "So all that's happening might help me fly." Her smile turned into a grin as she pretended to flap her arms. "I'm afraid it won't work. I'm not a bird."

"True, but maybe all that fighting will help you do what you're supposed to do."

Louisa appeared to be weighing the suggestion. "One thing it's doing is strengthening my resolve," she said at last. "I won't let cowards drive me away. Until the town can find a new doctor, I'm going to do everything I can to keep people healthy."

That was Louisa. Strong. Resilient. Remarkable. Josh smiled at the woman whose determination inspired him. "That's my girl."

Chapter Thirty-Five

"You gotta help me!"

Louisa rushed out of her office and into the hallway at the sound of the woman's cry, alarm making her heart pound.

The four days since she'd found the snake had been uneventful, the tedium broken by the arrival of a few patients, but, mercifully, no unwanted creatures. That had helped calm her nerves. While she still inspected each corner of the office every morning when she entered it, despite having changed the locks on both doors, the terror she'd felt had subsided, perhaps because she'd told no one other than Josh—not even Emily—about the snake. Not wanting to relive those horrible moments was part of Louisa's resolution to ignore what had happened. But now it sounded as if another woman was experiencing the same kind of fear that she had. Fear and something more, perhaps desperation.

Though the hallway was darker than her office, having no natural light, Louisa had no trouble recognizing Millie Colter. Strands of the woman's light brown hair had escaped the tight bun, she was panting, and her face was flushed as if she'd run the block and a half from her home. What startled and alarmed

Louisa was that this was the woman whose husband had been outspoken in his disdain for lady doctors, the woman who'd announced to a group of women that she agreed with him. Whatever had brought Millie here must be extremely serious for her to have defied her husband.

Though her own pulse was racing, Louisa kept her voice calm as she addressed the distraught woman. "Why don't you come in and tell me how I can help you." Louisa gestured toward the room she'd just left, wanting Millie to sit and catch her breath. While it was possible that Millie herself needed medical assistance, Louisa's cursory examination revealed nothing more than a very worried woman.

"It's Farnham Junior." The words came out in short bursts. "He's burnin' up. I put cold compresses on him, but they weren't no good. Now he's seein' angels." Millie's face crumpled, and she began to sob. "Oh, Louisa, I'm scared. I don't wanna lose my boy."

"It sounds like a fever." Last night at supper Craig had mentioned that several children hadn't been as alert as usual and that he feared they might be on the verge of an illness.

"Why's he seein' angels?"

"A high fever can cause delirium." Louisa maintained a neutral tone in an attempt to calm the anxious mother. "It'll only take me a minute to get what I need." She pulled the jar of meadowsweet from the shelf and opened the lid, relaxing a bit when the whiff of an aroma similar to wintergreen confirmed that the herb was fresh. She'd checked her supplies last week, but Louisa was taking no chances with the boy's life.

"Can you save him?" Millie gripped the edge of the desk so tightly her knuckles whitened.

Though she doubted the boy was close to death and wanted to reassure his mother, Louisa knew better than to make promises until she'd examined her patient and determined the extent of the illness. "I'll do my best." She slid the jar of meadowsweet into her black bag. Only when she'd placed the "doctor is out" sign in the window and locked the door behind them did she speak again.

"Does your husband know you've called me?" No matter how angry the man might be, Louisa would not refuse to treat the boy, but she wanted to be prepared.

Millie shook her head. "I love Farnham Senior with all my heart, but sometimes he's a stubborn old coot who won't admit he's wrong." She brushed back the hair that had tumbled into her eyes. "I don't care what he says. I ain't gonna let my son die just because his father don't believe women should be doctors."

Blinking to keep the tears that had welled in her eyes from falling, Millie gave Louisa a long look. "I was wrong to tell Nancy and the others that you ain't a real doctor. I heered how you saved Alice Grant's daughter. You gotta do that for my son. I trust you."

Those final three words warmed Louisa's heart and strengthened her resolve. Today was proof that helping people in need was why God had brought her back to Sweetwater Crossing.

When they reached the Colter home, Louisa found Farnham Junior thrashing on his bed as he muttered "silver wings" and "angels." Though his eyes were open, he did not appear to recognize his mother. No wonder Millie was frantic. It took Louisa only seconds to confirm that the boy had a high fever and the rapid pulse that accompanied many fevers.

"What can you do?" Millie's question was little more than a wail.

"I have something that will help, but I need you to clean a teapot, boil a quart of water, and let it sit for two minutes. When you have it ready, call me." In the meantime, Louisa would stay with her patient, checking for symptoms his mother might have missed.

As soon as Millie had the water at the right temperature, Louisa opened the jar of meadowsweet and spooned the dried flowers into the teapot, infusing them in the hot water. Few looking at the creamy-colored flowers would suspect they had a potent therapeutic effect.

"What's that?" Though suspicion did not taint Millie's voice, Louisa knew she was concerned as well as curious.

"It's meadowsweet. It'll help lower Farnham Junior's fever."

"Doc Sheridan always used willow bark."

As did many physicians. "This tastes better. That makes it easier to convince patients to drink it." When he'd introduced her to meadowsweet, Austin had had Louisa sip both it and willow bark. There was no comparison. That was the reason she'd ordered it soon after she'd taken over Doc's office.

With Millie supporting her son's head, Louisa was able to get the boy to swallow almost a full cup. Exhausted, he fell back asleep, his limbs continuing to move restlessly.

"It ain't doin' no good." Millie's voice was heavy with discouragement. Like many, she expected immediate results from a medicine.

Louisa laid a hand on her shoulder, hoping the woman would take comfort from her touch. "We have to give it time. Meadowsweet and willow bark need a while to take effect."

Knowing Millie would not leave her son's side, Louisa asked her to bring two chairs into the bedroom. When they were both seated, she encouraged Millie to recount stories of Farnham Junior's childhood. As she'd hoped, that gave Millie something to think about other than her son's condition.

Half an hour later, the boy seemed slightly calmer. "Hold him up again," Louisa directed his mother. "It's time for him to drink some more meadowsweet."

They repeated the process every half hour, and with each dose of the infusion, the patient's condition improved. By midafternoon, his fever had broken, and though he was still very weak, Farnham Junior managed a smile when his mother clasped his hand between hers.

"Don't cry, Ma," he said as tears rolled down her cheeks.

"Them's happy tears," she assured him. When he fell back asleep, Millie rose and hugged Louisa. "Thank you. You saved my boy."

What a difference a week had made. Josh tried to control his grin as he emerged from the church. Last Sunday he'd seen the way Louisa had looked at the other parishioners, searching for a clue to who'd let the snake into her office. Today she was surrounded by smiling women, listening intently as Millie Colter extolled Louisa's medical skills.

"Even Farnham Senior agreed that Doc Sheridan wun't have done no better." Josh knew it was no coincidence that Mrs. Colter raised her voice as she made that announcement. "He ain't easy to convince, but that there's the proof." She pointed toward her son playing tag with three other boys.

"It looks like the town has finally realized what we've known from the beginning—that Louisa's a fine doctor." Craig joined Josh at the bottom of the steps, his smile leaving no doubt that he was almost as pleased by the change in public sentiment as Josh himself.

"My leg is proof of her abilities."

"But it took people who've lived here their whole lives to convince others." Left unsaid was the fact that opinions could change again. "Judging from the number of women talking to her, Louisa's going to have more patients than she knows what to do with."

"Which is nothing more than she deserves. I'm glad that her future is secure." At least for a while.

"What about yours?" Leave it to Craig to raise the question that continued to weigh on Josh.

"I'll know in a month." It was hard to believe that his time in Sweetwater Crossing was coming to an end. The last two and a half months had passed more quickly than he'd thought possible. Even more surprising was the way he'd gone from resenting the accident that had kept him here to enjoying the new challenges each day brought.

"Have you thought about staying?"

More times than he'd admit to anyone, but each time the thought had surfaced, he'd known there was only one answer. "I can't. I owe it to my father to be part of P&S."

"What about you? Is that what you want?"

"Yes. Of course it is."

Wasn't it?

Louisa smiled and increased her gait when she saw two women waiting outside her office, one with a small child clinging to her hand. Three days had passed since Millie Colter's show of support, and the difference was remarkable. While Raymond ignored her as if she were invisible and Tina had glared at her on Sunday, others were kinder, and each day brought Louisa more patients.

Not surprisingly, there'd been no men, confirming what Austin had told her, that men rarely sought medical care unless they were seriously ill. While the men stayed away, women had begun consulting her over small ailments they were experiencing and had brought children suffering from rashes, fevers, and sprains. Thankfully, there'd been nothing serious, but the confidence Sweetwater Crossing's women were displaying had turned this into the most exhilarating time of Louisa's life.

Each day she returned to Finley House tired but confident that she'd done her best. As much as she relished the fact that she was making a difference in people's lives, there was another advantage to being so busy: it kept her from counting the days until Josh left.

"I'll be with you in a minute," she told her waiting patients as she fished the key from her reticule. "Just let me open the examining room."

With a quick check for sleeping reptiles, Louisa crossed the room to open the shutters, then paused at the sight of the chair that was normally pushed all the way to the desk. Odd. It looked as if it had been moved.

Concerned that she'd had another intruder, she checked the back door. When she found it still locked and all the windows closed, she dismissed her concerns, telling herself she must have knocked the chair when she was leaving yesterday. It had been a particularly tiring day. Perhaps that had made her clumsy. There was no reason to be alarmed.

Fixing a small smile on her face, she approached the two women who'd taken seats on the bench in her entry hall.

"All right, ladies. Who was here first?"

The older one pointed to herself. "I was, but you should see Mrs. Fellowes first. Her daughter's been coughing."

And so another day began. As she examined Adele Fellowes's throat and prescribed cough medicine for her, Louisa gave a silent prayer of thanksgiving that God had brought her here and given her the ability to help others. This was where he intended her to be.

Chapter Thirty-Six

"When we were growing up, I could usually read your emotions." Emily handed Louisa the rose she'd just cut. "Now I'm not sure. At times you look happy. Other times you're sad. Are you sorry you refused Raymond?"

Careful not to prick her finger on the thorns, Louisa laid the fragrant flower in the basket. When Emily had suggested she join her in the garden, she suspected her sister wanted some private time, but she hadn't expected this.

"No," she said firmly. "It was the right thing to do. I'm sorry that I hurt him, but I know he'll recover." Louisa pointed to another rose, waiting until Emily had cut it before she continued. "What bothers me most is not seeing Tina. I looked forward to my time with her, and I thought she genuinely cared about me. Now I feel as if she viewed me as nothing more than a wife for her nephew. She wouldn't even let me explain why we wouldn't have been happy together."

"But you were right. You wouldn't have been happy together. Raymond doesn't make you glow the way Josh does." Emily propped one hand on her hip as she focused her attention on Louisa. "What will you say when he asks you to marry him?"

Though her sister sounded confident that he would, Louisa wasn't as sure. "I don't believe he will. He's practically engaged to Winifred, and even if he weren't, our futures are in different places."

"You've said that before, but I'm not as convinced as you seem to be. You could be a doctor in New York." That was Emily, asserting her role as the oldest daughter to solve her younger sisters' problems. It might have worked when they were children, but today her words fell flat.

"Porter wives aren't doctors or midwives. They're part of society." Louisa frowned at the images her words conjured. "I wouldn't fit into Josh's life in New York. I can't imagine myself hosting parties the way his mother did."

"But you're not his mother. You're a woman who can do anything she sets her mind to."

Once again, Emily had more confidence than Louisa. "How can you say that when you know I've failed at so many things? I wanted to be able to cook like you and Mama, but the best anyone can say about my meals is that they're edible. I wanted to play the piano like Joanna, but I didn't get far past scales and five-finger exercises."

Emily laid her shears down and faced Louisa. "That's because you were trying to discover the talents that only you have. Once you found that wounded bird and tried to fix its broken wing, your path was clear."

Unlike the rabbit that had hopped away before Louisa could set its leg, the mockingbird had been unable to fly. It had, however, pecked at her hand when she tried to splint its wing. She'd been only moderately successful, but after a few days, the bird managed to fly to a nearby tree, never to be seen again. Louisa had been so excited that she'd barely eaten supper that day, waiting for the perfect opportunity to tell her family that she was going to be a doctor.

"Our parents didn't agree. They did everything they could

to discourage me." The memory of how often they'd urged her to cultivate more womanly skills like cooking and embroidery still hurt.

As if she sensed the pain that had yet to fade, Emily wrapped her arms around Louisa. "They knew how difficult it would be, and they wanted to spare you disappointment and heartache if you didn't succeed. They were protecting you."

Louisa weighed her sister's words, trying to view the past from her perspective. "I wish they'd told me that's what they were doing. It might have made life easier."

"But you persevered despite their efforts, and you're stronger because of it."

Louisa smiled, remembering Josh's story of seagulls flying against the wind. "You're right. I am stronger now, and I've found my purpose in life: to be a healer in Sweetwater Crossing. Even if the town can find a fully trained doctor, I want to stay here, possibly as his assistant, maybe as a full-time midwife. The one thing I'm sure of is that my future is here."

Emily lowered her arms and gave Louisa an appraising look. "Even though you love Josh? And before you try, don't deny it. I'm not blind."

"I won't deny it. I do love Josh and I hate the thought of a future without him, but I know that life in New York isn't right for me. For better or worse—and I think it's for better—this is my home. I'm not going to leave."

"Are you sure?"

"Yes."

Emily's smile turned so bright that it could have ignited a fire. "You've just made me the happiest woman in Sweetwater Crossing."

"Because your pesky sister is staying?"

"Because my talented midwife sister is staying."

Louisa stared at Emily as the implication of her words registered. "Do you mean what I think you do?"

"Yes. I hope I'm not mistaken, but I believe I'm expecting a baby." Emily, the woman who never giggled, giggled with happiness. "I didn't want to tell you until you'd made your decision, because I didn't want to influence you, but I'm so glad you'll be here to deliver your first niece or nephew."

Louisa flung her arms around her sister as joy welled up inside her. "This is one more sign that I made the right decision."

Though she thought the excitement might have waned after a night's sleep, the next morning found Louisa still elated by Emily's announcement. As she straightened the office in the lull between patients, she tried to imagine how thrilled her sister must be. If Emily was right, and in her heart, Louisa believed she was, George had been wrong. Emily wasn't barren, for it was possible she'd conceived the first month she and Craig had been married.

If only Emily hadn't married George! If she hadn't, Louisa's sister would have been spared so much pain and anguish. Fortunately, as horrible as her first marriage had been, it was over, and as the Bible promised, God had turned a bad situation into a good one. Because George had left her penniless, Emily had been forced to return to Sweetwater Crossing. It hadn't been a happy homecoming, but there was a happy ending, for she'd met Craig, the love of her life, and a glorious future awaited them.

"Louisa."

As if Louisa's thoughts had conjured her, her sister's voice echoed through the hallway, and Emily rushed into the examining room, worry etching lines on her forehead. She was no longer the happy bride and expectant mother who'd cut roses with Louisa only a day ago.

"Are you having morning sickness?" Though Louisa had asked her about that yesterday, Emily had denied experiencing the most common symptom of the first few months of pregnancy.

"I wish I were. It's Noah. He's running a fever. It came on suddenly, and cold compresses aren't doing anything to help."

Fortunately, it didn't sound like Noah's fever was as serious as Farnham Junior's had been. "We'll give him meadowsweet."

Louisa pulled the jar from the shelf, sniffing the contents after she'd unscrewed the lid. That was odd. Trying not to frown and worry her sister, she poured a small quantity onto a sheet of paper.

It took only a cursory glance to confirm what she feared. There was no question about what had happened. The chair that had been askew hadn't been the result of Louisa's clumsiness. Somehow, someone had broken into the office and contaminated her medicine.

"Is something wrong?"

"Very." Louisa pointed to the tablespoon of what should have been pure meadowsweet. "Someone mixed digitalis with this. See the green powder? That's digitalis. It's made by pounding foxglove leaves into a powder. The creamy flowers are meadowsweet."

The worry lines on Emily's face deepened. "What would have happened if Noah had drunk an infusion of this?"

Even though the truth would upset her sister, Louisa would not lie. "It could have made him sicker, possibly even killed him. Digitalis is used to treat the heart." The powerful medicine was designed to stimulate a sluggish heart, not be administered to a child with no cardiac problems.

Emily sank onto one of the chairs as if her legs would no longer support her. "I don't understand who would have mixed your medicines or why."

"I don't know the who, but I imagine this was intended to discredit me. Fevers are common, and after Millie Colter told everyone how meadowsweet helped Farnham Junior, other women have asked for it. If I had been less careful, Noah could have been very sick."

"But you are careful."

Louisa shuddered to think of what might have happened if she'd simply handed the jar to her sister. "I'm going to be even more careful starting right now." She gestured toward the cabinets. "I've already changed the locks on the outside doors, but that doesn't seem to be enough."

Louisa had no idea how someone could have entered her office, because she'd given no one other than Josh a key. When he'd offered to check the office occasionally to ensure that no snakes or other unwanted creatures had entered, she'd given him the spare key to the front door. "I'm going to put locks on these cabinets. Meanwhile, this is willow bark."

Louisa opened another jar and poured a small quantity into one of the envelopes she kept specifically for dispensing powdered medicines. "It won't taste as good as meadowsweet, but it will help reduce Noah's fever. I'll come home to check on him in an hour."

As soon as Emily left, Louisa locked the office behind her and crossed the street to the mercantile.

"How soon can you get me some locks?"

"C'mon, Zeus. It's time for a long ride." Josh settled the saddle onto his horse, grateful that he could once again ride comfortably. Tonight, more than ever, he needed a ride to calm his nerves.

When he'd returned from Porter's, he'd been disappointed to learn that Louisa had been called away by a woman who'd gone into labor and that she probably wouldn't be home until tomorrow morning. Disappointment had changed to alarm and anger when Emily recounted what had happened to the meadowsweet. Though she wasn't aware of the snake that had been planted in Louisa's office, Emily couldn't hide her concern. "Who would have done such an awful thing?" she demanded.

Josh wished he had the answer. Whoever it was was both persistent and willing to harm others as well as Louisa. That combination was dangerous. The escalation in the attacks—for that was the way he viewed them—worried Josh, making him wonder if whoever was behind them was totally sane.

"What do you think, Zeus?" he asked as he swung himself into the saddle. "Are we dealing with a crazy man?"

The horse snorted.

"That's what I thought too. So, what can we do about it? I have only a little more than two weeks before I leave for New York. Somehow, I need to find a way to protect Louisa."

This time Zeus was silent.

When he reached the corner of Center Street, Josh turned right, heading north. He couldn't explain why. When he'd saddled Zeus, he planned to go west, since Emily had said Louisa's patient lived that direction. If the baby arrived sooner than she'd expected, he might encounter her on the road and be able to accompany her back to Sweetwater Crossing. But, almost as of their own volition, his hands tugged the reins in a different direction.

"All right," he said to himself as much as to Zeus. "We'll go north." It was the first time he'd been on this road since the day Louisa had found him lying at its side.

Settling back in the saddle, Josh let Zeus set the pace. He had no destination in mind, and so there was no reason to rush. All he wanted was a chance to clear his mind.

But far from clearing, his mind was soon filled with whirling images. Instead of the lush green countryside of the Hill Country, he envisioned the crowded streets of Manhattan, the incessant clamor of chattering people surrounding him as he opened the front door of P&S the way he'd done so many times. Inside, the din lessened, but he was still bombarded with sound.

It was only when he entered the stairwell and began to climb to the top floor that his ears stopped ringing.

He took a deep breath, trying to cleanse the scent of too many different perfumes that had invaded his nostrils as he'd crossed the first floor. It must be worse than usual. Otherwise, he would have noticed how the various perfumes clashed.

Josh shook his head. "I'm the crazy one, Zeus. For a minute, I thought I was in New York."

He bent forward to touch the horse's neck, smiling when Zeus whinnied with pleasure. But as he sat back, the images resumed. He'd reached the door to Grandfather's office, a door that was normally closed but that now stood open. The big desk that had been Grandfather's for decades was still in the center of the room, but today its surface was clean. The pen and calendar that had been there for as long as Josh could recall were gone. So too were the pictures that had hung on the walls, the unfaded squares of wallpaper the only sign that the walls had once borne paintings and photographs. The room was waiting for Grandfather's successor to leave his mark.

"I'm ready, Father." Even though he was no longer addressing Zeus, Josh spoke aloud. "I did what you asked. The rest is up to Grandfather."

The horse was silent.

"What's the matter, boy? Don't you agree? I've done what the commandment says. I've honored my father—" He stopped in midsentence, remembering there was more to the commandment. *Honor thy father and thy mother.* Had he done that? Had he honored both of his parents?

"I'm not sure I have." Once again, Zeus remained silent, seemingly waiting for Josh to make sense of his thoughts. He'd spent his whole life trying to fulfill his father's wish, but what about his mother?

Unbidden, the memory of an afternoon walk he and his mother had taken in Central Park emerged from somewhere deep inside him. Josh had been twelve years old, convinced he was too old to be walking with his mother, but she'd been insistent that they spend the afternoon together. And so he'd gone, dragging his feet both literally and figuratively as they entered the park.

For a while, they'd said little to each other, occasionally commenting on their surroundings. But then the tenor of the conversation had changed.

"You're old enough to be thinking about love." The intensity of his mother's voice was etched on his brain. "If you remember nothing else that I tell you, remember that true love is more important than anything else in your life. It's like the glaze on a piece of fine porcelain. It protects the delicate painting and makes the colors shine more brightly."

Josh must have appeared unconvinced, because she'd continued. "You'll know it when you find it. There'll be no doubt."

"Is that how you felt when you met Father?"

"Yes. My love for him was born that day, and it's never wavered, nor has his for me."

Josh stared at the countryside, his eyes registering the flight of a hawk overhead while his mind tried to arrange the fragments of his memories. They were like pieces from a broken plate, needing to be reassembled before he could see the whole design.

Why hadn't he recalled that day in the park until just now? Was he wrong in believing that the polite way his parents treated each other was because their marriage had been nothing more than a business arrangement? If his memory of the day in the park was accurate—and he believed it was—the love his parents shared had been true. It brought them both happiness.

What a fool he'd been!

Though he'd been trotting, Zeus stopped abruptly and tossed his head.

"Is something wrong?" Zeus never simply stopped. Had he

reacted to Josh's thoughts, or was there another reason he'd done something so unusual?

When the horse remained immobile, Josh looked around. That old oak looked familiar. So did the large prickly pear.

"This is where it happened, isn't it? This is where you threw me?"

When Zeus neighed, confirming Josh's thoughts, he dismounted and walked to the side of the road. Once again, memories flooded back. Attempting to stand but failing. Unable to quench his thirst. Fearing he would die. But he hadn't. Louisa had found him. She'd saved him.

A sense of rightness settled over him. What might have been the end of his life had become the beginning. Josh started to laugh at the realization that the Bible was right. All things did work for good. The laughter continued as he stared at the place where he'd drifted in and out of consciousness. At the time, he hadn't recognized its beauty. Now the prickly pear that had appeared ominous was covered with blossoms, their delicate yellow petals contrasting with the thorny pads. The oak's branches provided shade and seemed to beckon him to sit beneath them.

He stood there, his heart lighter than it had been in months, perhaps ever. Was this the way seagulls felt when they took flight—confident of the direction they'd taken? Josh would never know what it felt like to fly, but he now knew how it felt to be free of the past. The future that had once seemed cloudy was clear. He knew what he wanted. More importantly, he knew what he needed. Only one question remained: was Louisa willing to share that future with him?

As eager as he was to ask her, he wanted the timing to be perfect, the setting to be worthy of her. That meant he'd have to wait until tomorrow. Tomorrow evening as the sun set, he would ask Louisa to be his wife.

Chapter Thirty-Seven

Not again. Louisa frowned as she opened her office door and spotted a piece of paper on the floor. As much as she was tempted to ignore it, she couldn't. There was always the possibility that someone needed her and, since the problem hadn't been urgent, had left a note rather than looking for her at Finley House. It was also possible that this was like the first note she had received. If it was, it might hold a clue to who had threatened her.

Louisa unfolded the sheet of paper, her frown turning into a smile and happiness bubbling up inside her as she read. This was neither a threat nor a summons to a patient. It was something much better.

My dear Louisa,

I beg you to join me for luncheon today. I have many things to tell you.

Sincerely yours,
Tina

What she had hoped for had happened: Tina's anger had faded and she sought to resume their friendship. Louisa knew their relationship would never be the same as it had been before she refused Raymond's proposal and dashed Tina's hopes, but she was grateful for a second chance. She would close the office as soon as she finished checking her supply of medicines.

Nothing was missing. Nothing was out of place. Nothing was contaminated. Last night's delivery of a small but healthy baby boy had been successful, and now Louisa had a chance at reconciliation with the woman who'd been so kind to her. What a wonderful day!

Half an hour later, she hitched Horace to the post in front of Tina's home and climbed the porch steps.

"I'm glad you came." Her eyes bright with excitement, Tina ushered Louisa into the house and gestured toward the parlor. Though it was a weekday, she wore the dress she normally reserved for church, her attire telling Louisa this was a special occasion for her.

"Please sit down." When Louisa settled in the chair Tina had indicated, her hostess continued, "I'll be back in a couple minutes."

While she waited, Louisa sniffed, trying to guess what Tina was planning to serve for lunch. To her surprise, no aromas wafted from the kitchen. Perhaps Tina had arranged another cold collation.

"Thank you for inviting me," Louisa said when Tina took the chair across from her. "I've missed our time together."

"So have I." Tina pursed her lips as she slid her hand into her pocket. "You probably wondered why I invited you."

"You said lunch."

Tina shook her head. "We have things to discuss. I had such high hopes for you, but you disappointed me, Louisa."

"I know I did, but my decision was the right one for both Raymond and me."

Tina shook her head again, this time more violently. "You're wrong. At first I was angry, but then I realized you must have acted in haste. Your mother said you were often impulsive. That's why I decided to give you another chance."

The gaze Tina fixed on her made the hair on the back of Louisa's neck stand up. There was a gleam in her eyes that she'd never seen before, a glassiness that wasn't the result of a fever.

"Another chance at what?" Surely Tina didn't think she could persuade Louisa to change her mind. Louisa kept her voice calm, not wanting to ignite Tina's anger again.

"A chance to marry my son."

Her son? Tina had no sons, and yet she spoke as if she did and that Louisa should have known it.

"You and Raymond are meant to be together."

"Raymond is your nephew." Perhaps Louisa's original assessment had been incorrect. Perhaps what she'd believed to be excitement was illness. Perhaps Tina had a fever that was impairing her cognitive function. That might explain why she was confused.

Tina pursed her lips again, her expression saying she considered Louisa to be a child with difficulty understanding even the simplest of explanations.

"That's what everyone was supposed to think," she declared. "His father was an itinerant peddler who promised me the world but left as soon as he'd gotten what he wanted from me."

Louisa's brain whirled as she realized that while the revelation was startling, it made sense. The strong physical resemblance she'd noticed between Raymond and Tina was because he was her son, not her nephew.

Keeping her right hand inside her pocket, Tina rubbed her midsection with the other, as if recalling the time her belly had swelled with new life. Louisa did a quick mental calculation, deciding that Tina must have been no more than fifteen or sixteen when she'd given birth to Raymond. While it was true that some women had their first children at even younger ages, Thea had told Louisa that young mothers did not always make the best parents. "They're still children at heart," she'd said. "If something goes amiss, they're less able to handle the grief."

Louisa started to speak but closed her mouth when she saw that Tina wasn't finished.

Still stroking her belly, she continued. "When she realized what had happened, my sister was angrier than I've ever seen her. Mabel screamed at me, saying no one could know what I'd done or the family would be disgraced. She was going to send me away, but she changed her mind."

Tina stared at the far wall for a few seconds. "Later I wondered if the reason she was so angry was that she was still childless after six years of marriage, but I'd conceived after one night. Once her anger subsided, she devised a plan. I would stay at home when I could no longer hide my condition, and Mabel would pad her clothes. When Raymond was born, she claimed him as hers."

The sorrow in Tina's voice confirmed how much that decision had cost her. "It was the hardest thing I've ever done, watching him grow up and not letting him know he was mine. I hated keeping the secret." She glared at Louisa as if she were at fault. "Mabel should never have insisted. Raymond was mine, not hers, but she wouldn't relent. That's why when Adam and I married and he suggested we move to a different town, I agreed."

For the first time since she'd begun the tale, Tina relaxed, and a faint smile curved her lips. "Then we had Tillie. She was mine, all mine, and no one would take her away. But God did."

According to Father, Tina had become fragile after that. When she'd first heard him describe Tina that way, Louisa had thought he was wrong, since Tina's physical stature could never be described as fragile, but Father had been referring to Tina's nerves.

Tina wasn't finished. "After Tillie died, I begged Mabel to let

Raymond come here. I promised I'd never tell him the secret, but I needed to have one of my children close by."

Recalling the story Raymond had told about the Bentleys offering him eventual ownership of the mercantile and how he hadn't been interested, Louisa guessed it hadn't been easy to convince him to leave Mesquite Springs. Tina had been fortunate that the parsonage needed rebuilding and that the town needed a skilled builder, because that was what had kept him in Sweetwater Crossing, not the desire to live with his aunt and uncle.

"It was wonderful having him here, and when you returned and he was so taken with you, I knew it was the hand of God. God saw my sorrow over Tillie and was offering me a second chance at happiness. When my son married my best friend's daughter, I'd have both a son and a daughter."

In Tina's mind, it had all been simple, but Louisa hadn't played her part.

"Now that you know everything, you'll marry Raymond, won't you?" Tina leaned forward, imploring Louisa to agree.

The fire Louisa had seen in her eyes had intensified, telling her Tina was on the verge of losing control of herself. She had to get out of here. "Raymond is a wonderful man," she said as she started to rise. She wouldn't run, because that might inflame Tina more, but she couldn't stay here, not with this woman who'd become so unstable.

Tina stood and shook her finger at Louisa. "Yes, he is. He's perfect for you. You must marry him."

Perhaps if Louisa kept talking, Tina wouldn't notice that she was moving toward the door. "You want your son to be happy. So do I."

"And he'll be happy with you. I know he will." Louisa's ploy failed, for Tina mirrored each step she took. "You'll see that I'm right. You have to."

When Louisa was only two feet from the door, Tina lunged

in front of her, blocking her escape. "You're not leaving here until you agree to marry Raymond. I haven't heard you say that yet." She pulled a pistol from her pocket and pointed it directly at Louisa's heart.

Though that heart was pounding with fear, Louisa forced her voice to remain calm. "Put the gun down, Tina. You don't want to hurt me." Killing Louisa would defeat her plan, but the fact that Tina had her finger on the trigger told Louisa she wasn't thinking clearly. Trying to disarm her would be more dangerous than simply going along with whatever Tina had in mind. She wouldn't lie and say that she would marry Raymond, but once they were out of the house, she would find a way to escape.

"All I want is for you to see that I'm right. Your mother said you could be stubborn. I was afraid of that, but I know how to convince you." Tina gestured toward the door with her other hand. "Come on, Louisa. We're going for a walk. Now, open the door."

When Louisa complied, Tina stood behind her, the gun pressing into Louisa's back. "If you're thinking about running away, forget it. I unsaddled your horse. And don't think I won't use this gun. I will."

Louisa could duck. She could sprint to one side. She could spin around and try to knock the gun from Tina's hand. Any one of them might work, but the odds were against them. At such close range, Tina wouldn't miss if she fired the pistol.

"Where are we going?"

"The smokehouse."

The day that had been unpredictable from the beginning had just become more bizarre. "What's there?"

"You'll see." Tina's laugh was little more than a cackle. "When I misbehaved, my mama used to lock me in our smokehouse. She knew I hated the dark."

Moving as slowly as she could with Tina prodding her back, Louisa approached the small wooden structure where the Bentleys cured their meat. It would be dark, and the odor of smoke might be overwhelming, but there was no reason to fear being shut inside there.

"I'm not afraid of the dark."

"But you are afraid of other things. I thought the snake would convince you to give up pretending to be a doctor and marry Raymond, but it wasn't enough, was it? Open the door."

Knowing she had no choice, Louisa lifted the heavy bar that secured the door and pulled the door forward.

"In you go." Tina shoved her into the darkness and slammed the door behind her. "I didn't want you to be lonely, so I left you some friends," she shouted.

Her eyes had not adjusted to the darkness, but there was no mistaking the sound of the friends Tina had left. Louisa was locked in a small space with a swarm of bees. Angry bees.

Chapter Thirty-Eight

"I'm glad you enjoyed the canned oysters so much, Mrs. Albright. They're very popular with our customers in New York."

The gray-haired woman whose husband was the wealthiest man in town nodded. "I hope you'll keep them in stock, because Wilbur likes them too. He's not one for trying new foods, but he ate every one of the oysters I served him and asked for more."

That was the kind of endorsement a shopkeeper liked to hear. Josh smiled when he took Mrs. Albright's payment, then escorted her to the door. Although she could easily open the door herself, whenever he could, Josh extended small courtesies to his customers, knowing that they helped instill loyalty. As he started to return to the counter, he stopped abruptly.

Louisa needs you. The voice echoed through him. He looked around, even though he knew no one had spoken.

"What's wrong, Josh?" Mrs. Sanders abandoned the cans she'd been arranging on a shelf and took a step toward him. "You're as white as a sheet."

"I don't know exactly. All I know is that Louisa needs me." The words had faded, but the conviction that she was in danger had only heightened. He grabbed his hat and plunked it on his head. "I don't know when I'll be back."

Her office was closed. Somehow, he wasn't surprised. He'd formed no picture of the danger, but his instincts told him Louisa wasn't here. Still, he had to check. He pulled out the spare key she'd given him when she'd had the locks changed and opened the door. The office felt empty, confirming his suppositions. Yet he couldn't leave without going into each room.

His first stop was her office and examining room. As Josh had expected, there was no sign of Louisa. The only thing out of place was a piece of paper on top of her desk. With two quick strides, he reached the desk and grabbed it.

An invitation to have lunch with Tina. There was no danger in that. But as he gave the note a second glance, his eye was caught by the extra loop on the letter *L*. It was the same anomaly he'd noticed on the threatening note Louisa had received weeks ago.

Josh's heart began to race as he considered the implications. This wasn't a coincidence, nor was the feeling that Louisa needed him. If Tina had threatened her once, and it seemed obvious that she had been the author of the note, the invitation to lunch might not be as innocent as it seemed. There was only one way to be sure.

Minutes later, he and Zeus were on their way to the Bentley farm, Zeus galloping, Josh praying.

Please, God, don't let me be too late.

Stay calm. Don't let them sense your fear. Louisa knew that other mammals reacted to humans' emotions. Bees weren't mammals, but they might do the same. If she was going to survive this, she needed to keep her wits about her and do nothing to provoke them. Though their buzzing frightened her, as long as they didn't sting her, she would be fine.

"Have you changed your mind?" Tina's voice carried clearly through the heavy door.

Not knowing how the bees might react, Louisa wouldn't respond. She wouldn't do anything that might alarm them. Instead, she tried to study her prison. Her eyes had adjusted after being in the sunshine, but there was little to see in the almost complete darkness. Still, there had to be a way to escape. She moved slowly, hoping to find something—anything—that would help her. But when the bees increased their buzzing, Louisa stopped. She'd have to wait until they were calm and no longer saw her as an intruder. Did bees sleep? She had no idea.

"You know what will happen if a bee stings you." Tina was taunting her now. "You'll die."

The temptation was strong to tell Tina that that would defeat her purpose, since Louisa wouldn't be able to marry Raymond if she were dead, but she remained silent, her thoughts whirling. There were so many things she wanted to do before she died, foremost of which was telling Josh that she loved him.

Please, Lord, don't let me die before I see him again.

Peace settled over her as she knew her prayer had been heard. The bees were quiet, and she was filled with renewed resolve. She would get out of here. She would see Josh again. There had to be a way.

She stared at the door, wondering how long Tina would wait before demanding an answer to her questions. She must be getting tired. Louisa pictured her holding the pistol, keeping it aimed at the door, and as she did, a glimmer of hope flickered inside her. It would be difficult for Tina to open the door while she was holding the gun. She was a strong woman, but the bar she'd slid across the opening was heavy. To move it again, she'd need to put the gun down. That could be Louisa's chance.

The bees were quiet. Even if her voice aroused them, she'd have a few seconds before they swarmed. It was time to make her move.

She'd have surprise on her side, but she needed more. She needed a way to overpower the woman who outweighed her by fifty pounds. Moving slowly to avoid alarming the bees, Louisa continued to explore the shed. When her leg bumped into a table, she stopped and ran her hand over it, almost laughing when she recognized the object on top. It was a decidedly unconventional weapon, but it just might work. Lifting it into her arms, Louisa turned back toward the door.

"I'm ready to talk."

Josh slowed Zeus as they approached the Bentleys' house, searching for signs of Louisa. Horace should have been hitched in front, but there was no sign of him. Perhaps Louisa hadn't come here after all. And yet Josh's instincts told him she had and that the danger still existed.

He squinted, looking at the outbuildings, his heart skipping a beat at the sight of a woman standing by one of them, a gun pointed at the door as if she were guarding whatever—or whoever—was inside. The gun-toting woman was Tina. The person inside had to be Louisa. Josh's anger toward the woman who was holding her prisoner ratcheted up a notch.

Quickly dismounting, he moved as silently as he could, planning to grab the gun before Tina knew he was here. But before he could reach her, she placed it on the ground, lifted the heavy bar, and opened the door. The instant she did, Louisa rushed out, clutching something in her arms. Seconds later a swarm of bees emerged. Bees that could kill Louisa.

Please, Lord, no!

Josh's anger turned to amazement as he watched Louisa slam whatever she was carrying into Tina, sending her tumbling down while the bees flew away. His prayer had been answered.

He blinked in astonishment as he identified Louisa's weapon.

If the situation hadn't been so serious, Josh might have laughed at the realization that she had ambushed her captor with a ham.

Before either woman could reach for it, he closed the distance between them, scooped the gun out of the dirt, and pointed it at Tina.

As the woman who'd tried to kill his beloved struggled to rise, Josh shook his head. "You're going nowhere other than to the sheriff's office."

She sputtered a curse that would have earned Josh a mouthful of soap when he was a child. Without taking his eyes off Tina, he addressed the woman who'd outsmarted her adversary, armed with nothing more than a piece of smoked meat. "It's all right, Louisa. I've got her covered." He whistled for Zeus. "You'll find some rope in the right saddlebag. We need to tie Tina's hands and feet."

"You can't do that!" Tina's anger turned to outrage a second later when she spotted the ham lying in the dirt. "Just see what you've done. You've spoiled perfectly good meat."

Josh had been half right when he'd told Zeus they were dealing with a crazy man. This was one crazy woman.

Louisa knelt next to Tina and grabbed her wrists. "If you stay still, this will be easier on you."

Apparently recognizing the truth, the older woman stopped struggling, but her voice was filled with anger as she said, "I'm not going to let you take me to the sheriff. What will Raymond think when he hears?"

"That you love him and will do anything to make him happy." When she'd secured Tina's wrists, Louisa turned to her ankles. "Do you want me to explain everything to him?"

It was a strange question on what was already a very strange day. Rather than ask what Louisa meant, Josh kept his eye on Tina, taking comfort that, despite being unable to rise, she was becoming calmer.

"No." Her voice was low but filled with emotion. "No one

must know. Adam will take me away from here. We'll start over somewhere else. Just don't tell anyone."

If Tina thought she would get away scot-free, she was mistaken. Josh glared at her. "The sheriff needs to know that you tried to kill Louisa. I saw those bees. They didn't go into the smokehouse on their own." Fortunately, they'd flown away and were no longer a threat to Louisa.

"I wasn't trying to kill her. All I wanted was to scare her a bit. That's why I rubbed an old honeycomb with lemon. Bees love lemon." This time Tina sounded like an unhappy child, trying to explain why she'd misbehaved.

"You did scare me," Louisa assured her. "But you know I can't marry Raymond."

So that was what it was all about. Grandfather would have said Tina was two eggs short of a dozen if she thought intimidation would convince Louisa to do anything.

Tina's gaze moved from Louisa to Josh and back to Louisa. "Because you love this one."

"Yes, I do."

They were the words Josh wanted to hear, but this was neither the time nor the place to tell her how they thrilled him.

"We need to notify the sheriff."

"No, please!"

Ignoring Tina's pleas, Josh addressed Louisa. "I'll watch her while you summon him." He would take no chances with Louisa's safety, even though Tina was immobilized. "Take Zeus. He's faster than Horace."

"And he's saddled."

That explained why Josh hadn't seen the other horse. Someone—probably Tina—had removed his saddle and put him in the paddock behind the house.

Louisa lowered her voice to a whisper. "Don't hurt her. She's not in her right mind."

"You're right on both counts. My mother would be horrified

to see me treating a lady like this." Even if the so-called lady had tried to hurt the woman he loved. Handing the gun to Louisa, he bent down and hoisted Tina into his arms, carrying her to the porch and settling her into a chair.

"We'll wait for you here."

Louisa was still trembling as she mounted Zeus. She knew it was the normal aftermath of being so frightened and that the terror would subside, but it still took until she was almost back in Sweetwater Crossing for her breathing to calm and her thoughts to become less turbulent. Once they did, she knew what she had to do. Instead of going to the sheriff's office, she entered the mercantile.

"You need to come with me." She wasted no time on polite preambles.

Adam's eyes widened, perhaps because of her disheveled state. "What did Tina do?"

It was almost as if he'd expected Louisa's announcement, but surely he hadn't known what his wife was planning.

"Did she hurt you?" Genuine concern colored his words.

"No, but I'm going to let her tell you what happened. We need to get back to the farm."

Adam was silent on the ride, though the way his lips moved made Louisa think he was praying. So was she—praying for wisdom, for mercy, and for this day to have a peaceful ending.

When they reached the farm, Josh and Tina were seated on the porch, talking about Tina's honey. It could have been a normal conversation if Tina's hands and feet hadn't been bound and if Josh hadn't been holding a gun.

Adam leapt off his horse and bounded up the porch steps. "What did you do?"

His wife's face crumpled. "I wanted her to marry Raymond. Oh, Adam, she was supposed to marry him. It would have been perfect. Louisa would have been the daughter I wanted, but she won't marry him. She won't." Tears streamed down Tina's cheeks. "What am I going to do? Everyone will hate me." She stretched out her hands, heedless of the rope tying them together. "Take me away. Take me somewhere where no one knows what I did."

Adam looked at Josh, then turned his attention to Louisa. "What did she do?"

It was Josh who responded. "She tried to frighten Louisa. When a note didn't stop her, your wife put a snake in Louisa's office. Next she mixed some of her medicines. That could have killed an innocent person."

Adam blanched and turned to his wife. "Did you take the extra key?"

When she nodded, he explained that he always kept spare keys for every lock he sold, since customers occasionally lost theirs. "Obviously, that was a mistake."

"So was what she did today." Josh's voice was no longer calm but was filled with anger. "She locked Louisa in the smokehouse with bees, knowing full well that a bee sting could be fatal. This can't continue."

Looking like he'd aged ten years in a minute, Tina's husband nodded. "I agree. I've been worried about her ever since Tillie died. I thought the move to the farm and having Raymond here would help, but it hasn't. Now I don't know what to do."

When neither Louisa nor Josh spoke, Adam continued. "If you tell Sheriff Granger, he'll want to lock Tina up. That will kill her. Me too. I can't imagine life without her. Despite her faults, she's my wife, and I love her."

He was silent for a moment before he said, "When we lived in Mesquite Springs, I heard a man talking about a hospital near Philadelphia that treated people with problems like Tina's. If you agree, I'll take her there."

Louisa looked at the man whose words and actions proved

how seriously he honored his marriage vows. For better and for worse, in sickness and in health. Today would have been a challenge for anyone. Some might have abandoned their spouses, but Adam Bentley would not. He would stand by Tina's side, trying his best to help her. If Louisa insisted on telling the sheriff what Tina had done, Adam would suffer as much as his wife. Maybe more. And Louisa couldn't let that happen.

"No one else needs to know if you promise to take her there. I've heard of that hospital, because the doctor I worked with in Cimarron Creek once lived in Philadelphia. He mentioned a place near there that treated diseases of the mind and how effective their programs were. If anyone can help Tina, it's the doctors there."

"You'd forget this happened?" The hope in Adam's voice was so fervent it made Louisa's eyes tear. That was love. True love.

"I can't forget, but I can—and I do—forgive her." As Adam managed a small smile, Louisa turned toward Tina. "My parents taught me that one of the greatest gifts we could give others and ourselves is forgiveness. I'm sorry you felt you had no choice other than to do the things you did. You hurt me."

"I know." For the first time, Louisa saw remorse on Tina's face.

"I forgive you." As she uttered those three words, Louisa felt her spirits soar. Her parents had been right. She'd given herself a gift.

Once again, Tina stretched out her hands to her husband. This time he clasped them between his. "Take me away, Adam."

"I will, my love, I will. Just as soon as I can." He waited until Louisa met his gaze before he said, "I don't know how to thank you. I wouldn't have been so generous if someone had hurt me. Please know that I'll never forget this."

When Louisa nodded slowly, acknowledging his words, he turned to Josh. "You have no reason to help me, especially since you're planning to leave soon, but you're the only person in town who can do this. I need someone to take care of the mercantile. I don't know how you'll go about it, but I hope you can find someone to run it. I don't want to close it, because the town needs a mercantile."

Josh gave Louisa a quick look, then returned his attention to Adam. "I agree. A mercantile is a vital part of any town. And you needn't worry. What you're asking won't be a problem. I know someone who'd be willing to buy it."

He did? Louisa raised an eyebrow, but Josh did not respond.

Adam seemed less surprised. "Tina and I will leave as soon as we can pack."

Josh handed the pistol to Adam, then bent his arm. "Ready to go, Louisa? I have something to ask you."

Chapter Thirty-Nine

It wasn't twilight. They weren't standing on the bridge, watching the creek flow beneath them. He held no bouquet of flowers. This wasn't the way he'd envisioned it, but he couldn't wait any longer. As he and Louisa rode into town and approached Creek Road, instead of turning right toward Finley House, Josh tipped his chin forward.

"Let's go on a bit farther."

Though she was obviously puzzled by the suggestion, Louisa simply nodded, making him wonder if he ought to reconsider his plan. After all that she'd endured today, she might not be receptive to his proposal. And yet, as he remembered the peace he'd seen on her face when she'd forgiven Tina, he had the sense that this might be the right time to reveal his heart. Somehow, Louisa had overcome the fear she must have felt when she'd heard those bees buzzing and had managed to put it behind her. If she could do that, he hoped she was ready to consider the future.

They rode silently for another five minutes until they reached the stretch of road that had caught Josh's attention the day Louisa had brought him into Sweetwater Crossing. Despite the pain he'd experienced then, he'd been struck by the way the live oaks formed a canopy, sheltering travelers from the bright sun, and had wished he'd had a similar shelter after Zeus had thrown him. It was a peaceful spot, one that lingered in his memory.

"Let's stop here," he said as he tightened the reins. Another woman might have questioned him. Louisa simply nodded, her expression saying she trusted him. It was a promising beginning to what Josh knew would be the most important few minutes of his life.

He dismounted, helped Louisa off Horace, then gestured toward their surroundings. "I thought this was especially beautiful." The perfect place to bring the woman whose inner beauty outshone the oaks. Even though it was true, he wouldn't tell her that. Not yet.

"It is beautiful." Louisa took a deep breath and smiled, those blue eyes that rivaled priceless sapphires sparkling with pleasure. "I used to call it the green cathedral. My mother laughed when I told her this was where I wanted to be married."

A green cathedral. Though he hadn't used those words, Josh realized that he'd had the same feeling about this place. To others, it might seem ordinary, but to Louisa and him, it was special. His last doubts vanished, and his heart leapt with the sense of rightness. His original plan of a twilight proposal on the bridge might have been good, but this was better. Unknowingly, he'd been led to the spot that had figured in Louisa's dreams as well as his.

"I'm not laughing," he told her. "I think it's a good idea. If you can't be married here, you could become betrothed here. Will you marry me?"

Before she could respond, Josh let out a rueful laugh and shook his head. He may have found the perfect location, but that wasn't the way he'd planned to propose. And, judging from the way she'd blinked in surprise, a proposal was far from what Louisa had been expecting.

"I'm sorry, Louisa. I promised myself that when I asked a woman to be my wife, I'd find a romantic setting and would woo her with gentle words. Instead, I blurted it out like a schoolboy." He reached for her hands, feeling encouraged when she let him hold them. "Will you let me try to do it right?"

She gave him a short nod.

It was a good thing Josh didn't expect her to speak, because Louisa's heart was pounding so fiercely that she doubted she could get a word, even a simple yes, past her lips. She felt as if she were in the midst of a dream, the most wonderful dream of her life. The man she loved with every fiber of her body had brought her to one of her favorite places.

From the time she'd been old enough to ride, this was where she came when her heart was overflowing. She had cried here. She had laughed here. She had shared her hopes and fears, her dreams and disappointments with the oaks, never failing to find comfort. Somehow, Josh understood how special this place was and had come here to ask her to marry him. If this was a dream—and, oh, how Louisa hoped it was not—she didn't want it to end.

Josh held her hands in his, their warmth sending shivers of delight up her spine as he said, "You are the most incredible, most wonderful woman I've ever met."

She couldn't be. And yet the fact that Josh saw her that way made her almost believe it was true.

When she started to shake her head, denying the praise, Josh shook his. "Let me continue. I want you to know everything that's in my heart."

His expression was somber, his voice ringing with sincerity, as he said, "I thought my world was ending the day Zeus threw me to the ground. Instead, it was just beginning. Because of you. You healed my leg, Louisa, but more importantly, you healed my heart. You showed me that love is real, not simply a story for gullible children. Thanks to you, I now know what is most important in life."

Josh paused and raised her hands to his lips, pressing a soft kiss on her knuckles.

"What's important isn't money or control of a company. It's not prestige or power. It's love. I love you, Louisa Vaughn, from the depths of my heart."

He loved her! He loved her the way she loved him! Louisa's heart sang with joy at the realization that this was no dream. This was real.

"When I try to picture my future, only one thing is important, and that's that you're part of it." Josh paused for a second, his eyes dark with emotion. "Will you give me a chance to show you how much I love you? Will you marry me?"

He'd said nothing about his grandfather's challenge or where they'd live, but it didn't matter. Josh was right. What was most important was love. Louisa knew that, but before she could answer, there was one more question.

"What about Winifred? I thought you were promised to her."

To Louisa's surprise, Josh laughed. "It seems Winifred reached the same conclusion I did—that we weren't right for each other—but she came to her senses first. The day I wrote her a letter, saying I wasn't the man she should marry, I received one from her, announcing her engagement to someone else."

A soft breeze stirred the oaks, setting their leaves to rustling. In the distance, a bird called to its mate. And here, under the canopy of arched branches, the man Louisa loved more than anyone on Earth was smiling at her.

"I'm happy for Winifred and hope she'll always be a friend," he continued, "but you're the woman I want as my wife. Will you marry me?"

Louisa returned his smile, hoping he'd see the love shining from her eyes. "Yes, Josh, I will marry you. There is nothing

I want more. When Tina locked me in the smokehouse and I heard those bees, I knew I might die before the day ended." She shuddered, remembering the moment when she'd realized what Tina had done. "I was frightened, but mostly I was sad, because I hadn't told you how much I love you."

This time, Louisa was the one who lifted their clasped hands and pressed a kiss on his knuckles. "I love you, Josh Porter, and I'll go anywhere your dream takes you."

Though he smiled, she saw doubt in his eyes. "Even to New York?"

"Even to New York. As much as I love my sisters and want to be the one to deliver Emily's baby, as much as I love being able to help the people of Sweetwater Crossing, I love you more. I feel like Ruth in the Bible, telling Naomi 'whither thou goest, there I will go.'"

The doubt vanished from Josh's eyes, replaced by something Louisa might have called wonder. "I was wrong again," he told her. "You're even more incredible than I realized. I can't wait to show you New York, but first there's something I want to do even more."

He released her hands, then drew her close to him and lowered his lips to hers.

"Oh, how I love you!" he murmured when at last they drew apart.

"Well, Mrs. Porter, what do you think of New York?"

More than three weeks had passed since that unforgettable afternoon in the green cathedral. They'd been the busiest days of Louisa's life, days filled with preparations for her wedding, days filled with plans for their future together, days filled with more kisses than she could count. And now here she was, Mrs. Joshua Porter, a newly wedded woman standing in the middle of the largest city in the country.

"It's overwhelming," she told her husband as he helped her out of the cab at their final destination. "There are so many people, so much noise, so many smells, and yet it's exciting at the same time. I can understand why you find living here appealing."

Louisa gripped Josh's hand and gazed at the face she loved so dearly. "Are you sure you made the right decision?" There was still time for him to change his mind, but once they mounted the steps and entered the building that had been his home for more than a decade, it would be too late.

"I have no doubts at all. Let's go inside. It's time for you to meet my grandfather."

Leaving the luggage the cab driver had deposited in front of the brownstone mansion for servants to carry, Josh urged her forward.

The house where he'd grown up was very different from Finley House but magnificent in its own way, its leaded glass windows and intricately carved oak door leaving no doubt that a small fortune had been invested in its construction. When they'd discussed what Josh called the confrontation, she'd suggested it occur at P&S, but he'd wanted it to be here. Now that she stood on the doorstep, Louisa understood his reasons. This was the family home, the place where Jed lived with his wife, the place where Josh was expected to live with his.

"I want Jed's wife to be part of the meeting," Josh had explained. "Julia wouldn't have been invited to the office."

A man whose formal livery announced that he was the butler opened the door and then nodded briefly. "They're waiting for you in the drawing room."

"Thank you, Higgins."

Josh wrapped his arm around Louisa's waist as he escorted her into the coldest room Louisa had ever experienced. It wasn't a matter of temperature, for the June day had warmed the air, but the dark wood paneling, the heavy burgundy velvet drapes, and the obviously uncomfortable chairs made her want to shiver. Instead, she kept a smile fixed on her face as she looked at the room's occupants.

Josh's grandfather was frailer than she'd expected, his thinning hair gray, his blue eyes clouded with age, his expression as stern as she'd expected. Though Jed's resemblance to Josh was unmistakable, he lacked Josh's warmth. Or perhaps it was merely the circumstances that made him appear cold and a bit forbidding. The only smile came from the woman at Jed's side, a pretty blond who glowed as if she, like Emily, was expecting a child.

The old man gripped the chair arms and glared at his grandson. "It's about time you got here, but you're too late. Winifred is married."

The way Josh's hand tightened on her waist told Louisa how much his grandfather's harsh words hurt him. Instead of a welcome, he'd been berated. If this was the way Jeremiah Porter had treated Josh and Jed all the time they'd lived with him, it was a wonder either had wanted to stay. But, she suspected, today's apparent hostility was the result of the man's frustration that one of his grandsons hadn't met his expectations.

"I know." Though Josh's voice was as cold as his grandfather's, it warmed as he said, "Winifred's not the only one who's married. So am I. Grandfather, I'd like to introduce you to Louisa. She's been my wife for over a week."

The old man stared at her, as if just now seeing her. "Married?"

"Yes."

While Jed and his grandfather remained immobile, Jed's wife rose and extended her hand to Louisa. "Welcome to the family."

Taking his cue from her, Jed rose to stand next to his wife. "Yes, welcome."

"Thank you both." Louisa acknowledged their kindness with

a smile, then turned toward Josh's grandfather. "I know this must be a shock for you, sir, but I love Josh."

"And I love her." Josh kept his arm around her waist as if to protect her from an attack. It came almost immediately.

"Love!" The scorn in Jeremiah Porter's voice turned the word into an epithet. "Who cares about love? What are her connections? And where is your proposal?" The old man struggled to his feet and glared at Josh.

"I don't have a proposal for you."

Louisa had had three weeks to realize that Josh's decision was not one he'd made lightly, but his cousin and grandfather had had no warning.

Blood drained from the old man's face, and he tightened his grip on his cane. "What do you mean, there's no proposal? You said you were working on one." The shock of Josh's marriage had been eclipsed by his latest declaration.

Though Jed's eyebrows rose in surprise, he said nothing. Only Julia seemed unconcerned by Josh's announcement.

"I was working on a proposal," Josh told his grandfather. "In fact, I had two ideas. At first I wasn't sure which I should present, but then everything changed, and I knew what I would do." He turned to his cousin. "I'm going to leave one of my proposals with you. I believe it has potential, but you're the one who needs to decide whether or not to use it—not Grandfather."

When the import of Josh's words registered, Jeremiah Porter stared at him as if he were an unfamiliar animal in a zoo. "You're not going to fight for what you want?"

Shaking his head, Josh said, "I already have what I want, and so do you, Grandfather. Jed is the right man to continue the P&S legacy that your father began. He'll lead it into its next hundred years."

The day he'd told her what he planned, Louisa had been as shocked as his grandfather, but Josh's explanation had alleviated her concern that he was sacrificing his own dreams for hers.

"I didn't expect it," he'd admitted, "but I like living in a small town. Almost from the beginning, Sweetwater Crossing felt more like home than New York ever did. And creating Porter's was one of the most satisfying things I've ever done."

He'd smiled at Louisa. "My grandfather will be scandalized by the idea of my staying here, but it's what I want—a life with you. You'll have your patients. I'll have Porter's and the mercantile. And, if God blesses us, we'll have children. That's the future I want. That's my dream."

It was a dream they shared.

Louisa knew that Josh's decision was the right one, but the rest of his family was shocked. While Jeremiah remained speechless, Jed exchanged a glance with his wife, their surprise and relief evident. "Are you certain? You don't know what I proposed."

"I don't need to." Josh's voice was filled with confidence, the smile he gave his cousin as warm as the June day. "I know you. We may not have always agreed, but I always knew you cared for the company and would be a good leader."

That was one of the many things Louisa and Josh had discussed when he'd told her what he intended to do.

"Are you sure?" she had asked. "You once said you didn't think you could live with some of Jed's decisions."

Laughter was Josh's first response. "But I won't have to live with them. P&S will be his; I'll have my own life. A better one," he'd added.

After a moment's silence during which he and Julia exchanged another glance, Jed said, "There'll always be a place for you at P&S. Just as you'll always have a home here."

Josh had explained that his grandfather intended to leave the brownstone mansion to the next head of P&S, claiming it was only right that the man who ran the company have a suitable place to entertain.

Josh smiled at his cousin. "Thanks, Jed, but I know where

my place is. I'm going to run a tea shop and specialty store as well as a mercantile in a small town in Texas."

Clearly horrified, Jeremiah Porter stared at his grandson. "You're giving up everything for that?" He thumped his cane on the floor to punctuate his words. "I didn't think that I'd raised a fool, but clearly I did."

Though the condemnation had to have hurt, Josh's expression remained neutral. "I've deferred to you in the past, believing you were older and wiser, but you're wrong, Grandfather, just as you were wrong to treat my father as if he were second best simply because he wasn't your firstborn. He spent his whole life trying to prove that he was as good as Uncle John. When he couldn't do that, he begged me to do everything I could to gain your approval."

Never taking his gaze from his grandfather, Josh continued. "It took being thrown from my horse and breaking my leg to show me what was important and what I wanted most in life. I'm not settling for second best, I'm not a fool, and I'm not giving up anything. Quite the opposite. I'm gaining everything I've ever wanted—a future with the woman I love."

"Love? Balderdash! Only a fool believes in love."

This time Josh's lips tightened in anger. "That's twice you've called me a fool. I'm not the one who's a fool."

His grandfather hissed at the unmistakable implication, but he said nothing.

"Love is real," Josh continued, his voice firm. "Louisa showed me what love is, and now that I know how wonderful it is, nothing you can say or do will keep me from spending the rest of my life showing her how much I love her."

"She married you for your money, just like Julia married Jed for his."

For only the second time since Louisa and Josh had entered the room, Jed's wife spoke. "That's not true, Grandfather Porter. I married Jed because I cared for him. At the time,

I didn't know what love was, but now I know. It's what Jed and I share."

"And what Josh and I share. We may not be wealthy, but we'll be happy. That's worth more than the biggest bank account in the country." Louisa turned so she was facing her husband. "I love this wonderful man with all my heart."

Then, though she was breaking one of the cardinal rules of etiquette and would probably shock his grandfather, Louisa pressed her lips to Josh's.

Love was real. She and Josh were the proof of that.

Author's Letter

Dear Reader,

Thank you for joining me for the second Sweetwater Crossing story. With each word that I write, I picture you and hope you'll fall in love with my characters—except for the not-so-admirable ones, of course—and that you'll be smiling by the time you turn the last page.

Some of you know that I'm a plotter, which means that I outline my books before I begin writing them. In theory, that means I know everything that's going to happen in a story, but sometimes things change, and I find myself going in unexpected directions. That happened with *Against the Wind*. When I first envisioned it, Raymond was far different from the character you met. To be blunt, he was obnoxious. I didn't like him, and I didn't like the way he pursued Louisa, so I changed him into someone I hope you found likeable.

Similarly, I changed the person responsible for the threats to Louisa, in part because that gave me a secret to unveil. After all, you can't have a series called Secrets of Sweetwater Crossing without a secret, can you?

There's one major secret yet to be revealed, and that's what happened to Clive Finley. You'll find the answer to that in the final Sweetwater Crossing book, which will be released next summer. For a sneak peek at the opening, turn a page or two.

And while you're waiting for that book, if you were curious about Austin and Thea, Louisa's mentors from Cimarron Creek, you might enjoy reading their stories. Austin is the hero of the second Cimarron Creek book, *A Borrowed Dream*, while *A Tender Hope* tells Thea's story.

You'll find more information about them and my other books on my website, www.amandacabot.com, as well as a sign-up form for my monthly newsletter. I've also included links to my Facebook and Twitter accounts along with my email address.

It's one of my greatest pleasures as an author to receive notes from my readers, so don't be shy.

Blessings,
Amanda

Turn the page for a sneak peek at Amanda Cabot's next adventure in Sweetwater Crossing!

COMING SOON

FRIDAY, SEPTEMBER 14, 1883

Dreams weren't supposed to die, but Joanna Richter's had, all except one.

The concerts at Munich's glorious Odeon and Vienna's incomparable Musikverein had nurtured the dream she'd cherished for almost as long as she could remember, but it had crumbled, destroyed by something the doctors told her was invisible to the human eye. The majesty of the Swiss Alps had sown the seeds of another dream, one that had withered before it could fully flower. Now there was only one left.

Joanna smiled as she entered Sweetwater Crossing. It might lack the museums and monuments that Grandmother Kenner had called the essentials of a civilized city, but this small town in the Texas Hill Country had something far more valuable: home.

She slowed the buggy, wanting to savor the first few minutes of her homecoming. Other than the new parsonage that had been built after the last one burned, the town looked the same, and oh, how comforting that was. She'd once sought change. Now she valued stability. Being here would provide that.

Warmth flooded through Joanna's veins as she turned onto Creek Road and approached her destination. It was there, just as she remembered it. Her smile broadened as she gazed at the building where she'd spent most of her life. The stone that Clive Finley had chosen for the three-story house was strong and durable, unlikely to crumble or burn, giving her a feeling of safety and security. The columns that supported the verandah stood tall, as though proud that their role was more than decorative, or so Joanna had claimed when she was a child. The double staircase served as a reminder that there was more than one way to reach a destination, and the three dormer windows seemed to herald the presence of the three Vaughn girls, even though she and her sisters never used those rooms.

Her sisters had laughed when she'd described the house that way, saying she was being fanciful. Perhaps she was, but this was Joanna's home, her beloved home. It hadn't changed, though she had, as one by one her dreams had vanished.

She frowned at the memory of why she'd been so eager to leave Sweetwater Crossing. The disappointment that had verged on despair. The overwhelming sense of failure. The realization that there would be no happily-ever-after with a handsome rancher for her. That dream had been the first to die. Fortunately, she had told no one—not even her sisters—what she'd dreamt. And now there was no need.

As she had so often in the past, Joanna guided the buggy between the stone pillars marking the entrance to Finley House and along the curved drive that led to the house itself. When she'd reined in the horse, she inhaled deeply in an attempt to calm nerves that were unexpectedly ragged, regretting the action a second later. It was only when the pain subsided that she could climb out of the buggy, and even then her hands had begun to shake. Reminding herself to take shallow breaths, she mounted the front steps and knocked on the door. After a year and a half, Joanna Vaughn Richter was home.

It seemed forever but was no more than thirty seconds before the door opened and a petite blond with deep blue eyes stared at her.

"Joanna?" The woman's voice trembled more than Joanna's hands had, and her eyes widened in what appeared to be shock. "Is it really you?"

Joanna nodded. "It's me, Emily."

The last time she'd seen her older sister had been only hours after Emily's wedding, when she and her handsome groom had left Sweetwater Crossing to return to George's ranch. Emily had been beautiful then—everyone in town acknowledged her as the prettiest of the Vaughn girls—but that beauty paled compared to the Emily who now smiled at Joanna. There was a new softness to her sister's face, a gleam in her eyes that hadn't been there before, turning her into the picture of a happy woman.

"I can't believe it." Emily took a step forward and wrapped her arms around Joanna's waist as she'd done so many times when they'd been children. It had become more awkward once Joanna grew to her full height—half a foot taller than Emily—but Emily had always persisted in her efforts to soothe Joanna when she'd been distressed. Today it was Emily who appeared distressed. "Louisa and I've been so worried about you."

"I'm sorry." Though the words were inadequate, they were the only ones Joanna had. "I should have written, but I couldn't." For so many reasons.

Emily broke the hug, then reached out to take one of Joanna's hands and lead her indoors. "It doesn't matter. Nothing matters except that you're back and safe."

Despite the warmth of the September day, the house was cool. That shouldn't have been a problem, but something triggered a coughing spasm, the first Joanna had had since she'd arrived in Texas. The doctors had warned her against becoming overly excited. Perhaps that was the cause, because there was no doubt that she was excited to be home. Excited and at the same time a bit apprehensive.

She bent over, trying to stop the coughing. When she could again breathe freely, she looked at her sister. "I'm sorry," she said, wondering how many more times she would have to apologize.

Emily's blue eyes, so different from Joanna's brown ones, reflected concern. "You're ill. What can I do? Should I call Louisa?" As if she'd only just registered the unrelieved black Joanna wore, Emily asked, "Why are you in mourning? Was it your grandmother?" She shook her head. "Oh, listen to me. I should be helping you, but instead I'm bombarding you with questions."

"It's all right, Emily." When they were growing up, Emily had felt that her role as the oldest meant she had to care for Joanna and Louisa, and that caring had included what had sometimes felt like an inquisition. "I should probably sit down and drink a bit of water." The air here was heavier than it had been in the Alps, and that could make breathing more difficult.

"Of course." Emily wrapped her arm around Joanna's waist again. "Let's go to the kitchen. I've got pudding on the stove, and if I leave it too long, it'll be a scorched mess."

Once Joanna was seated at the kitchen table with a glass of water in front of her, Emily began to stir something that smelled like chocolate. "We have a few minutes to talk before Mrs. Carmichael and Noah come back from their walk." She paused and turned to look at Joanna. "Noah's my son—my adopted son—and you remember Mrs. Carmichael. She takes care of Noah while Craig is at school." A chuckle accompanied Emily's explanation. "There I go again. If you got my letters, you know all that. Craig tells me I'm prone to chatter when I'm excited."

There was no missing the smile that crossed Emily's face when she spoke of her husband. Her second husband.

Joanna brushed aside thoughts of George. Nothing good would come from thinking of him, just as nothing good would come from remembering how often she'd wished she'd been a petite blond like Emily instead of a tall brunette, especially when George had had eyes only for Emily. "The last letter I received said you were going to marry the schoolteacher and that Louisa brought a man with a broken leg to recuperate here."

"Oh my." Emily made no effort to hide her dismay. "That was months ago. So much has happened since then. Louisa did more than set Josh's leg. She married him."

Little sister Louisa was married. Joanna knew she shouldn't have been surprised, and yet she was. Before she could speak, Emily continued. "I don't understand why you didn't receive my letters. I thought it took only a few weeks for mail to reach Munich."

That was easier to explain than her reaction to the changes she was discovering. "I haven't been in Munich since early February." Though she tried to suppress it, Joanna coughed again. "I caught scarlet fever." And had almost died, although she wouldn't worry Emily with that information. "It turned into pneumonia. That's when Grandmother took me to Switzerland, because the air was supposed to be better there. She arranged for mail to be forwarded, but it appears most of it wasn't."

Abandoning the pudding for a moment, Emily gave Joanna a quick hug. "My letters don't matter, but I hate that you were sick and so far away. I wish I'd known."

It might have been comforting to have had Emily or Louisa with her during the long recovery, but they would have tried to convince her to return home, and at that point, Joanna had still entertained dreams of an illustrious career and hadn't wanted anyone to try to dissuade her.

"There was nothing you could have done. The sanatorium was one of the best in Europe, and the treatments helped." As much as they could. Joanna paused, debating whether to tell her sister the final prognosis, then decided she might as well be honest. "The doctors warned me that my lungs will always be weak"—too weak to allow her to continue her training and eventually embark on a concert tour of her own—"but if I'm careful, I can live normally."

Emily fixed one of her appraising looks on Joanna. "I'll make sure you're careful, and so will Louisa."

Joanna smiled, knowing they would. Emily would cook meals she was certain would strengthen her, and Louisa would study medical books to determine whether anything more could be done.

"I'm so glad you're home again." Emily returned to stirring the pudding. "The important thing is for you to rest, and there's no better place than right here."

Though her sister's gesture encompassed more than the kitchen, Joanna studied the room where she'd spent so many hours watching Mama cook and then helping her wash the dishes. The curtains at the window were new, but that was the only change she could see. The wooden table where she'd eaten cookies after school still had the small gouge from a broken glass, and the cupboards still had mismatched knobs after Louisa had unscrewed one and lost it in the yard. It was a simple room compared to some of the châteaux she'd visited, but that simplicity was a balm to Joanna's spirits.

"I feel better just being here."

Emily tasted the pudding, then added another spoonful of sugar. "I hope you're not angry that I turned our home into a boardinghouse." For the first time since Joanna had entered the house, her sister's voice held a note of uncertainty.

"How could I be angry? You did what you had to to save our home. Now that I'm here, I can help you, if you still have a room for me, that is."

"No helping until you're fully recovered, but of course there's room for you. Beulah's in your bedroom. I could move her, but I'd rather not, now that she's become accustomed to it. Would you mind moving into my old room or Louisa's? She and Josh have taken over the third floor."

More changes. The thought of returning to the room she'd had for as long as she could remember had buoyed Joanna during the long journey from Europe. Now it appeared that that dream had also died.

"Beulah?" Rather than upset Emily by admitting her disappointment, Joanna seized on the familiar name. "Beulah Douglas lives here?"

Emily nodded. "I thought I'd written about that. She stays here during the week so she can attend school, then goes home on Friday afternoon. It's been a good arrangement for everyone, especially Noah. He misses her on the weekends."

A shadow crossed Emily's lovely face. "There I go again, talking about other things. You haven't told me why you're in mourning, but I assume it's for your grandmother. When did she die?"

"A few hours after my husband."

"Stop! I can't do it."

Burke Finley stared at the woman seated next to him, not bothering to hide his shock. That was the last thing he'd expected Della Samuels to say. Not once during the ten days they'd been traveling had she complained, not even when the accommodations were at best mediocre and the food barely edible. Now that they'd reached Texas's Hill Country and were within an hour of the town that she claimed was the one place on Earth she wanted to visit before she died, it seemed that something had changed her mind.

"What's the matter, Aunt Della?" The petite woman whose brown hair had silver wings, making people believe her older than her forty-one years, wasn't his aunt, though she would have been his aunt by marriage if his uncle had lived. Still, for as long as Burke could recall, he'd addressed her as Aunt.

"I can't do it." Della's eyes, the same light blue as the dress she wore today, filled with tears. "I can't bear the thought of standing by Clive's grave. I was a fool to believe I could."

Burke gave her a professional assessment. Her color was a bit high, but she was showing no signs of heat distress, and her respiration was steady. "There's no need to visit the cemetery."

Though others made weekly pilgrimages to their loved ones' final resting places, he rarely spent time at his mother's grave, preferring to remember her alive. There was no question of visiting his father's grave, for he was buried on a battlefield hundreds of miles from home.

"We don't have to go to the cemetery, but I thought you wanted to see the house he built for you and talk to the man who's living there."

According to the stories Burke had heard, the house Clive Finley had designed for his bride-to-be was larger and more beautiful than the one on the plantation she'd called home. Legend had it that Della's daddy was so opposed to his daughter's moving to Texas that he wouldn't agree to the marriage unless Clive could give her the same luxury she'd had. And so Burke's uncle had built a house that rivaled those the plantation owners used to flaunt their wealth.

There should have been a happy ending to the story, but there wasn't. Though Clive's house had been finished, he'd died before he could return to Alabama to claim his bride and had left the house in the care of his closest friend.

"I thought I wanted to see it," Della admitted. "Now the whole idea seems overwhelming." Her breathing grew ragged, making Burke doubt his previous assessment of her health.

"Let's get out and rest a bit," he said, gesturing toward a large live oak tree. "The shade looks welcoming." One way or another, he had to convince Della to continue, for while she might be ready to return, he was not. There was nothing waiting for him in Samuels, Alabama. Nothing good, that is.

She shook her head. "Just turn around."

She'd regret it. Burke was certain of that, and so he said, "I never thought you were a coward." He was the coward, not wanting to relive that horrible morning. Though Felix had insisted that no one would know the truth, Burke did. According to Felix, everyone made mistakes. Burke had made his share, but never—ever—one of that magnitude.

Trying to block the memories that he knew would haunt him for the rest of his life, Burke fixed his gaze on Della. "You don't really want to go back, do you?"

Della stared at the live oak, then slowly shook her head. "You're right. I'm not a coward and I don't want to go back, but I'm afraid. I've had the image in my mind for over twenty years. What if it's wrong? What if I'm disappointed?"

Though he wished it were otherwise, Burke couldn't make any promises. All he could do was encourage her. "There's only one way to know."

This time she smiled. "You're right. You know, Burke, if you weren't such a fine doctor, you could be a minister. You're good at comforting people."

"It's a nice thought, but any skills I have are for healing bodies." And those were in question. He'd always found being a physician rewarding, but even before the morning when everything had changed, Burke had begun to wonder whether serving the residents of a small town was his true calling. He was no longer needed in Samuels. Felix could handle the practice, especially since he planned to let Edna assist him.

Had Della realized that? Was that why she'd suddenly decided to come to Texas and asked Burke to accompany her? He wouldn't ask. All he knew was that he needed a new direction for his life. Perhaps two weeks in the Hill Country would help him find it.

"How much farther is it?"

Burke was heartened by the anticipation he heard in Della's voice. "Less than five miles."

Her smile broadened. "Let's go. I owe it to Clive and to me." Her apprehension apparently gone, Della leaned forward and studied the countryside, giving Burke a running commentary as they approached their final destination.

"Clive was right," she said softly. "I like the Hill Country."

So did Burke. The rolling hills with their limestone outcroppings, the meadows ringed by live oak trees, the fields bright with wildflowers were all appealing. And when they reached Sweetwater Crossing, the appeal only increased.

The town Clive Finley had chosen was more attractive than Burke had expected, its main street lined with well-cared-for buildings. The mercantile, mayor's office, and church occupied one side of a block, with the dressmaker, post office, and a doctor's office on the other. Burke gave the doctor's office a longer look than the other buildings, noting that the front door had been freshly painted and that the windows gleamed. Whoever the town's physician was, he cared about appearances.

"Do you want me to ask for directions?" Burke asked as he and Della approached what appeared to be the center of town, a corner that housed the church, the school, and a restaurant as well as the doctor's office.

Della shook her head. "I'm sure we can find it on our own. Clive said it was next to the creek."

As he guided the buggy into the intersection, Burke looked both directions, grinning when he spotted a bridge a block and a half to the right. "That must be the creek." He turned toward it, silently praying that Della would not be disappointed. Though she'd begun speaking of it a scant two months ago, she'd admitted that she'd dreamt of coming here for many years. It was only after her father's death that she'd decided to make her dream come true.

"Which way do you want to go?" Burke asked when they reached the corner of Center and Creek streets. If the house was next to the creek, it would be on the north side.

Della shuddered when she saw the cemetery on the northwest corner. "Not that way."

Burke turned east, remaining silent as they passed a small house, then a larger one on the south side of the street. Though he would have expected similar homes on the northern side, there were none, simply a large expanse of grass and trees. Then he saw it.

"That's it!"

Della's excitement matched his own. The house his uncle had built was magnificent, far larger and more elaborate than anything Burke had seen in Sweetwater Crossing. While the other buildings were situated close to the street, this one was farther back, with a curved drive leading from the wall that marked the front of the property to a three-story house. A double staircase led the way to the front door, while four columns supported a second-story verandah. Della's home in Alabama was beautiful, but this one surpassed it in both beauty and grandeur.

"Oh, Burke. It's just the way Clive described it." She leaned over the side of the buggy, pointing to the pillars that marked the ends of the wall. "Look. They say Finley House." Tears glistened in her eyes as she turned to Burke. "Thank you for insisting that we come. I'll remember this for the rest of my life." She paused, then asked, "Do you think Pastor Vaughn will let us go inside?"

Burke smiled and repeated what he'd said less than an hour ago. "There's only one way to know."

"Your husband?" Emily's eyes widened with shock. "You're a widow?"

The tremor in her voice reminded Joanna that Emily had been a widow when she'd returned to Sweetwater Crossing a year ago and was probably remembering the grief of the first few months without her beloved husband.

"Kurt and I were married in July, two months ago today." It had been a wonderful day, one of the happiest of Joanna's life, but the happiness had been almost as short-lived as her first dream of marriage and happily-ever-after.

"He and Grandmother died a month later. According to the doctor, it was spoiled chicken." If Louisa were here, she'd want more details, but that should be enough for Emily. "My stomach was queasy that day, so I didn't eat any, and Sophie didn't like the spices, so she had only a little. The doctor said that's why she survived."

As she continued to stir the pudding, Emily raised an eyebrow. "Who's Sophie?"

"Kurt's sister. She was at the sanatorium too." If it hadn't been for Sophie, Joanna would not have met Kurt, and if she hadn't met Kurt, she wouldn't have known the wonder of love and marriage.

Before she could say more, the back door flew open, and a young boy raced in, then flung his arms around Emily's legs. "Me saw new horse, Mama!"

The brown-haired boy, whom Joanna guessed to be three or four years old, must be Noah, the schoolmaster's son.

"I'm sorry, Emily. You know how he gets around horses." Joanna recognized the gray-haired woman who'd followed Noah into the kitchen as Mrs. Carmichael, the widow who'd lived in the parsonage once the Vaughns moved into Finley House. A few inches shorter than Joanna, her back still straight despite her seventy years, Mrs. Carmichael was one of the kindest women Joanna had ever met. It was no wonder Emily had welcomed her as a member of her newly forged family.

The widow glanced at the table, then stopped, her surprise evident. "Do my eyes deceive me, or is it really Joanna Vaughn?" She bent down to give Joanna a hug.

"Your eyes are as sharp as ever, Mrs. Carmichael, but I'm Joanna Richter now."

"Come see horse, Mama." Ignoring the other adults, Noah tugged on Emily's skirt.

His stepmother shook her head. "Later. Remember your manners, Noah. This is my sister Joanna. What do you say to her?"

"Is it your horse?"

She probably shouldn't have laughed at the boy's single-mindedness, but Joanna did. "Yes, it is." She was about to tell Noah that she'd introduce them later when she heard a knock on the front door.

"I'll answer that," Joanna said. Emily had pudding to cook, and Mrs. Carmichael appeared tired from her walk. Even though she had only recently returned, this was still Joanna's home. Greeting visitors was partially her responsibility.

She rose and walked through the hallway that bisected the first floor, wondering whether she'd recognize whoever had come to call. Perhaps the Albrights, who lived across the street, had seen her arrive and wanted to welcome her back. But the couple who stood on the front porch were strangers.

The man appeared to be close to her age with auburn hair, green eyes, and a square chin that kept him from being conventionally handsome. Though the woman at his side appeared old enough to be his mother, Joanna saw no resemblance between them. What she saw was apprehension on the woman's face and in the way she clung to the man's arm.

"Can I help you?" Joanna asked, unsure whether she should invite them inside. Perhaps they were simply lost and needed directions.

"We're looking for Joseph Vaughn. I understand he lives here."

Joanna's first thought was that the man's voice was deep and melodic, making her wonder whether he sang in a choir, but it was overshadowed by the pain the name evoked. Joseph Vaughn was—or, rather, had been—her father.

Before she could explain that he'd died more than a year ago, Noah raced into the hallway, his rapid footsteps followed by Mrs. Carmichael's more deliberate ones.

"Me see! Me see!" Apparently Noah wanted to greet the visitors.

As Joanna reached out to keep him from catapulting himself onto the porch, Mrs. Carmichael stopped and put her hand on her heart. Blood drained from her face as she stared at the doorway.

"Clive! Clive Finley! You're back!"

Amanda Cabot's dream of selling a book before her thirtieth birthday came true, and she's now the author of more than forty novels as well as eight novellas, four nonfiction books, and what she describes as enough technical articles to cure insomnia in a medium-sized city. Her stories have appeared on the CBA and ECPA bestseller lists, have garnered starred reviews from *Publishers Weekly* and *Library Journal*, were a *Woman's World* Book Club selection, and have been finalists for the ACFW Carol, the HOLT Medallion, and the Booksellers' Best awards.

Amanda married her high school sweetheart, who shares her love of travel and who's driven thousands of miles to help her research her books. After years as Easterners, they fulfilled a longtime dream when Amanda retired from her job as director of information technology for a major corporation and now live in the American West.

"Such beautiful words flow from Amanda Cabot's pen—words that lead characters from tattered situations to fresh beginnings and culminate in tender story endings that make a reader sigh in satisfaction. I've never been disappointed by a Cabot tale."

—Kim Vogel Sawyer, bestselling author

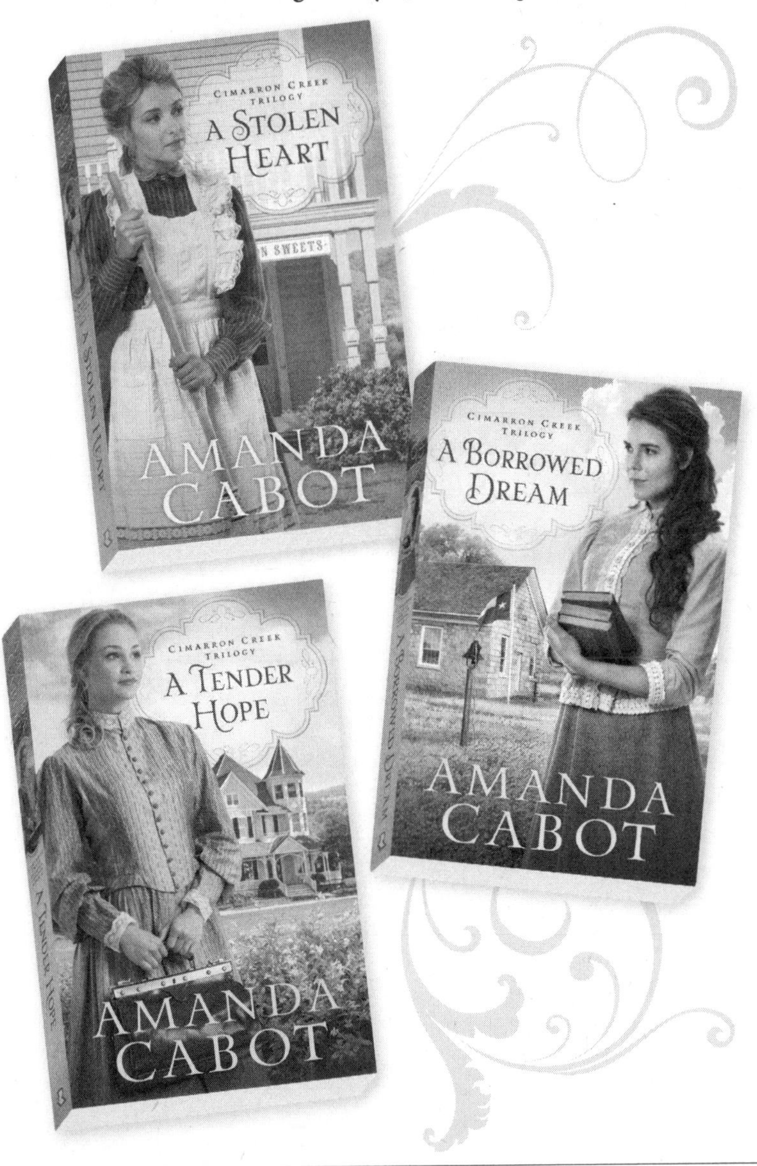

"Amanda Cabot offers a delightful read, and as I turned the pages I was swept away with a story of love, courage, and sacrifice. Recommended!"

—**Tricia Goyer,** bestselling author of *Beyond Hope's Valley*

VISIT

AmandaCabot.com

to learn more about Amanda,
sign up for her newsletter,
and stay connected.